KV-374-831

JO NESBO

Jo Nesbo is one of the world's bestselling crime writers. When commissioned to write a memoir about life on the road with his band, Di Derre, he instead came up with the plot for his first Harry Hole crime novel, *The Bat*. His books *The Leopard*, *Phantom*, *Police*, *The Son*, *The Thirst*, *Knife* and *Killing Moon* have all since topped the *Sunday Times* charts. He's an international number one bestseller and his books are published in more than 50 languages, selling over 60 million copies around the world.

Sign up to the Jo Nesbo newsletter for all the latest news: jonesbo.com/newsletter

ROBERT FERGUSON

Robert Ferguson has lived in Norway since 1983. His translations include *Norwegian Wood* by Lars Mytting, the four novels in Torkil Damhaug's Oslo Crime Files series, and *Tales of Love and Loss* by Knut Hamsun. He is the author of several biographies, a Viking history and, most recently, *The Cabin in the Mountains: A Norwegian Odyssey*.

ALSO BY JO NESBO

JO NESBO

Blood Ties

TRANSLATED FROM THE NORWEGIAN BY
Robert Ferguson

VINTAGE

3 5 7 9 10 8 6 4 2

Vintage is part of the Penguin Random House group of companies

Vintage, Penguin Random House UK, One Embassy Gardens,
8 Viaduct Gardens, London SW11 7BW

penguin.co.uk/vintage
global.penguinrandomhouse.com

Penguin
Random House
UK

First published in Vintage in 2025
First published in hardback by Harvill Secker in 2024

First published in Norway by H. Aschehoug & Co. (W. Nygaard), Oslo, in 2024
with the title *Kongen av Os*

Copyright © Jo Nesbo 2024
Published by agreement with Salomonsson Agency
English translation copyright © Robert Ferguson 2024

The moral right of the author has been asserted

Penguin Random House values and supports copyright.
Copyright fuels creativity, encourages diverse voices, promotes freedom
of expression and supports a vibrant culture. Thank you for purchasing
an authorised edition of this book and for respecting intellectual property
laws by not reproducing, scanning or distributing any part of it by any
means without permission. You are supporting authors and enabling
Penguin Random House to continue to publish books for everyone.
No part of this book may be used or reproduced in any manner for the
purpose of training artificial intelligence technologies or systems. In accordance
with Article 4(3) of the DSM Directive 2019/790, Penguin Random House
expressly reserves this work from the text and data mining exception.

Printed and bound in Great Britain by Clays Ltd, Elcograf S.p.A.

The authorised representative in the EEA is Penguin Random House Ireland,
Morrison Chambers, 32 Nassau Street, Dublin D02 YH68

A CIP catalogue record for this book is available from the British Library

ISBN 9781529940442

Penguin Random House is committed to a sustainable future
for our business, our readers and our planet. This book is made
from Forest Stewardship Council® certified paper.

MIX
Paper | Supporting
responsible forestry
FSC® C018179
www.fsc.org

1

EVERYBODY HAS THEIR WEAK SPOT.

Dad drummed that into me when he taught me to box. I was smaller than the other boys, but he showed me that even the most frightening opponents have a hole in their defence, some place that's not covered, a mistake they're doomed to repeat. He also taught me that it isn't enough just to find that spot; in addition you have to have a heart that's cold enough to exploit it without hesitation. And right there you had my weak spot. A heart that bled for people like me, that recognised all weakness as my own. But I learned, and my heart chilled. And now you could say my heart is an ice-cold, stone-dead volcano that had its last and final eruption eight years ago. And even then it was cold. Cold enough to make me a killer already back then.

That's what was going through my head as I stood on the steps outside a villa with a garage and an orchard tinged in autumn colours in Kjelsås, in northern Oslo. That I'm a killer.

It was Saturday night, almost eight o'clock, and I'd just pressed my thumb against the bell on the front door. Directly beneath the bell was a heart-shaped ceramic shell that said 'The Halden Family Live Here', along with a smiley.

I don't know whether I was thinking about being a killer because I already had a guilty conscience, or to reassure myself that what I was about to do was something I was capable of doing. I'd done worse before.

My heart started beating faster as I heard the footsteps inside. Easy now. Just think *fuck everything* and get it over with.

The door opened.

'Yes, good evening, can I help you?'

The man was tall, a lot taller than my 175. Slender, almost skinny. Grey hair, youngish face. Forty-one – I'd checked. I saw two snowsuits hanging on hooks behind him, with shoes for adults and kids strewn across the floor in typical organised chaos. According to the registration information I'd found on the net they'd owned the house for four years. I guessed Bent Halden's wife wanted the place because they needed more room once number two was on the way – at least that was how I interpreted her Instagram account. And he'd always wanted something a bit higher up the hill because it was closer to running and skiing country. A Google search turned up his name as a participant in several local ski and orienteering events. But the last one was a few years back, so there was presumably less time now for that kind of thing than he'd planned. Partly because two kids are more than twice as much work as one, mostly because the company he'd started with a colleague named Jon Fuhr took up more – not less – of his time than before they became their own bosses. It's just a guess, but I doubted I was too far off. Their company was called GeoData and they had been commissioned to examine the geology around Todde in connection with the tunnel being built to replace the road that ran straight though the middle of Os, as it had done as far back as people could remember, long before it was classified as an A-road in 1931.

I moistened my lips.

'Roy Opgard. Don't know if you remember me?'

I tried to give him my friendly, maybe slightly anxious country-bumpkin-in-the-big-city face. Not my speciality. I'm guessing I looked like a Roy anyway. A bit dark, closed, reserved. Fortunately for me it seems to be a type Norwegians trust, probably because we think there's some correlation between being shy and socially inept and honesty. Well, that's the way I think too, so that's OK.

Bent gave a long-drawn-out 'Aaah' that was somewhere between a 'Yes' and a 'Not sure'.

'I fixed your car when you were working in Os,' I added.

Bent swished his finger through the air.

'Of course! And you made a really good job of it too.'

The skin in his forehead folded into several V-shaped rows. 'Didn't the money come through?'

'Oh yes, yes.' I tried a little laugh. 'Sorry, I probably should have called you first, but that's the way we do things out in the sticks, you know. Just turn up on your doorstep and ring the bell. But I've been in Poland, just got back, and since I was in town I remembered I had something of yours in my glove compartment. This.'

I held it up in front of him. And sure enough, I could see

3

that Bent hadn't the faintest idea what that shiny little metal object was.

'Found it after you got the car back. Must have just forgotten to put it back again. Of course, the car works without it, but much better with it. Where is the beast?'

'The car? Now? No, really, I'm sure I can fit it back myself. What is it, anyway?'

'Well, if you don't know, how are you going to do that?'

Bent looked at me. Smiled and shook his head. 'Good point.'

'I've been paid for a job that, for once, I haven't done properly. It'll only take five minutes. Where . . . ?'

'In the garage,' said Bent, stepping out of his slippers, lifting the keys to the Audi from a hook and pulling on a pair of trainers. 'Camilla! I'm just going down to the garage!'

From somewhere inside the house came the shouted reply: 'Sigurd's off to bed now.'

'If you get him ready then I'll read to him!'

'You got kids?' Bent asked above the scraping noises as we walked the gravel track that led down to a large, white-painted garage. I wasn't expecting the question and just shook my head and tried not to think that she would have been seven years old now. Not that I knew it would have been a girl, but I'd just grown more and more certain of it. I swallowed back a lump. It was a little smaller with every passing year, but it would never quite disappear completely.

'So you run that garage in Os?' His voice was friendly.

'No, closed down a long time ago. But I'm a certified car mechanic, so now and then I take on a repair job just for the fun of it. I run the petrol station next to it.'

Bent held up his keys when we arrived at the garage and the

door opened automatically. I could see it was the expensive type. Bent Halden would probably have chosen something different if he was buying today.

'Yes, now I remember the local guy who recommended you told me. You're what's-his-name's brother, that . . .'

'Carl Opgard,' I said.

'Yes.' Bent laughed as we walked in. 'The king of Os.'

I noticed he immediately realised how patronising that sounded. As though Os was some shitty little town where Carl swaggers round like some pantomime king. King of the dungheap.

'I didn't mean . . . I just gather that he owns most of the village.'

'He owns most of Os Spa. Open the car?'

'Yes, but doesn't that make him king of Os?'

I slipped into the driver's seat and Bent got into the passenger seat. I pulled out a screwdriver, flipped off the panel under the steering wheel and started turning the screwdriver. Bent watched, pretending to take an interest. 'So what's the news?' I said as I moved the leads. 'From the preliminary reports I saw that your firm thinks the mountain at Todde looks OK?'

'That's right.'

'I see. How sure are you?'

'Pretty sure.'

'Is that possible, when you can't see *inside* the mountain?'

'Yes. Though, of course, there's always an element of uncertainty when it comes to interpreting the seismic data.'

'And it's your firm – or actually, in fact, you – who does the interpreting and then presents the conclusion, would that be right?'

'Well, yes, in a way. Along with my partner.'

'Jon Fuhr.'

'Jon, yes. We're the head geologists.'

'You own sixty per cent, he owns forty, so what happens if the two of you disagree?'

'Well, I must . . . you sure know a lot about us. How—'

'Oh, all you have to do is check the company registration records up at Brønnøysund. You know, just recently I was going to check the financial status of an American company that makes roller coasters. But it wasn't that easy, and it struck me then how we take transparency for granted here in Norway. We're such a trusting nation Americans would almost certainly say it bordered on the naive. But it's precisely because we can see everything that we're able to trust each other. It's like it is out in the country towns and villages. Everybody knows everything about everybody in Os. Just about. It's not that everybody likes everybody, but we just take it for granted that people are more or less telling the truth. The way the Highways Department trust that the conclusion you and Jon have come to is the truth.'

'Well, yes, we do have a good reputation.'

'But finances are a little tricky at the moment.' I looked up with an apologetic smile. 'At least, according to Brønnøysund.'

Bent returned the smile a little stiffly. 'Things came to a bit of a halt during the pandemic. What are you actually getting at here?'

I went back to concentrate on my work. 'I'm wondering how sure you can be that it's possible to bore this tunnel and stay within the budget that's behind the decision to reroute the main road. On a scale of one to ten, for example.'

'We-ell,' said Bent. 'Eight, perhaps. Nine if we say that it wouldn't cost more than twice the amount.'

'Why not ten?'

He didn't answer, just looked at me.

I held up the screwdriver. 'What would it take to make you change your mind?'

'What do you . . . it's Roy, isn't it?'

I smiled. 'I apologise, Bent. The questions are from a scientifically based technique of persuasion. The idea is to ask questions and let the other person convince himself that you are right. My brother gave me a book about it, it's the way he works.'

'He persuades people?'

'Yes. Selling projects and things like that. He's good at it.'

'So, you're here to . . . sell me something?'

'Yes, I guess you could say that. But I'll drop the sales pitch.'

'Oh yeah?'

'Yes. And instead persuade you the good old-fashioned way. I'll give you and your partner twelve million kroner if you say in your report to the Highways Department that the tunnel can't be built.'

Silence.

'Are you trying to bribe me?'

I nodded. 'Yes. I know it doesn't sound good but that's probably the correct term.'

Bent stared in disbelief. 'And what on earth makes you think that'll work?'

'Because, in the first place, you're using the present tense.'

'What?'

'If you were dismissing the idea completely you would have said, "What makes you think that WOULD HAVE worked?" They write about it in that book, that our choice of words reveals what we're thinking, often before we ourselves even know we're thinking it.'

Bent snorted. 'And what else?'

'What?'

'You said "in the first place".'

'Oh yeah!' I opened the glove compartment, took out the vehicle registration card and held it up. 'I took a look at it while I was working on the car. Says here you don't own the car. So it must be a company lease, right? Leasing's a bad business practice right now, you know that?'

'So what?'

'There were three unpaid fines there too, all of them overdue. And that tells me just one thing. That you and your company have a cashflow problem, Bent.'

'So that makes you think I can be bribed? Listen, Roy, I'd rather let the company go under than do anything criminal.'

He'd raised his voice, but I doubted he was as morally indignant as he was pretending to be. I shook my head as though I was weighing things up. 'Well, just how criminal is it, actually? No one knows exactly what's inside that mountain. Could be water. Could be porous. Eight out of ten, that's to say there's a twenty per cent chance the provisional report is mistaken. Quite a lot, don't you think? You just have to look at it from a slightly different angle, see if there are other ways of interpreting the data. Right?'

Bent didn't reply.

'Sure, you can declare your company bankrupt, but not your family up there.' I nodded in the direction of the villa. And saw from the flicker in his eyes that I'd found it. His weak spot. The family. Same as my weak spot. But I pushed aside anything you might call sympathy, I kept my heart cold.

'I checked in the land registry archive,' I said. 'This whole dump of yours is mortgaged to the hilt. So is your partner Jon's house. Guess you had to go that extra mile when you started the company.'

Bent's head didn't move, but I could see he nodded assent with his eyes.

'And then along comes the pandemic.' I sighed. 'Okay, the advantage is that it won't be all that difficult to persuade Jon to go along with it.'

Bent's eyes opened wide. 'You're crazy. Jon has—'

'—a previous conviction for fraud,' I interrupted. 'And one for violence.'

Bent's jaw froze open.

'Yes, the verdicts are in the public domain,' I explained. 'Didn't he tell you that? Sure, it was just a bit of loose change, when he was a student working in a bar, but he got six months conditional. So he's got what it takes. That's why I came to you, Bent. And you can take it up with him. Shouldn't be that difficult really.'

Bent swallowed. His head dropped and he looked crestfallen. Resigned. But I recalled what Dad used to say, when he told Carl and me how they break wild horses in America. That the most dangerous moment was when the horse looked as though it had given up and was standing quite still. That was when you had to watch out, because that bronco had another buck coming.

'I could declare the company bankrupt and get work anywhere as a geologist the next morning,' Bent suddenly said in a sharp voice. 'And get better money than I'm making today.'

He was right, I knew that. But I also knew that money wasn't what made him tick. What made him tick was the need to make something of himself, to be his own master. When he said that I was the guy who ran the car workshop I had to stop myself correcting him, that I was the guy who *owned* it. I had even said that

9

I ran the petrol station, not that I *owned* it. Because it sounds so pompous and boastful. I remember Mari, Carl's first girlfriend, asking how come we were so different, why I didn't go around bragging about things the way he did. I told her it was probably because I was happy enough with my own idea of who I am. Which was, of course, a lie. Because I'm not. Never have been. In my own mind, in my own head, I'm a hayseed, nothing but a fucking peasant. A dyslexic and socially dysfunctional loner with no more education and no more refinement than I've been able to pick up for myself in a remote mountain village. With a brother who had everything I didn't. Good at school, good with girls, good with people in general. Carl never needed the book to find out which buttons to press, he *was* the book.

'Trust is good,' I said as I pushed the panel beneath the steering wheel back into place. 'It's what's best about Norway – it's more valuable than our oil. Naturally, the authorities will trust your report. The same way they trusted the weather report that said there were so-and-so many foggy days over in Hurum and so they decided to build the main airport at Gardermoen instead. Remember? That was in 1994. A lot of people stood to gain by it being at Gardermoen. And then that engineer – Wiborg – started making a fuss, telling everybody the measurements were wrong. Two days before he was due to present his own data to the Storting he dies, right? Suicide, they said. Even though no one could really explain how, alone and naked, he was able to smash his way through the Thermopane window in his fourth-floor hotel room.'

Bent blinked and blinked again. I felt for him, of course I did. The same way I felt for those guys who wanted to start something at the dances at Årtun because Carl had been flirting with their girls. They were jealous, nothing strange about that. And usually they weren't from the village and couldn't know that Carl had a big brother – even though he was actually a smaller big brother – who would pretty soon sort them out. I mean, *really* sort them out. It didn't bring me any pleasure back then, and it didn't bring me any pleasure this time either. It was just something that had to be done. For the family.

Bent released the air from his lungs and stared through the windscreen at the garage door. Oh yes, he was well and truly caught, he must have realised that. This stuff about mysterious violent deaths was, of course, just talk, something to give him an extra argument in the discussion he would be having with himself later that evening. So that he could say this wasn't about greed, oh no, it was about looking after your own health. Was he finished? Was my work here done? I truly hoped so. Because I really didn't want to have to play my last card. In a casual way mention his wife's name, and the names of his kids, and which schools they went to. And anyway, once you bring family into it, there's really no telling what might happen.

I held up the metal object. 'Ah!' I said. 'Guess I forgot to put it back again this time too.'

2

CAN ANYONE BE A KILLER? Or do some people – maybe even most of us – have some kind of mental or moral fuse that prevents us from taking another's life? I'm not talking about killing in self-defence or in anger, but whether you can get normally decent people, someone like Bent Halden for example, to kill another human being in cold blood for no other reason than that it will make their own lives a little better, a little easier. Thoughts such as this were what occupied my mind as I ploughed through the darkness in my Volvo V60.

The drive from Oslo to Os didn't take as long as usual this late in the evening and it was just past midnight as I pulled over to the side of the road and stopped on the ridge from where, in the daytime, you can see both the county sign and the part of the village that lines the shore of Budalsvannet. Os is a small settlement of around a thousand inhabitants, part of a county with a total population of three thousand. It lies six hundred metres above sea level, the summers are short but warm and dry, the winters hard and intense. The settlement itself and most of the farms – because this is farming country – lie in the lee of the valley, while other farms – like Opgard – are located up on the mountainside, with a lot of grazing and not much arable land. I guess the cliché would probably say that the people here are taciturn and tough, that they've learned how to survive in a harsh environment, and that's not too far off the truth of it. Maybe it's conditions like these that create a community that's balanced somewhere between sticking together, and a claustrophobic backbiting and envy. The major sources of income are related to the tourist industry, mainly the sale of land for building holiday cabins, on Os Spa, and on the camping site, which also rents out cabins. The building of Os Spa was what made Carl king of Os. Before him Willum Willumsen was the town's top dog, with his second-hand car business and his cabin sales. But the real power in Os was the mayor, Aas, who had held office for the Labour Party for decades until he decided to call it a day and retire. Aas is still the power behind the throne, and someone whose voice any new mayor has to listen to.

A pale moon shone across the Ottertind peak and the night was starry and clear. I don't know all that much about the stars, it's all too big and far off for me. But if I'd had someone sitting beside me in the car there I could have told them a fair bit about Os. Pointed, and told her exactly who lived in which house, those lights in the landscape below us. For a brief moment I lost it and imagined it was her sitting in the passenger seat beside me, with our little girl in the back seat, listening. Telling them, there, girls, there where all the lights are, that's the market square, and that light directly above it, that's the big house Uncle Carl is building for himself.

But I pulled myself together and dragged myself back into the real world. I'd been away three days and was feeling homesick already after two. I don't know why. I'd lost everything I ever had in that little town. But then it had given me everything I'd ever had, too. I hated that place, but I loved it too. And in the final analysis, what more could you ask of a home town?

I put the Volvo into gear and turned onto the main road. Past the first settlements, past my car workshop and petrol station, Smitt's house, with its windows grimed with road dirt, and a big hoarding on the wall advertising haircuts and the solarium, in a way that made it look as though you could get both done at the same time. A hundred metres beyond it was the Gospel Hall. Paint flaking off the white walls now, but then things went up and down with that place. Ever since I could remember waves of religious revivalism had passed through the town at irregular intervals, and for a while there would be a period of enthusiasm for all things spiritual, fundraising and a new coat of paint for the Meeting Hall. For as long as that lasted, then the devil got the upper hand and the place lay empty and deserted again, in darkness, the talkers in tongues and the promises of salvation echoing from the walls. There was something creepy about the place and about those smiling travelling preachers who would appear suddenly and live there for a few months. It was as though things happened behind that door with the cross above it, things that no one ever spoke of. Along with all the delightfully scandalous things people *did* gossip about and which probably never happened.

I slowed down when I came to the centre – if that's what you could call the little square – lowered my window and peered up at Fritt Fall, the only place to go to on a Saturday night in Os. I recognised Erik's florid handwriting on the pavement sign outside the club: DJ ERIK. HAPPY HOUR EVERY HOUR. The sound of the bass from the music inside could move even the air out here; sounded like a good night, lot of customers. Back when I bought Fritt Fall for a song from Erik Nerell it wasn't exactly because I thought there was money to be made in the nightlife business, but because I wanted to get my hands on the real estate. One day – if everything went according to plan – it was going to be worth a good deal more than Erik had been forced to sell it for. It was his own fault, he just never ran it well enough. As part of the deal Erik kept his job there, but I made Julie the manager – she'd shown she was smart enough to run the petrol station the times when I had to be away. She'd thrown out the billiard table and brought in a pizza oven and an espresso machine and extended the range of beers to include twenty brands from all parts of the world. Open from ten to ten, one o'clock on Fridays and Saturdays. And it actually worked. It wasn't a gold mine but it did something for Os, it was a sign of life after five in the evening, and one should never underestimate the synergic effect something like that can have. Due west, and right now silhouetted against the moon, I saw the outline of the house Carl would be moving into, once it was ready, in about six months' time. People referred to it simply as the Palace because it really did look like some kind of stately home, like in that Springsteen song 'Mansion on the Hill'.

I took a right, passed Nergard. Noticed – the way locals notice things like this – that Grete Smitt's car was parked up behind

Simon's. Began the narrow ascent to the summit. Changed down through the turn at Japansvingen and then finally rounded Geitesvingen. Pulled into the yard and parked between the barn and the little farmhouse, next to Carl's BMW.

Opgard. Home.

Carl was still up. He hadn't changed out of his suit and was sitting in Dad's old rocking chair out in the winter garden with a beer. It was Dad's idea to have an American porch in that otherwise modest little house he'd built up in the mountains. And Mum's idea to glass it in and call it a winter garden. It probably tells you something about where they came from. She'd worked as a maid and housekeeper for a shipping family in the city, and she liked things to sound English and upper class, the *haaall* was what she called that porch of ours. It smelled like a cowshed. Dad grew up in sodbusters Minnesota, with all the Cadillacs and Methodist churches and the pursuit of happiness, he'd even given me and Carl middle names after two Republicans. I got Calvin, after President Calvin Coolidge, Carl was Abel, after Abel Parker Upshur, the guy who annexed Texas. From our winter garden we could look out over the whole village. We couldn't see Os Spa, directly behind the hill in the west, but it took just a quarter of an hour to walk there across our own land, as quick as it was to drive down to the village and then follow the sign up the asphalt road to the hotel. I'd asked Carl why he always drove, why not use his legs instead and maybe get rid of a couple of those kilos he was putting on, an extra one every year. As for me, I just got thinner. But his view was that the hotel boss should arrive for work with a certain amount of style, and those extra kilos gave him a certain dignity.

I sat down beside Carl, pulled out my tin of Berry's chewing tobacco and wedged a pouch in under my lip. The lower lip, not the upper lip like the people round here did it, as my dad always told me. And it had to be Berry's, not that Scandinavian crap the others chewed.

'Well?' said Carl.

'We'll see,' I said. I picked up the last unopened bottle of beer from the windowsill and flipped off the cap. It tasted good. One bottle of beer always tasted good. It was the thirst for more that was the difference between me, and Carl and Dad. I was the sober one, always the 'designated driver' for Carl from the time I was old enough to drive – up here in Os that could well be a couple of years before you're old enough to take your tests. From the time I was sixteen I'd driven Carl and Mari to the dances at Årtun, waited and drank Coke, fought, drove them back home again. It was all over between them after Mari's best friend – Grete Smitt – started bragging about how she'd had it away with Carl. Carl had gone to the USA to study. He'd come back home fifteen years later with a wife and his plans to build a spa in Os. Eight years had passed since then, the wife was no more, but the hotel got built. A five-star gold mine of a mountaintop hotel, pride of the village and its sole claim to fame.

'But what do you think?' said Carl as he suppressed a belch.

I shrugged. 'Ninety million kroner for a roller-coaster track is a lot of money.'

'I mean the geologist, did he accept the proposal?'

'Don't know. I gave him time to think about it.'

'Oh? Does that mean he has his doubts?'

'It means fortunately that he has his moral doubts.'

'Fortunately?'

'Yes.' I took a swig from the bottle. 'If he has his moral scruples now then they won't suddenly crop up afterwards.'

'Which is good for us?'

'It means that when he says yes we don't run the risk of him regretting it and changing his mind. And since he *has* a moral sense it means he won't say yes just to trick us.'

'Sometimes I swear people might think you were the smart one of the two of us,' said Carl. He raised the bottle to his mouth and drained it.

He said it like it was a joke, because there really weren't that many who thought I was smarter than Carl.

'We've had a reply from the safety division of the Highways Department,' he said and got to his feet. 'Beer?' I lifted the bottle to show him I already had one. He disappeared, and from the kitchen I heard the sound of the fridge door opening and closing. Typical Carl dramaturgy. Put something out there then leave a pause for the expectations to build. It worked well when he was trying to sell some new project, but I was so used to it I neither died of excitement nor got impatient and annoyed. I heard him open another bottle out there as my gaze turned towards Geitesvingen. It was bathed in moonlight. The exact line where the public right of way ended and our private property began was something we'd been discussing with the Highways Department for years. Our view was that it was their job to erect a crash barrier along that turn with a sheer drop of a hundred metres down to Huken, a narrow ravine that never liked to let go once it got hold of something, whether people or goats. Or cars. I was almost eighteen, Carl still not seventeen when Mum and Dad died. We had watched as they entered the bend in Dad's black Cadillac DeVille and disappeared over the edge. If there'd been a crash barrier there it would never have happened, the Highways Department agreed with us about that. But another two cars had to drive over the edge before they swallowed their pride and accepted responsibility for the safety of that stretch of road.

Carl returned and sat down.

'They're starting work this weekend.'

'Wow,' I said. 'That's good news. How did you finally manage to persuade them?'

'Just by being Carl,' he said solemnly. 'What they're wondering now is what colour we want the crash barrier painted.'

I laughed. We raised our glasses to each other.

'Not such good news is that they want to fetch the cars up first.'

I nearly choked on my beer. 'You're kidding?'

'Nope. They said they'll be using two crane trucks and some kind of winch arrangement. I don't understand how those winches work but I guess you do.'

I nodded. I do know how forces work, even though I only sat the theory part of the mechanic's exam, and the letters don't jump around so much for me when there's only three or four of them in a formula. What Carl understood was the world of business. After he finished secondary school and after the break-up with Mari, Mayor Aas arranged for a scholarship for Carl from an association of Norwegian-American immigrants in Minnesota. I only heard from him when he needed money and for fifteen years I never saw him. But after he came back from the USA about eight years ago hardly a day had gone by without my seeing him. People thought it a bit strange that the two of us – two adult brothers – would want to live together on a farm on top of a mountain. A lot of the old stuff, the old rumours, began cropping up again. Most of them to do with me. In a place like Os, once you pass thirty and still haven't started a family, people start to wonder. One rumour was that I'd abused my kid brother when we were in our teens. There were even hints we were a couple. The rumours faded a bit after I turned seventeen and people started gossiping about how I was having it away with Willum Willumsen's wife. And Carl was too much of a skirt chaser to be an out-and-out homo. He'd even brought a wife back from the USA with him. People believed so much and knew so little. And that was fine by us. Because no matter what they did believe, it couldn't be worse than the truth.

'Relax,' said Carl. 'They'll take the cars straight to the breaker's yard.'

'Think so?' I said. 'You're the one who said it was bad news.'

'I was thinking that *you* would take it as bad news. I'm thinking it's a good thing to get rid of the cars. That way we won't have it hanging over us like a sword of Sisyphus.'

'Sisyphus is the guy with the stone. The guy with the sword is Damocles.'

Carl laughed. 'It was really funny, how you suddenly knew all that bloody stuff when I came back home. As if, like, you'd suddenly gone to some kind of school that nobody knew about.'

'Nobody did know about that school,' I said quietly, peering at the label on the beer bottle.

'True. But Rita Willumsen can't have taught you all that in such a short time.'

'No, but she started something off, you could say. And I don't know much about "all that bloody stuff", it's just that all you hicks are so fucking easy to impress.'

'Impress? It makes us throw up, surely you realise that?'

We both laughed. Carl was in the good zone now. And when

he was there I would think about how lonesome it would be after he moved into that mansion of his. But I also knew that another couple of beers could be enough to tip him over the other way, into the Dad zone. That dark, sullen, black zone that had always been my domain, but Carl – the guy everybody thought was the charming, carefree extrovert of the two of us – was visiting it ever more frequently these days.

'Dammit, she was something else, Rita,' Carl said, staring dreamily out through the window.

'She still is,' I said and took another drink.

'Oh yeah? You getting anywhere with her?'

I grinned. 'She and Kurt Olsen got engaged last week, so I'm thinking you must be talking about the camping site.'

'Naturally.'

'The ball's still in her court, and I haven't heard anything.'

'She won't get a better offer. But if GeoData deliver a report and it says the Todde tunnel can't be built, then the price is going to rocket.'

I nodded. Property prices in Os had dropped like a stone once it became known that the new highway wouldn't be going through the village after all but bypassing it. They recovered slightly after Os Spa was finished, but there are limits to what a hotel can do for an isolated rural community with no major road, even one with less than three thousand inhabitants. And while property prices in Os stagnated and fell, the rest of the country had been experiencing record growth in the private and commercial sectors, in the towns and cities. Putting it simply, once people heard that the new road was, after all, still going to run through the centre of Os then the village had twenty years' growth to catch up on and it would happen more or less overnight. And the camping site – right next to the lake and just two hundred metres from the square – would be a prime piece of real estate and the price would rocket, no question about that. So yes, it was a matter of urgency to get that deal concluded.

The late and lamented Willum Willumsen didn't just live up to all the clichés about used-car salesmen, he exceeded them. When I asked Dad once if it was true what someone at school had said, that Willumsen had completely shafted him when he bought that run-down old Cadillac DeVille from him, all he had said was: 'Opgard folk don't haggle over prices.' There were, it seemed to me, equal measures of bitterness and pride in his reply. Plus a little embarrassment.

'She's going to be at the game tomorrow,' said Carl.

'How do you know?'

'*Everyone* is going to be at the game tomorrow. If we win, we go up.'

'We do? What division would that be?'

Carl groaned. 'You know, it's OK not to be interested in football, but this is, like, *our* team.'

That was only partly right. On Carl's initiative, Os Football Club had become a corporation in which Os Spa owned eighty per cent of the shares. As I'd sold most of my shares in Os Spa to Carl a couple of years ago, my ownership of the club was minimal. Pretty much like my interest in football. Not that Carl had been such a fan either, he just wanted people to love him and had this idea that the way to the village's heart went through support for the local football team. First we sponsored it, then Carl got the idea of incorporating and owning the club, so we could buy and pay a couple of good full-time players plus employ a trainer. Apparently this was unheard of for a 5th division club like ours.

People laughed and said the only people who fucking *owned* a football club were sheikhs and oligarchs. But they changed their tune when the club bought a top Nigerian striker, employed the club's former star player Kurt Olsen as part-time trainer, and Os FC AS won promotion to the 4th division practically without losing a game. And were about to go up to the 3rd, if my maths were correct.

'Fine, I'll be there,' I said. 'Any other news?'

'I finally got that German company to install that specially designed kitchen I want up in the house. And a wolf's been seen up by Steinssetra.'

'Really?'

'No, well, who knows, it was Simon Nergard who saw it.'

We laughed. Nergard was our nearest neighbour, even though his farm lay on the fields far below ours. He was a notorious liar and gossip, like his sweetheart Grete Smitt, who ran the village hair salon and gossip centre.

'But Erik Nerell found a sheep's carcass yesterday in the same area,' said Carl. 'Obviously a predator, according to him. But not much of it was eaten, so he reckons that if it was a wolf then it was on its own, not with a pack.'

I shook my head. 'There haven't been wolves here for fifty years. Must be some stray. Wouldn't surprise me if it was that Rottweiler of his, and he's crying wolf so his own dog doesn't get the blame.'

Carl chuckled. 'But suppose it is a wolf. Something like that in an area where the hotel guests like to go walking, is that good or bad for business?'

'Your guess is as good as mine. Anyway, it's not going to be around for long.'

'It'll move on, you mean?'

'It'll die. A wolf lives off large prey and that means it has to hunt in a pack.'

'So pretty much like us then?'

'Pretty much like us,' I replied, and took another swig of beer. I felt warm, tired. It was relaxing to sit there and chew the fat with the one person on earth who you knew better than anyone else, knew so well it was like talking to an extension of yourself. Three or four words into a sentence I'd know where Carl was going to end it, and vice versa, so we often made do with just those three words. It was almost like being alone. You saved your energy and your vocal cords.

'So no other news then?' I asked.

'No. Or, well, sort of. We've employed a new head of marketing. Young girl, local, smart.'

'Oh yeah?'

Carl did it again. Took a slow drink, kept me waiting. Took a deep breath. And what came out wasn't a name but a long burp.

'Jesus, Carl.'

'Sorry. Moe's daughter. The roofer's daughter.'

'Natalie?'

'You remember her? Oh, right, that business there, I'd almost forgotten.'

Maybe he was lying to himself, because Carl hadn't forgotten, at most he'd just suppressed the memory. Because 'that business' was something I'd only ever told Carl about. It happened just after he came back. Natalie Moe was at secondary school and that pale, skinny girl with the frightened eyes came a little bit too often to the petrol station to buy a packet of EllaOne, a morning-after pill. I asked Julie, who worked in the shop and was in the same class as Natalie, if Natalie had a boyfriend, and that Julie should suggest they use condoms, but Julie reckoned Natalie was just sleeping around. I don't know, it just didn't seem to add up to me. Then one day her father, Moe the roofer, came in, and he asked for a packet of morning-after pills too. As soon as I read the shame in his eyes I got the picture. And when I couldn't persuade Sheriff Kurt Olsen to do anything about my suspicions I took matters into my own hands. I went out to Moe's place, beat him half to death and said I'd be back to finish the job off if he didn't the very next morning send his daughter somewhere she could be far away from him. And if he did as I said, then I'd keep quiet about what I knew.

So Natalie finished her schooling at Notodden. Once, when I was there, I saw her in a cafe, sitting with some friends. I didn't speak to her, just noticed that she no longer had that same frightened look on her face.

'You speak to the Frenchmen?' I said, changing the subject because there are certain things Carl and I agree never to talk about.

'Every day,' said Carl. 'They like our operating margins and our figures, they love the drawings for the new wing and they're sending two structural engineers who are coming to inspect the hotel on Wednesday.'

'Good,' I said. At first the plan to extend Os Spa had been greeted with scepticism at the annual general meeting, which consisted entirely of local investors and me. Behind it was a well-founded unease about what the tunnel and the rerouting of the main road would mean for the number of guests the hotel could expect. But Carl's argument won us round. He described any talk of consolidation as defeatist, and said that if the hotel were to become a good enough reason to make a detour to Os then we had to think offensively, think big, be spectacular. 'Increase or die,' was how he put it.

'We can be a five-star boutique hotel. It's vital that we're visible and on the map, and that doesn't just mean we think quality, it means we have to get above the critical mass in terms of size too. I want this whole part of the county to be synonymous with the name of Os Spa, not just this village. When people hear the name Os Spa they shouldn't just think *hotel and hot tubs*, they should think *experience*. And that means investment, not retrenchment.'

This had been followed by a short but intense discussion about whether it was right to focus the share issue on outsiders, but common sense won the day. There were limits to how much capital could be raised in Os. The French hotel group Alpin now owned fifteen per cent of the hotel after Carl – who knew the CEO at Alpin from his years in the real estate business in Toronto – had invited them in during the refinancing that took place following the fire. Now Alpin were being offered shares that would take their holding in the company to forty-five per cent. It meant that control of the company was still safely in the hands of Os, but with the risk now spread. The French could also perhaps contribute some of their expertise in marketing the hotel internationally. As soon as the price per share was agreed on, the deal would go ahead and the building work could start. And obviously, if in due course the report from GeoData meant that there would be no tunnel, then the French would be willing to pay a considerably higher price for the shares.

'I'm off to bed,' said Carl and got to his feet.

'OK. Goodnight.'

'You're looking thoughtful.'

I nodded. 'You know what I was thinking when I rang on that doorbell for Bent Halden?'

'That you were going to take one for the team?'

'Yeah. But most of all I was thinking that I'm a murderer. That *we* are murderers.'

Carl looked at me, his eyebrow raised. 'Sleep tight,' he said and left. Like I said, some things we just don't talk about.

I sat there a while longer, looking out into the night, listening to his footsteps from his bedroom above.

Seven murders.

Altogether, Carl and I have killed seven people. Plus a dog.

I emptied the rest of the bottle.

No. I didn't like the thought of those wrecked cars being winched up into the light of day.

3

I WAS IN POLAND THE evening before I was at Halden's and offering him twelve million kroner to write a false report. To be specific I was in Zator, a town of around four thousand inhabitants in the south of the country. To be even more specific I was in Energylandia, an amusement park, the biggest in Poland. And to be even more specific, I was in a car that was being pulled up to the top of the largest wooden big dipper in the world. Although, strictly speaking, the track was a hybrid of steel and wood. At least that's what the builder, Glen Moore from Rocky Mountain Constructions, explained to me above the shrieking whine from the tracks. The sound made me think of chains being dragged through the snatch block of a boat weighing anchor. Or rather no, the chains in a slaughterhouse where the carcasses of the animals get hauled up to dangle in mid-air. I tried to listen to what Moore was saying about the technical details, but it's hard to concentrate when you know that in a few seconds time you're going to be free-falling about sixty metres.

He looked at me, and I realised he'd just asked me a question. 'Sorry?'

'I asked if there's much wind.'

'Yes,' I said.

'Low temperatures?'

'Yes. It's in the mountains.'

'Then I would not recommend wood, but steel.'

'No,' I said. 'It needs to be wood.'

Moore gave me a puzzled look. I hadn't had time to explain, even if I'd wanted to, because right then we reached the top. The rattling of the chains stopped and I no longer saw the tracks in front of us, just the drop, and Polish fields stretching as far as the eye could see to the horizon. But if I'd had time to give a concise explanation, then one name would have done it: Shannon Alleyne.

The carriage stopped almost on the brink of the drop, as though overcome with dread itself. Then, slowly, it began to point its nose downwards. And downwards. I could already feel the acceleration tickling my stomach and assumed we were now vertical, but the tracks continued to disappear out of sight below us, almost as though they were running *inward*. I thought, that's how it must feel, to be sitting in a car that can't handle Geitesvingen, that feeling of losing contact with the ground, tipping forward on account of the heavy engine in front, staring into the abyss that was Huken. I closed my eyes. When Shannon Alleyne came hurtling into my life eight years ago I was thirty-five years old, single, and a mass murderer who was absolutely ready to start a family. I say 'absolutely ready' because it wasn't a conscious thought of mine until the day she suddenly told me she was expecting my child, and from my own reaction I realised it must have been something I really wanted. I was, as they say in America, 'over the moon'. Now, it's perfectly possible that I didn't want a family per se, as they say, and that what changed things was that Shannon Alleyne was the mother.

Because Shannon was perfect. A small, pale wisp of a thing with the face of an angel, the voice of a baritone and a mind so sharp you had to have all your wits about you just to keep up with her. She was from Barbados, from a heavy-drinking, white lower-class family of redlegs, descendants of emigrant Scots and Irish who'd left their home country a few centuries earlier. No one in the family was educated much beyond the level of primary school, but Shannon had defied the odds, gone off to study architecture in Canada and generally been regarded as someone with a very bright future. She was as tough as old boots, sentimental and crazy. She knew she was different and special, and she was uncompromisingly ambitious. Not so much on her own account as for her creations. That was why she had fought like a lioness for that minimalist masterpiece of an Os Spa she'd designed, defied those local investors who wanted something cheaper, tamer and more traditional. Oh yes, when it was about her ideas, and people she thought of as family, then Shannon was loyal to the death, a warrior, someone you wanted on your side, not facing you. And so hot, sweet and hungry in bed that it was more like fighting a battle than the lazy, dozy lovemaking with Rita Willumsen. Shannon Alleyne was, as I say, perfect. There was only one snag.

She happened to be my brother's wife.

At the time Shannon became pregnant Carl was in a bad way

and on his uppers, both personally and financially. Os Spa was in the process of being built, the budget was out of control and he'd taken out a secret loan from Willumsen at a ruinously high rate of interest. On top of which Shannon was on at him the whole time about how her drawings had to be followed *exactly and in every detail*. It's possible that all that pressure was a partial explanation for why Carl beat Shannon every now and then. I was desperately in love, had been for over a year, and she was the same. So even without knowing it we'd been heading towards the inevitable that time we ended up in bed together in Notodden. That's when I noticed the bruises on her body. Was that when I finally managed to hate Carl? Or did that come later, when I discovered that as security for the loan from Willumsen Carl had put up my share of the kingdom? Or did I not even manage it then? Was the debt and the guilt from our childhood still too great?

Then, one New Year's Eve, Os Spa burnt down. Must have been a stray rocket, people said. Insurance fraud, others hinted. But Carl told me he'd dropped fire insurance to save money. So in taking up that loan he'd risked not only his own inheritance but mine too. I owned just a small part of the hotel. The plan – which was now in ruins – had been to buy me out once the business was up and running, so that I could buy the petrol station I was manager of.

Something had to be done.

Willumsen's loan fell due and his Danish hit-man torpedo turned up in Opgard driving a white Jaguar. It was a cold winter's day, and I added yet another murder to our list when I emptied a bucket of water across the road and watched as it froze to mirrored ice. Sheriff Kurt Olsen had a lot of questions about the accident, as he had done when Willumsen was found dead in his bed. I told him that accidents do happen. So do suicides, all you had to do was look at Kurt's own father, the old sheriff. I saw the hatred in Kurt's eyes but, just like his father, he couldn't prove a thing. Police from KRIPOS had arrived from Oslo to look into the case, and thought they'd found proof that Willumsen's own hit man had killed him.

So the immediate problems at Opgard were solved and out of the way.

All except one.

Carl.

I can't remember now whether it was Shannon's idea or mine, but we both understood that there was only one way forward if we were to be together and rescue what remained of my finances. And that was to get rid of Carl. It wasn't an easy decision, but once made it proved easy to come up with a plan. You just do the same thing that worked for you before, so it wasn't especially original. I bled the brake fluid on Carl's car so he wouldn't be able to handle Geitesvingen. That day, before he drove down to Opgard for an investors meeting for the rebuilding of Os Spa, Carl confronted Shannon and told her he knew she was pregnant. Told her he knew who the father was, it was an American who'd been paying court to her, a man whose name he'd seen in the hotel guest list at Notodden that time she'd spent the night there. She'd started laughing, and in a blind rage Carl struck her over the head with an iron. And then she confessed. Not the name of the father, but to the fact that it was her who had set fire to the hotel. So that it would have to be rebuilt, only this time it would be rebuilt the way she wanted it. So Carl hit her again. And after that she didn't laugh any more. She didn't breathe either.

And then he did what he'd done when he'd killed the old sheriff. Phoned me, and begged me to help him clean up the mess.

We sat Shannon behind the wheel of Carl's Cadillac DeVille, turned on the ignition and then let it freewheel down towards Geitesvingen and over into Huken. I stared at those red rear lights until the car disappeared over the edge, carrying with it the woman I loved, and our child. I let Carl cry on my shoulder.

As I opened my eyes again in Zator, Poland, I saw the skeletal structure hurtling towards us as the red rails twisted and turned in front of us, almost as though they were trying to escape. But we held on tight. Suddenly we were upside down. I'd been told that the course had three of these 'inversions', and they gave the strangest feeling of weightlessness. Another sharp turn, I felt as if I'd pulled a muscle in my side.

A minute after we'd been up at the top it was over. The car braked through a gentle right turn and we came to a stop.

'What do you think?' Moore asked.

I nodded approvingly. There had been several steep sections, but nothing like that first fall. Nothing is like that first fall.

4

FIVE MINUTES TO KICK-OFF. We parked Carl's BMW behind the wartime barracks built for the Germans that had ever since the liberation been used as changing rooms for Os FC. Dad always said that the road system and infrastructure in Norway wouldn't be what it is today without the five long years of the German occupation. And that the average lifespan in Norway had gone up, not down, as the English and the Americans and Russians fought the war for us. After another couple of beers we always knew pretty much what was coming next, usually in a voice trembling with anger:

'Did you boys know that more Russians died fighting the Nazis on Norwegian soil than Norwegians? On *Norwegian* soil! Biggest bunch of cowards in the whole of Europe. Just a handful took up arms to defend their own country, while two million

Americans crossed the pond and risked their lives to save our asses! Come on!'

Then it was grab the Remington rifle from its hook above the back door and out onto the steps and target practice at whatever Dad pointed at.

'This place here is our kingdom!' he would bellow. 'And if anyone comes along and tries to take it, we defend it with the last drop of our blood. You got that?'

Carl and I would nod and start shooting imaginary Nazis and commies hidden in the heather. Now we got out of the car behind the German barracks and walked past the other cars parked there.

'Like I said, she's here,' said Carl as we passed Rita Willumsen's Saab Sonett 58-model, a roadster, and the only cabriolet in the village. You need a degree of panache to drive around somewhere like Os in an open Saab Sonett without looking like a jerk, and Rita Willumsen had that in spades.

We rounded the corner of the barracks just in time to see the teams run out. Os FC in red shirts with the sponsors' logos, and the biggest of them all right across the chest – Os Spa. The players jogged out onto the grass to scattered applause and cheers. At a quick guess I estimated the crowd at about three to four hundred, which wasn't bad. Most were standing along the touchline on the west side of the pitch, where the barracks provided a little shelter from the wind, along each side of a seven-metre wide and two-and-a-half-metre high wooden stand. The stand was a sort of unofficial VIP lodge for the club's backers. The manager of Os Sparebank sat next to the mayor, Voss Gilbert. The former mayor, Aas, was of course there too, along with his daughter Mari and son-in-law Dan Krane. Krane was editor of the local newspaper, the *Os Daily*, so I figured he was there to cover the promotion, if it happened. I nodded to the manager of the Co-op as we climbed up through the tribune and took our places next to Rita Willumsen. Most people were dressed in sensible outdoor clothing and parkas, but Rita was wearing an elegant burgundy-red cape. Along with the high-heeled boots and the upright carriage you'd have to say she looked queenly. She had a place in the VIP tribune both as a club sponsor through Willumsen AS and as a board member of Os Spa, but something tells me Rita Willumsen would have ended up there anyway.

'Not often we see you at a game,' she said.

I shrugged. '*Oh when the Os, oh when the Os, oh when the Os go marching in . . . !*'

'Very good. But it's years since we sang that.'

'I know. I'm just doing it to show my senority as a fan of long-standing.'

'Seniority.'

I grinned. That summer when Rita Willumsen and I used to meet in deepest secrecy up at the converted mountain cabin farm they owned seemed like an eternity ago, almost like it had never happened. But all the things she taught me about – the correct way to speak, proper manners, art history, love and literature – were proof that it really had. She used to say that our relationship was like one long Sant Jordi, a Catalan festival in which, she said, women gave books to their lovers, and their lovers gave them roses in return. Whatever, I'll never forget that summer, the summer of Petrarch's sonnets and Rita's Sonett.

'Thank you,' I said quietly.

'Don't say thank you too soon,' she said in an equally quiet voice. 'They've started.'

I looked up. Sure enough, they'd kicked off.

'Who are we playing?' I whispered.

'Sometimes I wonder the same thing,' she said.

'Doesn't Kurt tell you?'

I nodded across towards the other side of the pitch, where Sheriff Kurt Olsen, with his mane of blond hair, stood in front of the bench where the subs and the backup team sat, cigarette dangling from the corner of his mouth, arms folded. No, not many believed all the rumours about Rita and a seventeen-year-old back then, but maybe Rita's fondness for young men was a bit more obvious a couple of years after she became a widow, when she hooked up with Kurt Olsen, who'd been in the class below me at school.

'Kurt has a duty of confidentiality,' she said. 'And I think he plays a different game from you and me.'

'And what game do we play?'

'That's what I've been wondering about, Roy. You haven't told me what you want to do with the campsite.'

'Run it for campers?'

'Please, don't underestimate me.'

'Is this why you still haven't accepted my offer? You want to know more, so you can raise the asking price to what you think the place is worth *to me*?'

'There now, that's a bit more like it.'

'What if I just want to own it?'

'Don't talk nonsense. A field has no value in itself, you need a return on it.'

'We're farmers. Owning land is everything to us. It's in our blood, like a disease.'

Rita smiled. 'Do you want to own more of Os than your brother? Is that it?'

I shrugged. 'Sibling rivalry is as good a motive as any.'

'Aha,' she whispered.

'Aha?'

'You're trying to make light of it because I hit the nail on the head. Fine, now I know. And because I know it's worth more to you than what you're offering, how about we raise the price ten per cent?'

'So five and a half million? That's your price?'

'And if it is?'

There was a roar from the crowd around us. Apparently we'd scored a goal already.

'Fine,' I said and held out my hand. 'Then we have a deal.'

She looked at my hand but didn't shake it.

'No bargaining?'

'Up at Opgard we don't bargain.'

'No, Willum told me. Well, maybe you should, because now I think I can go even higher.'

'I thought we just had a deal.'

'No, I was talking about a *hypothetical* ten per cent rise.'

'Dammit, Rita, now you're starting to sound like Willum.'

She gave a short laugh. 'We all have our teachers, Roy. You had me, and I had my husband. And, by the way, I would prefer it if neither you nor your brother mentioned Willum's name, thank you very much.'

The smile was intact, but her eyes had darkened. There had been a number of uncertainties surrounding her husband's suicide eight years ago. But it had been no great mystery to her. Directly after Willum was found in bed with a pistol on his pillow, a letter turned up in which he summarily discharged Carl's debt to him of thirty million kroner, and loaned him another thirty million. Without that money, Os Spa would never have been built. With it, Rita would never have had to sell the campsite. So maybe it was not so strange that when Carl offered his condolences at the funeral she'd leaned forward and whispered the word 'murderer' in his ear.

But since Rita missed the millions more than she did that fat, old, jealous villain of a used-car salesman husband of hers, and money can never reap as much hatred as true love, it looked like she'd been able to put most of the vitriol behind her. But I wasn't naive. If Rita thought she could screw things up for anyone from the Opgard farm then she would. The way she was doing it to me now.

'Ten per cent more,' I said. 'Tomorrow's Monday, my offer is open until four o'clock. After that it goes back to the original price.'

'The price is one thing,' she said. 'How you're going to pay is another. I very much doubt you have that amount in cash, and you'll never manage to sell a petrol station that's about to lose its main road.'

'You do know that that isn't the only thing I own?'

'Yes, yes, I suppose you could pay me in Os Spa shares, but you won't want to.'

'Why not?'

'Because you know that if I get more than six per cent that'll give me eleven altogether, and when Alpin comes in that would give us a boardroom majority. And then Carl Opgard's days as hotel boss would come to a sudden end and he'll be replaced by some nodding little yes-man for the French. So, Roy, where are you going to get that money from?'

I had to smile.

'Guess I'll have to borrow it then,' I said, with a nod towards the back of the stand.

Rita looked at me. Let her eyes glide up and down just the way she had that warm summer day an eternity ago when she'd come into my workshop in her high heels and I, a seventeen-year-old kid, was standing there bare-chested and oil-spattered. I had just turned on the ignition of her Saab, and she raised one of her painted eyebrows and wondered if there was anything else she could get me to turn on for her. That was then. The look now was more like some kind of credit assessment check.

'Good luck with that,' said Rita, and turned back to watch the game.

I moved a couple of rows up the stand. Even in his padded anorak the bank manager, Asle Vendelbo, looked exactly like a bank manager. I'm not saying all bank managers look alike, but Asle Vendelbo really did look like one. Friendly, smiling, spoke in a sweet, soft voice. His father used to run the village funeral parlour and he'd inherited some of the old man's discreet manner. I stood next to him.

'Hello, Roy. Think we'll win?'

'Depends.'

'Depends on what?'

'If we dare to attack.'

Vendelbo glanced at me.

'I'm thinking of asking for a loan of several million,' I said.

Vendelbo kept his eyes on the pitch, bounced on his heels,

hands folded behind his back, lower lip sticking out. It's curious how we can inherit even tics and habits, because what I saw then was Vendelbo senior, standing at the back of the church during the funeral for my mum and dad.

'I feel as though I want to make one of those whistling sounds,' said Vendelbo. 'But I can't whistle.'

'What d'you think?'

'That it all depends on what you need it for.'

'I mean, generally speaking.'

'Generally speaking?' He studied my face. Didn't see much there. 'Generally speaking I would say that in any case it's a very large amount for a small bank like ours. So it boils down to what you would be able to put up as security.'

'And if I can provide security?'

'Then we'd have to carry out a risk analysis on the basis of that. In any event, a loan that size would have to be made via head office.'

'Thought so.'

'You've got me curious here, Roy. What manner of project is this?'

'You'll find out when the time is right. I just wanted to give you a heads up that I might be asking you to call a meeting in the not too distant future. But for the time being, I'm hoping I can count on your discretion as regards our little chat?'

Vendelbo nodded and said something that was drowned out by an angry roar from the crowd. I glanced at the pitch. One of our star professionals was out for the count but the referee had obviously allowed play to continue. I said so long to Vendelbo and moved further along the stand. Shuffled past the Aas family. Old Jo Aas smiled. Mari too. Most village folk – young as well as old – got more bloated with each passing year, but Mari just got thinner. I could no longer make up my mind if she was still pretty, or if it was because I'd seen her back when she was the village princess and automatically read beauty into that bony face. After the break-up with Carl she'd gone to Oslo and studied political science, which was where she had met Dan Krane and brought him back to Os. Dan Krane was skinny, like Mari, with a prominent Adam's apple and veins in the close-cropped temples which gave a pretty good indication of what was going on behind those cold, blue eyes. Like the Aas family he was politically active, and I'm guessing that when he came here he had plans to one day take over the mayor's gavel, and that he saw the job as editor of *Os Daily*, the Labour Party newspaper, as a springboard to that. And for a long time things had gone as planned. They lived in a village where there was no Carl and no other echoes from the past, raised a couple of kids and, if not exactly popular, Dan was at least respected. He worked hard at fitting in, acquiring his hunting permit and walking around in wellies with the tops turned down. But no matter how friendly people like Mari and Dan try to be, wearing flannel shirts and dropping their aitches, they're never quite able to hide the fact that they feel as though they're just a cut above the rest in a place like Os.

Then something unexpected happened: Carl came home from the USA. He brought a wife with him and shouldn't have posed a threat. But he looked like a million dollars. And talked like ten million when he stood up there on the stage at Årtun and presented his plans for Os Spa which, he said, he wanted the whole village to own. He said the hotel would be the village's response to the planned tunnel at Todde. Now, nobody ever thought of Mari as being a slut. Quite the opposite, as the mayor's daughter she was considered something of a prude. On the other hand, I've sometimes thought that there is something in women like Mari that makes them feel a compulsive attraction towards any alpha male. In fact, I'm not even sure they try that hard to resist it, maybe feeling that it's logical and fated, that they're part of what makes power what it is. And since Carl was so definitely an alpha male, the saviour who had returned to his flock, it was only a question of time before the two of them resumed their relationship behind everyone's back. Not, of course, counting Grete Smitt, a shark that could smell blood a kilometre away.

But Dan's humiliation didn't end there. When Mari gave birth to her third, a little girl who was now six years old, the resemblance to Carl was so striking that even Jo Aas – according to Grete – had taken his daughter to one side and asked what was going on. Dan surely realised it too, but either he pretended he didn't know, or he let it go out of consideration for the kids. Amazingly, the marriage survived, but Dan was a broken man.

I had never liked Dan Krane – though that's not saying much, because there's not many people I do like – but with a kid who looked like a chip off an old block named Carl I had started to feel sorry for him. Gone were the firm strides, the straight back and those inspired editorials in the newspaper, their place taken now by a head one saw a little too often bent to a morning glass of beer at Fritt Fall, and badly written editorials that were neither angry nor stirring, just dull.

I tried to make eye contact to at least exchange a 'Hi', but from where Krane was standing, one step up from me, I had no luck. Instead he was following events on the pitch with a thousand-yard stare, as though he actually cared a fuck about what was going on down there.

I stood next to Carl. Looked over in Kurt's direction, on the far side of the pitch. From that distance it was easy to imagine he was staring right back. Staring at the Opgard brothers. A lot of people wondered why he had moved the substitutes' bench over to the far side of the pitch. For one thing it meant the reserves and backup staff had to run the width of the pitch at least four times in the course of every game, not to mention sitting with the west wind blowing into their faces for ninety minutes. Some said it was because Kurt didn't want to hear all the mud-slinging from the supporters who always gathered in the shelter of the barracks. Others claimed to have heard him say that it was to keep him distant from the club owners and sponsors in the VIP stand – he wasn't going to have anybody overruling his tactics and substitution from that quarter. But I think there was another reason: Kurt Olsen didn't want to sit with his back to me and Carl. He wanted to be able to look us in the eye. See what was coming. Show us what was coming.

An unexpected and chilly blast of wind flapped the Spa pennants on both sides of the stand.

'There's a lot of hate here,' I said.

'Typical derby game,' said Carl with a nod. 'They should have had at least two yellow cards.'

I sighed. Glanced at my watch. Thirty minutes to go. And that was just the first half.

5

PROMOTION WAS CELEBRATED AT FRITT Fall that same
evening.

Everyone was there, as they say.

Really I would rather have spent the evening alone with the
drawings of the big dipper and the ninety-second video I took
with my phone while whizzing round on those rails in Poland.
I'd read up on the background physics of the operation. Speed,
weight, friction, air resistance, temperature and so on. There's
an interplay of forces operating in different directions, acting
to keep each other under control, and you need to keep your
eye on it or risk the whole thing going to hell. Fortunately it's
all fairly predictable, physics being more law-abiding than
we humans. And I loved studying those drawings. The rigid,

squared geometry of the supporting structure against the elegant curve of the rails outlined against the horizon, like a replica of the mountains behind them. This wasn't one of those monsters they'd started building in Asia and the USA, 140 metres tall, a doom-drop of steel capable of speeds of up to 240 kilometres per hour. Even though a run built on the drawings I had would have been the world's highest wooden construction, it was above all about aesthetics, the fusion of art and physics. I wanted the whole experience, from the moment you saw the big dipper to the point at which you found yourself up in it, and under it, at the mercy of forces you had no control over, to be like a concert where you just have to open up your senses and be receptive to everything.

Opening up like that is definitely not easy for a person like me, but life has taught me a lesson or two about that as well. Moore had been sceptical about building a track based on plans his company had not designed itself, but he'd promised to have a think about it.

It was Carl who pointed out that I was under some obligation to attend the party.

'You're a sponsor, people are going to wonder why you aren't there.'

So I stood there at the bar and watched as the people and the players jumped up and down on the dance floor, bellowing along with Freddie Mercury and 'We Are the Champions'.

'Isn't this great?' shouted Julie, who was busy pulling a beer for someone.

'You bet,' I said. 'We'll probably make more this evening than we do in an average month.'

'Idiot!' She laughed and gave me a punch on the shoulder. 'We got promotion, Roy! Be happy.'

I shrugged. 'I'm happy enough, Julie. Sorry I can't manage to get hysterical about us moving up from one shit division to another. I'm more excited about that there.' I pointed to the bulge in her belly.

'Me too,' she said. 'They say it's easier second time around.'

I nodded. Everything's easier second time around. I looked at her. She was twenty-five now. Gone was that innocent and at the same time cheeky and defiant kid who started working for me at the petrol station as a seventeen-year-old. She'd put on a bit of weight, and she'd acquired that calm self-assurance some women don't get until they become mothers.

'What's on your mind?' she asked as she moved out of the way of Erik Nerell behind her with a tray of empty glasses.

'Thinking about back when you were seventeen and had to call me over every time someone wanted to buy tobacco,' I said. 'How you've changed.'

She smiled. No one could smile like Julie.

'Talking of change,' she said, 'have you seen Natalie Moe?'

'No. I just heard that she's got a job at the hotel.'

'Taken up a position, is what you say when it's head of marketing. And talking of jobs – we were wondering whether to ask if you'd be a godfather?'

I had a coughing fit and nearly choked on my beer.

'Again?' I said. 'Didn't you notice the last time how completely unsuited I am to the whole thing?'

'Oh yeah,' said a voice. 'But we figure it's best to have a heathen. Don't want to risk having kids who turn out Christians.'

An inebriated Alex had glided in behind Julie and given her a hug. He still had that close-cropped hair that looked like it was painted on his head, with a parting and gel, like an Italian footballer, but there the similarity ended. In a pre-season article in *Os Daily* in which all the players had been asked to characterise themselves in a single sentence Alex had replied with: 'Not technically good *but never gives up.*'

'Get over on the right side of the bar!' Julie said, pulling herself free.

'Hey, I'm a player!' Alex complained with a grin.

'So what?'

'Today you just dig us.' He leaned towards her and pouted his lips.

'Dig this,' she said as she slapped his face with a beer-soaked cloth. 'Shove off!'

Alex sighed and looked at me as though hoping for support, but I shook my head. He came round to the front of the bar.

'Saw you up in the stand.'

'Oh yeah?' I said. 'You were good today.'

'I was on the bench.'

'That's what I meant.'

He laughed. 'You prick.'

'Once a prick, always a prick,' said Kurt Olsen. He was standing on the other side of me. 'A beer, Julie.'

If people change, Kurt Olsen wasn't one of them. He was still the same slender, hollow-cheeked guy with the trailer-trash moustache and the Boris Johnson mop of blond hair he'd inherited from his father. Always the same sun-bronzed glow that came courtesy of his season ticket to Grete's solarium, supplemented by a winter holiday in the Canaries. They say the way a man is dressed the first time he gets a girl is the way he stays dressed for the rest of his life. If that's true then Kurt must have had his first girlfriend sometime back in the nineties. That was when all the city hipsters were listening to alt-country stuff like Wilco and the Jayhawks, and people out in the country were listening to Garth Brooks. Kurt Olsen's dress style suggested he could have played for both teams, with those tight-fitting jeans that accentuated his bow-legged walk, and the snakeskin boots he'd inherited from his father, the old sheriff. People used to say that in his playing days Kurt had been Os FC's best player. That he wasn't just good technically but could keep going for the whole ninety minutes, never gave up. That he should have played at a higher level. But he'd never accepted any of the offers he'd apparently had, probably figuring it was better to be a star in Os than to wear out the bench in a higher league. And when he did his knee in at the age of twenty-eight that was the end of his playing career anyway.

'Congratulations on promotion,' I said. 'You gonna sweep through the next division too?'

'Most people in Os say "we" when they're talking about the club, Roy. Not "you".'

He watched as Julie pulled another beer. 'And no, the next division up is for the big boys. So we're going to need that brother of yours to cough up some more money.'

'For what?'

'We need a quick defender.'

'Alex here is a defender. Free, and local.'

'I said a *quick* defender,' Kurt said without looking up at Alex. 'Success in football is never free, Roy. Any number of research articles all show the same thing, that the team that wins most has the highest wage bill. That's the simple, brutal truth of it.'

'So, not the team with the best trainer then?'

Kurt Olsen took the beer glass from Julie and had a sip. The music changed from Queen to the White Stripes' guitar riff. Everyone howled along, a-a-a-a-a. Kurt wiped the froth from his moustache and set his beer down on the bar.

'I know you don't have a clue, Roy, so let me just say that not even Mourinho can make a good player out of one with no talent.'

I lifted my own beer glass.

'Then it sounds like the logical thing to do is fire a trainer that gets paid and use the money to pay a wage to Alex, for example. As a way of increasing the wage bill, I mean.'

I took a gulp and heard Alex laugh. And Kurt telling him to get lost. As I put the glass back on the bar Kurt had his gaze fixed on me.

'There is a certain similarity between a trainer and a sheriff,' he said. 'Know what that is, Roy?'

'Is this where I'm supposed to say "no, do tell me"?'

His eyes narrowed. 'The job is preventative. I make sure trouble and difficult situations don't arise. I give the number 10 shirt to the best player; but the captain's armband goes to the player most likely to follow my tactical plans. I tell Stanley Spind that as the team's doctor he can wear our training gear, but not shower with the lads. In order to act—'

'—preventatively?'

Kurt turned his beer glass in his hand.

'I saw you talking to Rita during the match.'

'You *saw* that? So you thought the match was pretty boring too?'

Kurt put his hand on my shoulder and squeezed.

'I know Rita fooled around with you a bit when you were very young. It meant nothing to her, and she's told me how bad you were in bed, Roy. You weren't just inexperienced, you had no talent at all.'

'So even if she'd been Mourinho she wouldn't have managed to get me up to speed?'

'Roy . . .' He squeezed harder, dug his thumb in under my collarbone. 'Could be I'm not a hundred per cent sober right now, and that's why I'm finally spelling this out for you. But if you ever approach Rita again I will absolutely and completely fuck you over.'

'Whenever you like, I'll spread my cheeks for you.'

Kurt grinned a spray of spittle and beery breath into my face.

'You hoping I'm going to stick one on you, Roy? Really? Give you the chance to use that famous right of yours? Oh yeah, I remember you were a good fighter once, but it's a long time since we were teenagers at the village hop, Roy. I'd wipe the floor with you now. Don't believe me? Take the first shot.' He pointed at his chin. 'Hit a sheriff, then we'll finally be able to get you where you belong – behind bars.'

He sucked in his cheeks as though he was gathering a glob of spit. But instead of spitting he pulled my head towards him and whispered in my ear: 'In prison, Roy. A fucking life sentence. Just a shame for you that the statute of limitations was repealed. It means I'm going to be after you both till the day you die.'

He let go of me and laughed.

'Rita says you're after the campsite. If there's any more discussion on that offer, it goes through me. Got that? And I'm talking money *up front*. I don't fucking trust you.'

He picked up his beer and walked off, so rolling and bow-legged it was hard to tell just how drunk he actually was.

'What was all that about?' asked Julie, who had obviously seen us but not heard what was said.

'White Stripes,' I said. 'Good riff, isn't it?'

6

IT WAS SIX IN THE morning when I entered my petrol station.

There were times when I had to remind myself like that, that it was mine. I'd managed it for the oil company for so many years that the feeling of being just the guy who worked there was hard to shake.

'Morning , boss,' Egil said from behind the counter. He'd been working here for ten years and I couldn't recall a single time when he hadn't greeted me with exactly those words. It didn't matter that I only worked there now and then and handed over a lot of the responsibility of running the place to him. We were a station that stayed open nights and Sunday night/Monday morning could be busy, on account of all the cabin owners driving back to their city homes. On arrival I'd seen that Egil had tidied up and washed around the pumps, but a little further off there were still hot-dog wrappers and cigarette butts, over where the new generation of boy racers usually hung out. Fair enough, someone working nights alone shouldn't leave the station shop more than was absolutely necessary.

'I'll deal with it on my way out,' said Egil, who'd read my thoughts. He hadn't always been a lad you could rely on, Egil, sneaking off work, petty thieving. But something had happened when instead of sacking him the way he expected I'd given him a second chance. Things had worked out well for a while. Such a long while that when he did give in to temptation yet again he got another chance then too. In time I'd handed more of the responsibility over to him. He'd thrived on it. After I gave him a bonus based on the annual results he'd shaped up. The bonus wasn't big but it was enough for him to look me in the eye at last and get rid of his cap-doffing, peasant attitude. And when we took on new youngsters he'd hung that poster up again, the one I'd hung on the wall of the staff toilet.

DO WHAT NEEDS TO BE DONE. EVERYTHING DEPENDS ON YOU. DO IT NOW. Explaining to him that it wasn't anything to do with shitting.

'Great we got promotion, eh?' said Egil as he worked the till. I heard the chuntering sound as the printer in the office started to print out the day's takings. 'Did you go to the do at Fritt Fall?'

'Was there for a bit.'

'You hear anything about us getting that striker from Notodden?'

'Nope,' I said, and noticed that the rolls had defrosted and risen during the night and were now ready to serve. 'Probably the most interesting thing I heard actually was the White Stripes.'

' "Seven Nation Army"?'

I recalled that Egil was a football nerd. Manchester City supporter, unless I was much mistaken.

'I'm just surprised at football people having such taste. It's actually a good tune. Is it your team's song maybe?'

'No, no, ours is "Hey Jude".'

'The Beatles? Aren't Manchester people supposed to hate anything that comes from Liverpool?'

'Oh yeah. But that's the trick, right? You take the best thing the enemy has and you use it *against* them.'

'Eh?'

'Like with "Seven Nation Army". That was Club Brugge's song, they sang it when they beat AC Milan in Italy. But by the time they played at home against Roma a couple of years later the Roma supporters had learned the lesson and they sang "Seven Nation Army" *against* the home fans. And they won the game.'

I nodded. Steal your enemy's weapon. There was something in that, I just didn't know exactly what. But maybe it was something I could use.

Egil fetched his jacket from the mess room, said Daniel would be taking over at two o'clock, and left. Naturally, I let Egil play whatever music he liked, but as soon as he was out the door I switched to JJ Cale's *Stay Around*. The album was released six years after JJ Cale died, and yeah, there are good reasons to be sceptical about an album that's the result of someone going through an artist's unreleased sketches after he or she is dead. How good is it, *really*? It isn't easy to be objective about your own dead heroes and heroines. Had I been objective enough when I found those drawings for the big dipper, or did I love them because I'd loved *her*? I imagined Shannon must have made the sketches while sitting in the kitchen at Opgard and waiting for work to begin on Os Spa. Looked at the mountains, at the lines. To judge from the drawings with Budalsvannet and Ottertind in the background, it was also clear that she'd seen the campsite as the location. Carl had looked astounded the first time I mentioned the idea of a big dipper to him, so clearly she hadn't shown the drawings to him. Because why should she? The very idea of something that big up here in the Norwegian mountains was quite simply crazy. I'd weighed the pros and cons of telling Carl about the drawings I had, and that they were Shannon's. But for one thing, I was afraid he knew me too well and would know why I – the always cautious pragmatist – had suddenly come up with an idea I just *had* to complete. That it was about something more than simply the synergy between Os Spa and a roller coaster made of wood. And I doubted he would go along with the plan if he found out it was Shannon's vision. After Shannon died Carl hadn't even gone through her papers, just asked me to throw everything away in a cold, decisive voice: 'I want every trace of that whore gone.'

But was it really true, what I was telling myself, that I wanted to build that big dipper to honour the memory of the woman I loved, a memorial monument I could actually visit, since Shannon herself lay buried in the ground in her Barbados homeland? Or was there something else in me, something not quite so selfless? Kings built churches not to show how great God was but how great they were themselves. Dad had been fascinated by the Viking Age, when men were men and all that, and I remember especially the story he told us about two brothers, Øystein and Sigurd, who shared the royal power in the country. Øystein was the clever one of the two, charming and extrovert, and he erected several monuments to himself, including that enormous royal stopover in Dovre. Whereas Sigurd, the dark, introverted one, built just the one monument – the cathedral in Oslo. The two must have had a complex relationship, with Øystein the one who most people thought of as the real king. But when Øystein died they had to accept Sigurd as sole ruler, and Sigurd is the one still remembered down through history, as Sigurd the Crusader.

I looked at my watch. Rita Willumsen still had ten hours left.

A quiet start. Locals who filled up, paid up and left without expecting small talk. The driver for Nor Tekstil, who collected the dirty linen from Os Spa every weekday, stopped in for a coffee and two words before heading on to the dry cleaner's in Skien. Dagur, the Icelander who drives one of the two taxis in Os, stopped in to fill his red Mercedes and revealed that he was thinking of going over to a hybrid, same as Lillabeth and her husband who owned the village's other taxi, a white Toyota hybrid which had cut their running expenses by twenty per cent, or so they claimed. I nodded and said I had plans to add another two quick-charging bays.

It was now almost eleven, and it had been a good day, right up until I saw Grete Smitt standing on the far side of the major road. She was wearing Crocs and a T-shirt. Regrettably, she looked both left and right before crossing the road in my direction. The electric glass doors gave off a hoarse wheezing noise as they opened for her, and all I could think of right then was Darth Vader.

When we were growing up Grete was pale grey with flat, lifeless hair. Later she wore it in a perm like a fright wig. With a nose that looked like someone had put an axe through her head and left the blade sticking out she could have frightened the life out of the devil himself. Now being pretty isn't a human right, but when it came to Grete the good Lord had been downright mean. For that reason, if it had been anyone else you might have said it was divine intervention that Grete had what you might call *flowered* after she got herself a man. But Grete Smitt wasn't anyone else, she was such a nasty piece of work that the good Lord owed her sweet FA, and that went for me too. All the same, she was my very own Darth Vader, and she knew it. With all the things she knew about me and Carl she was a bloody landmine of a woman, waiting for the right moment to blow the balls off us both. A landmine just waiting for the moment when it *paid* to detonate.

'So, what are you going to do with the campsite, Roy?'

She plonked herself down in front of me, didn't even make a show of coming in to buy something.

'Have you been cutting Rita Willumsen's hair today?' I said.

'No, Kurt was in. Wondered if I knew anything.'

'So even the police do their detective work in your gossip salon these days?'

'I'm thinking you'll be relieved it wasn't a police investigation, Roy.'

I gave up in the staring contest that followed.

'A bun, Grete?'

'No.'

'Dieting?'

'Come on, Roy.'

I coughed. 'Even if I'm not going to run it as a campsite, exactly why should I tell you what I'm going to do with it?'

'Because I just told you Kurt's on the lookout for information, so quid pro quo, right?'

It was so unusual to hear Latin spoken in the village I had to ask her to repeat it. Maybe it came from that courtroom drama thing on Netflix that Simon thought was so good for the brain.

'Then let's say for camping and call it quits,' I said.

She stared at me. 'You're lying,' she said.

I shrugged. 'Three buns for the price of two?'

Grete Smitt turned, the soles of her Crocs screeching on the floor. Stopped for a moment in the open doorway as the cold wind swept in.

'By the way, Natalie Moe is back.'

The doors glided shut behind her with what sounded like a sigh of relief.

At twelve o'clock Kurt Olsen rang. His voice was hoarse after last night. He got straight to the point.

'If you can go up another million the place is yours, OK?'

'That's a lot,' I said. 'Think I'll stick at five and a half. Goes down to five after four o'clock.'

'Jeez, so it's not true then. You're always going round bragging that you people up at Opgard never haggle.'

'You're the one doing the haggling, Kurt. Does Rita know you're calling me?'

'Does . . . Why wouldn't she?'

'Because I doubt whether she'd handle the negotiations in the same cack-handed way you are.'

'What the fuck do you mean?'

'Rita would either beat about the bush for a while to see how high I was willing to go or just say no and leave it up to me to raise my bid or not. Whereas you slap a price on the table and that tells me you do want to sell. And if you want to sell, it's not a case of you being well pleased with six and a half million

59

but uninterested in five and a half. No one knows what that site is going to be worth after the Todde tunnel, and people aren't exactly queuing up to buy camping sites in the middle of nowhere.'

Silence at the other end. I heard a sound, like fingernails scratching an unshaven chin. Saw an image of a badly hung-over Kurt Olsen, and heard a sort of rustling sound that could have been the sound of Kurt Olsen thinking. And since thinking was not exactly Kurt's thing it went on for quite a while. Actually, it took a little too long, because by the time he responded it was already too late.

'Actually, that's *exactly* what's happening,' he said.

'Really?' I said.

'Yes. We've had an offer of six point four.'

'Just like that, out of the blue?'

'Oh no, I called someone I know is interested.'

'In camping?'

'Maybe.'

'And who might that be?'

'Naturally I'm not at liberty to disclose that.'

'But I'll know anyway once he's bought the site.'

Kurt didn't answer. He was lying, naturally. He must have known I would understand that. Now I didn't hate Kurt Olsen the way he hated me, mostly because I didn't have the same good reasons for doing so as he did. So I said nothing, to give him time to sort himself out and take the chance to beat a reasonably dignified retreat. But as the seconds passed I realised he wasn't going to take the chance. I could feel the doubt creeping up on me. Was I mistaken? Had they really got another buyer? But then who the hell would buy a camping site that was on the verge of being cut off from the rest of the civilised world?

And then it hit me.

Only someone who knew that wasn't what was going to happen.

'Let me think about it,' I said.

'You do that. You've got until . . . what, let's say four o'clock, shall we?' I could hear the malicious glee in his voice.

'OK,' I said.

'One other thing, Roy. I don't trust you for a second, so I'll want it in writing.'

'Will do.'

I hung up and rang Carl.

7

I DROVE FROM THE PETROL station at ten past two, into the centre and then up the road that connects the hotel and the village. Three hundred metres higher up I turned in at the front of the main building. Os Spa doesn't look all that spectacular at first glance. There isn't much front to it, and the oblong-shaped wings follow the curve of the land and blend in with the landscape. The old mayor, Aas, used to say it reminded him of the German bunkers he could recall from his childhood during the Occupation. Not that the association prevented him from investing in the place once the hotel returned as a joint-stock company after the fire. Him, and over a hundred other villagers too. Small investments, but enough to give them a feeling of ownership and to be able to call themselves 'hotel owners'. The returns had been solid enough, but over the next seven years no bonuses had been paid.

Carl had explained to the shareholders that this was usual when a company was in the growing stage. And because no one knew in advance just how much the rerouting of the main road would affect the hotel, it had proved difficult to sell the shares on. The new wing, to be built using a mixture of grey cement and blond wood, was ready to go, machines and carriers sporting the AUB logo of the Lithuanian building firm were in place. Voss Gilbert, who people still called the new mayor even after ten years with the gavel, said he couldn't wait to dig the first shovelful of dirt to the sound of a brass band.

I walked into the lobby. Granite, glass and wood. A bust of Jo Aas. Nothing to honour the one who'd designed the place, even though I was struck by the brilliance of the design every time I entered the place. Practical, clean lines, simple but at the same time sophisticated, in a warm, inviting way. Like Shannon Alleyne herself.

I nodded a 'Hi' to the receptionist and entered the lift. Carl's combined office and conference room was up on the third floor, which was, for one thing, extremely impractical, given that all the administration took place on the ground floor, and for another thing, it stole what could have been the second-best suite in the hotel, with a view of the mountains that almost matched the one from the Bridal Suite, with its view across Budalsvannet.

But Carl had been adamant. His idea was that he could invite loyal or important guests to lunch or dinner up there, the way the captain of a cruise ship will invite lucky passengers to dine with him.

Carl stood by the panorama window looking out as I walked in without knocking.

'This new wing is going to be *amazing*,' he said without turning round. 'I've just had a meeting with Lewi.'

'Lewi?'

'The Lithuanian. Head of AUB. He says the drawings are so detailed and complete that they don't even need to revise them. All they need to do is follow the instructions, make a start and get it built.'

He walked over to a chair and hung his suit jacket on the back of it.

'She was a genius, did you know that?' He looked at me. I just nodded and sat down at the long conference table. 'I've been thinking, Roy. We ought to name the new wing after her. What d'you think?'

'After Shannon?'

'Yes. The Alleyne Wing.'

I gulped.

'I thought you wanted to wipe out every trace of that . . . I think "whore" was the word you used?'

Carl sighed. 'Time heals all wounds, dontcha know.'

The fuck it does, I thought. Yours, maybe, but not hers. And not mine.

'Anyway,' he added, 'it occurred to me that it might seem odd, possibly even suspicious, if I, the widower, don't do something in memory of the dead. See what I'm getting at?'

I opened my mouth just slightly, just enough so the whole musculature of my jaw wouldn't tense and give me away.

Carl slumped down into his luxurious black leather office chair. 'So . . . any news?'

I told him about my phone conversation with Kurt Olsen. And that, if he was telling the truth, then the other bidder had to be someone who knew there was a fair chance the main road wouldn't be rerouted after all.

'Are you saying it's *me*?' said Carl. He pressed his fingers to his silk tie and gave me that rascally grin, the one that had melted all hearts, men and women alike, from the time when he was just a little lad. It was a joke, of course, but I nevertheless felt a little jolt at his words. Because the thought was troubling. Even though Carl and I had our shared economic interest, our financial destinies weren't quite so intimately bound up with each other as they had been once I'd sold my holding in Os Spa. The thought of Carl and me bidding against each other was out of the question, but still, we were no longer in the same boat. At least not when it came to money. If you're talking about life sentences in prison, well, that's another matter altogether.

'Could be GeoData,' I said.

Carl shook his head. 'Given that nothing here is listed perhaps the rules about insider trading don't apply when it comes to buying up property they know is going to go up in value once their report is published. But it would be a criminal offence nonetheless.'

'One of the partners has been done for fraud before.'

'Five million is a lot of money for that campsite even *with* the major road running past it, Roy. I can't see a couple of geologists suddenly deciding to invest in the tourist trade in some place they know nothing about.'

'They know I've got something going on and they want to sell it back to me at a higher price.'

'Come on, Roy. Maybe there are a few small pike in the waters here. Like Rita Willumsen, and possibly that partner in GeoData. But there are only two sharks, and that's you and me.'

'Perhaps you're right,' I said. I stood up and walked over to the window. God, how beautiful it was, with the heather glowing in autumnal reds up in the mountains, and the sky high and blue. 'But someone is out fishing for shark. Someone is using big hooks. Attached to a crane. I was talking to Kurt at the party last night. He was drunk, but he is definitely after us, Carl. He used the words "life imprisonment". Said straight out that we wouldn't be walking around as free men forever.'

'He said that?' Carl looked thoughtful.

'I can't imagine he's got anything new on us, but it's obvious he's expecting to find something in those cars when they lift them out.'

Carl nodded. He squeezed the skin below his chin between his thumb and forefinger.

'Anyway, I was thinking I'd give Kurt another contract suggestion this week,' he said. 'But maybe I should go a little higher than I was planning to.' Carl leaned over the desk which, he once claimed in jest, was made of wood from a threatened species of palm tree in Tuvatu. He picked up a fountain pen he had been given as a present by Jo Aas.

'I have always believed,' he continued, accentuating each word with the pen, 'that there are no limits to what people are willing to do or, as in this case, not do – if you just pay them enough. It could be money, sex, drugs, or power and glory. Mostly the latter. *No* limits.'

'You're beginning to sound like Dad,' I said.

The pen stopped tapping. My eyes met Carl's. I felt the chill.

'Sorry,' I said, and raised my palm. 'But for Kurt Olsen this is about him wanting to know how his father really died, right? And family trumps money. And power. And glory. Agreed?'

Carl looked tense as he sat staring at me from the high-backed chair.

'Agreed,' he said finally. His shoulders relaxed. 'Jesus, Roy, I have got to stop drinking.'

'What, again?'

'Before I only used to get angst afterwards,' he said, ignoring my remark. 'Now I get full paranoia too. Last night I dreamed the French took over here, kicked me out and I had to ask you for a job at the petrol station.'

'That's interesting. What did I say?'

'Can't remember. Or I woke up. What are you going to do about these offers?'

I shrugged. 'I think probably Kurt called me behind Rita's back to show her that he's up to squeezing me for an extra million. And I'm thinking it was probably me who gave him the idea that other buyers might be interested in offering, which he liked. Just spent a couple of seconds too long savouring it, so his bluff was exposed.'

'Bearing in mind we want to keep Kurt happy, maybe we should give him what he wants?'

I nodded. Carl's phone began to vibrate.

I turned to the window and made a call myself while Carl answered his.

'Yeah?' came the hoarse-voiced reply.

'OK,' I said. 'Six and a half it is.'

'In writing,' said Kurt, scarcely able to hide his relief. He'd probably been worrying he might have fucked up the deal Rita already had with me.

'You can have that, but I want to see the other offer first.'

'I already told you what it was.'

'I want to see it in writing.'

'Now listen here—'

'You don't trust me, Kurt, and I don't see any reason to trust you either. If you've made up an offer just to get me to raise my price then that's a valid reason for me to cancel the offer. Didn't Rita teach you that?'

I should have just left it and let Kurt piss all over me. But I couldn't resist it, I'm weak like that.

'The offer is verbal, and the buyer wishes to remain anonymous,' said Kurt.

'Then get it in writing. I don't need to know the name, it'll be good enough for me if I know Rita has seen the offer and confirms it. Because her I do trust.'

Kurt reeled off a few curses. You'd have to be a native of Os yourself to know which particular circles of hell they were consigning you to.

'Six o'clock,' he said. 'At Rita's house.'

Carl looked quizzically at me but got up and kept talking away on the phone in his broad Midwestern American when I signalled I needed to use his computer. I tapped in the offer in a couple of brief lines and signalled to Carl to read them – I didn't want to give Kurt any excuse to crack a few dyslexia jokes. Without lowering the phone from his ear he peered at the screen and corrected two spelling mistakes, then I sent the text to the print room on the ground floor and left.

I held the lift doors for a middle-aged couple who came flip-flopping along the corridor in white dressing gowns. The doors slid shut and we stared stiffly past each other.

While they continued on down to the spa section I walked

through reception and made my way to the administration section. The print-room door was open and I queued up behind a fair-haired girl who was standing there sorting the pages as the machine spat them out. She had a cup of coffee on the side of the machine, and her head was bobbing to the music from the headphones she was wearing. I coughed, to announce my presence, so she wouldn't jump and tip over the coffee cup when she turned and saw me. But the music was obviously too loud. The sounds leaking out were familiar. It was the riff from yesterday.

I coughed louder.

The girl turned. Gave me a big, open smile.

'Nearly done!' she shouted unnecessarily.

'Take the time you need,' I said, also smiling. Waited for her to turn back to the printer but she didn't. Just kept on looking at me.

'Roy Opgard?'

'Yes,' I said.

She took off the headphones. I could hear now that it wasn't the White Stripes but something classical, at any rate something with a lot of wind instruments and violins in it.

'Don't you recognise me?'

I gazed at her. The intense eyes seemed too big for the narrow face with the high cheekbones. And there was something about the colour of them, as though the irises were layered with a greenish tinge at the bottom that glided over into blue, and into light blue at the top. It wasn't just the colour that was special, it was the expression in them. 'Crying eyes' was what Carl and I used to call it. Eyes with something wounded and vulnerable in them. Yet this girl – whom I put at somewhere in her mid-twenties – didn't seem especially vulnerable or frightened but continued to hold my gaze with that nice, unwavering smile of hers. And that was the reason I hadn't recognised her.

'Natalie Moe,' she said.

'Natalie Moe?' I echoed in disbelief before I could stop myself. 'Of course. My brother told me you'd started work here. Sorry, it must be . . . what do they call it again? Alz . . . ?'

'No need to apologise,' she said. 'I'm pleased when people round here don't recognise me from before.'

'You are?'

She shrugged. 'I think you know the reason better than most, Roy.'

I nodded. Gave that slow Os nod that can mean everything and nothing. Up and down. Nodded finally at the headphones.

'What's that you're listening to?'

She gave a quick smile, realising I was keen to change the subject. 'Bruckner's Fifth Symphony.'

'Jeez. Not many people in Os listening to stuff like that.'

'Nor me either, actually. I'm just, I suppose, sort of . . . searching.'

'Searching,' I repeated. I could not stop that damn nodding I was doing. Fortunately I noticed that the batch she was printing was finished, and the sheet with my offer on slid out.

'That's probably mine,' I said, pointing. She stepped to one side and I grabbed up the sheet.

'It's good to see you back, Natalie. Where . . . ?'

'No, I'm not living at home with my father,' she said. 'He's on his own now, you knew that, didn't you?'

'I heard he was a widower, yes,' I said. Maybe she put a little bit extra into telling me how he was alone now, but I didn't need to know that. It was enough just to look at her now, a grown woman, no longer that frightened teenager who'd needed help. Help to get over the shame, to get out of the village. Get out of that house.

'See you around then,' I said.

'Roy?'

It was strange to hear her say my name that way. Natalie and I had hardly exchanged a word back when she lived here and came in to shop at the petrol station, and yet we had this thing that bound us together at the same time as it separated us. That time I'd seen her in the cafe in Notodden she'd pretended she hadn't seen me, and I'd been glad.

I turned in the doorway and looked at her. She said something, one word, but so quietly it was drowned out by the printer which, at that exact moment, announced with a shrill beep that it was finished. I smiled and signalled that I really had to be on my way.

The autumn air was cool and gentle against the warmth of my forehead as I stepped out into the car park. I got into the Volvo and turned on the engine. I'd read the word that formed on her lips.

Natalie Moe had said *thanks*.

8

DRIVING PAST NERGARD AND BEGINNING the climb I saw something moving high up on the rock face below Geitesvingen. It took a few moments for me to realise that what looked like a large beast clambering slowly up the overhang was a car. I stopped and took a closer look. Sure enough, it was the first car, the wreck of the black Cadillac DeVille, the 1979 model Dad had bought 'without haggling' from Willum Willumsen, who had claimed that the car had been carefully driven along nothing but straight highways in bone-dry Nevada and that it was rust-free and as good as new. It had its first visit to the workshop inside just two weeks and over the next few years it gave me my education in car mechanics. But the most important lesson I learned was that it was actually possible to repair things. For a time I believed that applied to everything. I don't believe that any longer.

By the time I reached Geitesvingen the salvage crane had already winched the Cadillac up and deposited it onto the bed of a waiting truck, on top of Carl's '85-model DeVille and the white E-Type Jaguar that belonged to Willumsen's Danish hit man. The men standing there watched me. I recognised one of them, the only one not wearing a hi-vis jacket. I stopped next to him and lowered the window.

'Gilliani?' I said. 'You working for the Highways Department now?'

The crime-scene tech smiled and pushed the nerdy pair of glasses he was wearing higher up his nose.

'You've got a good memory, Opgard. How long has it been? Seven years? Eight?'

That was back when Kurt Olsen had demanded that KRIPOS send a team to investigate the bodies down in Huken. KRIPOS hadn't found anything to suggest they hadn't all died as a result of injuries sustained in the drop. And when they also found a type of gunshot residue on the hit man's hand that tied him to the gun found on the pillow next to Willumsen's body they decided they could close that case too: the hit man had killed Willumsen. Motive? KRIPOS said there were several to choose from when a debt of thirty million was involved, but saw no reason to continue the investigation now that both parties were dead.

Apart from the fact that now, seven or eight years later, they clearly saw a reason after all.

'I'm guessing it was Kurt Olsen who called in KRIPOS,' I said.

'Could be.'

'I see. You gonna be taking all three cars back to the lab with you?'

'That's the plan.'

'What for? Some new developments in the case?'

'New and improved technology,' said Gilliani.

'Oh yeah?'

I recalled the fancy equipment he had with him back then, that gunshot residue detector that looked like a hairdryer.

'But what do you need the old Cadillac for?'

'The statute of limitations no longer applies. But I guess you probably know that.'

'No,' I lied. And remembered the day Carl and I sat listening to the radio and heard that the government had voted to change the law.

'Murders committed within the last twenty-five years ago can all now be prosecuted throughout all eternity,' said Gilliani.

'You don't say?'

'It's true. And Olsen says it's less than twenty-five years since the first car went over the edge here. That's correct, isn't it?'

I nodded. Remembered how Carl and I cursed as the reporter on the radio outlined the consequences of the resolution. If the change had come just a few years later, we would have had three fewer murders to worry about.

'What sort of clues could you expect to find after so many years?' I asked.

'We'll see. Neither rain nor sunlight penetrates that far down into the ravine, and DNA is more robust than people think.'

I looked at Gilliani, trying to read his face. Was he trying to scare me, or was he talking so openly because Carl and I had been so completely ruled out as suspects the last time KRIPOS were here?

'Good luck,' I said, and added that I had coffee in the kitchen if they were going to be up there for a while. Gilliani grinned and shook his head.

I was on my third cup of coffee and the Highways Department was busy boring holes for the struts for the crash barrier that was going to go up. The thin glass of the kitchen windows shook and rattled so loudly that at first I didn't hear the phone ringing.

'Yes?' I shouted above the din.

'This is Halden.'

'Wait a moment,' I said, and moved to the living room where we had installed proper windows. 'That's better. So, made up your mind yet?'

'Where can we meet?'

He sounded nervous. I thought about it. Nervous was good. If he'd gone to the police he would have sounded a lot calmer. He didn't suggest a time and place, left that to me, so it was unlikely to be a trap. It was anyway less than two days since my visit to him and I figured the police would need more time than that to work out a plan.

'Notodden,' I said.

'Isn't that a bit close to Os? If someone you know sees us together . . .'

'The Brattrein Hotel,' I said. 'Wednesday at three. Room 333 unless you hear to the contrary, go directly there. And come alone.'

'But Fuhr wants—'

'Alone. He can come along if he likes but he'll have to wait in the car.'

There was a pause, and I got the feeling he was exchanging

looks with someone listening in on the conversation. Fuhr, I guessed.

'OK, Opgard.'

'Good. See you there.'

.I hung up. Stared ahead. Why had I said Room 333? Was it only because I knew what it looked like, the layout of the room, where the bathroom was, for example? But all the rooms were probably alike, so it must have been sheer nostalgia, that I wanted to see once more the room in which Shannon and I had made love for the first time. Or was it because this was a place that was already cursed, the place where I had betrayed my own flesh and blood and started down the road towards becoming what I had turned into during these last eight years – a cynical sinner who had lost the moral compass that had once sustained in him the desire to become a somebody, to stand for something, to count? To be there for Natalie Moe when no one else lifted a finger to help. Twice 333. A number that suited the new Roy Opgard.

I called Carl. 'I'm meeting the tunnel guy tomorrow.'

'Oh yeah? What did he say about—'

'We'll talk about it this evening.'

We hung up. I sat down in Dad's old wing chair, the one that Carl, strangely enough, had insisted we keep after we'd redecorated the place. I stared at the phone. I had avoided any mention of GeoData or Halden and made certain Carl didn't say too much either. Had Kurt's threats got to me? Was it because I had had KRIPOS quite literally on my doorstep? Or was Carl's paranoia beginning to affect me too?

I w____d back to the kitchen, found a pen next to the bread bin _____ the offer. Looked at the stove pipe that ran from the _____ through the hole in the ceiling to where the two of us had slept in our first-floor bedroom, with just enough of a gap in the floorboards to make sure the house didn't burn down. Carl had gone on about how we should upgrade the kitchen too; I really don't know why I had objected. He wanted to keep the wing chair, and I to keep the wood stove with the chimney. Neither one of them represented happy memories for us. But ties to things from the past can be an enigmatic business.

It was six o'clock exactly when I pressed the doorbell at Rita Willumsen's house.

It was, for the time being at least, still the largest detached house in Os, and – with those two ridiculous pillars on either side of the front door – the nearest thing to a stately home in the village. As I waited it occurred to me that in the course of my forty-four years in Os this was the first time I had ever stood in front of this door. That the only time I had been inside this house before I had entered via the cellar door.

The door opened and there was Rita, towering above me.

'He's waiting for you up in the bedroom,' she said as she stepped to one side.

'Bedroom?' I said as I entered.

'You know the way, Roy.'

Before I could ask what all this nonsense was about she had disappeared into the living room. I climbed the broad staircase. On the wall above the landing hung a portrait of Willum Willumsen. Even though the artist had edited out some of the double chins and tried to make his subject look dignified rather than villainous, the end result was as unappealing as the man himself had been in life.

The door to the bedroom, which I had also only entered once

before in my life, was open. I stuck my head inside. Kurt was lying on the bed. Sure, he was fully clothed, but his pose and general appearance were undeniably reminiscent of the iconic photograph of the naked Burt Reynolds lying on a bearskin rug that had once appeared in *Cosmopolitan* magazine. Another difference being that a cigarette rather than cigarillo dangled from his lips, and his head was supported by the left and not the right hand. His right hand was held out towards me.

I handed him the sheet of paper with the offer on it. He read it quickly then pushed it under the blanket.

'Thought you might like to take another look at the scene of the crime,' he said.

'Oh, but Rita and I never fucked in here,' I said.

Kurt tensed and the veins in his temples stood out.

'This is where you shot Willum Willumsen,' he said.

'And you got me up here to see how I would react?' I said as I looked around. As far as I could gauge, nothing had changed. But of course, back then it was winter, and so early in the morning it was dark. I sucked my teeth.

'How d'you think your X-ray vision is working, Kurt?'

'You're a cold fucking fucker, Roy.'

'Two fucks in the same sentence. Which reminds me, I want to see that other offer.'

'You said it was good enough for you if Rita saw it.'

'OK, so get her up here then.'

'Nah, I'll let you look.'

He pulled another sheet of paper from under the blanket. Placed his hand over the lower half of it and held it up for me to see. I peered at it. A few brief, handwritten lines, with a concluding *Yours sincerely*. Kurt's hand covered the name. He was about to put the sheet of paper away again.

'Wait,' I said.

'Oh, sorry,' said Kurt. 'I forgot, you're dyslexic.'

I looked at it. Sure enough, the offer was for 6.4 million, and it didn't look as if the figure had been altered. I read the short text again. *For the campsite owned by Rita Willumsen I bid the sum of 6.4 million Norwegian kroner. Yours sincerely.* Something stirred inside me. Something about the note. Something that could be worth more than the million Carl thought I should pay to keep Kurt sweet.

'Fine,' I said.

'And the moola?'

'You'll get it once the deed has been signed. That's the usual procedure. I would expect you as sheriff to follow the usual procedure.'

He grinned. 'It's Rita's money, and I don't know much about that kind of stuff. But now I have this . . .' He tapped the blanket above where my offer lay. 'And if you don't pay up . . .' He ran a finger across his throat.

'Quite the hit man, aren't we?' I said. 'Apropos, if it wasn't the hit man who knocked off Willum then maybe you did it. I mean, look at where you are now. Maybe it was all part of a cunning plan.'

Kurt Olsen made a face. 'As though your soul wasn't ugly enough already, Roy.'

'I'll see myself out,' I said, and left the room before he could get to his feet.

As I passed the living room I popped my head round the door.

'I've just bought your place, Rita.'

'Congratulations,' she said without looking up from the thin book she was reading, probably some great literary classic. If she'd been hoping Kurt would be as receptive to stuff like that as I was then she'd probably been disappointed. But then I guess he must have had other qualities.

'Why d'you leave the dealing to him?' I asked.

Finally she looked up. She seemed tired.

'He wanted to.'

'Wanted to impress you? Or just screw me?'

Rita Willumsen sighed. Her thick hair was braided and bound in a tight knot. Maybe the idea was to stretch the wrinkles that were beginning to show.

I heard Kurt coming down the stairs.

'You've seen the other offer?' I asked.

'Six point four,' she said. 'Looked just about good enough.'

I waited to see if she was going to expand on that *enough*. Until I remembered that I was content, both with what I'd bought and what I'd acquired into the bargain. So I nodded and left by the front door.

9

IT WAS SEVEN IN THE morning when Carl came into the kitchen.

'Thought you were working today,' he said as he poured himself a cup of coffee from the pot that had been quietly puttering away for the last hour.

'Got Egil to cover for me,' I said. 'Rita and I are signing the deed at the bank today, I want to get there a bit early and go through things with Vendelbo.'

'Vendelbo's a good man to have on your side,' said Carl. He slurped his coffee, and the sound reminded me of Dad. He used to pour coffee into his saucer to cool it down, then slurp it up with a noise you could hear all the way up through the hole in the floor to the bedroom where Carl and I slept.

'Apropos good to have on your side,' said Carl. 'I've been think-ing about Natalie Moe. What do you think of her?'

'What do I *think* of her?'

'I think it might be a good idea to involve her in the campsite project. We need someone who's good at marketing.'

I crossed to the window.

'Maybe. But maybe a bit young for such a big project? Maybe someone else.'

'Young is what we need. They know the networks, they under-stand what works. Did I tell you she had a job offer from an Oslo-based chain when we snapped her up?'

'I'm sure she's good,' I said. 'But . . .'

'But?'

'Are you certain she's reliable?'

'As in?'

'As in, you tell her something and it won't get spread around all over town. As in, if she works for us two then we can't have someone who digs a bit too deeply into . . . private matters.'

'Natalie's the real deal. She's a serious young lady. I prom-ise you.'

I thought about it. I don't know why, but it bothered me. Natalie obviously felt she owed me something, but all the same. Or maybe that was exactly the problem. It could easily get too personal.

'I don't know,' I said. 'It seems a bit early to be thinking about marketing.'

'Early?' Carl opened his arms wide. 'You've got your campsite now. You've got the plans and a builder who's going to build it for you. As soon as the report is published showing we're going to keep the main road then all that's left after that is to sell the idea to Vendelbo and the bank. And I'll handle that, you know that.'

82

'Do I?' I said. The clouds dragged above Ottertind, rain was forecast. 'What if they say no?'

'They won't.'

'I mentioned the potential size of the loan to Vendelbo at the match. He didn't exactly faint, but he did say it would be about security.'

'Exactly. When the news breaks that the road isn't going to be rerouted after all then the price of our properties will rocket, and we can give the bank security from here to the moon and back. And once we've got the loan, then suddenly it's show-time, the cat's out of the bag. Then it's going to be about how to get news of the project out into the media in the right way. Use professionals like Natalie and we'll get the full-blown *wow* effect. You only get one chance to make a good first impression, right?'

I gave a reluctant nod.

'OK?' asked Carl.

I sighed. 'OK.'

He crossed the room and stood beside me at the window. Rested a hand on my shoulder and took another slurp of his coffee.

'Looks like we're going to get a crash barrier,' he said.

'Looks like it.'

Os Sparebank occupied the same featureless eighties building that housed the county administration, the sheriff's office and the doctor's surgery. Asle Vendelbo, the bank manager, and I watched Rita as she read through the sales contract. Vendelbo had established that there were no outstanding debts on the property, that it wasn't subject to licensing, and that the money had been transferred from my account to the bank's and was ready to be paid over to Rita.

'Standard formula all the way,' said Vendelbo as Rita flipped through the pages. 'The only thing I've added just for the sake of formality is that there was an offer of six point four, since I gather neither of you wants a separate record of the offers with the names of the other bidders?'

Rita and I nodded.

Vendelbo called in his assistant as a second witness as Rita and I signed the deed with copies and sale documents. And when everything was signed, sealed and witnessed Vendelbo congratulated us both on the transaction and showed us out.

'Actually, Roy, could I have a few words with you on another matter?' Vendelbo said as he held the door for us.

I nodded, and Rita looked a little relieved that she wouldn't have to leave with me. We stood watching her as she left. Sometimes I suspect women of adding an extra wiggle when they know they're being watched by men, but not Rita Willumsen. That's just the way she walks. Like a cat.

'Thanks for helping me with the sales contract,' I said. 'And for approving the loan application so quickly.'

'Usually we wouldn't allow that much on a campsite,' said Vendelbo. 'But since it only involved transferring an existing loan from one customer to another we didn't want to complicate things unnecessarily.'

We watched as Rita stepped into the Saab Sonett. Amazing what good condition they were in, both of them. Style, I thought. Lots of style. The last thing Rita Willumsen would give up.

'The reason the bank is allowing the same size of loan is that it's being transferred from a slightly risky borrower to one that's more secure,' I said. 'I'm assuming you've seen Willumsen AS's books. I'm thinking you'll be glad she's selling and getting rid of some of that debt.'

Vendelbo merely gave a thin smile. Bank manager's discretion.

He coughed.

'I just wanted to inform you that I raised your query about a loan in the hundred million class with head office. And that, unfortunately, they're a little sceptical about a loan financing something that is going to be so far off-centre. Or to put it another way, that the security being offered is out here. Because, of course, your financial worth is in property in Os, and head office has noted the fall in prices since the decision on the Todde tunnel. Their assessment is that prices will continue to fall.'

'Can't they see that things are happening here?' I said. 'Os Spa is really thriving, it'll do just fine without the main road.'

Vendelbo sighed, swayed on his heels, tugged at the belt on his suit trousers.

'Os Spa by itself isn't going to be enough, Roy. The village is suffocated. In another three or four years it's not even certain the bank will still be here. So from my point of view I welcome anything that can breathe new life into the area. But head office doesn't see its job as giving special treatment to Os. They've already started looking at projects in Todde.'

'Todde? There isn't anywhere named Todde.'

'No, but there might be.'

'Oh? And you want to be bank manager in . . .' I pursed my lips as though I was going to spit. '. . . Todde?'

Vendelbo thought about it. 'Actually, no, I don't.'

'No. Anyway, thanks for the heads up.'

I buttoned up my Levi's jeans jacket with the fur collar. Julie told me they were coming back into fashion. Well, I'm still waiting.

My phone rang on the way out to the car. I didn't recognise the number, but it didn't get flagged as a sales call either so I took it.

'Yes?'

'Hi, this is Natalie. Carl asked me to call.'

I swore silently. Quite OK for Carl to be on top of things, as they say, but he was rushing too far ahead, always did. And when he tripped up it was always me – the big brother – who had to catch him.

'There's a project you want to discuss, I gather?'

'Yes,' I said. 'Sort of.'

'OK. When does it suit you to meet up?'

I thought about it. Looked at my watch. I was off to Notodden in the morning. The day after that I'd promised to do a double shift in exchange for Egil covering for me today. Maybe best to get it over with.

'How about now?'

'OK. Where?'

'At the campsite. You got a car?'

'Yep. I'll be there in ten.'

Nine minutes later, watching Natalie as she walked towards me from a dusty Mitsubishi, I realised she was pretty. She probably had been even as a teenager and I just hadn't noticed it. Or she'd kept it hidden, with her cowed walk and her head bent so that she could hide herself behind the black fringe. Not like Julie was back then, with her earthy, extrovert ways and her already womanly curves, glowing with self-confidence and playfulness and already hot stuff for all those boy racers who hung around the petrol station like predators around a watering hole. Which is not actually a good image, since these young sprouts danced to Julie's tune. No, the real predators in Os stayed in their caves, behind four walls.

And yet I couldn't help noticing that Natalie Moe had something of the same hip-swinging walk as Rita Willumsen.

'Long time since I've been here,' she said, again with that very direct gaze, as though looking people in the eye was something she'd decided at a certain point in her life she was going to do, and practised doing it, and had obviously mastered it. It seemed very natural to me, at any rate. I'd often wished I had it, that outgoing manner, Carl had it too. Maybe Natalie had always had that brightness in her, and it was only the situation she found herself in that had darkened and stunted her ways. Whereas I had grown up in the dark and always been dark, from the very beginning. And I had never kidded myself I was going to be capable of some great metamorphosis, as people say.

Quite automatically we headed off walking between the small wooden camping huts in the direction of the lake. The grass needed cutting, the cabins a lick of paint. The season was over, but Rita had let me know which of the twenty cabins were booked and still in use. The arrangement was for keys, bedclothes and towels to be handed out and handed in at the petrol station for the autumn.

'You know, we used to come here to swim in the summer,' said Natalie. 'Actually my dad wouldn't allow it, he was worried about the boys on holiday here. So I asked Mum, pointing out that the camping site had the only good beach on the lake, and she said it would be OK.'

'Smart lady.'

'Maybe,' said Natalie with a smile. 'But it was a lie – of course it was to meet boys here.'

We laughed. It reminded me there was a before and an after in Natalie's life, a time of innocence, before the beast of prey struck.

'What about you?' she said. 'Did you and Carl come here when you were growing up?'

'Sure did,' I said. 'That was before there were any cabins here, when people stayed in caravans and tents. I made a friend here one summer. So I came down the following summers, hoping to see him again, but he never came back. Or actually, one summer I did see a boy who looked like him, and I went up to him and said his name. I mean, the name of my friend. The boy looked at his pals and laughed, and asked me where my banjo was. I didn't come down here again after that. Until a couple of years ago.'

She didn't say anything, and I suddenly thought that was a strange thing to tell a person you hardly knew. I'd only ever told the story to one person before, and it didn't even occur to me how lonely it made me sound. Because Shannon already knew.

I cleared my throat.

'The reason I came back here, of all places, was that I had this idea. And I found some drawings that made it clear I could make that idea a reality.'

I saw no reason to tell her that things had actually happened the other way round, but registered that I'd just told my first lie to Natalie Moe.

'A roller coaster,' she said.

'Damn,' I said. 'Carl?'

'Yes.'

'I was hoping to see the look on your face the first time I mentioned it.'

'Why?'

'To get some idea of where, on a scale of insane ideas, you were going to locate it.'

She laughed.

'Carl thought I didn't look all that shocked.'

'No? And there's Carl telling me you're a serious-minded, highly professional person.'

'I am!' She was still laughing and her laughter reminded me of her. Of course. Now and then I catch myself wondering when I'm going to stop looking for her among the living, but the thing has taken hold inside of me, it's like a bloody virus, not always active, but always there, in the blood. I tried to ignore the memory.

'That's typical of all original ideas,' said Natalie. 'The first time you hear them they sound crazy. And then if they catch on we think the only crazy thing about it was that no one had thought of it before. Tell me about it.'

'I'm not sure how much Carl has told you.'

'Only that it's a roller coaster made of wood. And that it's to be built here.'

I nodded.

We sat down on one of the wooden benches by the jetty in front of the boathouse and I told her that the idea was for something that would complement Os Spa. Something aimed more at whole families. As things were, the hotel didn't have that much to offer kids and young people. A small swimming pool, the chance to see a fox or a deer during a mountain walk, these things were all well and good, but families with children who wanted to swim preferred to go to Sommarland in Bø, just the other side of Notodden, and if they wanted to see wildlife they headed for the Zoological Gardens in Kristiansand. I told her how I'd been in Poland and seen Zadra, the world's biggest wooden track.

'It's in a village named Zator, it's no bigger than Os and it's way out in the sticks, a seventy-minute drive from Krakow. But it's got Poland's biggest amusement park. They've got all sorts of other things of course, but it's the roller coaster that's the big draw. That's why dads are prepared to drive for over an hour on a Sunday.'

'So you're thinking something similar here too? An amusement park catering to the whole family?'

'Yes. But the track has to come first.'

'Of course,' she said.

I glanced at her. Time for the first test.

'Why "of course"?'

She replied without hesitation.

'Because a roller coaster will show the level of ambition your park has. It'll create headlines and expectations about the rest of the park too. And the best recipe for success is to create high expectations and then meet them. Even a partial success can be enough if the expectations raised in the first place are high enough. That even beats modest expectations that are exceeded, if you get my meaning.'

'Why is that?'

'Because expectations influence perception. There was a famous example from the US, of a delicatessen that sold its own cheese in two different wrappings. On one of them it just said "Sliced Cheese" and on the other it said "Delicatessen Sliced Cheese". When customers were asked what they thought of the cheese, people who had bought the "Delicatessen Sliced Cheese" were most pleased. But there are limits, of course – if an amusement park promises a lot more than it delivers then customers are going to punish it all the harder if it fails to deliver.'

I gave that slow Os nod. 'So what you can help with would be . . .'

'. . . building up the great expectations. Delivering them will be up to you.'

'I see. And how will you do that?'

'Today I just wanted to hear what you plan to do, then I'll think a little more about my bit, OK?'

'Actually,' I said, and almost dried up in the face of her unexpected self-assurance, 'it was Carl's idea I should talk to you, I'm really not sure I need anyone to do the marketing at all at this stage. And Os Spa and this are two separate enterprises, so you don't have any obligations here.'

'I know that.' She smiled. 'So if we go ahead then I'll work on it in my spare time and invoice you at an hourly rate.'

'Oh shit,' I said. 'Is the meter running?'

She laughed. 'Not yet.'

'OK,' I said. 'Let me think about it.'

We stood up and headed back towards the cars.

'You've lost some of your accent after studying in Oslo,' I said.

'That's not the only thing I lost in Oslo,' she said. Glanced over at me with one eye half closed. I thought of Shannon's congenital, heavy-drooping eyelid – a condition which she called *ptosis*. I couldn't tell whether the look was an encouragement to delve deeper, or a warning not to, but I let it go anyway.

A fat man wearing underpants and a T-shirt emerged from one of the cabins. Belched and scratched his upper arm as he watched us walk past. I stood next to the Mitsubishi as Natalie got in. Music came on as soon as she turned the ignition. Violins again, but not classical. This time the sound of a Hardanger fiddle.

'What's that?' I asked.

'Odd Bakkerud. You like it?'

I listened. A whining caterwauling. Dad had always turned off the radio whenever folk music came on. It reminded me of something, but what the hell was it?

'Psychedelic,' I said. 'Is it new?'

She laughed. 'From the fifties. When he played at local dances, before he changed his style.'

Jimi Hendrix. That was it. 'Purple Haze', from the Woodstock concert. That's what it reminded me of.

'Saturday morning,' I said. 'OK for you if we meet then?'

'Weren't you going to think about it?'

'I already have. Ten o'clock OK?'

'Fine.'

'You know where Opgard is?'

'Course I do. Want to know what my hourly rate is?'

'No, but I'm guessing you're not proposing to bankrupt me either.'

Natalie put her head on one side and gave me a strange look.

'It's not just me. I think you've changed too, Roy Opgard.'

'Oh? In what way?'

'I don't know,' she said. Then she told me her hourly rate, raised the window and drove off. As I watched her go I realised it was time to rethink that business about Opgards never haggling over money.

10

ON WEDNESDAY MORNING I PHONED Vera Martinsen at KRIPOS.

She'd been in Os in connection with the death of Poul Hansen, the Danish hit man. We'd liked each other. Some might even have called it a relationship, because she'd visited Os a few times after that, and I'd been to visit her in Oslo. It had been enjoyable and certainly therapeutic, but from my point of view it was just too soon after Shannon for me to summon up any strong feelings. The last I'd heard was that Vera had met a guy at work and now they were living together, had even moved into a new house. After chatting briefly about our respective lives – and there she had more to tell than I did – I got to the point. Or rather, she did.

'You're wondering what's happening with the checks on the cars?'

'Yes.'

'And you know I'm not allowed to tell you that?'

'Yes.'

'But you're asking anyway.' I heard the note of rebuke.

'I suppose I am. They were my parents, Vera. You'd want to know too if anyone was responsible for their deaths.'

'I probably would. Especially if I was in danger of being a suspect.'

I tensed. Back then Vera had ridiculed Kurt Olsen's accusations. Called them conspiracy theories. Explained to me that KRIPOS had made the trip to Os because it was Oslo policy to show support for small, local sheriffs' offices. Had she changed her mind?

'I didn't mean it like that,' she said. 'All I'm saying is that no matter what we find, that sheriff of yours will think up some way to connect it to you and your brother. He seems as keen on it now as he was back then.'

'OK,' I said.

There was a pause. She said nothing.

'*Have* you found something?' I finally asked.

'Roy . . .'

'I know. Sorry. It's good to hear your voice again, Vera. And I'm pleased to hear things are working out for the two of you. Good luck with the new house. And be careful it doesn't turn out to be grounds for a divorce.'

'I will. Say hello to the golden plover from me.'

'Will do.'

I didn't hang up. She didn't either.

'They found blood,' she said. 'And hair.'

I waited. There wasn't any more. She'd hung up.

On the drive to Notodden I listened to JJ Cale. But after a while I pulled over to the side, got out my phone and navigated to the name Odd Bakkerud. I connected the first tune that came up – 'Fanitullen' – to the sound system and drove on. I'd heard it before – everyone in Norway knows it – where the fiddle player now and then raises his bow and plays the strings with his left hand. But this wasn't as wild as the music Natalie had played in the car.

There was still half an hour to go before three when I pulled in and parked behind the Brattrein Hotel. There weren't many cars there, and only one with an Oslo plate. And it wasn't Halden's Audi. But when I asked at reception for the key to Room 333 she told me my guests had already arrived.

Guests. Plural.

Shit. Police? I waited by the lift. Time to get out of there?

Even before visiting Halden in Oslo I'd tried to read up on bribery or so-called deal-influencing, which I guessed was how this would be described. It was as well to know what the potential outcome could be for Halden, Fuhr and me. As I understood it, both parties to an agreement like this could face up to three years in jail according to the Criminal Law Code, paragraph 389. But all it said there was that it was punishable to accept a bribe. There was nothing about planning or discussing it. The lift doors opened and I made my way to Room 333.

Halden was sitting in a chair by the desk and Fuhr – whom I recognised from an image search on the net – was in an armchair by the window. Both stood up. Halden and I shook hands.

'I know you would have preferred me to come alone,' he said, 'but my partner insisted on being here. After all, there's a lot at stake for all of us here.'

'Jon Fuhr,' said the man next to him.

I looked at Fuhr and at the proffered hand. He was a different type from Halden. Crew cut, army-green bomber jacket. Compact, muscular, a couple of pimples that hinted at the use of steroids. Bent nose, possibly into martial arts. There was a completely different vibe about him. He looked cold, challenging, self-assured. Like the sentence for embezzlement, his conviction for violence had been conditional. Something about it being in self-defence, but unnecessarily brutal.

'Hi,' I said and shook his hand.

'It is *Roy* Opgard, right?' said Fuhr.

I nodded, and wondered why a straightforward forename three letters long should cause him difficulties. I tried in vain to meet his eyes.

We all sat down, me on the edge of the double bed where Shannon and I had lain. At least, I assumed it was the same bed. Nothing in the room seemed to have changed since that last time.

'So what's it going to be then?' I said as I looked at Halden. He blinked, seemed nervous, not surprising really.

Fuhr cleared his throat. 'Before we answer, we need to get a couple of things clear. That OK?'

'Fire away,' I said.

'So you, Roy Opgard, intend to bribe us, GeoData, with an offer of twelve million kroner in exchange for our delivering a false report on the Todde tunnel to the Highways and Parks Department. Is that about right?'

I stared at him. Even though that's its proper name, no one

actually *says* Highways and Parks, they drop the 'parks' bit. I lowered my gaze. The fabric in his bomber jacket was so thin I could see the light from the screen of his phone in his inside pocket.

'Excuse me just one moment,' I said. I stood up and went to the bathroom.

The towels at least had changed. They were pale blue, back then they had been white. As white as Shannon's Irish skin. She'd looked naked as she emerged from the bathroom with the towel around her. I turned on the tap and studied myself in the mirror. What did she mean, Natalie Moe, about me being different? It's obvious people change over eight years – for one thing we get older. But she'd meant something else, hadn't she? I took out my phone, tapped the screen, then wedged it halfway down a glass and turned it facing the door. Took hold of one of the small towels, wrapped it around my right hand, turned off the tap and went back into the room.

There are a couple of things to note about fighting. One is that it doesn't matter how good you are at martial arts, if you come up against someone who spent much of his youth getting into fights at dances then it's not going to help you much. Mostly because in martial arts you're taught to wait for a signal to start from the referee. I didn't stop to close the bathroom door behind me, I used my speed and did as Dad had taught me back when he taught me how to box at the punchbag in the barn: hip forward, use your shoulder. Given that Jon Fuhr was seated and the chair was wide, it had to be a low hook. His head was resting on the chair back, meaning he couldn't move backwards or sideways to roll with the punch.

When I hit his nose it sounded like a bag of crisps being

crushed. Halden screamed, Fuhr just grunted. He didn't have time to get his guard up before my second blow landed. Same place, but now without the crunching sound, his nose was obviously gone. Fuhr had his guard up now, forearms bunched in front of his face, fists raised, head bent. I stepped to the side of the chair, reached down into his jacket pocket and fished out his mobile phone. Samsung, same make as mine. I looked at the bouncing wave graphic of the sound recorder that was turned on. Pressed Stop and deleted the recording. Tossed the phone into Fuhr's lap. He flinched, probably thinking a punch to the stomach was on the way. Then he slowly lowered his arms and a pair of eyes wet with tears of pain came into view. And then an even more crooked nose, and blood that ran from his nostrils and dripped down over the protruding upper lip and onto the chin, and from there onto the bomber jacket. It was like the spring ice melting on a mountain.

'If you're going to set a trap,' I said, 'always make sure the trap isn't more stupid than the victim.'

Fuhr studied me, looked like he was considering getting to his feet, wondering if he could take me. But then wisely dropped the idea.

'We . . . we just wanted it as insurance,' said Halden.

I looked at him. He looked pale, like he was seasick.

'In case we handed in the report and you didn't pay us,' Fuhr grunted. A whistling sound came from the crushed nose, it gave his voice a nice double tone, like the sound of Bakkerud's Hardanger fiddle.

I scoffed. 'In which case you would threaten to go to the police with your recording? And get three years in jail for all of us? Doesn't exactly sound a likely threat to me.'

They looked at each other. Fuhr continued.

'If you didn't pay then, technically speaking, there has been no bribe. And in that case we could go to the police and tell them we handed in the false report as a trap for you. That we had done it without involving the police beforehand because the police aren't allowed to solicit a criminal act like that.' Fuhr managed a little smile, the prick. 'Say something about how important it was for society that people contribute to criminals being caught, especially skilled criminals. And that we were prepared to deliver the genuine report.'

'Which you already have?'

Fuhr wiped below his nose with the sleeve of his jacket and nodded. 'You would have provided backup yourself, Opgard,' he double-wheezed.

He was right. Backup. Sure, we thought alike. If not, then maybe I wouldn't have suspected something when he started in on that exaggerated and overexplicit description of the situation – the 'exposition', as they say in the movie business – asking me to confirm my full name and that stuff about the Highways and Parks. But it was the very amateur nature of it all that persuaded me to believe them. I unwrapped the towel from my right hand and held it out to Fuhr.

'Listen,' I said as I sat back down on the side of the bed, 'we're not bandits here, any of us, we're just doing what we have to. And we're doing it for something that's bigger than ourselves. You guys so that your employees can keep their jobs through difficult times, and me because I want my village to survive. Right now we have a situation in which we can both achieve our goals, but if we are going to manage it then we're going to have to be able to trust each other.'

It wasn't easy to see how my pep talk was going down, but I carried on anyway.

'*Leap of trust*,' I said. It was an expression I'd used once before, the time Willum Willumsen and I shook hands and agreed not to try to kill each other. And it had worked. At least, for a while.

'And as a sign that we're willing to take that leap,' I said as I pulled the thick envelope from the pocket of my parka and tossed it onto the little round table between them, 'here's a little advance for you. There's two hundred thousand there.'

They peered at the envelope. I was guessing Fuhr would be the first to pick it up. I was right.

'And the rest?' he asked as with studied nonchalance he flipped through the thousand-krone notes.

'Fourteen days after the publication of the report.'

'Why so long?'

'Because that's how long the bank needs once they receive my loan application.'

'Loan?' asked Fuhr. Again he and Halden exchanged looks. 'Why wait for the report before you apply for a loan?'

'Because the report is what means they're going to give me the loan. I own a petrol station and various other properties in Os that are suddenly going to be worth a lot more and can be offered as security once it becomes clear the main road will still run through the village.'

Fuhr didn't look too happy, which was probably not easy anyway with a freshly squashed nose.

'Like I say, we need to be able to trust each other.'

Fuhr glanced over at Halden. They nodded.

'The report will be published on Thursday next week,' said Halden.

I stood watching them from the window as they walked across the car park and got in the Mercedes with the Oslo plates. We had gone through the most important points of the report and they had stressed that the data wasn't completely false, the facts had simply been distorted slightly. If the highways people were to commission a second, independent assessment they would reach the same conclusion, or at least be unable to take issue with Geo-Data's conclusion: that the tunnel at Todde wasn't viable. In their day, both the old and the new mayors had travelled to Oslo to argue in the Storting for another and cheaper solution involving an upgrading of the already existing section of road. But that wouldn't make the travel time from A to B any shorter, and, let's face it, Os was neither A nor B. But if the tunnel idea disappeared there was every chance that the idea of improving the section of road that ran through Os would be revived and the village would not only be spared the fate of isolation, it would also come closer to the population centres of Drammen and Oslo.

The lights on the Mercedes came on, and away they drove.

I walked into the bathroom, where the door was still open, and bent to the glass containing my phone and in my best impersonation of a chat-show host's voice said:

'This is Room 333 at the Brattrein Hotel, where we have just seen Bent Halden and Jon Fuhr, partners in GeoData, accept two hundred thousand kroner in part payment for submitting a false survey report on the feasibility of the Todde tunnel.' I took the phone out of the glass and stopped the video recording. Went back into the room, lay on the bed and played over the recording from the beginning. Halden didn't appear in it, but you could see my back, and see Fuhr counting the money. See him stick the envelope in his pocket. And you could hear the conversation. Like I say, both they and I thought the same way about backup.

I closed my eyes and felt my own weight against the mattress. It was the same one all right.

On the drive home I came across an album called *Warg Buen*. Recent stuff. Two Hardanger fiddles duetting, sounded more like racing to my ears. Good stuff. Turned it up good and loud and drove too fast, overtaking twice on the edge, had to ease down. Oh yeah, now Halden and Fuhr had taken the money, the die was cast, there should be some kind of celebration. If not on my own in the car, then with whom? Carl? Yes, had to be, there was no one else on our team. And the plan, what was that? To build that roller coaster, OK. But then what? What was the *plan*? Jesus, was I going to beat myself up over that again? It's like asking what the meaning of life is. You'll spend a lot of time wading around in that bog before you reach dry land again. That is, *if* you reach dry land again. Because when you realise that what you do, and what you are, are without value, then perhaps you're better off putting a bullet through your forehead. That was a thought I had managed to keep at a reasonable distance. I say reasonable, because there's a comfort in that too, that there is always that way out. After Shannon died, and everything lost its meaning, I'd come to realise that the only thing that could reawaken an appetite for life was danger. To be constantly reminded that life could be taken from you actually made you cling all the harder to it, like a kid throwing away a toy who starts to howl hysterically when some other kid picks it up. Maybe that was why I had walked into the hotel room with such a feeling of pleasure, of being ready to encounter anything at all, maybe even my own demise. That's why down in Poland I had half hoped the carriage would come off the rails. That's why my scalp felt a tingle when Vera Martinsen had said *they found some blood and hair*.

Because naturally there had been blood and hair in the cars that went over the edge into Huken with four, no, five people inside. So naturally it was something she could have told any journalist who called her, and without breaking any oath of confidentiality. So naturally that wasn't what she had meant when she said it to me. Vera had wanted to tell me something without saying it in so many words. The way she'd said '*And hair*'.

Did she mean my hair? If they'd found it in either or both Cadillacs there was nothing suspicious about that, I'd sat many times in both cars. A stray hair of mine in the Jaguar would be a little more difficult to explain, but I doubted it. When I was down in Huken and brought up the hit man's gun, the one I later used to snuff out Willum Willumsen in his bedroom, I'd been careful not to leave any fingerprints or any other biological traces. And my hair wasn't exactly an unusual colour, and anyway there was no way they could already have completed DNA tests on any hair they found.

I drove close up behind a tractor that had evidently come straight from the field, huge lumps of dirt spun up from its wheels and one landed on the bonnet with a thud. I was in no special hurry to get anywhere, but I stuck close behind him on the corner and waited impatiently for the straight stretch of road I knew came directly after it. Noted how the clod of earth defined the centrifugal forces and stayed where it was, on the bonnet.

And that was when it hit me.

Hair. Hair that was so platinum blond, long and thick it could only have come from one of two places. Kurt Olsen's mane, or the man he inherited it from, the old sheriff. In my mind's eye I saw again Sigmund Olsen, leaning over the edge of the precipice over twenty years ago and peering down into Huken at the wreck of Dad's Cadillac. Carl takes one step forward and pushes him. I see it as clearly as though I was there, see it even more clearly. Because in my imagination I can slow the whole incident down, I can let the fatal decision take several seconds whereas in reality it was the split-second impulse of a desperate, terrified teenage boy. Sigmund Olsen being pushed with sufficient force that the body slowly turns over in the air and he lands on his back when he hits the car down below. Not on the bonnet but on the under-body, since the car had also turned a half-somersault as it fell. I was in the workshop when I got the call from Carl, he was close to tears, I had to get there straight away.

And I went. Like I always did when my little brother needed me. Not because I'm some kind of altruistic idiot but because we were already tied by the same blood, guilt and fate. So in one sense it was very symbolic when we tied one end of that hundred metres of rope to the Volvo 240 I had back then and the other end to me, and Carl reversed, and I dropped down into Huken. Sigmund Olsen lay half across the car, his body skewed at a ninety-degree angle where it had landed. He looked like a puppet with no joints, a scarecrow, his upper body and head hanging down in front of the licence plate and the boot, the blood still dripping from his mane of hair and down onto the stones with a low, soft spattering sound. But he wasn't much of a scarecrow, that old sheriff, because a raven was sitting on his belly with its claws around the large buckle of his belt, and it didn't fly off until I started throwing stones at it.

Carl and I managed to hoist the body up and we pulled off his snakeskin boots and that same night I put them in the bottom of his boat and shoved it out onto Budalsvannet. We put his body in the grab of the tractor which we filled with Fritz Industrial Cleaner – now illegal – which dissolves absolutely everything it touches – diesel, asphalt, even calcium. Of course, it was a shock when the boat was found drifting and everything suggested the sheriff had drowned himself; but everybody knows men like him don't go round telling anybody who'll listen how depressed they are either. But Kurt Olsen never bought into that suicide. He fixed his gaze on me and Carl and that's where it's stayed ever since.

But it didn't quite add up that they had blood and hair on the outside of the car. And more than twenty years after what we'd come to know as the Fritz night? Out in all kinds of weather? Sure, Huken was sheltered from too much sun and rain, but there are insects in the ground that feed on blood, and the occasional gust of wind would have blown away any stray hairs. I dismissed it again.

The road straightened, I indicated, glanced in the rear-view mirror, put my foot down, checked the mirror and the tractor had already shrunk to almost invisibility. I turned up the Hardanger fiddle music again. Sure, sure, everything was going to work out just fine.

11

IT RAINED UNTIL THE WEEKEND, then the weather brightened, with a clear sky and the air sharp. On Saturday morning I went to check the new crash barrier on Geitesvingen. They seemed to have followed all the recommendations and instructions and it certainly looked solid enough. I peered at the road where it twisted its way down towards Nergard. Walked back and over the low ramp up to the hayloft. Switched on the light, stood in the middle of the floor and looked around. For years Carl and I had talked about what we should do with the barn and the goat paddock. Whether to do it up, pull it down and build a new house, or just let it stand there until it blew down. Lately Carl had been in favour of the last option, he thought there could be a lot of insurance money in it. I had disagreed, said there should be some bloody limits on how low we were prepared to sink. Now I wasn't quite so sure any more. Insurance money or not, I really had no objection if an autumn storm were to blow up and wipe away everything stored in the great book of memories. The punchbag still hung there, where Dad had punched until his fists bled, and I'd followed in his footsteps.

I looked at the wall below the light switches. Dad had left the shotgun there that evening, with shells in both barrels. For me to do what had to be done. And I'd let him down, and not just him but the whole family. I looked at the floor. Because it was here, on this very spot, that Dad had knelt with Dog, in his arms. Carl had just hit him with a stray bullet and I had finished the job off with a knife because Carl couldn't.

No, not much here to hang on to.

I looked over at the windowless west wall of the main house. When people built up here it wasn't light that was a priority, it was protection against the north-westerly wind. The entrance was at the back of the house, facing due north. On the other side – the sunny side – was Mum's winter garden where Carl now sat reading the newspapers on his computer.

I pricked up my ears. Checked the time again. Walked out into the yard.

Yes, it was a car all right. Changing down, probably just rounding Japan Corner now. When I was a teenager it was still possible to tell the make of a car from the sound it made, at least if they weren't brand new. But nowadays I had no chance, it was easier to guess what make of tyres they were using. But as the car rounded Geitesvingen I saw it was Natalie's Mitsubishi.

She climbed out.

'So this is the famous Opgard,' she said.

'Never been up this this way before?'

She shook her head. 'This is the only place the road goes to.'

'I was thinking maybe if you were walking in the mountains.'

'We didn't walk in the mountains. Hey, look, you've got fresh snow!' She laughed and pointed up towards the outfields. A thin scattering of snow had decorated the heights in the night, like icing sugar on a cake, and now it glinted dully in the sunshine. 'It's really lovely up here, Roy.'

'Yes, we're very lucky.'

I don't know why, but I felt a certain pride. Oh yeah, the land we were looking at belonged to Opgard, but a farmer's pride isn't based on aesthetics, it's based on how good the grazing is, what the forestry is like, and in those respects Opgard didn't have much to boast of, to put it mildly. Rocky hillocks, mountain birches, heather and so on, terrain that only goats can thrive on.

'So you've never gone walking up here?' I asked.

'I don't know, I probably have, at some time or other. But I don't remember. Anyway, I should get to know it, the walking up here is one of the hotel's selling points.'

'Amen to that. Coffee?'

'Love one.' She gave me that happy, open smile of hers, but I wasn't ready for so much joy and openness and pretended to be still studying the landscape.

I led the way into the house. She sat down at the kitchen table while I put the coffee on.

'Hi, Natalie!' Carl called from the winter garden.

'Hello, chief!'

He laughed, sounded contented.

I turned from the worktop. Saw her sitting there. Saw the notes

I'd made still on the kitchen table. And it struck me how small the kitchen was. We could of course use the living room, but that was still littered with the remains of yesterday's pizza and Carl's empty beer bottles.

'You know what?' I said. 'Since you have to get to know the terrain up here anyway, how about we put the coffee in a flask and go for a walk?'

She automatically glanced down at her tight-fitting jeans and thin Converse shoes.

'You can borrow my mum's old walking boots,' I said.

I found the boots in the chest in the porch, and while Natalie laced them up I looked at the Remington rifle hanging above the door.

'Remington 700 CDL?' I heard her say.

I turned. Natalie was standing now, had zipped up her Patagonia jacket and was ready to leave.

'You know your guns?' I asked.

She shook her head. 'Just that my dad had one exactly like that.'

'Does he go hunting?'

'He used to, yes.'

'But he never took you with him?'

'No. And I wasn't allowed to touch the rifle either, only look at it. Especially not after I got a little soldering iron for Christmas and drew a tiny little heart here.'

She stood on her toes and ran a finger over the end of the walnut stock.

'You could hardly see it but Jesus, I got such a telling-off.'

'A strict man,' I said, my hand on the doorknob.

'Oh, it was Mum did the telling off, she was the one who said I wasn't allowed to touch the rifle.'

I brushed aside a number of questions that occurred to me, opened the door and the light flooded in.

We waded through the heather. I noticed how she alternated short and long strides, almost hopping, as though she wasn't sure how to deal with the terrain. She was already out of breath by the time we reached the top of the first rise and could see the hotel.

'You're a real mountain goat, aren't you?' she said.

'Not sure about that,' I said.

'Oh yes you are. You look like you're walking slow and even, but you romp ahead. Same as Ola.'

'Who's Ola?'

She put her head on one side, closed an eye and peered at me.

'Someone. Someone I've been hunting with.'

'Aha! So you *have* been out shooting?'

'Nope. I haven't got my hunting licence so I was just a spectator there. Shall we keep going?'

'OK. Where to?'

She smiled. A wide mouth, soft lips and white teeth.

'To the top, of course.'

We walked on. I walked slower and a little to the right of the indistinct path so she could walk along beside me.

'Apropos shooting,' she said. 'I really don't want to shoot down that idea of yours for an amusement park in Os before it's even started, but I've been doing some research.'

'Shoot.'

'Successful amusement parks in Norway have one thing in common. Know what that is?'

'I could guess, but go ahead, tell me.'

'They're all close to a major road. The four biggest – Tusenfryd, Kongeparken, Dyreparken and Hunderfossen – are all next to motorways. Sommarland's next to an A-road. And it does well enough, 150,000 visitors a year. It has enough attractions to beat Hunderfossen. It's all about access. So once Os loses its major road access the likelihood of a big amusement park being a financially viable enterprise isn't all that great, in my view. So my first question is: have you considered a small park?'

'I have,' I said. 'And dismissed the idea.'

'Why?'

'Because a roller coaster costs hundreds of millions of kroner to build, so it's obvious you need a few thousand visitors every year if you're going to make a profit.'

Natalie nodded like she understood, but I could see she didn't.

'You're wondering whether I have a practical business idea, or if this is just an *idée fixe* about building a track.'

'Well, is it?'

I looked at her. She was looking me right in the eye. There was something, there really was, that told me she could read me. Read me the same way I had read that abused teenager who came to my petrol station to buy her morning-after pills. And to see her read me like that gave me the strangest desire to tell her everything. Well, no, not everything. But some of it. Though of course I couldn't.

'The maths is a little broader,' I said. 'You've got the synergy effects. Not just between a family-themed amusement park and Os Spa, but also the effect on the petrol station, on Fritt Fall, on property prices round here. It's about a critical mass, to start a self-increasing reaction with the roller coaster as the catalyst.'

'OK,' she said, but still didn't seem convinced. Maybe it was because she hadn't taken a course in science and mathematics with chemistry at her secondary school in Notodden, or because she just didn't believe in the arithmetics of my big picture. 'Well, you haven't employed me to assess a business idea, but I just need to be clear that this is what you really want. Because there are certain ground rules about how to market something like this.'

'Such as?'

'Everyone knows that big, expensive projects require more marketing in purely monetary terms, but not that it's going to take up a bigger percentage of the whole investment too. Take the movie business, where each film is its own project. For small, indie films the marketing takes maybe ten or twenty per cent of the total budget, but for blockbusters it's more like fifty per cent, or even more. Do you have that kind of money?'

'No,' I admitted.

'I thought not. So, bearing in mind that Os is far from any sizeable town, is on the point of losing all its through traffic, and that you don't have the money to persuade the mothers—'

'The mothers?'

'Research shows that they're the ones who decide where the families spend their holidays and weekends.'

'OK.'

'So, I've been thinking, and I've come up with an idea and I want you on board with it.'

I nodded, said I was still listening.

'You, Roy Opgard, need to go all-in on one card.'

'Eh?'

'You're supposed to say: "And that is?"'

I rolled my eyes. 'And that is?'

She held my gaze again, then said, slowly and distinctly: 'The. Biggest. Roller. Coaster. In. The. World.'

I had no idea what was going on when she grabbed my hand, pulled my arm towards her and pushed up the sleeve of my parka.

'You see?' She laughed and ran her fingers up and down the soft underside of my arm.

'See what?'

'Goosebumps. That's your one card.'

'Goosebumps?'

She let go of my arm and I pulled the sleeve down again.

'A limited promotional budget doesn't just put a cap on how loud you can shout, it also limits what you can say. And the only thing you have to say is: "The biggest . . ." ' She directed me with both hands and I realised she wasn't going to desist until we both chorused it. '. . . roller coaster in the world.'

'Those six words are your message. They need to be repeated each and every time you advertise or say something to the media.'

'You think that'll be enough to attract people?'

'The only times attendance figures at Tusenfryd have been over a million were the two years when they presented a new roller coaster. And this wasn't even the biggest in the world. With the world's biggest in Os, even Dad's going to want to vote for where the family goes. Not to mention all the roller-coaster nerds in the world who'll turn up for the ride. In the USA they have roller-coaster clubs with thousands of members who travel round the world.'

'You could be right,' I said. 'But this won't be the world's biggest, it'll just be the world's most beautiful. The track itself, and the surroundings.'

'The aesthetics will probably be what attracts the nerds, but not the general public. The general public want to be able to cross it off their list, that they've ridden on the world's biggest.'

'So then what you're saying is . . .'

'. . . you have to build bigger.'

'Only to find out in two years' time that someone in Dubai has built an even bigger one?'

'Attendance figures at amusement parks tend to be fairly stable, which means that the first year gives a pretty good indication of what's going to happen over the next twenty. It's a bit like the opening weekend of a blockbuster film. If you get it said enough times from the opening onwards that this is the "world's biggest", that's what people will remember, and they'll remember it long after you can't say it any more.'

'Well, that's certainly something to think about,' I said, scratching my chin. This morning I'd dropped my electric shaver and had to use my old safety razor, and it felt odd.

'Shall we drink our coffee up there?' said Natalie, pointing up at snow-coated Nesaksla.

'It's probably a bit further off than it looks,' I said.

'So what?'

I shrugged. 'Well, if you like cold coffee . . .'

Natalie smiled. 'Shall we go up to the snow and make our own iced coffee?' And without waiting for an answer she walked off. I stood there, waiting for her to turn. But she didn't, and after a few moments I headed up after her.

The sun glided through the sky above us as we trudged through the snow towards Nesaksla. Natalie was a quick learner too when it came to hiking across uneven terrain and very soon I was able to walk at my normal speed. We talked more about the amusement park, and I began to realise that there were a lot of things I hadn't thought about. Not because she claimed to have the answers, but because she had so many good questions. And after a while the conversation turned to what we could see around us. I pointed to the different peaks and told her their names, and how high they were, and I could tell her about the birds that flew above us. I knew the names of the different mountain shielings we passed, and she could tell me about the milkmaids' songs and cattle calls. About the milkmaids who spent their summers up here alone and sang to the animals. Or had tunes written about them.

'*Do you know Kari Midtgard from Tinn?*' Natalie sang in a light, vibrant voice that touched the blue notes with immaculate precision. '*She doesn't let the boys in.*'

It sounded so lovely it made me stop. And maybe gape too – it made her laugh, at least. And place a hand behind her ear when the vidda responded, a single note, lonesome and sad, that seemed to hover in the air.

'What was that?'

'A golden plover,' I said.

'A golden plover? Is that a kind of bird?'

I nodded. 'We can't see it because there's two of us. But if you're alone it shows itself to you. The golden plover is the companion of the solitary.'

'So that's what it is,' she said, nodding to herself as though she'd just realised something.

'What what is?'

'That note. I recognise it. You and the golden plover have seen quite a bit of each other, haven't you?'

Instead of meeting her gaze, which I knew was fixed on me, I looked at my watch.

'Sure you don't want to turn back?' I asked.

'I don't have any plans for today. Do you?'

I shook my head and we carried on walking.

We'd been walking for over three hours before we finally reached the snow. It had started to melt, chuckling sounds came from all the small, new streams, and up on the sloping mountainside rock faces and patches of heather showed through. We found two dry rocks to sit on and I opened my rucksack, pulled out the flask and poured coffee into two plastic cups. There was still a little warmth left in the sun even though it had started to close in on Ottertin. A tiny little ball of a bird with a narrow beak and its tail feathers sticking straight up in the air stood on the stump of an upturned root and studied us.

'Does the golden plover want some company after all?' asked Natalie.

I shook my head. 'That there is a wren.'

'Ah. Does it have a nest nearby, d'you think?'

'I doubt it. As a rule the male builds in wooded areas where he can find the material easily.'

'So the male is the builder there too, right?'

'Oh yeah. And then the female comes along and inspects the nest and hopefully gives it her approval.'

'And what happens if she doesn't?'

I shrugged. 'Not sure. He has to build a new one, I suppose. Or she finds another mate with a better nest.'

'Is that why you don't have a girlfriend, Roy?'

The question took me so greatly by surprise that I could hardly summon an answer. 'Don't I?'

'I had my hair cut yesterday, and Grete said you haven't had anyone since the policewoman who used to come and see you, but that was five years ago.'

I laughed. 'Grete's grasp of the calendar is impressive. Better than mine is, at least.'

'So?' Natalie gave me that direct look of hers. 'Then why no girlfriend?'

I put the cup to my mouth, to give me a little time.

'Sorry if that's a bit too personal,' she said.

'No, no,' I lied. 'It's just that there isn't much to say. Time passes, and there's so much to be getting on with, right?'

She nodded, looking out across the empty, desolate landscape, where soon the autumn colours would be swallowed up by the dying light.

'I was just thinking that, with everything you know about me and my business, it might be a good idea to balance things out a bit. Would be for me, anyway.'

'I understand,' I said.

She threw what was left of her coffee into the snow.

'I need to pee,' she said. 'Can you make sure no one comes?'

It was a joke, but neither of us laughed.

'I'll make sure,' I said.

She disappeared up the mountainside and behind an enormous rock, while I sat and watched the sun and worked out that we ought to manage the return journey in two and a half hours now that we would be heading mostly downhill and Natalie had learned the technique of a steady and regular stride.

'Roy!'

The shout echoed around out there.

I turned.

'Come here!'

I stood up and walked the fifty metres to the rock. Natalie was standing behind it, pointing down at something in the snow. 'Tracks,' she said.

And sure enough, there was a paw print, four toes, a shape like a juggler's hat.

'Isn't that a wolf?'

'Could be,' I said. 'But it's probably a dog.'

'Isn't it too big for a dog?'

'Depends on the dog. In practice it's impossible to tell the difference.'

'A woman at the hairdresser's said wolves have been seen around here.'

'I think a fair amount of fake news gets produced in that hairdresser's. This is hunting country, there are lots of dogs around here.'

'But if it is a wolf? And the sun will be going down soon . . .' She looked at me with an expression of fear on her face.

'If it is a wolf it's a lone wolf,' I said, and tried to sound reassuring. Should be possible for a man who's almost twenty years older than this precocious young lady. 'It would be a male who's on his own because he lost a fight with the alpha male,' I went on. 'Ergo this is not the strongest wolf. Without a flock this is a starving, weakened wolf that's already sentenced to death. On top of that it's more scared of you than you are of it.'

'Wanna bet?'

A small smile showed up through the fear. *Was* she scared, or was she just messing me about?

'Next time we'll both bring our Remingtons,' I said once we'd packed up and were heading back down the mountain.

'It's illegal to shoot a wolf,' she said.

'In self-defence you can shoot anything you like.'

'Are you sure?'

She was walking in front of me and turned without slowing down. Closed one eye. 'If you're standing on the scaffold after you've been sentenced to death, are you allowed to strangle the executioner? If the king orders you to charge into the enemy's machine-gun fire, does that mean you have the right to shoot the king?'

I just shook my head.

'That's one helluva question,' she said in a fake, deep voice.

'Eyes ahead so you can see where you're stepping,' I said.

'Admit that you think that was one helluva question.' Amusement danced in those strangely coloured eyes of hers.

'I think,' I said as I pushed her forward, 'that that was one helluva question.'

Her laughter trilled out, trilled through the sharp, clean air beneath the pale autumnal sky.

Dusk had fallen by the time Natalie got into her car and drove away. Carl wasn't home. At the hotel, probably. I had some idea who with. I sat over the drawings until it was late. I had Zadra's measurements and was trying to work out how a general increase in every dimension would affect the physics of the track. I juggled the formulas for a while but had to admit it was beyond my capabilities, so before going to bed I sent an email to Glen Moore and asked if it was possible. And how much it would cost.

Before falling asleep I heard a distant sound, a long, sad note. I thought of the golden plover, but it wasn't that. Not a dog. Not a wolf. Not that I've heard a wolf, but this sounded too human. Like a song. I'd probably already drifted into a dream when the song was interrupted by a cold shriek from down in Huken. And I saw again the raven, sitting where it had sat that time, on Sigmund Olsen's belt buckle.

12

SUNDAY ARRIVED WITH WIND AND a low layer of scud that hurried across the sky.

We had another home game. Carl explained that the fixture list for Os FC was arranged so that all the team's home games were out of the way before November and the last autumn fixtures were all away games, down in the lowlands, where there was less risk of snow.

The pennants on the VIP stand were standing at full stretch as I climbed up behind Carl. I noticed how Mari Aas gave him a quick, formal smile, as though they hadn't just a few hours earlier been lying in each other's arms somewhere in Os Spa. His thing with Mari was something Carl and I never spoke of, almost certainly my choice and not his. I just didn't want to be any part of that clandestine stuff, and he'd probably gathered that.

Perhaps it made it easier for Carl – it's easier to pretend it's simply something inside your own head, if no one knows about it. That's the way it was with me and Rita anyway, back then. And with Shannon and me, of course. Yeah, Shannon . . . there were still times when I wondered whether it had happened at all or whether the whole thing had just been a dream.

Fewer spectators today, in the stand and around the pitch. Promotion was a fact, and that was reflected in the team selection too. I saw Alex pull off his training top, he was obviously going to start.

Before the referee and the linesmen appeared the announcer walked to the centre circle with a wireless mike in one hand and a coupon in the other. It had been Carl's idea before each game to give an award for the best player in the previous game, always a two- or three-hour spa treatment at the hotel.

Carl winked at me when the announcer called out the name, people clapped and Kurt Olsen jogged his way out to the centre circle.

'That's on top of the draft contract he received on Friday,' Carl whispered.

Kurt accepted the coupon, but instead of the usual 'thank you' and leaving the pitch Kurt took the microphone. The wind made an ugly scraping noise in the loudspeakers and the announcer turned Kurt so he had his back to the wind and the mike was sheltered.

'This is probably the first time a trainer's been named Best Player,' he said. 'But I couldn't agree more with the decision.'

Laughter from the VIP stand.

'But this is probably also a good time to inform the club and all you supporters that I have made my decision.'

Carl grinned and leaned back, hands behind his back and

stomach protruding. Only now did it occur to me that he was carrying more than the 'weight' he used to refer to. He actually had to lean slightly backwards in order to maintain his balance. And something else struck me too, that Carl wasn't far off the shape of the previous king of Os – Willum Willumsen – when Willumsen was the same age as Carl.

'I've decided that my work at this club is done,' said Kurt. 'I would very much like to have continued on the next leg of the journey, but the fact of the matter is that, as sheriff, I have another mission, a mission that, for various reasons, will occupy my time over the coming months.'

All that could be heard from the pitch now was the whistling of the wind and the flapping of the pennants.

'I have been offered a contract by the big shots up there.' Kurt pointed in our direction, and from down on the touchline came a single laugh, it sounded like Erik Nerell. 'And it's a handsome offer, as of course it should be, since they can afford it, and I'm such a bloody good trainer.' Again that single burst of laughter from Erik Nerell, Kurt's faithful disciple. 'But it is both my wish and my duty to concentrate on my obligations as sheriff from now on, and to hand the baton on to another. Thank you for having faith in me, goodbye.' He held up the spa coupon and spoke above the applause. 'I won't have time to use this, so someone else is welcome to it! Alex was good in training, so let him have the sauna!'

I glanced at Carl who stood there stony-faced, beating his hands together as though he were punishing them.

'What the fuck is the guy doing?' he hissed from the corner of his mouth.

'He's obviously got himself some kind of bomb,' I whispered as I continued to applaud. 'Now he needs to keep his distance.'

Carl nodded, he understood what I meant. Kurt had something that was dynamite, but he had to get out of the room himself before he detonated it. Get some distance between him and us, no links, no common interests. They'd found something in the wrecks of the cars, that was the only possible reason for his rejecting the contract and the chance of being a real legend in Os. Or rather, he still planned on being a legend in Os, just in another field. Being the man who not only solved the murder of his father but six others, seven killings in all, which Kurt had been investigating more or less on his own all these years. So I carried on applauding. Because sure, he deserved it, that tough bastard of a trench warrior, who kept at it even when winter came, and there was no news from the front.

Rita turned and looked up at us, and I saw something in her eyes I hadn't seen before. Cold, pure hate. It shot through my body like a fucking gamma ray, and I shivered. Because no matter how well you can explain away the fact that you are hated by a woman who once opened her heart and her bedroom door to you, you can never avoid the question: is she right? Are you really the repulsive, spiritual cripple you know she sees you as? But you can't always have been that way if she once loved you, or at least once cared about you. So just when did it happen, when exactly did you lose touch with your own humanity? Was it when you saw the Cadillac with Shannon inside it drive over the edge? Or before that, when the Cadillac containing your own mum and dad went the same way? Or before even that, when you were twelve years old and lay in the top bunk with your hands covering your ears and tried to think yourself away to somewhere else altogether?

Rita turned back to the pitch. The teams lined up for the

kick-off. The other team had more to play for than us, I gathered, as they were in the relegation zone. So it was the usual contest, between the one who is best, smartest and strongest, and the one who wants it most.

When we got back from the match I cooked some pasta and while we ate Carl and I discussed what kind of bomb it could be that Kurt Olsen had got hold of.

'Well,' said Carl, 'if your KRIPOS lady friend says they found blood and hair, and you think that means they didn't find it in any obvious place, well, then maybe they found something in the boot of my Cadillac.'

I noticed how he avoided mentioning Shannon's name. After Carl had beaten her to death he'd stashed her body in the boot of his car and called me for help. Naturally. It's still a mystery to me how I managed to reveal nothing when I realised what had happened, and my life tumbled to ashes. I said we should move her to behind the steering wheel, run the car over the edge and make it look like an accident. 'Yet another accident on Geitesvingen?' Carl had queried. In response I'd said that, statistically, half of all road accidents within the same calendar year happened at the site of previous accidents so three accidents at Geitesvingen over a period of eighteen years wasn't exactly a striking figure.

I dug my fork into the pasta. 'We washed that boot so thoroughly I doubt they would have found anything there.'

'Well, what could it be then?'

I shrugged. 'Maybe they just found a couple of hairs here and there and when they check it they'll find they're from the victim or else you and me, so there's nothing to worry about. Dessert?'

'Is there any?'

'Not unless you've been shopping.'

We looked at each other and laughed.

Carl went to bed early. I'd heard him come home the previous evening, he'd been late. God only knows who Mari had allied herself with and was using as an excuse. Her best friend from childhood Grete Smitt? Yeah, right, that would have been a terrific idea. Although actually, wasn't that exactly what the big nations had done before 1914, allied themselves with the countries they were most afraid of going to war with?

I sat there and thought about it. Had Mari entered into an alliance with Os's answer to the KGB? Because it was quite something to conduct an affair like that over so many years and manage to keep it more or less secret. And if that were the case, was there maybe something I could learn there?

I checked my emails. Moore had replied. He wrote that he would very much like to come and examine the site and discuss the project. That I had been right in my suspicion that it wasn't just a question of multiplying all the dimensions by the same factor, and that the marginal cost of building a bigger and higher track tended unfortunately to increase the cost of the whole project, not lower it. In reply I wrote that I had nothing in my diary that couldn't be moved and he could come when it suited him, the sooner the better as far as I was concerned.

After that I did a search for Norwegian folk music and Kari Midtgard but got no hits, so I sent a text to Natalie and asked for the title of the song she had sung.

Her reply came two minutes later.

'*Do you know Kari Midtgard?*'

I found the track on Spotify. An old guy, an old recording, not much there that reminded me of Natalie's pure delivery. But OK, it had soul too, just in a different way.

Then she sent another message.

Are you genuinely interested?

I rejected a couple of smart-arse replies (*define 'genuinely'* and *was just wondering if anyone lived between here and Nergard*) before sending a three-letter reply: *Yes.*

I didn't hear any more after that.

I went to bed, read a few pages of *The Magic Mountain* by Thomas Mann, it's a good and inexpensive sleeping pill, I'd been reading it for two years and never managed more than a single page before I was out like a light. So I was well on my way into the night when the message arrived.

Sorry about the late response, had a long phone call. If you want to hear more hardcore folk music you can come with me to a concert in Notodden on Wednesday. We need an audience.

Wednesday. Late shift. I tapped in my reply:

Nice idea but working at the petrol station. Hopefully some other time.

In reply I got a thumbs up.

Read another page of *The Magic Mountain*. And another. And another. Sighed, turned out the light and lay blinking in the dark. Tossed and turned. Thought how maybe it's not so strange you find it hard to get to sleep when you know the sheriff is on your tail and maybe a bomb is about to go off.

Then I guess I fell asleep anyway.

13

THE BOMB WENT OFF ON Tuesday morning.

It was ten o'clock, two of us were on duty; I was out in the pump area picking up the litter, drying off the pump nozzles, changing the paper towels and the soapy water. I heard a car change down, and the crunch of gravel on asphalt told me it had pulled into the station. Turned round. The car braked and I saw the man behind the windscreen. A pair of dull blue eyes stared at me from beneath a bald head with a few wisps of hair on it. The hollowed-out cheeks in the pale, drawn face suggested an hourglass. The man looked sick. But then Moe the roofer had looked that way for as long as I could remember. When Moe filled his tank he paid with his card, he never came into the station, not after the time I beat him up in his own kitchen. He sucked his cheeks in even more, as though thinking about spitting, but that would have meant winding down the window on the old delivery van, and that would probably have been too obvious. Instead he revved the engine, like a warning, before releasing the clutch and driving out onto the main road again and disappearing westwards.

As I stood watching him my phone rang. Dan Krane calling, from *Os Daily*.

I'll admit I tensed when he announced himself. There had been a leak. It would be plastered all over the front page of the newspaper the next day and would be the top story in the net edition within an hour. That there was a bomb – he actually used that image – and now he wanted to hear my response.

'First you're going to have to tell me what the "bomb" is,' I said, my mind racing. I'd read somewhere that technological advances now meant the police could get the results of a DNA analysis much quicker than before, so it shouldn't come as a surprise. After all, it was over a week since they'd hauled up the cars. What was surprising was that the press should have got hold of us before the police. And the leak, how had that happened? Kurt Olsen, of course. Otherwise the Oslo newspaper would have got the story before *Os Daily*. I should have realised Kurt already knew who the DNA results pointed to when he announced on Sunday he was retiring as trainer, realising it was a matter of urgency to get off the Opgard brothers' payroll. It wouldn't really surprise me if Kurt had leaked the news deliberately, using the Opgard hater Krane as his willing accomplice. He wanted to see us sizzle in the frying pan of publicity before we had time to hide behind our legal advisers. My heart was pounding.

'The bomb,' said Krane, and there was no trace of malicious glee in his voice, I'll give him that, 'is that the Highways

Department's report due to be published on Wednesday has been leaked, and the conclusion is that the Todde tunnel project isn't feasible and should be abandoned.'

'What?' I exclaimed, and there was no need for me to act more surprised than I really was.

'According to the report, the cost of the tunnel would be vastly greater than the amount allocated by the Storting. And even then, adequate safety of the tunnel couldn't be guaranteed. It's a bomb that blows the whole Todde project to pieces. I'm calling round looking for spontaneous reactions from people who will be most immediately affected. So as owner of the petrol station and several properties in the village, what is your response to the news?'

I let out a huge sigh of relief. Watched Egil behind the counter slipping three buns for the price of two into a paper bag and handing it to yet another satisfied customer. Saw his lips form a word. The price. That was something he got from me, from back when people still paid in cash, saying the price out loud. Now that everyone paid with a card and saw the price on the machine I'd stopped saying anything, but not Egil. 'A hundred and sixty-two kroner,' Egil might say, and now and then some irritable customer might mutter 'Yeah, I can see that', not that it bothered Egil. And that was fine. With the road still running through the village, Egil would still have a job to go to next year.

So I said something along those lines to Krane; I can't remember my exact words, but something about full employment and how, if the road wasn't going to be rerouted, then at least they could upgrade it.

'We've already spoken to Jo Aas about that and he agrees.'

Of course. Aas was involved again. During his time in office he had tried to warn the Transport Minister about the astronomical cost of tunnels, and the death of a local community, but to no avail. Well, he'd been right after all.

'I saw the announcement that you bought Rita Willumsen's camping site last week,' said Krane. 'Lucky with your timing there – suddenly that doesn't look like such a bad bargain after all.'

'You mean you think it looked like a bad bargain before the report?' I said it in what I hoped was a jocular way that would give Krane the chance to retract what he'd said, but he didn't.

'Six and a half million is a lot for a few acres with a major road running right by it, but to pay that for something that looked likely to end up a piece of waste ground? Some would describe it as complete stupidity. Any comment on the purchase and the timing?'

'No,' I said, unhooking a pump nozzle and wiping the petrol from the handle. 'Actually Dan, I'm sort of busy here at the moment.'

'All right,' said Krane. 'I'll call your brother for his response too. This is good news for Os Spa as well.'

'It's good news for the whole village,' I said. 'And for your newspaper too. Actually I'm impressed that you sound so calm about the news, Dan.'

Krane gave a brief laugh. 'Are you?'

I didn't reply. Something in his voice suddenly made me think he'd been drinking. And that brief, bitter laugh of his had revealed how much he hated the village, this place that held him prisoner, a cuckold with three kids and too profound a sense of responsibility for him just to walk away. Or maybe it was Mari, maybe it was his love for her that kept him imprisoned. Because love doesn't set you free, it walls you in and deprives you of your will.

I knew that from experience, and that's why I left love alone. Thinking about it, I always ended up with a certain sympathy for Dan Krane. And for the first time it struck me that maybe he'd looked on the Todde tunnel as his way out. Os without the life-blood of traffic would wither away, the newspaper would fold, he and Mari would have to move in search of work and a school for their children. That would be his escape, his reason for hanging on. The thought made me so sad I felt I had to end the conversation with a few cheering and even friendly words.

'Good luck,' I said and hung up.

I headed over to the little workshop behind the station. Walked past the grease pit, past the tractor that was parked next to it, minus its registration plates. Up there on a shelf – like a reminder – were two old tins of that poisonous Fritz Industrial Cleaner fluid which I was still trying to find a way of getting rid of. I entered the bedroom I'd built in there long ago. Called Carl and told him about the leak and that GeoData had obviously written the report we'd asked them to. The profit had already been discounted, as they say. I warned him that Dan Krane would be calling him for a comment.

'We need to talk,' said Carl.

'Sure, I finish at six.'

'Preferably before that.'

There was something in Carl's voice, he seemed stressed.

'Can you get up to the hotel at lunchtime?'

'OK,' I said. 'Is something wrong?'

'It is. Just a touch too wrong.'

We hung up. I looked at the rare licence plates I'd nailed up on the wall – Basutoland, French Equatorial Africa, Johor, British Honduras. Just then something occurred to me that I'd never thought of before. That I only collected things that didn't exist any more. That I had no photographs of friends, or people I'd known, or of me and Carl, not a single one.

I went back into the station shop.

It was OK by Egil if I popped out for lunch. 'So you can leave earlier this afternoon if you like,' I said.

Egil shrugged. 'Guess I'll stay, not that much to do these days.'

'No?'

'Bored to death at home. I mean, everyone's moved away.'

By 'everyone' Egil meant the two pals he'd gamed his way through his teens on computers with.

'You can work an extra shift tomorrow evening if you want it.'

Egil brightened. 'I can?'

I smiled. 'It's yours.'

Driving from the station shortly before twelve I decided to pay a very quick call on the bank before heading up to the hotel.

Vendelbo emerged and showed me into his office.

'You heard the news?' I asked.

'Of course,' he said. 'Heard it on the radio. Members of parliament from both Labour and the Conservatives have already given their reactions. They're saying that if the leaks are correct then a new motorway has to be back on the agenda. And that means no rerouting for at least fifteen or twenty years, and perhaps never.'

'So you might be staying here after all then,' I said.

Vendelbo smiled. 'Perfectly happy in Os, me.'

'Does this put my application for a loan in a different light?'

'That thought had already crossed my mind, yes.'

Vendelbo leaned back in his chair, hands folded behind his head.

'The petrol station is all paid up now, no encumbrances, isn't that correct?'

'Correct.' I mirrored his pose and clasped my hands behind my neck. I read somewhere that mirroring is supposed to be an unconscious expression of empathy, although I guess there must be exceptions to that.

'So are Fritt Fall, the campsite, twenty-five per cent of the building we're sitting in now, my shares in Os Spa and my part of the outfields at Opgard. No encumbrances anywhere.'

'Good. Shall we arrange a meeting with head office?'

At the hotel I was told that Carl had eaten lunch and was down in the spa section. I descended the stairs to the spa reception where the spangled and painted female face behind the desk told me Carl was in the sauna, and that she'd been told to tell me to go straight in when I arrived. I said that was only going to happen on condition she turned off the mindfulness music that dripped like syrup from the speakers. She just smiled as though she thought I was kidding and handed me a towel.

I disrobed in the changing room and found Carl in the sauna. As I pulled open the door the steam whirled out and for a couple of seconds I saw him sitting naked on the topmost bench before the door closed behind me and he disappeared once again inside that dense white fog.

I sat on the bench below him, tried to convince my body that it wasn't dangerous to breathe in air that was almost a hundred per cent moisture, and waited. Heard Carl draw in his breath with a rasping sound.

'The Transport Minister is quoted on the net as saying she won't comment until she's read the whole report.'

'Reasonable enough,' I said. 'But she'll conclude that the Todde tunnel is dead.'

'Yes. Heard anything about the loan application yet?'

I stared into the whiteness but didn't reply.

'Relax, we're alone in here,' said Carl.

'It'll be approved,' I said. 'I'll be sending the project description and budget to Vendelbo later today. As soon as they have an up-to-date valuation of the property I own we can have a meeting. Vendelbo's got his foot down hard and reckons it'll all be done by early next week and the loan signed off on the week after that.'

'That late?'

'I told GeoData it'll take fourteen days before they get their twelve million, and they accept that. What are you worried about?'

'Am I worried about something?'

'Yes.'

I knew Carl wouldn't try to protest, he knew me as well as I knew him.

'Alpin,' he said.

'What about them?'

'They want out.'

'What?'

'They say their engineers found large amounts of hidden fire damage.'

'What kind of damage?'

'They weren't very precise in their definitions. Load-bearing constructions, damage that will, in time, ruin the foundations, they say. Enough for them not to want to risk an investment.'

'Really?'

I turned to look at Carl, but he was still hidden inside that fog.

'Really.'

'You believe them? You don't think we've fixed one false engineers' report only to get slapped round the face with another one?'

Carl gave a mirthless snort of laughter.

'I could easily suppose so,' he said. 'They are French, after all, so if they'd used the report to try to knock down the issue price I would have had my suspicions. But they're turning down the whole thing, full stop.'

'But we're going to be keeping the road. Maybe they'll change their minds when they hear that?'

Silence.

'If you're nodding or shaking your head I can't see it, Carl.'

'No,' said Carl. 'They won't change their minds.'

'Because?'

'Because I had already told them that the main road would still run through the centre of Os.'

'You what?'

'Yes. I discounted it for them.'

It was a business term, one of two favourite phrases he brought back with him from his business studies in the USA: to work out the value of future cash flows at today's prices. The other was 'pre-emptive strike', a tactic he claimed to have learned from me during those Saturday-night fights at Årtun. To hit first, to attack as soon as you think the opponent intends to attack you. I groaned.

'So now the French are sitting out there and know that someone – probably us – has paid for that report?'

'They can think whatever they like, but it doesn't matter to them, Roy. This is just one of a hundred hotel projects they're considering, most of them in lands that are more corrupt than Norway.'

Something was running over my body, I couldn't tell if it was sweat or condensed steam, but it tickled. Tickled in so many places. Tickled in the wrong places.

'So what are you going to do now? Cancel the new wing?'

'It's too late, the contracts have been signed and cancellation fees this close to the start will break us.'

'So?'

'So I was wondering about that loan you're going to be getting.'

Naturally. Naturally, there it was again. Carl fucks things up and big brother has to come along and bail him out. But not this time. I was done with that. Shannon was the last time.

'That loan is for the amusement park, Carl. You must understand that I can't use it to get you out of a mess.'

'Yet another mess, you mean?'

'That's not what I said, but OK. Another mess.'

'But you must know you owe it me.'

I turned again, stared into that white miasma, wasn't sure I'd heard him right. Sure, I felt I owed him, owed him some repayment for what had happened to him in his upbringing. But I was the one who felt that way, not him. It was crazy. It was as if he, the victim, had accepted, perhaps repressed his memories of those night-time assaults in the bedroom we shared, and that I was the one who couldn't manage to put it behind me. Sure, Carl had more or less consciously played on my feeling of guilt, but he'd never before said it in so many words, that I owed him. And there was a trembling bitterness in his voice when he said it that I'd never heard before either. As he continued, however, his voice was once again mellifluous and flattering, Carl in persuasive mode, the way I knew him.

'We're family, Roy. The hotel is mine, the park is yours; but one and one add up to more than two.'

'I know, but—'

'The bank isn't *so* bloody bothered about what the money goes on so long as they have their security and you pay the interest and the instalments. And it would be completely temporary, just for a month, two at the most, until I've found a new investor. The two Chinese concerns I said no to are still interested, I should be able to set up a bidding contest between them. I promise you you'll get your money back long before you have to pay for the roller coaster. What do you say, big brother?'

It's strange how when someone has a hold on you, even though you can see what it is they're doing, even though you can see from a mile away what the left hand is up to all the time they think they've got you watching their right, still, *still* they manage to get things their way. Because they have your heart in their hand, and it really doesn't matter which hand it is.

'I'll think about it,' I said.

'That's all I'm asking. I'll be home late tonight, but let's talk about the details after work tomorrow?'

'OK. Or, no, actually, I'll be going to Notodden.'

'Oh yeah? Doing what?'

'A concert.'

'On your own?'

'No. It's something Natalie thought I might be interested in.'

I said it in a casual, throwaway manner. Maybe so casual it sounded exaggerated. Anyway, I wasn't able to pick up any reaction from behind the wall of fog.

'Enjoy yourselves,' was all he said. 'Day after tomorrow then?'

'Yes,' I said. 'I need to get back to work.'

'OK. I'll stay on here for a while.'

I turned as I pushed the door, held it open as the white mass gushed out, enough for me to establish that Carl really was alone back there. Alone and naked, and giving me an impenetrable look. It's strange how someone you've lived with so intimately for so many years can suddenly look like a stranger to you. You think it must be the light, or that you're tired, that this is your kid brother, someone who can't hide anything at all from you. Before remembering that you don't even have complete insight into your own self.

14

'SO YOU WANT US TO make you look nice for Natalie Moe?'
said Grete Smitt as she massaged my scalp. I was lying more or
less defenceless on my back in her chair with my head in the
bowl and hoping that the two others in the salon hadn't heard
her. Grete was doing well, she'd employed a girl and I knew she'd
been looking around for more suitable premises somewhere
nearer the square.

'Just the usual,' I said. 'No need to make me look too nice.'

I don't know whether she picked up the implied insult or
where she'd got the information about Natalie and me going to
Notodden that evening, but I wasn't about to ask her. She gathered my hair in a towel, led me over to the vacant chair, combed
out the wet hair and began work with the famous Japanese

Niigata 1000 scissors which, at some point in her monologue, she would manage to reveal had cost her fifteen thousand.

'You never seem to get any older, Roy,' she said.

The compliment took me slightly by surprise. I studied my face. In a way she was right. A brutal, lumpy nose, wide mouth, square jaw, deep-set eyes and a thick head of dark hair that looked like it would never beat a retreat. Not all the way, at any rate. Was it maybe a train of thought involving a much younger woman that led to her remark about age? But there was something in the way she said it, an implied and unspoken continuation of the remark. Which I thought I understood anyway: *Not like your brother, Carl.*

I understood it not so much because it was true, because it *was* true, as because Grete was still hung up on Carl. Previously it had taken the form of a long and hopeless one-way infatuation which had resulted in a one-off fuck with a Carl smashed out of his mind. Now it looked like she was trying to gather evidence to prove how much more fortunate she was to have ended up with Simon Nergard. And even if Simon Nergard was a boring jerk, or maybe for that very reason, she was probably right about that.

'Is your brother heading off somewhere warm then?' she asked.

'Why d'you ask?' As soon as I said it I regretted I hadn't just said I don't know.

'This last week he's been in here for the solarium twice.'

'So what? A bit of vitamin D's good for the health, isn't it?'

'Oh yes, but people round here think that men who use the solarium must be gay. I mean, only three men come here. The bank manager, Stanley Spind and Kurt Olsen. And everyone knows Kurt likes the ladies. But in Os people are scared to death of anything to do with gay. I used to have that Adrian working here, remember?'

I remembered. A boy Stanley had met on holiday in Ibiza who'd come to live in the village. He'd stuck it out for eight months, an achievement in itself.

'Really good barber, but I just had to let him go. Even the women here are scared to have a homo fussing about with their hair.'

I had no idea where Grete Smitt was going with this and I didn't want to know either. I closed my eyes in what I hoped was a signal that I wasn't interested.

'But it's nice that Carl and Kurt can at least enjoy the solarium together. I mean, they aren't exactly the best of friends now that Kurt's given up training Carl's football team. Or am I wrong?'

Say as little as possible, I told myself. 'I'm sure they're both grown up about it,' I said.

'Didn't look that way when Carl left the sheriff's office yesterday morning,' she said. 'Someone told me he looked furious, swearing and cursing, speeding out the car park at a hundred miles an hour.'

I concentrated on breathing slowly. Why the hell hadn't I just asked Julie to give me a quick short back and sides in the office at Fritt Fall?

I cleared my throat. 'Probably gave Kurt an even better offer which he still turned down.'

The grinding sound from those Japanese super-scissors stopped. Concentration was clearly required to give this explanation a full examination.

'Could be,' she finally said. And the scissors started up again.

'Speaking of offers, a Notodden hairdresser phoned me last week wanting to buy my Niigata 1000 scissors. Guess how much he was willing to pay?'

I glanced at the mirror, at the clock on the wall behind me. I wasn't due to pick Natalie up at the hotel until six, so I had plenty of time. All the time in the world, in fact. And a thought that had occurred to me at irregular intervals over the past eight years was suddenly there again. That I had more time than I wanted.

It was raining lightly as we drove out of the village. 'Don't Go to Strangers' playing through the speakers. As always I glanced in the rear-view mirror directly after we passed the county sign.

'So,' said Natalie.

'Eh?'

'It looks like it reads Zo backwards. That's why you checked in the mirror, right?'

I had to smile. 'Thought I was the only one who ever noticed that.'

'Oh no, I was always happy when I saw that Zo, because it meant I was on my way out of this town.'

I nodded, not certain how to interpret this. Was it because that bad stuff had still been happening to her when she came back home to visit? I was hoping that wasn't the case. Not just for Natalie's sake, but for mine and for Moe's too. Because I'd sworn I'd kill him if he touched his daughter again, and I had every intention of keeping my word.

'What's this you're playing?' she asked.

'JJ Cale,' I said. 'Stuff from the seventies.'

'Is he singing *don't talk to strangers*?'

'Nearly.'

'That's what my aunt used to say to me. That I shouldn't tell anything to other people.'

For a few seconds there was silence between us. Only JJ and the beat of the windscreen wipers on the two and the four.

'She'd been abused by her grandad. Both her and Dad, she said.'

'What do you mean? That your aunt *knew*?'

'Yes. She gathered it, anyway.'

I could feel my pulse rate going up, noticed that I'd unconsciously stepped down harder on the accelerator. 'And all she did was tell you not to *tell* anyone?'

Natalie shrugged. 'If it had been your family, are you so sure *you* would've told someone?'

I could feel her looking at me. I didn't know what to answer; suddenly my throat felt tight, constricted.

'She told me it would stop one day,' said Natalie. 'That's what happened with her grandad. One day he'd just stopped. It never happened again, and after a few years it was as though it had never happened at all. Like when the body grows around a bullet wound.'

'I see,' I said. I'd eased off on the accelerator now. 'And is that true? As though it had never happened?'

She shook her head. 'No. No, it isn't. But I'm not afraid of him any more.'

'Why not? He's still physically powerful enough to . . .' I searched for another word, but then realised there was no point in avoiding it any more. I looked at her. 'Rape you.'

Natalie didn't even blink.

'Of course,' she said. 'But he can't control me any more. He's lost his hold over me. And after Mum died he lost what little control he had of himself as well. He's a sad man, Roy. Walks around at home and . . . I don't know. Waiting to die. I don't hate him. Or I do, yes, but I love him too. I know it's crazy, and that's what makes me so angry. That a man who doesn't deserve even a single one of my tears can make me cry just because I feel sorry for him. Because I *want* to hate him, you see? My brain hates him, but my heart betrays me. Understand?'

I nodded. Because I did understand.

We drove on. Let JJ Cale do his thing, slowing the pulse rate down. Until she asked the question I knew had to come.

'Why did you do it?'

'You mean, your father?'

'Yes. I mean, you weren't the only one who had their suspicions.'

'No?'

'No. But you were the only one who did anything. Why?'

'Must have been because I'm a responsible citizen, I guess.'

She peered out the window. It was dark now, the rain heavier, there was nothing to see out there.

Then she said it. Her voice quiet. 'Don't you want to talk about it?'

I saw my knuckles whiten around the steering wheel. Didn't I want to talk about it? Yes, we all want to talk about it. Talk about it, be understood. Get someone to help us feel like a human being again, so we can tolerate our own reflection in the mirror. But there was no one to tell it to. No one who could understand. No one I could trust to keep their mouth shut.

'Roy?'

Apart from Natalie. Who had been there. Who had family

secrets of her own. I took a deep breath, uncertain for a moment whether my voice would carry.

'My father was an abuser too.'

There. I'd said it.

I took another deep breath. 'That's what I recognised in your father. The shame. It weighed on him. Like a rucksack filled with rocks.'

'I thought it had to be something like that,' she said. 'How long did it go on for?'

I hesitated. Should I reveal that Carl had been the victim, not me? That I had been the big brother who lay in the upper bunk bed and pretended to be asleep, let it happen, because I didn't think I could do anything about it, that it was just the kind of thing that happens in families and that people keep quiet about. No, I couldn't give up Carl, he was her boss, it was his story.

'From when I was around twelve.'

'Same as me,' she said. 'And then it stopped?'

'When my parents died in that car accident.'

'Speaking of which,' she said. 'You're doing well over a hundred now.'

'Ah shit,' I said, and slowed down again. 'Thank you.'

She put a hand on my arm. I felt the warmth of it through my jacket and the flannel shirt. 'I'm the one who should say thank you. You know that, don't you, Roy? That you saved my life?'

'All I know,' I said, hoping she would never take that hand away, 'is that you gave me the chance to do something that was right.'

'To stand up to an abuser.'

I nodded. Looked at that middle finger protruding a little from the others on the steering wheel. The result of a *pre-emptive strike*.

That time in Moe's kitchen when I gave him my ultimatum – that I'd say nothing, on condition that his daughter left home – he had managed to crush the bottom joint of my finger with a hammer before we began to fight. But it ended with him sobbing in a foetal position on the linoleum floor, blood running in a rivulet that stopped when it came to one of the overturned chairs. And a few days later, Natalie left for Notodden.

She took the hand away. Turned up the volume. I lay my head against the headrest and fastened my gaze as far ahead as possible in the cone of the headlights. *Oh, woman, when in doubt, call on me.*

The concert was something else, unlike anything I'd ever attended before.

The place wasn't big. A bar, a few tables and a little stage. The audience of around fifty seemed to be either friends or relations of those performing. First up was a young guy in a full Hallingdal traditional costume, with the white jacket, red waistcoat, black knee breeches and white stockings. He played the Hardanger fiddle, with the drone string, and beat time with his foot, stamping the floor so hard the beer glass on the chair next to him shook. After two short numbers another young man stood up, this one wearing the traditional costume of Setesdal, with a wide-brimmed black hat. From the response of those in the audience and from his own charisma I gathered that this one was the star. A big guy with a steely glint in his eye, he announced in slurred Swedish that he was going to play something written by the man who had been his teacher. As he placed the fiddle into the base of his throat and placed his hand around the neck of the instrument I saw a cross tattooed on the back of his hand. He counted in, started on five, and I realised at once this was going to be something different. His play was hard and aggressive, and by the time the first number was over the stage lights were already glinting on the hairs that had come loose from his bow. Instead of beating time on the floor of the stage he pounded his foot on a stomp box that gave off a sound like a one-stringed bass guitar and bass drum combined. I closed my eyes. It was wild, big, deep, so familiar and at the same time completely new, like a girl you grew up with who comes back to the village as if a new person, a different person, like someone you only now start to understand. Or maybe it's yourself, maybe it's you who has, imperceptibly, one step at a time, been changing over those years, developing the insight you needed in order to be able to see, hear and understand something that's been there in front of your eyes for your whole life. I glanced over at Natalie and she looked back, raised her beer bottle to me, and I raised my glass of water in return.

Then the whole band was onstage. Drums, stand-up bass with two strings, accordion and two Hardanger fiddles. They played loudly, if I can put it that way. Everything else apart from those two fiddles was accompaniment. And the fiddlers reeled off overtones, inversions, bass lines, rhythms that raced apart and threatened to descend into chaos but still met up again, the way three and four meet up in twelve. Just when you thought they were heading left they took a right, and even before you'd got your breath back you found yourself tumbling again in a musical free fall. But like in a good, timber-built roller coaster you always sense an underlying harmony, an order, a meaning. The Swede tossed his black hat into the air to reveal hair that was close-cropped, apart from a glossy black fringe, swept over to one side and pulled through a big earring. I'd seen it before, in pictures of the old fiddlers, they called the fringe a *spir*. He bared his teeth, his eyes were popping, and when the playing was at its most intense he hissed in our direction.

After an hour, when we thought, and I'm sure some were hoping, it was all over, the Swede called Natalie up onto the stage. She picked a strange-looking wind instrument that looked like an ice-cream cone and was almost as tall as she was. It was the same instrument I'd seen on the poster outside, an illustration from the days of Norway's national romantic period, depicting a milkmaid blowing into a horn on a mountain farm. Somewhere before I'd seen the same image, with the band's name – Hell Spelemannslag – written in the same Gothic lettering, I just couldn't remember where.

Natalie put her lips to the narrow end of the horn, her chest swelled, and she blew into it. And now I knew what it was, that long, sad note she'd heard and recognised on our mountain walk. It was the call of the golden plover. She played three notes, over and over again, in the same order. The effect was hypnotic. Discreetly the Swede began to beat out the same slow rhythm on his stomp box. And then Natalie began to sing. There was absolute silence in the place, the only sound that beautifully pure, almost crying voice, and the steady rhythm, beating out like a slow, insistent heartbeat. I closed my eyes again and cursed inwardly. Because now I really was in free fall.

After the concert the band, including Natalie, disappeared through a door at the back of the stage. By the time they returned, most of the audience had left. Natalie and the Swede joined me at my table. The Swede had removed his jacket, and the white shirt was so drenched in sweat it lay plastered against the muscles of his chest. He placed a Thermos in the middle of the table with a heavy thump.

'Roy,' said Natalie, 'this is Ola.'

'So you're Roy,' the Swede said, holding out his hand to me. 'She was right.'

'Right?' I said as I took his hand.

'You *do* look like Leonard Cohen, but not as handsome. *Uddevallare?*'

He picked up the Thermos. The cross on the back of his hand rippled over the prominent veins.

'What is it?'

He grinned. I guessed he was just a couple of years older than Natalie, but already he had several gold fillings glinting in the back of his mouth.

'*Kaffegök,*' he said. '*Kaffedoktor.* Moonshine and coffee.'

'Thanks, but I'm driving.'

'OK.' He poured some into Natalie's glass and into his own.

'So what d'you think, Roy?'

'About?'

'About us, of course.'

I looked from Ola to Natalie and back again.

Ola grinned. 'About the band. The music, for chrissakes.'

'Oh, oh yeah.' I thought quickly. 'It was . . . powerful stuff.'

'Like an *uddevallare?*'

'Like a Jimi Hendrix.'

Ola gave a satisfied nod. 'That's good. You get it.'

He drank from his glass.

'At least, you nearly do.'

'Nearly?'

'We-ell, Natalie says you seem to know about music. You're

quite a bit older than us, and you're Norwegian, so I was thinking you might have maybe a more contemporary reference than Jimi Hendrix.'

'Oh yeah?'

'Oh yeah. After all, there's a direct line linking these two outstanding examples of Norwegian music. The folk music, and . . .'

He paused and stared expectantly at me, amusement dancing in his intense eyes. I racked my brains. No, wait . . . yeah, that poster. The penny finally dropped.

'Black metal,' I said. 'Burzum. That poster with the milkmaid is on the cover of one of their albums.'

Ola turned to Natalie. 'Pretty smart, your friend. I need to make an offering, guys.'

He put his tattooed hand on top of Natalie's, stood up and headed for the exit.

'Offering?' I said.

Natalie laughed and drank from her beer bottle.

'It's a local thing, a Setesdal thing. Not so long ago people on remote farms around here still made offerings of food and blood to the gods. Ola calls it offering when he has to go out and throw up.'

'Does he do that often?'

'Before every concert and sometimes afterwards. Nerves before, exhaustion afterwards. He's an artist, he makes huge demands of himself.'

'You mean this is what he does for a living?'

She smiled. 'No, of course not, there's no way he could live off it. He's a sexton at the church here in Notodden. But his music is what he lives and breathes for. He played a *nyckelharpa* when he was growing up in Bohuslän. Started playing when he was five years old.'

'A *nyckelharpa*?'

'It's sort of like the Swedish version of the Hardanger fiddle, only you press keys on it instead of fretting with your fingers. And it only has four strings. Then when he was visiting relatives in Setesdal he went to a music masterclass and discovered the Hardanger fiddle. Although actually it was an earlier version of the Hardanger fiddle they were using, but it still had the drone strings. And he was completely sold. He hooked up with one of Setesdal's best music teachers and moved out here.'

'And now he's a sexton, with church burners like Burzum as his musical role models?'

She laughed. 'Ola just listens to the music and the feelings. Everything else is just a distraction for him.'

I could hear the admiration in her voice and see the light in her eyes. Time to be getting home. I looked at my watch.

'Want to stay over?' she asked.

I looked up. 'Stay over?'

'There's a party. I'm staying at Ola's. There's room for you there too.'

I felt my stomach tighten. 'I've got to get back – I need to be in early tomorrow. You'll have to take the bus.'

I heard the way it sounded as soon as I said it. And it was too late to take it back. I could see in her eyes that she was on the point of saying something, giving an explanation, an assurance that she hadn't offered me a place to stay overnight just so she could get a lift back to Os. Instead she put the beer bottle to her lips, blinked and looked away. That hand she'd put on my arm in the car, that's all it had been: a hand on the arm. Now the conversation had painted us into a corner and we sat there in silence and suddenly I saw myself through her eyes, through Ola's eyes, the way everyone else in the club would see the middle-aged guy sitting there drooling over someone who was young enough to be his daughter. While her boyfriend was out of the room. Jesus, how pathetic can you be? I clenched my fist under the table. What was the matter with me? What I'd shown of myself to her was so embarrassing that for a moment I wished we'd skidded off the road on the drive over and died. No, not her. She and Ola looked like two people with a fair chance of making each other happy. Anyway, I'd get a second chance on the drive back home alone in the car. I laughed.

Natalie looked at me in surprise. 'What?'

'Nothing, I . . . I actually thought we might use the trip here to talk about the launch of the ride and the park now that it looks as though we're going to keep the main road. But it was more fun to talk about music and growing up. Apart, of course, from—'

'—the growing-up bit,' we chorused together. And now it was her turn to laugh.

I stood. 'We can do it on the phone over the weekend,' I said.

She glanced up and there was a look in her eyes, a victim's eyes, almost as though I'd slapped her.

'OK,' she said. 'Thanks for coming. Drive safely.'

Outside, on my way out to the car, I saw Ola and the guy in the white Hallingdal outfit quarrelling about something. Ola had his hands on the other guy's shoulders, so drunk now it looked like he was holding himself up. Neither of them saw me.

It was two thirty when I parked in the yard. Carl's car wasn't there. I went into the kitchen, grabbed two bottles of beer and then sat in the winter garden. About ten minutes later I was blinded by the headlights of Carl's BMW. He came in, also grabbed himself a beer and sat down next to me.

'Late,' I said. 'Celebrating the road?'

'Nope,' he said. 'Fucking Mari Aas. Again.'

We drank our beers, stared out into the night. It was still raining.

'You don't seem surprised,' he said.

'The only surprising thing about it is you telling me. Or actually, you telling me now. Why now?'

'Because I want to know what you think.'

'About what?'

'About her and me becoming a couple. Properly.'

'She and Dan get divorced, you mean?'

'Yes.'

'Is that what she wants? With the kids and everything, I mean?'

'Yes. Dan Krane wants to leave Os. She doesn't.'

'And you'll do as a husband and dad?' I raised my bottle and saluted in the direction of the Aasgård place somewhere down below. 'Good thinking of Mari Aas that is, to swap someone who doesn't deliver for the king of Os. Timing's right too, she'll be able to move into a brand-new castle just in time to take over the interior decor. And good for you too – you aren't exactly the type to live alone.'

'Stop it, Roy. It's not as if Mari and me haven't thought of it before.'

'Oh? Then why didn't you?'

Carl shrugged. '*She* was the one who held back. For all sorts of reasons. Pride, because I was unfaithful that time and everyone in the village knew about it.'

'Jesus, that was a lifetime ago.'

'Yeah, but it probably meant she couldn't completely trust me. I mean, we started meeting while Shannon was still alive, so she's already got proof I've been unfaithful twice. And the kids are very attached to Dan, she says he's a regular superdad.' He put his head back and rolled his eyes, meaning God knows what. 'Or was, anyway. He's fallen off the pace a bit there too.'

He leaned forward in his chair with his elbows on his knees, hands clasped around the beer bottle. 'I told her that now is a good time to do it, now when the road is the only thing people are talking about, it would go under the radar. She won't admit that things like that are important to her, Mari, but of course they are. Anyway, she seemed a bit more positive when we discussed it this evening.'

'Naturally,' I said. 'Because the main road suddenly means that Os is a place where she and the kids can settle, at the same time as she knows Dan can't stand the thought of staying on in a town where everybody knows he's a cuckold.'

Carl looked at me. 'So you think he knows, do you?'

'Dan Krane has got eyes in his head like everyone else, Carl. Anyone can see that the youngest is yours.'

Carl turned his gaze back out through the window again. 'Ah, shit,' he muttered.

'And you better watch out, cuckolds are dangerous.'

'Yes, well, you would know, wouldn't you?'

For a moment I was back in the car with Natalie again before I realised that the hand I could feel on my arm was Carl's.

'You know something, Roy?'

'What's that?'

'You're the best big brother an idiot like me could ever have.'

He said it with such warmth and intensity I had to swallow.

When two lives are as intertwined as ours are it becomes impossible to see and feel everything at one and the same time. You focus on particular aspects or parts of it, you can say 'hey, remember that time?' and for that brief moment that's all that has ever happened, and the only feelings that really exist are the memories aroused.

'Ha, I'm just as big an idiot,' I said, and I could hear how I should have cleared my throat first. He turned to me.

'What happened?'

I coughed, took a drink.

He squeezed my arm, kept his gaze on me.

So I told him. Told him about the evening in Notodden. How I had managed to lie to myself before suddenly realising what I was up to. Not even up to, because I wasn't up to anything. But what I felt.

'You're in love,' Carl exclaimed with a laugh. He rocked from side to side in his chair. 'Fucking hell, Roy! I mean, I've never seen you in love before.'

His words made my guts twist again. He looked so happy, and yet I couldn't tell him the truth. That I'd been in love before, with the woman who was his wife, and that I'd moved to Kristiansand just to get away, that when things were at their blackest I thought about throwing myself off a bridge and putting an end to it all. So instead I tried to laugh along with him.

'It'll pass, I expect,' I said.

'Ah, you'll get rid of that fiddle player,' said Carl.

'Aren't you listening?' I said. 'I don't *want* to get rid of anybody. This is Natalie Moe, the roofer's daughter. She was a teenager just *yesterday*! I'm going to sit very quietly in my corner until the whole thing blows over.'

But Carl persisted. 'Is he good-looking, this Ola guy?'

'That's a matter of taste. But he sounds like Jimi Hendrix. The competition would be tough, even for a smooth operator like you.'

Carl grinned happily. 'Come on, Roy, you're looking better than ever.'

'Idiot.'

We drank to each other. I checked my watch. In less than four hours I'd have to get up. 'But she did say to Ola that I look like an ugly Leonard Cohen.'

'That's a contradiction in terms.'

'And then on the drive back I recalled that story. New York in the late sixties. Leonard Cohen and this older Canadian are in town and hanging out on the folk scene. There's this lovely girl there with a fantastic voice, Joni Mitchell. He's on a date with her, they've eaten out and are on their way back to the Chelsea Hotel where they're staying when this limo glides up alongside them. A tinted window goes down and there's Jimi Hendrix. She gives him this huge smile. "Hi, Jimi!" He: "Hi, Joni, you wanna go for a ride?"'

'And?'

'And? Then I think fuck Suzanne takes you down and Hallelujah, here comes Purple Haze and Voodoo Child, and if I'd been Leonard I would have told Joni to get lost and I would have jumped in beside Jimi and got fucked myself.'

Carl took a deep breath. And started to laugh. It was liberating to hear, Carl's laughter. It said, shit, life isn't so serious. Nor is love. Nor is death either. You take the moments you get, everything is just temporary, nothing is real, nothing is genuine or lasting.

'What happened?' he said, wiping away a tear. 'Did she go for a ride with Jimi?'

'I don't recall. I should think she did.'

I stood up and went to the kitchen for more beers. It was going to be a long night.

15

THE FOLLOWING WEDNESDAY GLEN MOORE arrived in Os in a hire car.

I picked him up at the hotel and took him to the campsite. He was wildly enthusiastic. 'Wow, Roy, now I can see why you want the profile of the roller coaster to align with the mountains. And the lake! You know what? I think this could be a masterpiece, no matter the size.' He had a few questions about the geology of the site and the possibility of acquiring the surrounding land since he thought the site was on the small side. I answered as best I could and explained about the laws regarding the tied functions of certain farm properties and the possibility of concessions and exemptions.

'Anyway,' he said, 'visually it'll be great, for those riding, for on-lookers and for people driving by. Let me put it this way, they will want to stop. And go for a ride themselves.'

We agreed to head back to the hotel for lunch and to look at the drawings.

'Hunting season?' he asked as we passed three guys wearing camouflage gear sitting in deckchairs in front of one of the cabins. Two of them were cleaning rifles.

'Yes.'

'What do you hunt around here?'

'Mostly deer. Moose. Some roe deer.' And now and then people, I couldn't help thinking. I'd just seen Kurt Olsen cruise by in his Land Rover. I hadn't heard any more about the examination of the wrecks, so maybe all this about blood and hair was a false alarm. All the same, I felt a prickling between the shoulder blades, as it used to say in those Morgan Kane Westerns I read when I was a kid, a feeling that someone had me in their sights.

After lunch we adjourned to a meeting room. On our way in we bumped into a group coming out. Carl was among them and he gave me a secretive little smile. And when I saw Natalie emerging at the back of the group I understood why.

'Hi, Roy,' she said with a smile.

I smiled back. I hadn't called her after Notodden. Should have done, of course, if only to say that I wouldn't start thinking seriously about the marketing until everything else was in place – a builder able to construct the track, and a bank willing to give me a loan. I could have stopped and given the message there and then, but the meeting took me a bit too much by surprise. Actually felt my cheeks flushing slightly.

'Tell me, why are all Norwegian women so damned beautiful?' said Moore after we'd closed the door behind us.

I shrugged, and there was no follow-up question.

For the next four hours we pored over those drawings, Shannon's originals as well as Glen Moore's suggestions for a larger course that would keep the same basic shape.

'It will be the world's tallest timber track,' he said. 'It'll beat Zator, though only by two metres.' But he was doubtful it would beat Zator's top speed of 121 kilometres per hour. He explained that the colder air up here led to a greater friction between the wheels and the rails. He thought that would outweigh the fact that the air resistance this high up the mountain would be slightly lower. But that until the ride was built we wouldn't know just how fast it was.

'We're looking at twelve or thirteen million dollars,' he said when the discussion turned to the cost. I told it like it was, that I was dependent on a loan from my local bank, and that they would demand a workable budget, and that a realistic assessment of the expected income from the ride meant that I wouldn't be able to meet his price.

'Well,' he said, 'let's see what we can do. Every customer argues that their project is unique, that we should do it for less because it'll be a showcase for us. This is the first time that's actually true. This could be a very special roller coaster, Roy. I'd love, love, love to do it.'

I smiled. Thought about it. I'd just haggled over a price, hadn't I?

It was dusk as I walked back out to his car with him. The sound of a gunshot rolled over us, its echo tossed back by Ottertind. Glen Moore peered up at the mountainside.

'Let's hope the hunter can see what he's aiming at,' he said.

Yes, I thought as I watched his tail lights disappearing down in the direction of the village. Let's hope the hunter knew what he was shooting at.

Carl and I had a meeting with the bank on Friday, two days after the report on the main road and the Todde tunnel appeared. The media had already reported the leaks so thoroughly that the publication didn't make headline news. There were a few quotes from members of the parliamentary Highways Department committee, but no one seemed willing to challenge a conclusion based on expert knowledge. As a member of the Left Party put it: 'We should welcome this report, rather than regret it. Think of the millions saved for the nation, money which would otherwise have been wasted.'

Opinions were divided in the meeting room at Os Sparebank. The two from head office in Notodden thought it was bad news for the whole county apart from Os, while Vendelbo quoted the response of the Left politician. Carl was unusually silent and pale. It was only eleven o'clock but he'd asked me to drive, explaining that Lewi, head of AUB, had been in to sign the contracts for the new wing last night and that they'd celebrated afterwards with a few drinks at the bar.

'Those Lithuanians are tough,' he'd groaned.

I gave a PowerPoint presentation of the 'Os Amusement Park' project that had seemed more impressive when I had shown it to myself earlier, in the kitchen at Opgard. Even after I'd given a cautious estimate of the number of visitors and then the sexed-up figures with more traffic on an improved highway that would run literally a stone's throw from the roller-coaster ride, I saw no clear signs of enthusiasm on the listening faces, not even Vendelbo's. Carl obviously noticed this too, which is probably why he went somewhat over the top when it was his turn to speak, enthusing about how the knock-on effects of the park would benefit the bank's other customers, among them Os Spa. As usual, his enthusiasm was infectious, and even one of the Notodden guys was nodding his head. But once Carl was finished, and the bank guys started asking their questions, the stony faces were back. They pointed out, of course, that I had drawn the park on neighbouring properties that were farming land – how were we going to sort that one out? I replied truthfully that I had recently talked to the two landowners concerned, and that one of them was interested in selling if the price was right, and the other was willing to rent out his land on a twenty-year contract. That I was in dialogue with the council on a change of function in the use of the land, and that the signals I had received so far had been positive. This was, after all, something that could give a boost to the whole community. Vendelbo concluded the meeting by thanking us and saying we would have our answer early next week.

'That snotty little prick,' said Carl as we sat in my car. 'Did you see how much he was enjoying himself?'

'Vendelbo?'

'He hated it when we took over at Os FC and the name of that shit little bank of his disappeared from the shirts. But he sits there now in his cheap suit, serving Danish pastries and thinking that for once in his life he's got the power he deserves.'

'I think you're wrong about that,' I said as I pulled out of the car park.

'Oh?'

'I think Vendelbo's just doing his job. And that I didn't do mine. I didn't put on a good show.'

'Nonsense. They just don't get the big picture.'

'No one gets the big picture, Carl. I wasn't good enough. You did the best you could.'

'Of course I did, you're my brother.'

'Thanks, but the fact that we *are* brothers is probably part of the problem here.'

'For fuck's sake!' Carl slapped the dashboard with his palm. 'A good argument is a good argument, regardless of who makes it.'

Parking in front of the hotel restaurant I could see the lunch rush was already under way.

'Looks pretty full,' I said.

Carl sighed. 'Has to be to pay what it costs to have a chef that won the Bocuse d'Or.' He opened the passenger door. 'If Vendelbo doesn't give you that loan I'm going to ban him from using the sauna.'

'You think he'd regard that as a serious threat?'

'Oh yes.'

'OK. And Carl?'

'Yes?'

'Take a blast of this mouth freshener before you go in.'

He sniggered. Did as I told him. Patted me on the cheek before he climbed out and strode firmly towards the entrance. Not because he had an appointment to keep but – as he once explained to me – the same rule applies in business as in a backstreet in Caracas where you don't want to get robbed: look busy.

'The rest of your life,' Stanley Spind said in his southern accent as he looked at me across the narrow desk.

'I have to take these tablets *for the rest of my life*?' I asked in disbelief, staring at the prescription he had handed me. He'd explained that my condition was probably more a genetic disposition than the result of an unhealthy lifestyle.

'You and a hundred thousand other Norwegians with high levels of cholesterol,' he said. 'Unless you want to die of, for example, a heart attack. Like a hundred thousand others.'

'Thanks,' I said. I liked Stanley. He was wearing an Hawaiian shirt decorated with skulls under his doctor's coat. He bleached his hair and looked around thirty though he was actually the same age as me.

'Plus you should make some changes to your diet. And work out more.'

'I thought you said it was genetically conditioned and not lifestyle?'

'Yes, but that only means you must be even more disciplined than—'

'A hundred thousand other Norwegians?'

'Correct. You can pick up the tablets at any chemist's. The nearest one is er . . .'

'Notodden.' I sighed.

'I know,' said Stanley. He made a note on his computer, stopped abruptly and looked at me.

'Your petrol station is under the jurisdiction of the Food Safety Authority, isn't that right?'

'Yes it is.'

'Os is too small for anyone to open a chemist's here, but did you know you're legally entitled to sell medication from a petrol station?'

'Yeah, I already sell some prescription-free stuff. Paracetamol, morning-after pills and suchlike.'

'I mean you can take prescriptions and have the medication

sent from a chemist's. So people wouldn't have to drive all the way to Notodden. It means a bit of extra work, but it might pay off now that we're not going to be a ghost town after all. I suggested it to the Co-op, but they said they didn't have enough employees over eighteen. Asle promised me the bank would give a start-up loan to anyone wanting to open an outlet.'

'Thanks, but I don't want to use up my credit limit on that,' I said as I felt my phone vibrating in my pocket. I folded the prescription, thanked Stanley, left the consulting room and took the call out in the waiting room. It was Julie. Her daughter was ill and none of the usual casuals were available to take the evening shift at Fritt Fall.

'Surely Erik can handle it?'

'Not on his own, Roy. Not on a Friday night.'

'I wish I could spare you someone from the petrol station, but the only one old enough to serve alcohol is Egil, and he's at a bikers' gathering in Kongsberg this evening.'

'Egil? He doesn't ride a bike, does he?'

'No, but him and Børge have a club.'

'Børge Lid? Has he passed his motorbike test? When he left town he was blind in one eye. At least.'

'Neither of them has a licence, but Børge's got a deregistered bike.'

'And the two of them have a motorbike club?'

'Lid & Evensen. Pretty cool badge, haven't you seen it?'

Julie laughed. She'd quit smoking when she got pregnant the first time, but you could still hear the cigarettes in her bubbly, hoarse, infectious laughter that was its own reward if you made her laugh.

'I can do it,' I said.

'You?'

'I can pull a pint, change a barrel and handle the cash register. And be DJ.'

'The DJing is Erik's, I doubt he'll hand that over to you, but thanks, Roy, you're a star.'

'Well, that's my middle name.'

16

ERIK WAS SITTING AT ONE of the tables with the pavement sign in front of him as I walked into Fritt Fall. It was seven o'clock, the daytime customers had left and the evening crowd wouldn't be in for another hour or so. I stood behind him and watched as he chalked the board. He'd already written 'DJ ERIK FRIDAY NIGHT LIVE' in large, florid lettering and was now adding the words 'Hits only'.

'What d'you think?' he asked and tried to put his head on one side. I say 'tried' because Erik had such a small head on such a thick, muscular neck that the two things – head and neck – seemed like the same thing.

'Beautiful,' I said, indicating the sign. 'You've got your own style – that font should be named after you.'

'Well,' said Erik without looking up, 'at least I can spell.'

I saw the skin of his neck contract, as though he could hear himself that he had gone too far.

I laughed. 'One nil to you. Just tell me what you want me to do, boss.'

He finally looked up and gave me a sour little smile.

'Me? I thought you were the boss.'

'You know what, the owner and the boss are sometimes two different things.' I returned his smile, but I had a hunch it was going to be a tiresome evening.

It started off well enough. At about half eight people began arriving and by ten the place was full. I manned the beer pumps and had my work cut out. Erik's DJing involved him going through the playlists on his mobile phone. And he hadn't been lying when he wrote 'Hits only'. Or more precisely, a mixture of cheesy hits like 'Bombadilla Life' and stuff you couldn't argue about like 'Hungry Heart', along with 'Free Fallin'', the club's signature tune. Every time I got a short break I scanned the crowd. Don't really know how long I managed to kid myself that I wasn't looking for anyone special. Anyway, she wasn't there, and that was probably best. For a nightclub to succeed in a place like Os you can't try to appeal to a specialised taste, you need to attract all types, indiscriminately. Still, I was surprised to see Asle Vendelbo suddenly standing in front of me and ordering four beers. Not just because it was unusual to see the bank manager not wearing a suit, but also because he had a wife and two kids at home. I watched as he returned to his table and put the glasses down in front of three young lads. I recognised only one of them, a hot-headed kid people called Johnny Depp, not the sharpest tool in the box. Johnny because that was his name, Depp because he was Sheriff Olsen's deputy.

169

The lads took their beers but didn't seem interested in talking to Vendelbo, who was sitting beside Johnny, who was already knocking back his glass. Vendelbo put a hand on his shoulder, and Johnny looked at it like it was bird shit, stood up and with a gesture to the other two they moved to another table.

While Erik was out collecting empties from the tables I picked up his phone that was behind the counter, opened Spotify and tapped in Hell Spelemannslag, the name of Natalie's band. The band came up, although there was no picture, and I saw they had 137 followers and were listed with eleven tracks.

I selected one of them, 'Ihjælslått', turned up the volume on the speakers and pressed Play. The Hardanger fiddles went straight on the attack, and for a moment the club looked like a movie that had frozen. Then the rest of the band tumbled in and all hell was let loose. I draped a cloth over the phone and went back to the beer pumps as Erik came running back towards the bar.

'What the hell are you doing?' he shouted above the howling notes. 'You trying to empty the place?'

'Thought it might be good to try something local, something that doesn't smell of mould.'

'Mould? Does anything in the world sound mouldier than a Hardanger fiddle? Where the fuck is my phone?' He searched feverishly among the glasses below the counter.

'I'll find it for you as soon as I've pulled this one,' I said.

Erik gave me a furious look.

Hell Spelemannslag's tunes were mostly between two and three minutes long, and we got all the way through 'Ihjælslått' before we were back with Creedence. I emptied the washer for the second time that evening then headed onto the floor to collect the empties. Vendelbo was sitting alone, and as I passed I put the tray on the table and sat down.

'It's yourself, is it?' said Vendelbo with a faint smile. Didn't seem completely sober.

'Hi,' I said. 'So what did the guys from head office say after we left?'

Vendelbo turned his glass around in his hand. 'What do you think they said?'

'That they didn't have much faith in the idea.'

'Amusement park in a mountain village, Roy? You got to admit, it sounds like a project that could fall flat on its face.'

'Fair enough,' I said. 'But they really don't need to have faith, all they need to know is that I can put up the security.'

Vendelbo didn't respond. His T-shirt and jeans made him look older, not younger. But that wasn't what didn't add up, it was the look on his face.

'Right?' I added.

'Right.' He drank some of his beer. 'No, not right.'

I felt a creeping sense of unease. 'What are you saying, Vendelbo?'

The bank manager looked me directly in the eye. And his gaze was still wearing that suit. 'What it boils down to, Roy, is a matter of trust. I probably shouldn't say this, but the problem is that Carl seems to be involved.'

'Carl? Why is that a problem?'

'Os Spa hasn't been paying its instalments as punctually as it should, and head office doesn't think Carl's books tell the real story of what's actually happening in the company.'

I swallowed. 'But Os Spa and the amusement park are two separate companies.'

'As I say,' he said as his gaze swept around the club, 'it comes down to a question of trust. You two see the two companies as separate, but what we see is the collective debt. Perhaps you should try another bank, one that isn't already involved with Carl.'

'But . . . no other bank can appreciate the value of what I own here in Os.'

'They'll be more cautious, but if you give them time they're bound to make you an offer.'

'How much time?'

'Contact several. Give them each a month, or two months. Don't rush them, or they'll probably just say no.'

'But I don't *have* a month or two.'

'Sure you do. Building work doesn't start until the spring, you said.'

'Yes I know, but . . .'

I could feel my throat going dry. This was a bolt from the blue. But what the hell else could I say? That I needed twelve million to pay off a bribe within the next fourteen days?

'Asle,' I said, noticing myself how false it sounded as I used the name for the first time in my life, 'you can persuade head office that we can be trusted. Do it, please.'

Vendelbo bobbed his head from side to side. 'I probably can, Roy. The trouble is, I share their unease. Not about you, but Carl.'

I looked at him. Wondered whether to ask if they knew something else about my brother but didn't.

'When will you be making your decision?'

'At the credit meeting on Wednesday.'

'OK,' I said and got to my feet. 'I'll come up with something that'll convince you before that.'

Vendelbo gave another of those sad, wan smiles. 'Nothing would please me more, Roy.'

I looked down at him. Right now a part of me hated him. Another part felt sorry for him, he looked so out of place and lonely sitting there.

For the rest of the evening I stayed behind the bar and pulled beers while my thoughts whirled. If I showed Halden and Fuhr the recording of them accepting cash in the hotel room it might frighten them enough to exercise a little patience over the money. But of course, they knew that I had as much to lose as they did in any potential bribery scandal, so there would be limits to their patience. They had probably already finalised the genuine report by the time I talked to them, it was probably lying in a drawer somewhere. All they would have to say is that they had analysed the data again, something along those lines, and they were in the clear and wouldn't need to be afraid of anyone looking closely into the bought report. I had to talk to Carl, he had to know things looked to be heading for hell in a handcart.

'A beer here, Uncle Roy,' slurred a voice in front of me, followed by laughter from two others. I looked up. It was Johnny Depp. He was very drunk by now, his eyes swimming.

'Sorry, we aren't allowed to serve people who are intoxicated,' I said and hoped – all experience to the contrary – that that would be the end of it.

Johnny laughed. 'And what the hell makes you think I'm drunk, Uncle?'

'For starters you seem to think that I'm your uncle.'

'Not mine, you idiot. I mean some kid in Aas.' Johnny looked round for backup from his two wingmen. The three lads smirked, not laughing now, just eyeing me intently. David Bowie's 'Jean Genie' was playing – I'll give Erik that – and it was nearing the end, building up to a crescendo, as people say.

'But of course,' I said. 'Thinking back, it's quite possible I am your uncle after all.'

Just when 'Jean Genie' sounds as if it's going to start on a new verse it stops abruptly, and in the silence that followed Johnny stared at me. His jaw was working as he opened his mouth and then closed it again, like a fish in a bloody aquarium.

'No comeback, Johnny?' I said. 'With a reaction time that long you'd probably end up blowing into a breathalyser, right? How about a Coke? No? Coke Zero?'

Johnny Depp slowly shook his head, bent forward, as though he was about to butt something, the glazed pupils lurking up under his eyelids.

'Whatever,' I said. 'Anyway, say hello to your sister for me.'

One of his pals forgot himself for a moment and gave a brief, loud bark of laughter.

Johnny took a swing.

I was standing with one hand on the beer pump and the other holding a half-full glass, but that was no excuse. Those Saturday-night dances at Årtun had taught me enough about when a guy high on alcohol and hormones would snap. From his body language I knew he was getting ready to hit out, so why hadn't I stepped aside? Had I become too old, too slow, too dull, was that it? Maybe. But I'd pushed him, hadn't I, until, really, he was left with no choice? And wasn't it almost as though I'd invited the punch? I knew that with the counter between us, and with Johnny Depp's short arms, there was a limit to what he could deliver, although there was enough to feel it. Feel *something*. The punch was harder than I expected. I saw sparks, staggered back and suddenly found myself on my arse among broken glass and foaming beer that soaked into my trousers. Someone shouted. The music stopped. People swarmed forward.

'What the fuck's going on?' shouted Erik, who had pushed his way to the bar.

I got to my feet, rubbed my chin, and looked into Johnny's frightened eyes. They weren't glazed any more. Suddenly he looked stone-cold sober. Because, unlike Erik, he understood exactly what was about to happen. He probably already saw the banner headlines in *Os Daily*: DRUNKEN POLICE OFFICER ASSAULTS BARMAN. Given the number of witnesses queuing up in front of the beer taps Dan Krane wouldn't even have to tread carefully. Maybe Johnny was already imagining himself turning over the pages and looking for the Situations Vacant ads.

'Nothing,' I said. 'I just tripped.' I raised my voice. 'False alarm, people! Nothing happened! Let the dancing and the drinking resume!'

Scattered laughter.

Erik crossed to the amp behind the bar and turned the music up again. One of Johnny's pals had a hand on his shoulder and was trying to pull him away, but Johnny just stood there staring at me. I brushed the bits of broken glass from my trousers and leaned over to him, speaking so low only he could hear:

'Let's say we forget this, Johnny. So you can go on being Depp. But it means you owe me one. You got that?'

Johnny carried on staring. Blinked vacantly. Opened and closed his mouth before finally managing to put together a main clause, as they say:

'You sick fuck.'

He shook off his mate's hand, turned on his heel and headed unsteadily for the exit. I glanced at the time. Still not midnight. Erik turned up the volume on 'Macarena'. Ah yes, it really was going to be a tiresome evening.

Emerging into the night a little after two I pulled out my phone and saw I had two missed calls. One was from Carl. The other was a number not listed among my contacts but which I recalled anyway. A text had also come in from the same number: *Call. Doesn't matter how late.*

I pressed the call button and held the phone to my ear as I crossed the square to my car.

'Hi.' Natalie's whisper sounded sleep-drenched.

'Hi,' I said. 'Did I wake you?'

'Yes. Where are you?'

'I'm in the square. Been doing the evening shift at Fritt Fall. Didn't see your message until now.'

'Oh, I see. I just . . .' She interrupted herself with a yawn. I wondered whether she was whispering because there was someone else there but had no intention of asking. '. . . wondered if you might be interested in showing me how to hunt?'

'Hunt? Animals, you mean?'

Silence at the other end. But it was silence filled with something that told me she was alone.

'Natalie?' I was whispering now myself.

'Yes. I've never done it before.'

'But you think I have?'

'Haven't you?'

'Only two or three times. Not counting small stuff.'

'Small stuff?'

'You know. Hares. Birds. Things you can eat in just one night.'

She gave a low laugh.

'Lost you there,' she said.

'Could be,' I said as I got into the car. 'I'm still not sure we're much use to each other right now. And you're taken, of course.'

'Taken?'

'You have another job.'

'Yes, there is that,' she said slowly. Maybe I'd been mistaken, maybe it wasn't sleep but something else in her voice. She wasn't drunk, her diction was too clear for that. But high perhaps? Marijuana? MDMA? Pills?

'But of course I can teach you the little I know about hunting,' I said.

'When?'

'When is good for you?'

'I've got the whole weekend.'

The slow way she said it made it sound strangely formal, as if she was offering me not just two days but the rest of her life. It was a ridiculous thought, but that didn't stop my heart pounding in my chest. And me who was just beginning to get myself sorted out again.

'Tomorrow,' I said. 'Ten o'clock at the hotel. OK?'

'OK.'

We hung up and I leaned my head against the steering wheel. Damn.

17

IT WAS ONE OF THOSE warm October days that come like an unexpected gift to those of us who live way up here. A handful of white clouds drifted over the sky, and as soon as the sun disappeared behind them the temperature plummeted. But aside from that there was warmth enough in the old star.

Natalie and I took off our Gore-Tex jackets and pushed them down into our rucksacks before we'd gone more than a kilometre. I'd taken the rifle down from its place above the back door and carried it on a strap slung over my shoulder. As we walked I told her what I knew about getting a hunter's firearms licence, which wasn't much, since it hadn't become compulsory until after I'd gone hunting for the first time when I was about seven or eight years old.

'Probably Carl and I should have got licences, but my dad

wrote to the authorities and told them we were capable of handling firearms and enclosed a photo of me and Carl standing next to two dead goats, so we didn't have to.'

Natalie laughed.

We left the beaten track and scared up a few grouse, but I explained that while you could in theory shoot birds with a rifle, as opposed to a scattergun, what we were looking for were hares. There was no wind at all and we were able to take our first coffee break at a spot with a view in every direction. We sat there without our jackets.

'We have to teach you how to shoot,' I said after we'd drunk our coffee.

I loaded the gun and showed her the correct position to lie in. How to hold the gun. How to sight. How to breathe and how to fire. You pull the trigger, you don't grab at it.

She fired. The sound boomed around us and the echo didn't come back until several seconds later.

'And again!' she shouted.

I loaded the rifle.

'Now aim at something,' I said and pointed. 'Imagine that mountain birch over there is a Nazi.'

'Or a communist?' She closed one eye and pulled the trigger slowly backwards. At the third attempt – after she'd reloaded the rifle herself – the tree shivered slightly.

'You are a *natural*,' I said as she celebrated.

We marked the occasion with another cup of coffee.

'Think I could have killed someone?' she asked as she gazed out over the wilderness, warming her hands around her cup. 'If I was doing this for real, I mean?'

'Kill an innocent person, you mean?'

'Not necessarily innocent. And not in a war, because in war your choices aren't really your own. But to say to yourself, that life there, I'm going to snuff that out . . .'

'Depends on your motive, I guess. If you think the world will be a better place without that person, then maybe.'

'I've been thinking about it. If I'd had the opportunity to shoot a couple of heads of state who had caused and would go on causing suffering to other human beings, would I have been able to do it? And you know what? I don't think I would. I mean, I might wish to and want to, but do it? No. How about you?'

I moistened my lips as though I were debating the question with myself. 'Hard to say.'

'Yes, isn't it?'

She looked as if she wanted to pursue the theme, as they say, so I quickly coughed and asked if she thought her band might be interested in doing a gig at the Fritt Fall?

She screwed up her sweet face and shook her head. 'That's a real paradox,' she said. 'The smaller a place is, the less interested people seem to be in their own folk music.'

'Maybe,' I said. 'But maybe Ola might be interested in doing something, since it's his girlfriend's own home town?'

Natalie turned to me. 'What kind of hunting did you say this was?'

'Hares.'

'Is that where you have to stalk the prey?'

I just smiled. She smiled too, turned back to the view. 'Ola isn't my boyfriend. He's one of my best friends, we're more like brother and sister. We don't have any secrets from each other, we've seen the best and worst in each other, and we still love each other anyway.'

'Shame. Actually the two of you act like a comfortably married couple.'

'Married couple?' She snorted. 'Ola says he'll play at my wedding but only if I let him be best man. But there won't be any wedding.'

'Why not?'

She shrugged. 'You set me free. I want to carry on being free.'

'I didn't set you free,' I said. 'You did that yourself.'

'OK, but you held the door open for me.'

I didn't answer. Let my eyes wander across the red carpet of heather, and for a moment it seemed as though her thoughts were mine when she said: 'God, it looks as if it's on fire.'

We sat there in silence, each with our cup of coffee. Then, still without a word, we shouldered our rucksacks and headed on upward. An hour later we reached a lake in the middle of a stand of trees, mostly rowan and mountain birch. I don't know if it would be correct of me to say that what she said next took me completely by surprise.

'Swim?'

We built a fire before stripping off. Kept our underwear on though we knew it would mean being naked under our outer clothing afterwards – the fire wouldn't be able to dry the heavy cotton. I waded in first. The water was so cold that my legs immediately felt numb.

'Are you allowed to change your mind?' I asked.

'Not bloody likely!' Natalie shrieked as she raced by me and dived straight in, arms outstretched. Disappeared and then appeared again a few metres further out. I swore to myself and dived in too. Thought for a moment I was going to lose consciousness under the water. And when I surfaced again I found

Natalie desperately swimming back in, eyes wide open and lips already blue.

'Oh, was that it?' I said as I followed her back towards land.

We quickly dressed again and then sat more or less on top of the fire. Our teeth were still chattering and we huddled together and tried to rub a little warmth into each other. She stuck her ice-cold nose into my neck, pressed her forehead against my cheek. I was holding her, could feel the breathing – both hers and mine – begin to come a little more calmly. Then she lifted her face up to mine, and I looked into those wrong-coloured eyes. I looked and looked, and she kept her face there, unmoving, and I waited. And didn't kiss her until it was the only thing left to do. She opened my shirt. And I hers. She had goosebumps on her skin and was trembling, and at first I didn't know whether she was aroused or still feeling cold. But when she unbuttoned my trousers and then her own and pulled me down into the heather, then I knew. She sat on top of me, drops from her wet hair dripping onto me like tiny kisses. I wanted to say something, about how we didn't have to do this, that we ought to stop now, but as I drew breath to speak she put her hand over my mouth as though she'd read the words on my face.

'I don't use anything,' she whispered, then bent forward and guided me in with her other hand as her breath beat against my neck.

It felt both unreal and very real at the same time. The dream of making love with Natalie had been with me day and night, and now I was living that dream. But we didn't make love, we fucked. As though there was something we had to get out, as if we were each other's medication against something. The heather scratched my back as she moved on top of me, supporting herself with her palms on my stomach. I saw her in silhouette against the sky, the closed eyes, the face turned upwards and out, away. We were one, as they say, and yet she seemed so far away, so alone. As though she *wanted* to be alone. Then her breathing grew more staccato, she was rising up, I knew she mustn't be disturbed, I tried only to follow her rhythm and not get in her way but just reinforce what she was doing herself. She came with a long-drawn-out, raging, quivering groan. The hair swung down in front of her face and she collapsed onto me.

We lay like that, completely still. Her fingertips touched mine, but I got no response when I stroked them. I wanted to put my arm around her but didn't. She would come to me when she was ready. And so instead I listened to her breathing as it calmed for a second time. Somewhere a bird called, it sounded like a ring ouzel. I remembered something I had said one of the first times Shannon, Carl and I had talked together, that the males of mountain birds don't sing for the females, to them that's just showing off, that what they do instead is build the kind of nest that would impress her. 'Hotels?' she had said. 'Or petrol stations?' 'Looks like hotels work best,' I had replied back then.

Natalie moved position slightly. 'Oh,' she said, putting on a deep voice to imitate mine, 'was that it?'

I smiled.

'That's probably what you're thinking,' she said.

'No,' I said, and now I did put my arm around her. 'I'm thinking "so much, and this is only the first time".'

I felt a tension in her body when I said it and wished I hadn't.

'Relax,' I said. 'It was just something to say. I really thought it was good too. OK?'

I felt her body relax again.

'Thank you,' she whispered and kissed me on the cheek.

Shortly afterwards she stood up and began to get dressed.

'I'm going back now,' she said.

'Already?' I pulled my trousers towards me.

'Yes, now we've caught our hare.'

I knew it was supposed to sound like a joke, but neither of us laughed.

'I'll go alone,' she said. 'You carry on hunting.'

'No you won't, I'm coming with you,' I said as I opened my rucksack. 'But don't you want to eat first?'

Natalie shook her head. 'I've got a few things I have to do before the staff party. And, if it's OK with you, I'd sort of like to know what it feels like to walk in the mountains on my own.'

I must have looked pretty surprised, because she laughed.

'I won't get lost, Roy. I can see Ottertind and I've got a GPS signal. So is it OK then?'

'Of course it's OK,' I said, but added a question mark to the way I said it. She didn't say anything else, just packed her bag, gave me a hug and set off. I stayed by the fire, watching her, wondering what had just happened, what had gone wrong, was it my fault? Or was that the way she wanted it? Just the physical side, with as little intimacy as possible? It could, of course, be connected with the fucked-up start in life she got. It would be strange if it hadn't had some effect on her attitude towards sex. But in the end I decided there was nothing to be gained from overthinking it, maybe it had just been a lousy fuck. Or one that was quite all right but that she didn't feel any need to repeat. Or maybe that's the way things are nowadays, once you've got your hare?

As I watched she got smaller and smaller, until finally she

disappeared behind a bluff. I poured myself another coffee. The fire died down, the smoke drifted straight up into the air, that's how windless it was up there.

Almost an hour had passed, and I had managed to force myself to think about something else: how the hell was I going to persuade Vendelbo to give me that loan? And then I saw it. If I hadn't been sitting so still, or if there hadn't been water between us, there is no way it would have shown itself. I had not seen it coming, now it was standing on a rock on the edge of the lake, with just a hundred metres of still water between us. The coat was grey and black against the red heather, the ears standing up straight from the powerful head. The wolf thin, but big. Long front paws, broad chest.

We studied each other, both motionless. Two lone wolves in the same territory. My outfields, his hunting ground. What was it thinking? Could it think? If it was hungry enough, maybe it was considering me as prey, although I doubted it. I think it was trying to weigh up just how much of a danger I was. And then – as though deciding nah, he's not going to give me bother – it turned sideways on to me, strolled along the edge of the lake and then headed on up, in the opposite direction to Natalie, before disappearing from view.

Later, after I had poured water onto the fire and was making ready to leave, I heard the sound of a gunshot rolling towards me. It came from the same direction as the wolf had taken. Maybe it was tracking the same prey the hunter had just shot at.

It was still broad daylight as I came in sight of the hotel where I had parked my Volvo. Kurt's Land Rover was next to it. As I drew nearer both front doors of the Land Rover opened and Kurt and

Johnny climbed out. Both were wearing jeans and standard-issue hi-vis jackets. Both were carrying rifles.

'Police!' Kurt shouted, and the word bounced between the cars and the windows and into the restaurant. 'Roy Opgard, take the gun by the barrel and put it on the ground! Now!'

For an instant I thought Kurt was joking, or at least didn't mean it literally, and I was on the point of swinging the rifle off my shoulder and lifting it up to show them they didn't have to fetch it themselves, I was prepared to give it to them. But then realised from their body language that this was serious. That waving a rifle about was maybe the excuse Kurt Olsen had been dreaming of all these years. So I did as I was told, held the rifle high up on the barrel, bent down and carefully laid it on the ground. Straightened up again.

'Slide the rucksack down your back and put your hands up in the air where we can see them,' Kurt shouted.

I obeyed. Saw heads inside the restaurant staring at us.

'Now take four steps in my direction, turn round and lie on your belly with your nose in the asphalt! Now!'

It felt absurd. This wasn't the Bronx, it was Os, it was Kurt Olsen, the bow-legged sheriff with his Boris-mop, sounding probably the same way he did when he was telling his division 4 players what to do. But of course, I did as he ordered. As I took the prescribed four paces I looked into a wall of frightened faces staring out through the restaurant windows. And Natalie among them, standing between two tables, one hand covering her mouth.

I lay face down on the ground, breathing in the dust and thinking that if I did exactly as I was told then at least Kurt wouldn't have the excuse to humiliate me any more than an ordinary arrest would. As I should of course have known, I was wrong. The first thing he did was to squat on my back, as though I was his pony, bend my hands behind my back and snap a pair of handcuffs around my wrists. And then, since I was now incapable of getting to my own two feet unaided, he grabbed me by the collar and dragged me up. And as I was standing there, with Kurt clutching me by the neck, there was a flash directly in front of me. Dan Krane. He was standing five metres away, between the cars, and aiming his camera at me. Another two flashes came.

'Thanks,' said Dan, I'm not sure whether to me or to Kurt, and then lowered his camera and studied the results in the little pre-view window. All the while Kurt continued to hold me and wait. Dan looked up from the screen and gave Kurt a little nod.

'Come on, let's go,' said Kurt, and pushed me towards the Land Rover, where Johnny stood holding a rear door open. The car wasn't low, all the same Kurt laid what was supposed to be a pro-tective hand on top of my head as I bent to step inside, showing his audience that, here in the Os sheriff's office, we do things the right way, down to the smallest details. He probably even wished we had those Miranda rights so he could reel them off for me. Johnny tossed the rucksack and the rifle into the back and then got in beside Kurt. I saw another couple of flashes from Krane's camera as the car swung out.

18

AFTER WE'D BEEN DRIVING FOR a couple of minutes in silence I saw Kurt looking at me in the rear-view mirror.

'Aren't you even going to ask, Roy? Is it so obvious?'

I shrugged and looked out the side window. It was clouding over. It looked as if the weekend was going to turn out to be a whole lot worse than it had looked just a few hours earlier.

Johnny removed the handcuffs in the little sheriff's office and told me to wait in the small, windowless room they used as a cell. It was also used as a storeroom for a lot of folders and files piled up against the walls. Johnny came in with a cup of coffee for me and our eyes met. He was the first to look away. Kurt came in and sat down.

'OK if we record this?' he asked as he placed his phone on the table with the recording app already turned on.

'Sure,' I said. 'If I'm allowed to hear the recording afterwards.'

'But of course,' Kurt said with a smile. 'Can you tell me your name, date of birth and home address, so we have it on the recording?'

I did as instructed.

Kurt linked his hands and said a date, with a year. 'That ring a bell?' he asked.

'It's such a long time ago, Kurt. You and I were in our late teens then, but since you're the one who's asking, and since you've been trying to stick your father's disappearance on me ever since you became sheriff, let me guess it's the day he disappeared, possibly the day the empty boat with his boots in was found.'

'The day he disappeared, Roy. What were you doing that day?'

'You asked me exactly the same thing here eight years ago, Kurt. Check your notebooks.'

'I want you to check your memory.'

Ever since the arrest outside the hotel, Kurt had maintained a disquieting cool, something which told me he was holding a good hand. But now I could see his jaw muscles begin to move under the influence of all kinds of deep, inner pressures.

'And your conscience,' he added, his throat tight, a metallic ring to his voice.

I leaned forward slightly and spoke my words loudly and clearly. 'Then, for the purposes of this recording, I hereby announce that at this point in the interrogation, neither the person interrogating me, Sheriff Kurt Olsen, nor anyone else from the sheriff's office has given me any information about why I have been arrested, what my rights are, whether I am obliged to answer any questions beyond giving my name and personal details, how long they want to keep me, how long they are legally entitled to keep me and whether or not I have the opportunity to contact a lawyer.'

Kurt smirked and glanced over at Johnny, who stood leaning against the wall behind him.

'Don't play the smart-arse, Roy, we'll get to all that in due course.'

'Note for the recording,' I continued. 'Sheriff Olsen hereby confirms that he has started the interrogation before this information had been relayed to me.'

Kurt leaned forward, his face flushed now, and turned off the recording. 'Now don't get smart with us, Roy, it's not your game. Cooperate, or things will only get worse for you.'

'I hear what you say. Will you be deleting that recording, or can I have a copy too?'

'What do you think?' he hissed.

I didn't reply.

Kurt closed his eyes and took a deep breath. Julie told me once that Kurt was the only man who took part in the short-lived yoga course being held in the basement of the bookshop, so maybe this was some kind of Zen thing. It wasn't going down the way he'd probably imagined and now he wanted to get it back on track. He turned on the recorder again, and when he spoke this time his voice was smooth as velvet.

'In the first place we are entitled to hold you for forty-eight hours because what you are under suspicion of carries a minimum sentence of six months. If we wish to continue to detain you after that period then a custodial meeting will be required. You will be allowed to contact relatives, and you may speak to a lawyer. You are under no obligation to answer any of the questions we put to you. Is that clear?'

'Yes,' I said.

'You have been arrested on suspicion of having murdered Sigmund Olsen, the former sheriff in Os county, or of being an accessory to his murder.'

'OK,' I said. 'Is this still your moth-eaten private suspicion, Kurt, or have there been any new developments in the case?'

Kurt pursed his lips in what might have been a smile. I shuddered and steeled myself. They've found blood and hair, Vera had said. Didn't sound too bad. But I could see by Kurt's face that it wasn't looking good. For me, that is.

'The crime-scene technicians had a long and difficult search, but in the end they found blood in your parents' Cadillac,' said Kurt. 'Blood and three strands of hair.'

I shrugged. 'Hardly surprising in a wrecked car.'

'No, but they found these on the outside of the car, Roy. To be more precise, when they unscrewed the rear registration plate.'

It felt as though someone was tightening the skin around my skull. In a sudden flash I realised exactly what had happened. And it was catastrophic. I watched Kurt's mouth moving as the skin began to pull up from my eyes, my ears, my jaw. When Sigmund Olsen fell onto the Cadillac, his head had smashed against the underside of the car, directly above the licence plate. The blood that ran down and in behind the plate had carried with it these loose strands of hair, dried and glued them around the screws and bolts on the back of the car. That bloody DNA proof had lain there, patient and protected, for someone conscientious enough to want to look for it. Someone like Kurt Olsen. He looked triumphant now. Probably been dreaming of the look on my face when he told me. Which was probably why he couldn't leave it there but had to go on.

'The reason it took us a while to find out that it was my father's hair and blood is that we had no DNA profile on him and no source material either – back when it happened it didn't occur to anyone to take a hair from one of his jackets, everything went to the cleaner's or else was thrown out. Apart, that is, from one thing.' Kurt held up his index finger. 'Two, actually.' He grinned and held up his middle finger. 'His snakeskin boots. Which *you yourself* put in the boat so that it would look like he rowed out and then drowned himself. We didn't throw those out. I started using them, as a tribute to the best lawman this town ever had. Right? And that was our bit of luck, because we found tiny bits of toenail below the inner soles. His and mine.'

Kurt was grinning hugely now. The look on my face probably met all his expectations. My forehead was tight as a drum now. In another couple of turns of the screw my face would burst.

'Because we know my father was at Opgard the day he disappeared, and now we also know he never left it. That he ended up in Huken and bled onto the car already lying down there. At the time, you and your brother claimed that you saw him leave Opgard; well, what do you say now, Roy?'

I had to stretch my jaw a couple of times before I felt able to use it.

'What I say is that I'd like to call that lawyer.'

'The nearest one is in Notodden, they've got two on their list and I'm pretty sure both are going to be busy on a Saturday. But if you want to sit here the rest of the day and night and wait for someone to make the journey from there, or from Oslo, then be my guest. The alternative is that you answer a few questions now and then you'll be able to leave.'

'No.'

Kurt gave me a dead-eyed stare.

'Fine,' he said at last. 'We note that you decline to answer questions without a lawyer present. If you'll sign this document agreeing not to leave the area for fourteen days then you can go.'

'That's unreasonable,' I said.

'I agree,' Kurt said. 'You're free to walk out of here.' He leaned back in his chair, pulled a crumpled cigarette packet from his trouser pocket, flicked out a cigarette and put it between his lips. 'Since there's no danger of tampering with the evidence and I doubt whether you would consider fleeing the country, then we have no reason to detain you any longer.' He reached out a hand to turn off the recording and glared at me when I interceded my hand between his and the phone.

'I mean it's unreasonable to make me *walk*,' I said. 'You picked me up next to my car at the hotel, I demand that you drive me back there.'

Kurt scrutinised me. We were probably thinking the same thing. That to the people in the restaurant who had witnessed the arrest it might look like an admission of error from the police if they dropped me back at the same place half an hour later.

'The question is on tape,' I said. 'So?'

The hatred burned in Kurt's eyes like fire.

'Johnny,' he said, his gaze riveted on my forehead.

I followed Johnny Depp across the car park. Halfway to the car I turned. Kurt Olsen stood on the steps in front of the building. The day was beginning to darken and I could see the glowing tip of his cigarette as he watched us. The lights were all out in the bank, the doctor's surgery and the county administration office. Had Kurt had those DNA results for a day or two but chosen to arrest me on a Saturday because he knew it would be difficult to get hold of a lawyer? He must have arranged things with Dan Krane well in advance, because people with small children are always busy on the weekends. Kurt had maybe hoped I would talk but not actually counted on it. Still, he had achieved his main objective, which was to humiliate me. To tell the whole of Os, loud and clear, that I was a suspect. To get the village gossip machine turning over, get the vermin up out of the wood and into the light of day. Give another chance to anyone who might know something about what had happened back then but not reported it to him.

Johnny opened the passenger door of the battered old Honda Civic.

Wedged himself into the driver's seat next to me and started the car. It coughed itself into life, to the accompaniment of an unmistakable whining and ticking sound.

'You want to watch out for that,' I said.

'It's just a loose fan belt,' said Johnny and pulled out onto the road. 'I'll fix it.'

'You could maybe fix the fan belt, but that sound there comes from a worn camshaft belt. If that goes your whole engine goes.'

Johnny glanced over to see if I was telling the truth.

'Bring it into the petrol station on Monday,' I said. 'We'll change the belt at the workshop. Won't take long.'

Johnny went back to concentrating on his driving.

'That performance back there wasn't my idea,' he said. 'We drove to Opgard to pick you up but your brother said you'd driven to the hotel. And Kurt decided we should wait for you there.'

'And Dan Krane?'

'Kurt had arranged for Krane to take his pictures in front of the sheriff's office when we got back there. But once it got changed to the hotel Kurt called him and told him to go there instead. More drama, you know.'

I nodded. We drove for a while in silence.

'Thanks,' said Johnny. 'For not saying anything about yesterday.'

'If I was going to report it I wouldn't go to Kurt, I'd go to the station in Notodden,' I said.

He wriggled in his seat. 'Are you going to do it?'

I moved my head from side to side. I hadn't actually intended to report the lad, he'd probably learned his lesson. And I had plenty of other things to think about. The DNA samples. Natalie. A bribe and an investment arrangement that were looking seriously fucked up. Enough to drive any man to despair. Enough to get him clutching at straws. Maybe that's why I answered with a question of my own.

'What's this thing between you and Vendelbo?'

'Thing? What thing?'

'Him buying those beers for you and your mates?'

Johnny smirked. He hesitated, but guessed there was some link to the information I was asking for, that it would be a good idea to show a little cooperation.

'He wants to get his hand down my trousers. Nothing wrong with that but it ain't going to happen. But if he wants to throw beers, dinners and loans at me, that's his business.'

'Loans?'

'Yeah, but it's not happening, like I said.'

'Tell me.'

'Well, I showed him a picture of a used Porsche a couple of weeks ago. Lovely looking thing, somebody selling it over in Notodden. And he said he'd give me a loan at below market rates.'

My pulse rate – which had already had plenty to do in the course of the day – went up again. Could this be my straw? I swallowed. 'Just a casual remark, right?'

'No, no, he meant it all right.'

'How do you know that?'

'He sent me the offer in a text. Low instalments, rate close to zero. Said we could sign the contract after closing time in the bank. That he'd fix a way for me to pay. But I could see where he was going and so of course I said no. I like women, know what I mean?'

'I get you,' I said. 'He's probably sent you other text messages, hasn't he?'

Johnny grinned. 'Yeah, you could say.'

'Pictures too?'

'No, no pictures. Vendelbo's a married man, he can't take the chance of something like that getting about in the village, no way.'

'But these text messages, they do reveal what it is he's after?'

'You'd have to be pretty slow not to get it.' Johnny glanced at me again, and I saw the suspicion in his stupid eyes.

'Where are you actually going here?'

'To the hotel,' I said.

We drove on, but he'd slowed down, as though waiting and watching for whatever came next, whatever it might be.

'Johnny,' I said, 'what do you say you and me make a little deal?'

19

SUNDAY I WORKED AT THE station. If nothing else it gave the brain some brief respite from spinning round and round the question of the new DNA results and the fact that I had somehow to get hold of a hundred and twenty million. And twelve of them double fucking quick. On Saturday Carl and I had had a Zoom meeting with Liv Goebbel, a criminal law lawyer from Oslo. Goebbel was a sparky, no-nonsense woman in her fifties whom I'd met at a dinner at Os Spa. I keep the bar pretty high in such matters, but I had once felt she was someone I could trust. Now there she was on the screen behind her tidy desk, a view of the City Hall in the window behind her, a whisky laugh and a gift of high-speed speech so fast I had to concentrate hard to keep up with her. She explained that even without the toenails, the police would probably have discovered that the blood behind the licence plate was from Sigmund Olsen.

'With the analytical tools we have today a drop of blood from a pregnant woman can give us not only the DNA profile of the foetus but the profile of the *father* of the unborn child. In this case they could have used Kurt Olsen's DNA to show that the blood came from the father.'

She expressed her astonishment that the police hadn't also interviewed Carl, that they were probably only going for me. She asked me how old we had been, and when she found out I'd just passed nineteen, with Carl still not eighteen, she said that was the reason. Even though the age of criminal responsibility was fifteen, eighteen was also considered a clear line in terms of prosecution. It was difficult to get anyone under eighteen charged, prosecuted and imprisoned, so when dealing with a case as old as this the natural target for the authorities would be me. *Os Daily*'s online edition had a brief report of an arrest and the recovery of DNA relating to an old missing person's case without mentioning which case, my name or pictures of the arrest. Goebbel's view was that this was a result of the paper's own censorship process, that as long as I had been released, and no charges brought against me, society had no legal right to know more than that.

Carl and I had just exchanged exasperated looks. The Oslo lady obviously didn't know that everybody, absolutely everybody in Os, already knew who had been arrested, and for what. That Kurt Olsen was just waiting for someone to call who had information to share with him.

I hardly slept that night and it was a release when the alarm rang at six. Sunday was the busiest day at the station, with people from the hotel and the cabins further up the valley making their way back home. They didn't just buy petrol, they needed food and drink for the long drive. During the quiet interludes Egil told me about the MC meeting, and that it had been a great success. When I asked how success was measured at an MC meeting, whether it was about the number of bikers who attended, he said that didn't count for much, what mattered was that those who did turn up enjoyed themselves.

'More than expected?' I asked.

'Eh?'

'If you call it a success then it must have been more enjoyable than expected.'

'I think they were expecting it to be a success,' said Egil.

I had just handed five sausage-and-shrimp salad rolls across the counter when Natalie walked in. She'd gathered her hair under a trucker's cap and was wearing a hoodie with Tame Impala on it. She looked tired as she stood and waited over by the cartons of windscreen washer. Once the place was empty she came over to me.

'What'll it be?' I asked.

She gave me that direct look, right in the eye, and again I got that sweet, lost feeling. Dammit.

'Tell me what you've got,' she said quietly.

'We-ell.' I took a breath. 'I had a special offer on some tough old goat's meat. Old, but still pretty good I would say.'

She laughed quietly. 'I would say so too. But I think that meat got taken off the market yesterday. Is there a problem with it?'

I shrugged. 'Some say that around the time you were born the young goat butted the old sheriff and sent him tumbling down into Huken.'

199

'And did he?'

I shook my head. The door opened and a customer came in. Egil was busy out at the pumps.

'But the meat will have to be thrown out anyway,' I said, with my eyes on the customer. 'You best try somewhere else, where they have fresher meat.'

'Roy?'

I looked at her. She smiled, but only fleetingly, as if it was too difficult to keep it up.

'I'm sorry.'

I tried to smile. 'Nothing to apologise for. You must do exactly as you want, Natalie.'

'OK.' She took a deep breath. She looked as if she was standing on tiptoes. 'I want to . . .' She stopped. The customer had taken a carton of windscreen washer and lined up right behind Natalie. '. . . see you again. If you want that.'

I looked at her. She was so beautiful, like one of those songs that makes you want to cry. And it wasn't that I was so afraid of being used. It's often good for things to be used. But things had got too complicated, it wasn't something I could handle, on top of everything else. The problem was, the sight of her was like a shot of morphine to a body racked with pain, it was impossible not to want more of it. So I forced my gaze away from her and addressed the customer behind her.

'We're selling three of those for the price of two.'

'Wow,' the customer responded enthusiastically, and before I could say he could pick them up on the way out he was heading back to the shelf.

'Let's talk later, Natalie. When things have calmed down a bit, OK?'

I looked at her again. There was a glazed sheen in her eyes and the pupils were large and dark. Was she high on something? Or was she crying?

'When will things have calmed down then?' she asked, her voice cracked.

I swallowed. 'In five, six . . .' I began, not knowing whether I intended to say weeks or days. I saw a tear forming in the thin, short lashes over those discoloured eyes of hers.

'Hours,' I said. 'When I'm finished here. Meet me outside at six.'

At four I went out and cleaned up around the pumps and then strolled over to where a new generation of boy racers were parked in their trimmed cars.

'Pick up those butts,' I said, pointing to five cigarette tips scattered on the asphalt.

'OK, OK, Dad,' said the guy sitting behind the wheel, smoking. He was leaning on the bare arm that was sticking out of his cutaway denim jacket. A tattoo proclaimed No Mercy.

'Now,' I said.

'We'll do it when we leave,' he said with an embarrassingly relaxed drag of his cigarette.

'No way, I want this area kept clean.'

'When we leave, Dad.' He raised his Coke bottle and grinned. 'We're paying customers, right?'

I snatched the cigarette out of his mouth before he could react. Flicked it into the back seat where a young girl and a lad shrieked and tried to get out of the way.

'What the fuck!' yelled the driver.

'Now you know how I feel,' I said, before heading over to the crash barrier and the slope leading down to Budalesvannet. Pulled out my phone and called Asle Vendelbo.

'Yes?'

'I think I've got what you need to let me have that loan,' I said.

'Is that you, Roy?'

'Yes. Something's cropped up on my property list since the last time we spoke, something you can use as security. All right if I call in early tomorrow morning?'

'Well, that sounds like good news,' he said, though he didn't sound as if he was bubbling over with joy. 'But I gather you're a person of interest for the police on some matter?'

'A misunderstanding,' I said. 'But we can talk about that and other things tomorrow. Ten o'clock all right?'

'Tomorrow's a bit difficult, Roy.'

'A bit difficult is better than very difficult. Johnny Depp says hello, by the way.'

Silence at the other end.

'Ten o'clock?' I asked.

Vendelbo coughed. 'If we can get it over inside half an hour.'

'I'm guessing we'll be even quicker than that,' I said.

We hung up. The weak point. I'd found it. The question now was, was my heart cold enough to exploit it? I turned and walked back towards the petrol station. The guy wearing the jeans jacket was out of his car now. He stood waiting for me. Shifting his weight from foot to foot. A red-headed guy from one of the other cars approached and whispered something to him. He looked at the red-headed guy in disbelief, then at me. The redhead hurried back to his car and jeans jacket opened his car door ready to jump back in.

'Hey, hey!' I shouted. 'Butts first.'

He stared at me. Even from ten metres away I could see his Adam's apple bob up and down. Then he squatted and began collecting them from the asphalt. I don't doubt that the red-headed guy had told him I'd been arrested yesterday on suspicion of murdering the former sheriff.

'Boo!' I whispered softly as I passed the guy, making him jump and sending the butts flying.

Oh yeah, my heart was cold enough all right.

At six o'clock precisely I left the petrol station. Natalie was standing beside my car and shivering, her arms folded. I was a little surprised because it wasn't cold, actually quite the opposite.

'Been waiting long?' I asked.

She shook her head.

'You look cold. Want to take a drive?'

She put her head on one side. 'Is that what you guys used to do when you were young?'

'You bet. If you had a car and a driver's licence then, socially speaking, you had it made.'

She laughed. 'So you were the driver while the others drank and picked up the girls?'

'Is it really that obvious?'

'Maybe. You don't have somewhere where we can be alone, do you? Preferably indoors.'

'Sort of. As long as you don't object to the smell of oil?'

As I unlocked the door to the workshop it occurred to me that the last person I'd shared this space with was Shannon, when she was still alive. We sat in the room where I had lived for all those years, me in the Stressless chair, her on the bed. She was pale and trembling like a leaf, so I turned on the powerful fan heater

I usually used in the winter. Put the only Lou Reed album worth talking about – *Transformer* – on the record player and made some tea. The jar of honey had been standing in that cupboard over the stove for at least ten years, but since honey is like murder – there is no sell-by date – I put three spoonfuls into the piping-hot drink and placed it in front of her.

'You don't look too good,' I said.

'I don't feel so good,' she said and then took a sip. 'Thanks. What are all these?' She pointed to the wall.

'Licence plates from countries that don't exist any more,' I said. 'My uncle used to collect them, so some of them were here when I took over the workshop. The rest I picked up myself.'

'Basutoland,' she read aloud from one of the plates.

'Lesotho now,' I said.

'Lesotho?'

'Tiny little kingdom, an enclave in South Africa. I hear it's very beautiful. Up in the mountains, they get snow on the tallest peaks.'

'A bit like here then. A mountain kingdom. Who's the king?'

I took a plug of tobacco from the snuffbox. 'There or here?'

She smiled and took another sip of her tea. 'You say such strange things, Roy.'

'Can't remember the king's name,' I said. 'I know he took over after his father died in a road accident.'

'Oh?'

'Drove from the farm to check on the livestock, went off the road and straight over the edge of a cliff. Some say someone must have tampered with the car, that it was murder.'

'What do you believe?'

I shrugged. 'Conspiracy theories. Anyway, the son took over and he sits on the throne now.'

'What's his name?'

'Don't know.'

'Shall we google it?'

'Or shall we just leave it as an unknown?'

'Let's leave it unknown,' she said. 'Will you kiss me?'

It was different this time. Slow, tender, patient and searching. And when we found what we were looking for we carried on with that same, low-glowing languid intimacy. I had to hold her back a couple of times, and then she got the idea. And like two dancers we found each other's rhythm and wavelength, and only then could we gradually begin to increase the frequency. This time she came without a sound, crying and shaking against my shoulder.

We drank more tea. I turned the record over and we made love again. Afterwards we watched Peter Jackson's first film, *Bad Taste*, which we'd discovered we both admired. I picked up a frozen pizza from the petrol station and we heated it up in the oven. It was warm now but her teeth were still chattering. She didn't have a fever, though – quite the opposite – because when I held her, her body was cold with sweat.

'What kind of ill are you?' I asked.

'What do you think?'

'I think its name might be abstinence.'

She nodded.

'What are you using?'

She shrugged. 'I have my rules, but within those I'm flexible.'

'Which is to say?'

'MDMA, speed, cocaine. Microdoses of ketamine when I'm depressed. Weed when I need to sleep, ayahuasca when it's available and I can afford it. But never meth, morphine or heroin.'

'How hooked are you?'

'I'm not hooked. It's more like a *habit*, if you know what I mean. Every time I start up again I know I have to kick it, but that's something I can handle. Like now. It's fine, I'll be over it in a day or two.'

'Why do you keep starting up again?'

She filled her cheeks with air and emptied them. 'Good question. Because I get bored. Or depressed. Because it stops the traffic in my head for a while.'

'You're saying that ayahuasca stops the traffic?'

'Well, at least it's a different type of traffic.'

'Where do you get hold of your stuff?'

'I have to go to Notodden.'

'To Ola?'

She looked at me for a moment as though making sure I could be trusted, then nodded. 'How did you guess?'

'We-ell, Ola's a black metal guy with a fiddle, right?'

She smiled and shook her head. 'Wrong. Black metal boys are dysfunctional but disciplined straights in fancy dress, they're hard-working nerds from small towns. They're folk musicians living rock 'n' roll lives. And it kills them. It's always been that way. You know, I always carry a little bottle of ipecac on me because of the boys in the band. Ola especially, he's the one who does the most pills.'

'A bottle of what?'

'Ipecac. It's an emetic. Makes you puke. But you have to take it within an hour of overdosing, otherwise that's it.' She stopped. 'Am I scaring you?'

'Scaring me?'

'I use dope. I'm a victim of sexual abuse. I suffer depressions. Life's simpler if you keep away from people like me.'

'Oh, you mean like that. No, that's not a problem. I've got a couple of things of my own.'

I took the pizza out of the oven, put it onto a plate and began to cut it into slices. Heard Natalie move on the bed behind me.

'Apart from your father abusing you, what else?'

'Isn't that enough?' I asked without turning round.

'Oh yeah. But there's more, isn't there?'

'Hm. Maybe. I guess there's always more.'

I cut the pizza into six slices and put it on a plate on the duvet. Sat down beside her.

'If you can stand it, that is,' I said, nodding towards the pizza.

'I can stand it,' she said. 'Go ahead, tell me.'

'I meant—'

'I know what you meant. But I'd like to know.'

I pulled a slice free. The strands of melted cheese made it look as though it was clinging on desperately to its home and didn't want to leave, just couldn't let go. I took a bite, chewed as she watched and waited. Breathed in and out a few times as she still waited.

'Moshoeshoe the Second,' I said.

'What?'

'That was his name. The king of Lesotho. His eldest son is

Letsie the Third. A lot of speculation about how it could have happened, but no obvious conclusions. And Dad always used to call Opgard his kingdom. He was Moshoeshoe, I was Letsie who took over the farm. With one big difference.'

Natalie helped herself to a slice of pizza. 'And that is?'

'I don't think Letsie killed his father.'

20

I WAS ALMOST EIGHTEEN, CARL not quite seventeen. I had promised Carl Dad wouldn't abuse him again, that I would kill him. Dad knew it too, he'd seen it in my eyes, and welcomed it, probably longed for me to release him from the torture chamber of his own head. He'd been in our bedroom that night and now he was out in the barn. Punching and punching away at that punchbag, knowing I was standing behind him. He'd got the shotgun out, it was leaning up against the wall, loaded and ready, all I had to do was shoot him in the head from close up and leave the shotgun lying beside him. Sheriff Sigmund Olsen would conclude it was only another tragic case of the most common way of committing suicide for the men around here. But I couldn't do it. Could not bloody do it. Because no matter how much I hated him, he was still me, and I was him.

So it went on.

Until an evening later that same year when Carl and I were sitting in the old Volvo I'd been given by Uncle Bernard, parked in the yard in front of the winter garden. The Cadillac was in front of us, with Dad and Mum inside, heading down towards Geitesvingen. I knew what was going to happen. It had taken me half an hour to loosen the set screw and the bolt that attached the stem of the steering wheel to the rack-and-pinion, punch two holes in the brake hoses and bleed the brake fluid into a bucket. I hadn't reckoned on Mum being in the car with him, but there was a kind of poetic justice in it too. She'd pretended she didn't know what was going on and wouldn't listen when I tried to tell her. She'd always loved Dad more than Carl and me, maybe it was a biological anomaly as it's called, but that's the way it was. Not that I understood her, understood how all-consuming the shame must have been. But still, it wouldn't have been wrong if I'd got a death sentence for what I'd done to her.

I still remember how my heart pounded so loud I was sure it could be heard in the silence that followed, when we could no longer hear the crunching of the gravel under the car's tyres. Remember that red rear light staring at me, like the eye of a silent witness. And then it was gone. A hundred-metre free fall. I remember the surprisingly dull thud as the car hit the bottom of Huken, and how my first thought was that they may have survived. That in a few moments we would see Dad come crawling up over the edge of the drop, bloody but undead, with that familiar self-hating rage burning in his eyes. We sat there and sat there until we were completely sure.

'You did what you had to,' Natalie whispered. I'd spent a long time telling her the story, answered her questions and along the way opened a couple of old beers that still tasted OK. I hadn't protested when she rolled herself a joint to take the sting out of the abstinence, as she put it. Night had fallen, and we hadn't turned on the lights.

'Yes, I did what I had to do,' I said. 'And I would do it again.' Then, imitating her voice the way she sometimes did to me, I said: 'Am I scaring you?'

I sensed her smile in the dark. She ran her hand over my naked chest, my cheek, hair, neck.

'No,' she said. 'And now there's just one last thing I'm wondering about.'

'Yes?'

'How do you know you can trust me?'

I returned her smile. 'Who said I did? But you're naked, so I can see Kurt Olsen hasn't taped a microphone to you, and without a recording it would just be a she-said-he-said thing.'

She gave me a playful punch. 'Don't be silly. What if I take something more, more than this . . .' She held up the joint. 'And start talking too much? Not that I will, but you can't know that.'

I shrugged. 'I guess you just have to take chances in life sometimes.'

I couldn't see the colour, just the whites of her eyes and the silhouette of her head, her body. It was so dark that if I'd wanted to I could imagine it was Shannon. But I didn't want to. I didn't need to.

She leaned forward and kissed me. She tasted of weed and beer and Natalie. I returned her kiss, not because I was feeling horny but out of curiosity, to see whether she was. Her kiss grew hungrier and my response was instantaneous.

'Damn,' I said and let go of her.

'I know!' she cried and laughed.

I brushed the pizza crumbs from the duvet, stood up and ran the empty plate under the tap. Stood there with my back to her and asked myself what kind of a situation I'd got myself into. Had I confessed to murder as a declaration of love? Put my fate in her hands as a way of proving something to her? Or was I doing what Dad had done? Leaning a shotgun against a wall, loaded and ready, then turning my back and half hoping she would take the chance?

Maybe. Maybe not. Because I'd only told her about my first two murders.

They winched the bodies up out of the chasm, but left the Cadillac down there, getting it up out of there would have been too expensive and too dangerous. I hadn't told Natalie that when Sigmund Olsen began to suspect it wasn't just an unfortunate accident and had come up to Opgard talking about how he wanted to get down into Huken to check the car, Carl had pushed him over the edge. Or about the Danish hit man. Or Willumsen. Or Shannon and the baby. I pulled my hands away when it dawned on me that the pain I was feeling came from the water from the tap, it was scalding.

21

'BUT THAT'S ENOUGH ABOUT THE weather,' said Asle Vendelbo and looked at his watch, as though to remind me we only had half an hour at the most. 'You said something new had come up regarding securities on a possible loan?'

'Yes it has,' I said, looking out the window over the square. Traffic on the main road through Os on a Monday morning wasn't much more than a trickle. I waited until he asked.

'What kind of asset are we talking about here?'

I turned my gaze back to Vendelbo, sitting behind his desk with the family photos on it, saw him pressing his stubby fingertips together. The arms of his suit jacket were too short. I don't know why it is that bank managers in small towns always choose to wear cheaper suits than their counterparts in the cities do – as far as I know the pay is the same. Is it because they want the peasants they're dealing with to think they're grass-roots too, as people say? That to wear an Ermenegildo Zegna suit would seem comic, almost insulting, to the average inhabitant of Os?

'We're talking about so-called goodwill,' I said.

'Goodwill?'

'Yes. The property aspect of the balance which is immaterial.'

'I know what goodwill is,' said Vendelbo. 'But that is a collective term for everything that is not a tangible and concrete asset, so what kind of goodwill are we talking about? A trade name? A reputation? A patent?'

'A reputation,' I said. ' A good reputation.'

'Does this mean you have received an offer to buy your station at a considerably higher price than the actual value of its component parts?'

'No it doesn't,' I said.

Vendelbo sighed heavily. And, it seemed to me, as if a little relieved. His upper lip had been glistening with sweat when I walked into his office at five past ten. Coffee was ready on the desk and he had voiced a few pleasantries about the weather. He must have had his suspicions, wondered what all this was about. But now he looked a bit more self-assured.

'Then all we have is an assumption that the company possesses these extra assets. And the bank does not accept security in the form of goodwill based on reputation, because that's something that can vanish overnight. Particularly where . . .' He pinched his mouth closed.

'Particularly where what?' I asked.

Vendelbo sat up straight. Fixed his gaze on me in what he probably thought was an authoritative manner. 'Particularly where the owner of the company is the subject of a police investigation. But in any case, as I say, we can't accept security in the form of good reputation.'

'Even if the good reputation in question is not mine?'

'I'm sorry?'

'Even if the good reputation I have acquired as an asset is not mine, but yours?'

He swallowed. His voice rose higher: 'What on earth are you talking about, Roy?'

I placed my phone on the table in front of him and pointed.

'These here are emails and text messages you've been sending to a young man. That you're contemplating infidelity with a man is a matter for you and your wife, although, of course, it's possible she knows nothing about it. In which case – and if I forward these messages to her – you may find yourself having to change that family photo of yours there on your desk.'

A brake light seemed to have come on in Vendelbo's face as he stared down at the screen.

'But worse than your marriage going on the rocks is the likelihood of your career being over too.'

I swiped to the next page on the phone screen. I gave Vendelbo time to read his own words before continuing.

'You shouldn't have put that offer there in writing, Asle. You've given me such a thorough account of the bank's own rules of conduct for giving loans that even I can see this is just not on. To use the bank's money to offer a loan at well under market rates to a young man you've got the hots for, what are we going to call that? Corruption? Embezzlement? I'm not much of a wordsmith but I'm sure head office has one that covers it. Dan Krane at *Os Daily* certainly will.'

Vendelbo raised his eyes and stared at me. His voice, when he spoke, was so hoarse it was hardly recognisable.

'What is it you want?'

I nodded slowly, looked at my wristwatch. 'We've still got another twenty minutes in which to discuss the details and what has to be done,' I said. 'But here's the short version: I want a loan of one hundred million approved inside a week. If you manage that then I won't have to use that button there.'

I pointed to the Forward icon and leaned back in my seat. Waited. Watched Vendelbo, who was staring at a point some way in front of him and breathing hard through his nose. Finally he coughed. 'What rate did you have in mind?'

'Market rate,' I said as I folded my hands over my stomach. 'Opgard men don't haggle.'

On my way across the square I saw that Natalie had called.

'Hi, honey,' she answered when I called back.

It was a joke, naturally. All the same, the words gave me a warm feeling in my stomach. 'Working tonight?'

'No,' I said.

'If you like I can make us dinner this evening.'

'Would love that.'

'Seven all right?'

'Perfect. Want me to bring something?'

'Like what?'

'A bottle of wine, for example.'

She laughed. 'Drive all the way to the off-licence in Notodden, you mean?'

'You don't think I have any at home?'

'Am I wrong?'

'Yes.'

'Yes?'

'And no. I'll take one from Carl's cellar.'

Her laughter tickled my ear. 'Thanks, but not on my account, Roy. I'll stick to water this evening.'

'Understood. Wine wasn't a good idea. You said yesterday that as from today you were going on the wagon.'

'Compromise doesn't work for me. You like trout?'

'Caught it yourself?'

'Yes. From the fridge at the Co-op.'

'That's the way we like it, farmed, tame and stone-cold dead.' I made some feeble joke about how people said it cures chlamydia if you eat enough of it. I knew by now I'd have to pay for any bad jokes, but as long as they evoked that laugh of hers then I intended to carry on making them.

We hung up and I headed on into Fritt Fall. Erik was behind the bar, reading a newspaper. I looked around the inside of the club. Ten guests. Twelve if you counted the two old codgers sitting there filling out their coupons for the day's racing. Erik read my thoughts.

'Don't worry,' he said. 'Guess how much we took on Friday?'

'A lot,' I said. 'But then, you had a bloody good barman on duty.'

'It's the hits!' said Erik. 'I know you feel some of that music is beneath you, but it sure does hit the spot with that crowd. It's just about finding the right genre that's going to appeal to everybody, both sexes, as well as the other four we've got here in Os.'

Erik showed his two gold teeth in an even wider, conspiratorial grin, but I didn't ask what he meant. I'd heard him tell the joke before, and even though I didn't remember the punchline I remembered enough to know that I didn't want to hear it again.

'By the way, we've been in touch with the Highways Department for permission to put up one of those blue knife-and-fork road signs now that we're going to be able to offer a full menu. We're hoping to steal a bit of business from your station.'

'Go right ahead,' I said. 'If the sign is enough to remind motorists they're hungry then it'll be to the advantage of us both. Was that your idea or Julie's?'

Erik looked lost. 'Not sure. I guess I'd call it our idea.'

I gave that slow Os nod. All right then, so it was Julie's idea.

'Good ideas are welcome,' I said. 'So is initiative. We need it to get that profit margin up. That's part of the reason I've called in.'

Erik Nerell gave me a watchful look. Not surprising really, he was used to the fact that whenever I had something to say it usually meant bad news for him.

'I've been looking over the quarterly returns,' I said. 'The problem is not the variables but the regular outgoings. In the main that means the wages of the permanent staff.'

I saw in Erik's eyes that this was exactly what he had feared. Because Fritt Fall only had the two permanent staff, Julie and himself. And Julie was good, and she was pregnant as well, so I neither could nor would be letting her go.

'I haven't spoken to Julie yet,' I said. 'Wanted to talk to you about it first.'

'Talk about what?' Already there was a hard edge of despair and anger in his voice.

'I've been thinking of offering her part ownership of Fritt if she'll agree to a cut in wages. That way we're in the same boat whether things go well or not. Thought it was a good offer, now that we know the main road is still going to run through the centre of town.'

I could see Erik Nerell's jaw muscles working hard. 'And what about me?' he asked, his voice now hoarse.

'I thought of offering you the same,' I said.

'The same?' He looked at me in disbelief, or as though he expected that any further description of what 'the same' meant would turn out not to be the same at all but some crappy and uninteresting deal.

'That you, Julie and I go into partnership, each one owning a third share.'

Erik closed one eye, but not the way Natalie did, not curious, just extremely bloody suspicious.

'You want the two of us to buy in?'

'No,' I said. 'You'll both get a one-third share free. In return for which you accept a wage cut of fifteen per cent. If we base it on the last two half-years that'll raise Julie's income by twenty-five per cent and yours by twenty-eight per cent.'

'I'll earn *more* from this than Julie?'

'She has a higher wage than you, so a fifteen per cent cut is more for her. And as I say, you'll both get the same share of the profits.'

Erik Nerell looked as though he didn't quite know what to believe. 'Why . . . do you want to do this?'

I spread my arms. 'Like I said, I believe in us all sitting in the same boat. To give inventive and enterprising people some feeling of ownership in what they do each day. That what's good for them is good for me.'

Erik looked thoughtful. He shook his head. 'Well, I'll be damned.' He grinned, the gold fillings glinting in his teeth. I knew how he was feeling. I had felt the same way when I was at last able to buy the petrol station where I'd worked for so many years. What was mine had finally become *all* mine. There's a farmer in us all, we need to own, own our own land, stand on our own ground and, if possible, own more, it's like a bloody disease. And now it had caught Erik, and it was as though I could see his inner farmer staring out at me.

'But of course it's obvious,' I said, 'that when you're all sitting in the same boat, if one of you goes over then the others do too. So we all have to help each other.'

'Of course,' said Erik vaguely, his gaze already sweeping over the interior with different eyes, the calculating look of an owner who's thinking income and outgoings.

'For example, you're going to have to help me remember something that happened the winter I turned seventeen. You must have been fifteen.'

'Oh?' Erik looked at me again. 'Does this have anything to do with Kurt taking you down to the sheriff's office?'

I nodded. 'Now, I know that you and Kurt are mates . . .'

'We-ell, I don't know if I'd go that far. It's more like he comes to me when he needs help with something. Which he knows he'll get because the licence here has always been dependent on him vouching for me and for this place, right?'

'But you also know that Kurt has never been able to accept that his father drowned himself but he pursues these conspiracy theories about me and Carl having something to do with it, right?'

'Well, yeah – a few years back he wanted to winch me down into Huken to check on the car.'

'You see what I mean? So I need you to help me to help him reconstruct what happened when my old man got his Cadillac stuck in a snowdrift just outside the Nerell place when you were fifteen.'

Erik gave me a quizzical look. 'Did your father do that?'

'Sure. Don't you remember?'

He scratched his head. 'Well, no, I don't think I do.'

'I'm not surprised, it was a long time ago, and it wasn't all that dramatic either. But let's go through it step by step and we'll see if something comes back to you. That's the strange thing about some childhood memories, you know, they need to be actually woken up before you can remember them.'

Erik's mouth was half open, and he gave me a concentrated stare. Then he nodded slowly, *very* slowly.

'Could be,' he said.

22

'IT STARTED WHEN I WAS twelve,' said Natalie. 'When I had my first period. I don't know if there was a connection. I've tried to ask friends of mine who are psychologists about it, in a general way, I don't tell anyone in any detail about what went on at home back then. And they say yeah, sure, that obviously it's connected with the biology. But psychologists are like astrologers, they go for any and every easy solution and obvious pattern. And in this case the connection should have had the opposite effect. It isn't biologically smart to get your own daughter pregnant. My father understood that too. That was why he went to your station to buy those morning-after pills, when he thought he hadn't been careful.'

She made herself more comfortable on my arm. Her bed was as small as the one I had at the workshop, but in our relationship so far anything over a metre wide would have been wasted space anyway.

'Until I was twelve I was probably an outgoing and happy little girl,' she said. 'After that I became a silent, moody girl who no one wanted to be around after a while. And who didn't want to be around anyone either. But no one ever asked why, no teachers, no other adults.'

'Same thing with Carl,' I said. 'Although actually, when suspicions eventually did arise, I was the one they suspected, not my dad.'

'There you are,' she said. 'But I think it's hard to blame adults, most of us go through personality changes during those years. Maybe I would have been like that even without the abuse. Not that that's what I think, but I really don't know. Maybe that's just me. Same thing with getting stoned.'

'Oh yeah?'

'That was when I discovered alcohol. If it had been more easily available I would have drunk even more. I hung around the older boys, the ones who knew where to get hold of moonshine. Probably that's why I got the reputation of sleeping around. It was partly true. Anyway, getting smashed and being promiscuous are classic behaviour patterns in abuse victims, but then I really don't know what I would have been like if it had never happened. Maybe I just like to get smashed and sleep around.'

'Do you?'

She took a deep breath. 'No. Before last night I hadn't used anything for a year, so obviously I prefer being clean. And I've been with eight boys. Including you. I don't know how many you've been with, but eight makes me a nun among the kind of people I hang out with.'

'Eight is more than me, but it isn't that many in any case,' I said.

'OK, then, nine, including my father.'

There was silence for a few seconds, then we both burst out laughing.

'D'you think it's ridiculous that we can talk about it in such a distanced way?' she asked.

I shook my head. 'I think distanced is the only way we can talk about it at all.'

'It's weird,' she said. 'Like talking about something that happened in a parallel universe, as though it was a dream, or a nightmare. But then you'll come across evidence that it was real. Knickers he'd ripped. The smell of him on your bedclothes . . .'

She stopped, perhaps feeling how I tensed at the sudden white rage that always boiled up in me whenever I was confronted with images such as this. The mere sight of the bunk bed in our room was enough to make my pulse race.

'Is everything OK?' she asked.

I breathed in the smell of her hair and felt my pulse rate slow. Out in the square the sound of a car horn. Her flat was on the top floor of the Meierigård, the old dairy building. The bedroom, like the living room, was minimally furnished. There was nothing hanging on the walls. Like someone who had thrown herself completely into her job from the moment she started and had zero interest in how and where she lived. Or someone who had no plans to stay here long.

'I'm the one who should be asking are you OK,' I said. 'Go on.'

She kissed me on the shoulder. 'After I moved away from home I found myself wondering how it could have gone on for so many years. It was obviously because my father had free rein at home where we lived, alone, on a farm. I was an only child and my mother was already sick and spent most of the time in bed. There was very little social life, no neighbours or relatives. But all the same. I knew. It wasn't like that girl I met in Notodden who told me how her father got her to think that it was something she wanted. And even though she knew it wasn't true she still felt the shame of it. Yeah, my father did try the same thing with me. To make me more compliant, or to make sure I didn't tell anyone, I guess. But that wasn't why I didn't tell anyone. I was afraid, but not for myself. I was afraid for him. Isn't that crazy? To worry about someone you hate more than anyone else on earth?'

'Yes,' I said. 'But I suppose that's a definition of what close family means.'

'Sometimes he read aloud to me from the Bible. About God's men having sex with members of their own families. Abraham with his half-sister, Lot with his daughters, and so on. Dad was the God-fearing one of the family – he'd given up any attempt to convert me – and he used these stories to try to persuade me that we wouldn't burn in hell.'

'Sounds more like he was trying to persuade himself rather than you.'

'Could be. Anyway, he always tried to present what he was doing as being OK. Or at the very least, not exactly monstrous. I mean, you have to live with yourself.'

'Yes,' I said, and pushed in a plug of chewing tobacco. 'You do have to. Until the day you decide you don't.'

I listened to the autumn evening. The wind rustling through the leaves. The beautiful, two-toned sound of a car engine humming away. The screech of tyres burning off rubber.

'Your father and that shotgun against the wall?' she asked.

'If I wanted to punish him I should have let him go on trying to live with himself. But I had to. To save my little brother. If you look at it that way it was more assisted dying than murder.'

The car had gone now. I imagined it was a Volvo, one with two boys inside, now doing 120 on the highway, heading for the county border line, leaving Os behind. Then I answered her unspoken question.

'My mother . . . I don't know. Yes, I condemned her to death for not having done anything. But it was as though she knew what was going to happen. It was the night I had made up my mind to kill Dad, I'd taken my hunting knife to bed with me and was just waiting for him to come in our room. He did come, but maybe he sensed danger. At any rate he turned back. And then I heard the sobbing through that hole in the floor up from the kitchen. I went downstairs, and my mum was sitting there. We had never exchanged a single word about what Dad was doing with Carl, but that evening she said quite openly, like it was a prayer: "You know, Roy, that I love your father so much I can't live without him. If I had to choose between saving my child's life or his, I'd choose him. I want you to know that. That's the mother I am to you." '

'So you think she would have chosen to be in that car with your father?'

I blinked, tried to see into the darkness.

'I don't know. We're good at believing what we need to believe. I'm the same as your father that way.'

'Roy,' she said, snuggling close to me, naked and warm, 'don't ever mention yourself and my father in the same breath. Promise?'

'OK,' I said.

She got up to go to the bathroom, and when I switched on the bedside lamp to find my pants I noted a couple of tiny specks of blood on the sheet. Natalie laughed when she came back in and saw me looking at them.

'Something funny?' I asked.

'The look on your face,' she said and kissed me on the forehead. 'You look like you think you might've killed me. I just bleed a bit after intercourse. It isn't unusual, or dangerous.'

We pulled the duvet up over us and snuggled up close. Listened to the sounds from outside, to hear if anything had changed.

'Listen,' she said, 'did you go to Krakow?'

'Krakow?'

'When you were in Poland. You said it was close to the amusement park. Old Town in Krakow is supposed to be fantastic.'

'Yes, they said so. But . . . well, I was travelling on my own, so there was no real reason. I just checked out the park and took the first flight back home.'

'How about a weekend trip?'

'You mean, you and me?'

'Yeah. Take a break from Os. You need it.'

'Maybe I do,' I said.

'I'd love to go Friday but there's a staff party at work. But there are cheap flights from Oslo on Saturday as well. I checked.'

'You mean *this* weekend?'

'Why not?'

I blinked into the darkness again. Just her and me. In Krakow, of all places. Yeah, for chrissakes. Why not? How wrong could it be? Not wrong at all. Right. Absolutely and completely right.

23

ON WEDNESDAY AFTERNOON I GOT the call I was expecting from Asle Vendelbo. The loan had been discussed at the credit meeting. And approved. We talked briefly about the practical side of things, avoiding any reference at all to the other side of our deal. Nor was there any need for him to worry, for we were both in the same boat. If I went to anyone else with what I had on Vendelbo, it would come out that I had used it to blackmail him into giving me a loan, and that would mean the end of me as well. But there was something about that phone conversation, the way it was just like a normal conversation about a quite ordinary loan. In fact he even managed to offer me his hearty congratulations. Pure acting. As though he suspected the conversation might be wired. The thought hadn't struck me before. That the reason Kurt Olsen had arrested me was to give me a fright, to see how I would react. That he was spying on me, in the hope I would do something that would reveal I had a murder on my conscience I was trying to cover up. I had no intention of giving him a bribery case as some kind of bonus.

That was why I didn't call Bent Halden from my own phone but borrowed Egil's.

'Yes?'

'Good morning, Halden, this is Os Car Repairs calling, your vehicle is ready. Where do you want it delivered?'

In the silence that followed I heard Jon Fuhr's voice in the background. It sounded like he was finishing up a call of his own.

'One moment,' said Halden, his voice audibly shaking. 'I'll put you on to the co-owner.'

I heard the phone change hands and then Fuhr's voice.

'We should meet,' he said. 'And go through the delivery arrangements one more time. Just to be on the safe side.'

'OK,' I said. 'The hotel in Notodden?'

'No. Somewhere on the main road. I'll send you the coordinates. Tomorrow at zero five hundred hours, can you make that?'

'Five in the morning?'

'We've got a full day's work tomorrow, lot of meetings. And I think there's less chance of our being disturbed there. Take the phone I'm sending the coordinates to. That all right with you?'

I listened. As though there might be something in the network soundwaves that could tell me what Fuhr was thinking.

'Sounds all right,' I said and hung up.

Then I phoned Carl and told him the loan had been approved.

He cheered so wildly I had to pull the phone away from my ear.

*

In the afternoon I drove up to Opgard. As I entered the kitchen Carl stood grinning at me as he popped the cork of a bottle of champagne. It flew up and hit the ceiling and he filled two green champagne glasses which had been, according to Dad, the most idiotic wedding gifts ever, and had only been used once. Not when either Carl or I was born, but when he bought that Cadillac.

I sipped at mine and Carl drained his.

'OK,' said Carl. 'I've been talking to the board and here's what we do. You buy the entire share emission at five hundred kroner per share, fifty million kroner altogether.'

The champagne nearly came back up my throat. 'Buy? For fuck's sake, we're talking about a loan! A *short-term* loan.'

'Yeah, yeah, relax. *At the same time* as you buy the shares you get a sales option that gives you the right, but not the obligation, to sell the shares back to Os Spa six months from now at a price of 510 kroner. The six months will give us more than enough time to get new investors. The ten-krone difference should cover the interest you pay the bank plus a little bit extra. That means that no matter how much the share price falls, you can still sell them back to us without losing anything. And if they go over 510 kroner then you can hang on to them if you want.'

'I can't do that. In six months I'm going to need that money to build the roller coaster.'

'I know, and since there isn't exactly a liquid market for Os Spa shares, what we propose is to issue the shares at five hundred anyway and buy them back. How's that?'

I turned my glass in my hand. 'So this is a straightforward loan from me to the company?'

'Exactly. You won't make a lot on it, but at least you'll have thirty per cent of the shares in six months and a seat on the board.'

'That'll make thirty-six per cent with the shares I already own. With that many, shouldn't I be chairman of the board?'

Carl laughed. 'I think we'll manage to get through the six months without changing chairman, we're pretty happy with Jo Aas as it is. So what do you say, big brother?'

I pursed my lips. I don't really like champagne, but this tasted better than any I'd had before. I raised my glass.

'I love you!' Carl yelled, and clinked his glass so enthusiastically against mine that some spilled out.

We put a pizza into the oven and I told him about my conversation with Halden and Fuhr, and what I thought about it. He nodded and phoned Goebbel, told her I would be sending her some material.

We chewed our way through the pizza at the kitchen table. Carl complained about having to drink all the champagne by himself.

'I'm driving,' I said.

'Driving? You've got all night to metabolise if you're meeting Fuhr at five in the morning.'

'I mean I'm driving now, soon. I'm spending the night at Natalie's.'

He raised an eyebrow. 'Really? A three-night stand? Is she that good in bed?'

I shrugged and picked up one of the pizza crusts, Carl would never eat them.

'We're going to Krakow for the weekend,' I said.

'Oh yeah? Going to check out that roller-coaster track again?'

'No. Just . . .'

'Just?'

'Wander round in the Old Town and look. Drink wine. Eat good food.'

'You mean *you*?' He laughed. But it was like something had happened to his laughter over the last few days. It had lost that carefree spontaneity that made it so infectious. It had happened before the arrest, so it wasn't that which was bothering him. Was it Mari Aas and all the worrying about whether they should take the leap and become a couple? Was it the house, with all the things that had to be fixed and arranged, and the endless delays? Or was it just the job, the daily strain of putting a good face on things, at the same time as knowing he had to improve profitability before reaching a point at which the figures in red in his accounting could no longer be covered over? I could, of course, have just asked him. Why didn't I ask him? Had something come between us that stopped me from doing it? No, because what could that be? So I did ask him: 'What's bothering you, Carl?'

He looked at me thoughtfully.

'The total,' he said. 'The sum total of everything. You know what I mean. Look how even you get affected by stress.'

'Like how?'

'Like believing Kurt Olsen might've put a wiretap on our phones. That's paranoia, and it spreads until it touches everything.'

I nodded. 'You're right. We've got to keep our heads cool. Be cautious, don't give in to panic.'

I looked at my watch and stood up.

'You leaving already?'

He said it like something just off the top of his head but there was more of a plea in it than he had intended. I looked into the big, lovely eyes of my little brother, and for a moment considered calling Natalie and telling her Carl needed my company this evening. As I drove away it was as though I could see him standing in the winter garden watching me. See his face glow red as I braked turning into Geitesvingen.

And as I lay awake in Natalie's arms after we had made love and she had fallen asleep, I could hear Dad's voice echoing round and round in my head: 'We're family. We have each other, and no one else. Friends, lovers, neighbours, the villagers, the state – it's all an illusion, not worth a light when it really matters. Then it's us against them, Roy. Us against absolutely everybody else.'

24

AS I FOLLOWED THE COORDINATES and pulled in off the main road it was five to five. It was still dark. My headlamps picked out Jon Fuhr, leaning with arms folded against the only other car stopped there. It wasn't the same car as last time, this time it was a Suzuki Across. I saw the Bislet Car Hire logo. He'd chosen a good place, cars rarely stopped there. Maybe because there was something desolate and at the same time claustrophobic about it. Black, abrupt rock face blocking the view on three sides, and a scree behind the crash barrier leading down to a small, unattractive lake. Another twenty minutes' driving would get you to Os, where the lay-by had a little cafe, a better view and petrol pumps.

'What?' I said as I climbed out and peered down the sloping

scree where the moon was reflected in the black, motionless water. 'Halden didn't want to come?'

'Not necessary,' said Fuhr and scratched his chin. He'd got a couple more pimples since the last time I'd seen him. 'I'll just give you the IBAN and the account number the money is to be paid into.'

He handed me a sheet of paper. A raven cawed somewhere up on the rocks as I read it.

'Two accounts in the Cayman Islands?'

'Full anonymity. It will be to our mutual advantage.'

'I guess it will.' I folded the sheet of paper and was about to stick it in my pocket.

'I want that back,' said Fuhr. 'It's for you to transfer the money now.'

'Now?'

'You've got your mobile phone with you, I presume?' He snatched the paper.

Standing with his back to the moon I wasn't able to read the expression on his face. I rubbed my hands together, it was cold.

'What's the big hurry?'

'The big hurry is that you're a suspect in a murder case, and you're not going to be in any position to transfer the money if you're in prison.'

'Christ,' I said. 'Who told you that?'

'Some locals working on the Todde tunnel. Who *did* work on it, I should say. If the police really are investigating you that puts a completely different spin on the risk factor attached to our arrangement. Bent's view is that we should get out of it, reject the money and send in a revised report. And fuck you and your threat to push us out of the hotel window or whatever it was.'

'Yes, because there isn't much to be afraid of once I'm under lock and key, is that what you're thinking?'

Fuhr didn't answer. Watched as a trailer drove by.

'So,' I said. 'Halden is not here because the two of you are afraid of me. You thought that if I really am a killer then it's possible I'll wipe the two of you out now that the report has been published and not have to pay you the twelve million.'

Fuhr shrugged.

'And eliminate the possibility of a revised report too. Because revised reports aren't all that uncommon.'

'Is that supposed to be a threat?'

'No, it's a motive.'

Fuhr moved, transferring his weight onto both legs. He was ready for me now, I wouldn't be able to use the element of surprise to knock him out as I had done last time. He didn't seem all that scared either. Those fresh pimples suggested he might have upped his intake of steroids and raised his level of testosterone – was that the reason? Or was he armed? Too fucking right he was. There was something sticking up from the waist of his trousers beneath the bomber jacket that might have been all sorts of things but which I knew was a gun. My heart began to pound.

'Fine,' I said, hoping that Fuhr couldn't tell from my voice how afraid I was now. 'No need for us to stand here discussing irrelevancies.'

I pulled out my phone. 'Just a couple of taps here and the money's yours.'

'More than a couple,' said Fuhr. 'There are two transfers, so let's get in your car.'

'Two?'

'You saw two accounts. Six million into one, nine into the other.'

'By my mental arithmetic that makes fifteen.'

'The price has gone up, Opgard. As I said, now you've got the police looking at you that alters the risk for us completely.'

'So six into Halden's account and nine into yours, I'm assuming?'

'Come on, let's get in your car.'

I swallowed. It was so quiet. Not a single car had passed along the road since that trailer. Fuhr noted my hesitation and dropped his arms to his side, like someone getting ready to take a swing. I could feel his watchful eyes on me as I headed towards the car and got in behind the wheel. Fuhr glided into the passenger seat. A crazy thought ran through my head. That he hadn't yet taken out that gun, so if I started the car, locked the doors, lowered the window on my side and drove along the outside of the short crash barrier the car would be in the water before he had time to react and I could get out of the window on my side. Like I say, it was just a crazy idea, but the thought of an attack must have translated into my body language or something, because when I turned to Fuhr he was holding a gun. A pretty fearsome-looking thing too.

'Don't try anything, Opgard. Just get the money transferred now, while I'm watching, then we can both get back to our own lives and we need never speak to each other again. That sound like a plan to you?'

I nodded, staring into the mouth of the gun barrel and the promise of a quick and relatively painless death. Faced with that just two weeks earlier I would probably have felt afraid too, but in some wretched way also welcomed it. But now things were different. Not because I had a loan of a hundred million, a camp-site and a major road, but because I had two plane tickets to Krakow that had set me back less than a thousand kroner.

'Actually,' he said, 'open your phone and give it to me.'

I did as he said. Watched as he worked the phone with one hand and kept an eye on me. He handed the phone back to me. I saw that he'd deleted the text message with the map references he'd sent me.

'I get it,' I said.

'You get what?'

'I see what your plan is.'

'I just told you what it is.'

'Yes, that business about us never speaking to each other again is true, as far as it goes.'

He put the sheet of paper with the account numbers in my lap. 'Cut the crap and just punch in those numbers on your phone, Opgard.'

I didn't move, just looked down at the paper.

'Now!' he shouted. He pressed the gun barrel against my temple.

'I doubt you'll shoot me before I've transferred the money,' I said. 'Afterwards, maybe . . .'

A bus passed. Then all was quiet again. The only sound was that of two men, breathing in a small coupé. Who were *still* breathing.

'Start!' Fuhr hissed into my ear.

'Do it yourself,' I said and handed him the phone.

'What?'

'Don't you remember what I told you in Notodden, Fuhr? That when you're laying a trap, you have to make sure the trap isn't stupider than the victim?'

'What the hell are you talking about?'

'Your plan, because I feel pretty sure it's yours and not Halden's, is to meet me at a deserted spot with no witnesses and where you can leave no trace of your presence. That's why you've used a hire car and why I feel pretty sure you've left your mobile phone at home. Am I right?'

Fuhr didn't answer, just pushed the gun even harder into my temple.

'Obviously you delete the message on my phone with the coordinates that the police *might* have found, had it not been so obvious that what they were dealing with was a suicide. Because what could be more natural than that a guy, about to be arrested for a murder committed many many years ago, takes the easy way out? The whole thing is a classic "lonely-man-suicide" case. Before dawn, isolated spot, in his car, with a gun. And it looks like you've got the right angle for the shot here, Fuhr. I'm assuming you've got hold of a pistol that can't be traced. Some old gang associate, no doubt? That was when you picked up that conviction for violence, I'm thinking?'

I heard Fuhr change his grip on the pistol, as though he'd been clutching it so hard the lactic acid had started moving through his lower arm. He moved his other hand and pushed something down inside my jacket pocket.

'What's that?'

'It's your suicide note, Opgard. Just so there will be no doubt about it. But it isn't too late. All you have to do is transfer that money now and no one has to die here.'

'Oh yes they do. You think I'm stupid? You didn't write that suicide note to threaten me, you wrote it to use it. The only thing that can save me now is if I *don't* transfer the money.'

'There are worse things than a bullet through the head, Opgard.'

I laughed. 'See, you show your hand there, Fuhr. A bit of torture, you mean? With the jack? With the knife? But then it won't look like suicide any more, will it?'

'Fuck you!' It looked like blood had been pumped into those pimples of his. 'If you don't get that money transferred I'll kill you, and then I'll kill . . .'

His breath hissed against my ear and the smell in the coupé now – if American thriller writers are to be believed – was fear, testosterone or adrenaline. Possibly all of them at once.

'Then you'll kill who?' I asked. 'See, there's the problem. I might get arrested for murder so, looking at it like that, I'm not all that afraid of dying right now. But at the same time, there's no one you can kill who means more to me than myself. It's sad, of course, but lucky for me.'

He swallowed. Managed to regain control over his breathing, and over himself and the situation, he was probably thinking.

'You don't get it, Opgard. The best thing is for us to get the money. Next best is that you disappear, that this whole business disappears, that we're back where we started before you showed up. Understand? So unless you start tapping in those numbers within five seconds I'll shoot you. If you transfer the money then there is a chance I won't shoot you. Why not go for that chance, eh?'

'No. I'm now going to make you an offer you can't say no to,' I said. 'A way to sort this thing out that'll be best for both of us.'

'Oh yeah?'

'Go into my mail,' I said, with a nod towards the phone. 'Go to the Sent box. The most recent one, to Liv Goebbel. Then open it.'

With the gun against my temple, and to the sound of Fuhr working the keyboard, I stared straight ahead. Out of the windscreen and into the darkness. Was I mistaken, or was that a touch of grey in the black sky on the far side of the water? Anyway, I knew for sure that Fuhr was right now reading the email I had sent the previous evening: *Further to our phone conversation. In the event of my death or if I go missing for more than three days, as my lawyer Liv Goebbel is hereby authorised to click on the link below and open the attached video and acquaint the relevant authorities with its contents. Sincerely, Roy Opgard.* A few seconds passed, then I heard the voices from Room 333 at the Brattrein Hotel. Fuhr played the whole thing, including my concluding summing-up. The pressure from the pistol was now less and I looked at him. He sat with head bowed, staring down at the little screen.

'The good news,' I said, 'is that Opgard men don't haggle. So naturally I'm going to transfer the twelve million kroner. Because it was twelve, right?'

Fuhr kept on looking at the screen and nodded so slowly you might have thought he was a native of Os.

'Good, then we're even,' I said. 'Hand me the phone and we'll do it now.'

I should, of course, have seen it coming, but I guess I'd lost that feeling for when someone is about to break. Fuhr hit out. He used the gun to hit me on the forehead and I saw sparks. Blood ran down over one eye and down my face and there was a metallic taste when I licked it with my tongue.

'There,' said Fuhr as he handed me the phone. 'Now we're even.'

After Fuhr drove off I stayed on for a while, waiting until my pulse rate had slowed down. I reached into my jacket pocket and took out the note he had put there. He'd written the message in block capitals, no doubt so it wouldn't occur to anyone to compare it with my own handwriting: I HAVE HAD ENOUGH OF THIS LIFE. GOODBYE. OPGARD. Short and sweet. Actually I was sort of impressed. Because that was pretty much exactly what I would have written myself.

'Looks like a centipede crawling over my head,' I said as Stanley Spind held a mirror up in front of me.

'At least you won't need to buy a Halloween mask,' Stanley said as he packed away his stitching kit. 'And just so you know, Roy, I don't buy this about you walking into a doorjamb.'

'It was the best I could do,' I said as I stroked my fingertips across the stitches on my forehead.

'Don't touch,' said Stanley. He stood behind the chair and began wrapping a bandage around my head. 'By the way, what's all this I hear about you being arrested?'

Stanley was someone you could trust. He had no agenda that I could see and was blessedly uninterested in all the intrigue and gossip the rest of the village found so fascinating. He was an upfront guy, said exactly what he thought, asked straight out if there was something he wanted to know.

'We-ell,' I said. 'Professional secrecy?'

'If you like.'

'They found some of the old sheriff's blood on my parents' Cadillac. Kurt's trying to link it to people who are still alive. He doesn't like that story about his father taking his own life.'

'I understand,' said Stanley. 'That's what we humans do, we only accept stories we like. You do too I should think, Roy.'

I shrugged. 'We're all the hero of our own film, right?'

'I'm sure that's true. There, now, at last, Os gets its first inhabitant with a turban.' Stanley fastened the bandage with a couple of safety pins and sat down behind his desk again. 'How's your love life, Roy?'

I smiled. 'Don't you have patients waiting out there?'

'Indeed I do, that's why I'm asking.'

'Oh?' I said as I took my jacket down from the peg.

He folded his hands behind his head and grinned. 'That is my express-version health check. If people are in love, then as a rule their health is good.'

'Oh yeah? Got any empirical proof of that?'

'Only anecdotal. Which is, however, strong. Who's the lucky woman?'

I had to laugh. 'You're telling me you can *see* it in people?'

'I can see it in the blood pressure, the pulse and in the whites of the eye,' he said.

'Maybe it's the other way round, and healthy people fall in love more easily.'

'Maybe so.'

'How about your love life, Stanley?'

'We'll see, going out for a couple of days' walking this weekend.'

He wrote something down on a piece of paper and handed it to me.

'Painkillers. If you need them.'

I looked at the note. 'Listen, something I've been wondering about. Is it true you can take a paternity test during a pregnancy?'

'Oh yes. A simple blood test of the cells in the mother's blood can reveal the baby's DNA profile.'

'Clever.'

'Isn't it?'

As I walked out through the waiting room I saw Moe the roofer sitting there. He was staring stiffly down into a magazine and didn't look up. Probably heard my voice from the doctor's surgery.

I pressed down the pedal on the shiny little rubbish bin. Tossed the heavy condom down into it. Shivered a little as the lid slid closed.

'Your head glows in the dark,' Natalie said as I walked back into the bedroom.

''The Invisible Man,' I said.

'What?'

'Only the bandage is visible. If I take off the bandage I'm invisible and I can do whatever I want to you.'

'Seems to me you do that even *with* the bandage.'

I slipped into the warm bed, she turned her back to me, pushing out her bum. I kissed her on the neck and she gave a pleasurable moan.

'Can I ask you something?' I said.

'I would say yes, but when you start like that then I'm not so sure.' She stretched out her arms to pull me closer.

'It can wait,' I said. 'Or actually, it can be dropped completely.'

'No.'

'Yes.'

'Now it's too late. Out with it.'

'I . . .'

'Shoot!'

'Have you ever been pregnant?'

It was as though the electricity went. She let go of me.

'I don't know,' she said after a long pause.

'I know you used the morning-after pill, but was there ever a time when you *knew*?'

She shook her head, making a rustling sound on the pillow.

'Is having a child something you've thought about?' I asked, and felt her tense. 'No, no,' I hurriedly added. 'I'm not suggesting anything, I'm just curious.'

She was silent. For a long time. And I regretted wandering into such difficult terrain.

'Yes.'

'Yes? You *have* thought you'd like children?'

'No, I mean, I did know.' She turned towards me. 'That I was pregnant. Once.'

'By . . .'

'Yes, by *him*.'

'Did he know?'

'Yes. He was the one who sent me to the doctor. So I . . .' She searched for different words but soon gave up. 'I got rid of it.'

'Do you remember if they took a blood test back then?'

'No. Where is all this leading, Roy?'

'I don't know,' I said. I turned onto my back and looked up at the ceiling. 'I really don't.'

In the silence it was as though something had changed inside the room. As though an uninvited guest had crept into bed and was now lying between us. I knew I had to kick him out again, before he moved in on a permanent basis. Say something. I swallowed.

'I love you,' I said.

'What did you say?' she asked, and I heard her genuine surprise.

I coughed. 'Sorry about the unclear diction. It's not a word I've had much practice in saying. What I said was, I—' But her lips against mine stopped me there.

'Ow,' I said once she'd stopped kissing me.

'Oh, sorry. Your forehead.'

'We-ell, it doesn't hurt *that* much,' I said, and pulled her head towards mine again.

'Take me . . .' she murmured after a while.

'Nothing left,' I said.

'But I want you inside me. Only be careful. Ovulation.'

'Oh no, now listen here, I don't trust either one of us when it comes to that. We'll wait until Krakow. I heard Polish blobs are cheaper.'

I could feel her body starting to tremble.

'No wonder you can't wait,' I said. 'Neither could I if I was about to get fucked by me.'

She slid down next to me, still shaking with laughter. Best audience I ever had.

'Are you laughing because I am funny, or because you appreciate the fact that I'm *trying* to be funny?' I asked.

'Let's say it's a bit of both,' she said as she stroked my cheek.

A while later she turned and whispered in my ear.

'You're not allowed to say what you just said after only two weeks, you do know that? But OK, I love you too.'

Before falling asleep I thought how it's true, things really do work out. Jesus Christ, how they work out.

But, of course, that was then.

Two days later and everything was turned upside down again.

25

IT WAS SIX O'CLOCK SATURDAY morning and there was thick fog. On top of that, there was a layer of snow on the road down from Opgard, past the Nergard place and all the way down to the square. Temperatures were forecast to rise so it would melt during the day, but I was pleased I had changed to my winter tyres so we wouldn't have to crawl all the way to the airport.

Things in general had moved at a great speed over the last few days. Since the emission had already been agreed at the general meeting, a hastily called board meeting was enough to accept me as the buyer and the money – fifty million – had already been paid and the shares were mine. At least they were for six months, until I sold them back. I'd studied the emission agreement and the sales option carefully. Everything looked to be in order, but even so, a little unease in the stomach is only to be expected when such a large sum of money is involved. Standing outside the Meierigård I saw my image reflected in the door. My fringe covered most of the scab after I'd removed the bandage before leaving. I rang Natalie's doorbell again. I'd called her on the phone before setting off, and when she didn't answer I thought the most likely thing was that she was still sleeping after getting home late from the staff party at the hotel. I'd been woken up when Carl came staggering in at about three, and he was still snoring like a two-stroke when I left. But it worried me more when she didn't answer the doorbell either. I knew it jangled because I'd heard it once before, when she'd gone out to buy breakfast for us. It jangled like a school bell.

I checked the time. Alternative answers to the question 'what the hell's happened?' raced through my brain, but I brushed them aside. All except one. That she'd cracked and was lying inside either dead drunk or out of her head on something or other. I rang the neighbour's bell. And after a while a sleepy voice came through the cracked loudspeaker above the bell. I explained the situation, that Natalie didn't seem to be awake, and that we had a plane to catch. The neighbour sounded sceptical, which was not surprising, since I'd given my name and right now the only association people had with it was 'suspected of murder'. But when I told him Natalie had been out at a party he got the picture and – as was only to be expected here in Os – they held the keys to each other's apartments *just in case*.

I made my way up to the second floor where the neighbour had pulled on a baggy pair of sweatpants and a 'Don't Suck' T-shirt and was standing ready to open the door for me. He stayed out in the corridor while I went in. I don't know what I was expecting. But it was empty. And the bed made. And of course, a couple of alternatives then suggested themselves to me.

But none of it added up.

I went back out into the corridor and apologised for the disturbance, said I was sure I would find her somewhere else, then drove up to the hotel. The girl at reception said she'd been on duty all night and so hadn't been at the staff party, but yes, she'd seen her workmates come and go. She knew perfectly well who I was, that I was her boss's brother and a shareholder in the hotel. All the same, she hesitated when I asked when Natalie Moe had left. I showed her the plane ticket with Natalie's name, explained that she hadn't been home when I went to pick her up. The girl blushed and said Natalie had left the party early, around nine thirty if she wasn't mistaken, and got into a taxi. I could only guess what the blushing might mean, so before getting completely carried away I asked her straight out: 'Alone, or was she with someone?'

'Alone,' said the girl.

'Sober?'

The girl puffed out her cheeks and looked unhappy: 'No.'

OK, so that could mean she'd gone to someone. A lover? A girlfriend?

'And you don't know where?'

'No.'

'Which taxi was it?'

She worked the keyboard and checked the screen, probably to see if there was a booking registered. 'Was the car white or red?' I asked.

'Red.'

'Thanks.' As I walked out I was calling Dagur's number.

He answered on the second ring. I asked where he'd driven Natalie Moe.

'Sorry, Roy,' he said in his fine, lilting version of the Os dialect, 'but I can't tell you that.'

'I don't care a damn about who she was visiting, Dagur, I just want to know if she's OK.'

'I realise that, but it's a question of confidentiality.'

I snorted. 'Taxi drivers don't take any vow of confidentiality.'

'Oh yes they do. Not a lot of people know it, but we have a legally binding duty of confidentiality.'

'You're joking?'

'If I tell you anything I'm risking the law and my licence. Sorry, but you'll have to go through Kurt if you want me to pass on information about my customers. Got to hang up now, Roy.'

He ended the connection.

'Shit!' I realised I had thrown my phone away. I went over, picked it up, and saw the screen was shattered in a small rose shape up in one corner. I smoothed out the edges of the break with my thumb and was wondering what to do when the screen lit up. At first I thought it was my thumb that had activated the screen, but then I felt it vibrating and saw it was Natalie who was calling. It was like finally waking up from a nightmare.

'Is that you? Where are you?' I almost yelled. Or actually, did yell.

'Roy, I'm so sorry.' She wasn't slurring, but sounded distinctly nervous.

'Where are you? Is everything all right?'

'I won't be going to Krakow.'

'Don't worry about that. Where are—'

'But I think *you* should go.'

I stopped. 'You think . . . Why should I go there on my own?'

'Because . . . because I can't come with you.'

I listened out for sounds from others in her vicinity, anything that might tell me where she was. 'I know it all went a bit wrong yesterday,' I said. 'These things happen. But we can always take the trip another time and no harm done. Really.'

'Yes,' she said. 'Yes, there is harm done.'

I could hear now she was on the verge of tears. Maybe that was why I began to feel like crying myself.

'Not if you're all right,' I said. 'I've got the car here, let me come and pick you up.'

'No,' she said sharply. Too sharply.

'OK,' I said. 'OK. Sounds like you don't need me making a lot of fuss about this right now. Am I right?'

She didn't answer.

'Natalie? Call me when you're feeling better. Or . . . yes, just call me.'

'Roy?'

I didn't like the way she said my name, like the prelude to something I was going to like even less. 'Yes?' I forced myself to say.

'We can't see each other any more.'

I swallowed. Suddenly it was as if I hadn't woken from that nightmare after all.

'Why not?' I asked feebly. 'I mean, you said you . . .'

I didn't finish the sentence.

'Forget I said that, Roy. OK? Forget everything. The whole thing was a mistake. *My* mistake. OK?'

'But—'

'No buts, Roy. I'm hanging up now.'

251

'Is there someone else? Is that it?'

I heard her hesitate.

'Let's say that it's just the way I am, OK?'

'Look, I know shit happens, Natalie. We can talk about it.'

'No! No, we can't do that, Roy. I'm sorry.'

'Or not talk about it. We can—'

'Listen to me, Roy!'

It hit me then that if anyone should be shouting into the telephone it should be me. But I didn't feel like doing that either.

'I'm listening,' I said.

She took two deep breaths, hard and shaking.

'I want you to promise me one thing, Roy.'

'Yes?'

'Don't come to see me. Do you promise?'

I swallowed, and swallowed again. Moved my tongue, shaped my cheeks and lips until finally I managed to whisper the two wretched words:

'I promise.'

Chicken. That was how Ibsen described Aslaksen. As a chicken, a coward, a man without an ounce of courage in him.

'Thank you,' said Natalie, and she hung up.

I stood there in the car park. Then realised I was standing more or less exactly where I had fallen to my knees and let Kurt Olsen arrest me. I felt like I wanted to kneel again. Was this really happening? What kind of devil found his entertainment in playing with me in this fashion? It struck me that it must be a punishment. Punishment for seven murders.

'Hey, wasn't your flight today?' asked Egil from behind the counter as I walked through the door into the station shop.

'Cancelled,' I said, and carried on walking out into the back room.

'Because of the fog?'

I waved my arm in a gesture he could interpret any way he liked.

'Got a bit of paperwork to catch up on here,' I said. 'Call me if you need help with anything.'

'Will do.'

Egil watched me as if I were a bomb he was afraid might be about to explode. Work had always been my favourite medicine for melancholy. Like most medicines it cures nothing, it just dulls the pain. But the more I could keep my brain occupied with manual tasks like cleaning the car wash, or mental activities like going through the books, the less time my mind had for useless brooding over matters of the heart.

I hung my pea coat next to Egil's leather jacket. On the back it had two crossbones in a circle, with 'Lid & Evensen MC Club' written in Gothic lettering. Sat at the little desk that almost swayed under the weight of the paper piled on it, pushed the product samples to one side, and the coffee machine that didn't work, and started to go through the pile containing the figures for the last quarter which I hadn't yet managed to square. I was confused. It's not that I'm some kind of outstanding student of human nature. No, I think most people would describe Roy Opgard as a simple, practical man who looked for simple, practical solutions. So perhaps that's where the problem lay. That I lacked the power to understand how the mind – and the heart – of someone like Natalie functioned.

I tossed the quarterly figures to one side.

Because it wasn't true that I didn't understand people. It was the same as the reading, I was dyslexic, sometimes I read stuff wrong, but I could *read*, for chrissakes. So what was it that was lying hidden from me? If Natalie had got stoned and spent the night with some other guy, someone she wasn't planning on having a relationship with, *then so what*? She felt ashamed, that was obvious. It could, of course, be the case that she interpreted the fact that she had been unfaithful ... Unfaithful? Jesus, we hadn't even reached the stage of defining ourselves as a couple! Whatever, it could be she thought getting laid when she'd had a drink or two was a half-conscious way of telling herself that she wasn't ready yet for a close relationship of the type she was heading into with me. Damn, it was like those quarterly figures, I just couldn't get them to add up! She could have sat down and told me quietly that this – being with me – wasn't what she wanted. Without the drama and the hysterical shouting over the phone. So what *had* happened? When she said she loved me too, hadn't she meant it? I not only *believed* it, I had *felt* it. But then the rest didn't add up, just didn't add up at all.

I closed my eyes and clenched my jaw. Controlled my thoughts. Then I opened my eyes again, pulled over those quarterly figures, laid my finger against the first column. Took a deep breath. And began searching for the mistake.

It was ten and I had almost finished going over the reports from the preceding three months when I stiffened. From where I sat, with the door open and only a thin wall between me and the counter, I could hear Egil serving the customers. Suddenly I heard a familiar voice. Natalie's. I couldn't hear what she was saying, but I heard a little thud on the counter and then Egil's loud, clear voice:

'Three hundred and fourteen kroner.'

There's only one thing in the station that costs 314 kroner, we keep it right behind the counter, and that is the EllaOne morning-after pill. I gripped the edges of the desk, tensed my jaw. Gripped hard, as though clinging on, as though I was underwater and the current was trying to pull me away from here, out to her, where I would open my mouth to say something, and all that would emerge would be air bubbles, and she would be staring at me as I drowned before her very eyes. Not until I heard the pling of the doorbell that told me she had left the shop did I gasp for air and realise I had been holding my breath.

I put my head on the desk until I felt more or less myself again. Enough at least for me to manage to stand up and go out into the shop and get myself a coffee. Standing by the machine I looked out the window. Yes, most of the snow had melted, but the fog was still dense. I could just see Natalie moving along the pavement in the direction of the square, slow, and hunched inside an oversized parka that I had never seen before. Or had I? And then she vanished in the fog.

Egil was gazing raptly at his phone.

'The hose on pump number 2 hasn't been put back properly,' I said.

'I'll do it,' he said, looking up at me. His face was in hibernation mode, as if he'd just sold milk and bread to Natalie Moe and not a morning-after pill. Maybe not too surprising, since I hadn't told him I was going with anyone to Krakow, and he probably hadn't heard that Natalie and I were an item anyway. Either that or he assumed the pill was us being careless, no big deal. Right, then. I returned to the back room, sat down and carried on. Still hadn't tracked down that damn mistake.

A little before twelve a voice with an Icelandic accent came from the counter.

'I heard you and Børge were at a bikers' meet?'

'Yeah,' said Egil. 'Pump number 1. Seven hundred and sixty kroner.'

'I hope they behaved themselves. It's crazy in Iceland these days. Hell's Angels, Bandidos, Outlaws, they all go there.'

'To Iceland? Why is that?'

'Well, you know, everybody wants to be king of somewhere. You got yourself a bike yet?'

'Not yet, there's so few on the market.'

'True. Maybe you should think about buying mine? There's been so much taxi-driving since the hotel opened I've hardly had time to ride it. Could probably give you a good price.'

'Yeah? I've seen it, of course, but what sort of condition is it in?'

At this point Dagur started out on a description that I could hear was going to take some time. I got up and left through the back door that leads straight out into the area between the station and the workshop where my Volvo was parked. Rounded the station building and headed over towards the red Mercedes standing at pump number 1. Took a quick look over towards the shop and saw Dagur's back was still turned, then jumped into the driving seat. I'm no computer whizz, but I've sat in taxis in Os and noticed how previous rides show up on the display beneath the radio console. I touched the screen, it lit up, and – voilà – there was a list of the previous night's trips. Pickup point, distance driven, price. There were several pickups at Os Spa, but only one at around half nine, 21.23 to be precise. The trip mileage told me the ride had been longer than from Os Spa to Natalie's flat in the Meierigård. But not where it had actually been to. I touched the trip-line to see if any more information would come up, and it did. Not the destination, but the payment details.

Natalie Moe hadn't paid for the trip.

I shuddered when I saw it.

There was a name behind the credit card number: Anton Moe. The roofer. The father. And I remembered where I had seen that parka. Anton Moe had been wearing it. The wave of nausea came so violently I almost threw up. My mouth was hanging open, I couldn't breathe through my nose. I closed my eyes and opened them again. But no, if this was a dream I was still trapped inside it. I touched the Back button and climbed out the car.

'Stone me, I call that service!' Dagur said as he emerged from the shop a few seconds later and saw me drawing the soapy sponge across his windscreen.

'Good customers get good customer service, you know,' I said as I splashed on a little more water then got started with the squeegee.

Dagur stood next to me.

'Sorry I couldn't help you out this morning, Roy. You get it sorted?'

He had a big beard and such mild brown eyes, Dagur. Now you can't assume that all Icelanders are good, decent people, but speaking personally I've yet to meet one who isn't. Could be down to the fact that I've only met about three of them.

'Got it sorted,' I said. 'Natalie drank too much at the party and didn't remember a thing until she woke up at her father's house.'

Dagur laughed. 'Yes, I thought it was best to take her there.'

'*You* thought it was best?'

'Well, I know she lives in the Meierigård, but in the state she was in I thought the safest thing was for her to be with someone who could look after her, yes.'

I looked at him. 'That was pretty damn considerate of you, Dagur.'

He smiled warmly. 'Only natural. We live in a little town, and we all look out for each other, right?'

'True,' I said. 'I heard Anton came out, paid the fare and helped her into the house?'

'Yep,' said Dagur. 'She was completely out of it, poor thing, I had to help him. But he didn't yell at her, just helped her, the way a good father should. Top guy, Anton. I—'

Dagur fell silent, as though suddenly recalling his vow of silence.

'Yeah, well,' he said. 'Thanks for the windscreen wash.'

He got in, and I pushed the windscreen wipers back into place. Tore a piece of paper off the roll and wiped it along the edge of the squeegee as I watched the red Merc head off in the direction of the square.

Seven murders.

I had seven murders on my conscience.

I had hoped to be able to leave it at that.

26

'I HAVE TO FIND WHERE that damn mistake is,' I said.

'Oh yeah?' Egil watched from behind the counter as I filled my cup from the coffee machine.

'It's driving me crazy. So now I'm going to sit down in that back room with the door closed and I don't want to be disturbed under any circumstances. Not for anything. Understand?'

Egil looked at me in some surprise but nodded.

Before heading into the back room I turned up the music in the shop a touch.

'Good stuff,' I lied.

Once in the back room I locked the door and pulled on my jacket. As I was about to slip my phone into my pocket I noticed a missed call from Kurt Olsen. I hesitated. But only momentarily. Left by the back door then crossed to the workshop and let myself in. Walked past the tractor and the bicycle I had used to pedal up to Opgard on when I was young. Sometimes we'd time our rides in what Carl and I called the Tour de Opgard. I still, now and again, in the summer, used it to cycle to the good swimming places on Budalsvannet. Or did I? Right now I couldn't remember the last time I'd done that.

I took down the wire cutters from the tool rack, pulled on a pair of gloves and cut the bicycle chain, thinking as I did so of the conversation I had had with Moe that time in his kitchen, when I told him what I would do to him if he ever touched his daughter again.

'How would you propose killing me?'

'By smiting you, I was thinking. That's sounds appropriately biblical.'

I placed a rag over my knuckles, wrapped the chain a couple of times around my hand and bunched my fist.

Yeah, that was appropriately biblical.

I stuffed the chain into my jacket pocket. Went out into the fog, got into my car and started it with as little revving as possible, so Egil wouldn't hear. I drove out onto the main road, heading east so he wouldn't see me either. Turned off where the ancient milk ramp still stands, made a U-turn, then headed west. I drove through the square and behind the veil of fog saw light in the window of the second floor of the Meierigård. That light hadn't been on when I was there a few hours earlier. Good. At least Natalie was now out of the line of fire. I drove on westward.

It suited me well that the fog lay as thick as pea soup. With visibility that poor there wouldn't be many who could say for sure they'd seen what was definitely my car passing by. So, good timing then. On the other hand, what was that call from Kurt?

What did he want now? Pretty bad timing, to be killing someone just as the police were trying to get in touch with me.

Maybe that's what brought me to my senses. Or maybe it was suddenly remembering what Dad used to say when he was teaching me to box. 'You fall into a rage, you lose.' Because that was one of the advantages I had had at those Saturday-night dances in the local villages when I was confronted by guys who wanted to beat Carl up because he'd been flirting with their girls. They were furious; I was cool, calm.

But now I was the one who was in a rage.

I slowed down. Told myself to think this through. Even in a fog this thick it would be bloody difficult to get away with murder if I just drove straight to the guy's house and beat him to death. Especially in a place where there was only one villager already suspected of being a killer.

I slowed even more.

But despite knowing that what I needed right now was a cool head, I couldn't stop seeing an image of Natalie lying unconscious in bed with her dress pulled up past her belly and her father on top of her. Seeing her waking in the morning, alone, looking down and realising what had happened. What had happened *again*. Only this time blaming herself, her burden of guilt so heavy she couldn't look me in the eye and tell me what had happened. She thought of herself as damaged goods, not worthy of anyone's real, pure love. How did I know that? Well, I knew it because I was damaged goods myself.

I noticed I was driving faster again and eased off on the accelerator.

'You fall into a rage, you lose,' I whispered to myself, and tried to blot those images out. 'Harm him now. Killing him can wait.'

Moe's place lay in the flat fields three or four kilometres west of the square, on the upper side of the highway. I turned off and drove slowly up the gravel driveway towards the main house and the barn. With so much fog and several hundred metres of cultivated land between the farm and the nearest neighbour, I knew there was no way I could have been seen.

I parked between the barn and the main house and stepped out of the car. There was a light in the kitchen window, and Moe's van was parked inside the barn, where the door was wide open. He was home, no doubt about that. I climbed the steps and knocked on the door.

'Looking for someone, Opgard?'

I turned slowly.

Moe – with his hourglass-shaped head – stood in the barn doorway. Natalie was right, her father's rifle was a Remington. He was holding it at chest height, and it was pointing at me.

'I'm looking for you,' I said. 'Didn't think you'd see me coming.'

'No, but sound carries well in the fog. And I don't think it's me you're looking for, you're looking for Natalie.'

'Only you,' I said. 'We had a deal, remember?'

'I hear you've been chasing after her,' he said. His voice creaked and squeaked like a rusty hinge, and the wisps of hair danced on his skull, though there didn't seem to be any wind stirring at all. 'I guess that explains why you were so keen to send her away from home back then. You wanted her yourself, you just had to send her up to the summer pastures to fatten her up and wait for her to turn twenty.'

He stepped out of the barn doorway, out into the flat light of the fog.

'That about right, Opgard?'

'No,' I said hoarsely.

'Oh I think it is,' he said. 'But Natalie's a smart girl, so that's not going to happen. And you know what? I'm tired of walking around and looking over my shoulder and wondering what you might get up to. I mean, you're a fucking killer, or so I hear.'

I swallowed. Being confronted with a loaded gun does something to your bodily functions, and this was the second time it had happened, and so soon after the first.

'Here,' said Moe, nodding towards the barn door. 'We're going to take a little walk in here.'

I didn't move.

'Suit yourself,' said Moe, and held the rifle up against his cheek.

I walked down the steps.

'In there,' said Moe, moving out of the opening and keeping a safe distance from me, probably remembering how quick I was with my right.

I walked into the barn and stood beside the van.

'Further in,' said Moe, pointing with the barrel of the rifle.

I did as he said. Walked over to what had once been a pigsty. Moe walked past me so that he was now on the inside, and I was standing with daylight at my back. And it dawned on me that he intended to do it. Damn right he did. He was going to shoot me. My throat was so dry I had to try twice before I could make a sound with my voice.

'How you going to explain it afterwards, Moe?'

'Leave that to me,' he said. 'When they find a jilted killer who's broken in here with a knife in his hand, they'll come to the obvious conclusion it was self-defence.'

There was sense in what he said – all he had to do was place a knife in my hand afterwards. He dipped his head a little to one side so he was looking through the sight and then closed his other eye. Not easy to miss from two metres away, so I guessed he was taking such care with his aim because he wanted to shoot me through the head. That way he could be sure I would lie where I had fallen, making it easy for the crime technicians to reconstruct the sequence of events. His finger pulled back the trigger. Because he was aiming at my head, and I was standing against the light, he couldn't have seen my hand moving into my jacket pocket, taking hold of the end of the chain and pulling it out. I swung my arm down by my side and then forwards and upwards. I knew that a 116-link bike chain is 148 centimetres long, that my right arm measures 70 centimetres at full stretch, so it didn't matter much how long the barrel of the Remington 700 BDL was. There was a clattering sound as the chain wrapped itself around the barrel like a whip, I jerked my arm down, the rifle flew out of Moe's hands as the shot went off, and even before the rifle hit the ground I knew the bullet had caught me in the leg.

I read somewhere that getting shot doesn't hurt all that much. I've also read that you shouldn't believe what you read about how getting shot doesn't hurt all that much. I would say it hurts very much indeed. But not enough to stop me pulling the rifle and chain away before Moe, who had stumbled forward, could manage to pick it up.

What happened after that is a little unclear to me. What I do remember is Moe running for the door, and that I must have ignored the pain in my leg and given chase. Because moments later we were both lying on the ground next to the van. I got on top of him, sat astride his chest and locked his arms with my knees, then pulled out the rag, wrapped the chain around it and around my hand and then began to hit him. Not too hard to begin with, like I was warming myself up. Then there's another blank in what happened. Then I remember looking down at a face – or rather, what had once been a face, because a chain like that really can make an unpleasant mess – and it looked a bit like Dog's face, and I thought the same thing as I thought back then – that now I had to put the poor thing out of its misery. Dog whimpered before I killed him, and Moe whimpered too. The blind rage had faded in me, and when I still kept on hitting it wasn't to cause pain but to stop pain. I hit and kept on hitting until there was nothing left to hit, until I could feel the wooden planks *beneath* his head against my knuckles.

Then for a moment everything goes black.

Next thing I remember is standing and looking down at Moe, who was no longer breathing, and that the pain in my leg was unendurable. I could see the bullet hole in the leg of my trousers, and when I shifted my weight I could feel the squelching in my shoe. Blood overflowed from the top of the shoe and seeped down into the untreated wooden planks. That woke me up. Because that was my blood in what was now a crime scene. That right there was twenty years in jail.

The flight instinct twitched and surged as I tried to ignore the urgings of the amygdala and instead listen to what the rest of my brain had to say. It was telling me I had a choice. Either fuck everything, run, and be arrested later. Or stay there, be constructive, do what had to be done, and take the risk of being caught red-handed. Because it was true what Moe had said, about sound carrying well in the fog, and the neighbours on either side were bound to have heard the shot. If they didn't drive over here themselves Kurt Olsen would turn up within five or ten minutes of getting the phone call. Conclusion: run away and the result was guaranteed catastrophe; stay, and the result was likely catastrophe. So I chose likely catastrophe.

I looked around. Moe had a carpenter's workbench with a good selection of tools on the wall, and probably more in the toolbox on the floor. The first thing I did was take the roll of gaffer tape lying there, pull up the leg of my trousers and wrap the tape hard several times around the gaping hole in the leg. There was no hole on the other side, so the bullet had obviously stopped against the bone. I looked over the array of tools again. Hammers, pliers, saws. Four car tyres stood in a pile next to the wall, with a jack lying on top of them. Moe, or Moe's corpse, reminded me of those paintings by Pablo Picasso that Rita Willumsen had shown me, with the details of the face completely reorganised. Rita said that Picasso had used surrealism to paint more realistically than reality itself. And that's exactly what it was; surrealism and bloody realism, both at the same time. And I knew then that was what I had to do, I had to paint a picture. One that looked more realistic than the sick thing that had actually just happened.

27

I checked the time as I drove out from the Moe place. Forty minutes had passed since I had killed Anton Moe the roofer, and the fog still lay thick and heavy. Fortunately, because the weather forecast was that it would lift later in the day. There was another missed call from Kurt Olsen on my phone. Eight minutes later I drove past the petrol station, made a U-turn by the milk ramp, drove back, turned off the highway and cruised in behind the shop, out of sight of Egil. I got out, felt the pains shooting up my left leg, glanced at Grete's hair salon and hoped she had enough customers on a Saturday so she wouldn't be standing looking out of her window much of the time. I let myself into the workshop, opened one of the tins of Fritz Industrial Cleaner, dropped the bike chain into it and left the lid half screwed on so the tin wouldn't explode when the chemical reaction started. I didn't know how long it would take to dissolve the metal, remembering how long it had taken before all trace of the old sheriff had disappeared completely. Since I was unsure about the reaction time I placed the can in the grab of the tractor and raised it to its maximum height. Then I went out, locked up, and sneaked in through the station back door, unbuttoned my pea coat, brushed the straw from my shoulders, unlocked the door to the shop and walked in. Headed for the pill rack and took down a packet of paracetamol.

'Get it done?' asked Egil, looking up from his phone.

Even though I doubted that Egil, of all people, would so coolly and calmly announce that he had seen through my trick, I still had to admit I felt my heart skip beat.

'Found that mistake?' he added.

'Maybe,' I said. 'Anyway, I've got to go.'

I buttoned up my jacket as I headed for the door.

'The sheriff was looking for you.'

I stiffened. If Kurt Olsen had been here they must have knocked on the door. And discovered that both my car and I were gone, along with my alibi.

'I said you were busy,' said Egil. 'I've to ask you to call him back.'

I breathed easier. 'So he just phoned?'

'Yeah.'

'OK. Talk later.'

'You're limping,' said Egil.

'Shot myself in the leg this morning,' I said.

Egil grinned and went back to his phone screen.

I walked out, round the building to the rear, got back into the car I had just got out of, swallowed four paracetamol tablets on a dry throat, and left. That had been a close call with Olsen, and

Grete was obviously also a potential witness; but if I was able to finish painting the picture then hopefully I wouldn't need any alibi.

Nine minutes later I stopped in the yard at Opgard. No sign of Carl's car, he was probably at the hotel. I limped into the kitchen, opened our medicine drawer and five minutes later had bandaged my leg, which was already greatly swollen. I lifted the Remington rifle down, loaded it, opened the hatch and climbed down into the cold and damp potato cellar, one and a half metres from floor to ceiling. I closed the hatch behind me to deaden the sound then, in the darkness, fired a shot into one of the sacks of wood lying there.

When I climbed back up again I saw the fog had lifted, with just a few straggling patches lingering in the blue sky above. Dammit, I was too late. But rounding the corner of the main house I saw the fog still lay thick down in the valley. I limped as quickly as I could towards the car.

When I stopped on the highway below the Moe place it was still not possible to see either the buildings there or on the neighbouring farms. I lowered the window and listened. All was quiet. No sign yet of the alarm being raised. I drove slowly up the gravel driveway and stopped in the yard. Walked into the barn, past the van and past Moe without looking at the body, my heart pounding.

When I came out again, and was about to get into my car, I paused and looked at the main house. Had I touched the door handle? I limped across and wiped the brass knob with the sleeve of my jacket. Pulled it down. The door was, of course, open, no reason why it wouldn't be. I hesitated a moment. Then walked in.

A framed embroidery hung on the wall by the stairs to the upper floor. I read the text.

For what is a man profited, if he shall gain the whole world, and lose his own soul? Glanced up at where it must have happened. Then began walking up the staircase.

There were two bedrooms, an unmade bed in each. I pulled back the duvet, first on the double bed, then on the single. There was no blood on any of the sheets. But for all I knew it might have happened down in the living room, before she'd woken on the sofa in the middle of the night and made her own way up to her bedroom. I closed my eyes and thought about it. Thought how it was a pity I had already killed Anton Moe, because now it meant I couldn't do it again. When I opened my eyes I discovered that it was much lighter outside. Two minutes later I was back on the highway again.

The pain in my leg was agonising. The surgery was closed on Saturdays, so I called Stanley Spind's home number. A female voice said that the person I was trying to call was not available, and then I remembered that he was away on a walking weekend.

The wet asphalt sparkled, the sun was breaking through the fog now. Then – after driving less than a hundred metres – it did just that, and suddenly our village was bathed in columns of light that splayed out from a hole in the cloud layer, just like in those pictures of Jesus up in the meeting hall. And I too would probably have seen the beauty in it, had I not been so desperate, and doubted the possibility of salvation.

There had been a change of shift at the reception desk at the hotel.

'He's in the massage parlour right now,' the boy replied when I asked for Carl, since he hadn't been up in his office when I looked. I limped down to the spa and walked past the counter without any chitchat to the girl sitting there. I finally located Carl after first bursting in on two other massage sessions. The person on the massage table lay with a towel covering his arse and his face wedged in a hole, but I recognised the freckles on my little brother's back.

'We'd like to be alone,' I said to the masseuse in English. She stared indignantly at me.

'Please leave, sir—' she began, but Carl interrupted.

'It's OK, Petra, just continue. Roy,' he went on in Norwegian, 'she doesn't understand a word of what we're saying. What's up? Why aren't you on your way to Krakow?'

I crouched down and spoke to the nose and chin I saw protruding from the underside of the bench.

'Krakow was aborted,' I said. 'Natalie didn't want to go.'

'No? She's usually willing enough.'

I was surprised. But it was difficult to know what he meant since I couldn't see much of his face, and anyway your voice is distorted when someone is pressing down on your spinal column as you speak.

'Kurt was trying to get in touch with me,' I said. 'I don't know what about exactly, but I don't think it's by chance he's doing it on a Saturday. It would be a good idea to contact Goebbel.'

'So then do it.'

'She's your lawyer.'

'She's ours now. Just call her.'

'Thanks.'

'Thanks? Jesus, Roy, are you going soft?'

'Maybe,' I said. 'I just wanted to give you a heads up.'

'You could have just rung and given the same message.'

'As I said here the other day, I think we need to be a bit careful using the phone.'

'You said. Bit paranoid, isn't it?'

'A bit of paranoia never hurt anyone,' I said, and stood up ready to leave when an apropos thought struck me and I asked anyway the question I had intended not to.

'What do you mean, saying Natalie's usually willing enough?'

Carl didn't reply. The masseuse did some sideways chopping on the small of his back that made his arse move from side to side, like he was wagging his tail.

'Petra,' his voice scraped down to the floor tile, 'take a break and leave us alone for a minute, OK?'

With the masseuse out of the room Carl sat up on the table. The towel slipped off, and it looked to me as though he'd put on another couple of kilos since the last time I'd seen him naked.

'You look pale,' he said. 'Is something wrong?'

'Just a little trouble with my leg.'

'OK. In the first place, Natalie is a booty call, right?'

'Booty call? What makes you think that? I was supposed to go to Krakow with her, for fuck's sake.'

'But isn't that what you do with a booty call? Quick weekend, plane tickets costing just a few hundred, cheap booze, plenty of sex? I mean, if it's serious you take her to Paris or New York, right?'

I stared at him. Something in his doglike expression aroused a deep unease in me, deeper than the unease I was already feeling.

'What are you trying to tell me, Carl?'

'It isn't as though you two are *together* now, is it? You don't have any monopoly, OK?'

'Get to the point, Carl.'

I heard that my voice was shaking. Because I knew, I already knew.

'The point?' He gave a sheepish, guilty smile. 'The point is, well . . . er, I screwed her at the party yesterday.'

I swallowed. But it was too much to take in, it was just words, sounds.

'Tell me that isn't true, Carl.'

'It isn't true,' he said. Sighed heavily. 'But actually it is true. We both had a little too much, and . . . it just sort of happened.'

'At the party? How is that possible?'

'It was at a hotel, so there wasn't exactly a shortage of possibilities. That was probably part of the problem, I think.'

'Where and when?' I asked.

'The Bridal Suite was empty,' he said. 'It was early. Nine, maybe? Anyway, she emptied the minibar afterwards and got so drunk I suggested she sleep it off there while I rejoined the party. But she probably saw the scandal coming and insisted on getting home, so I got reception to call a cab for her.'

I felt empty, drained. Drained of strength, of feelings, of purpose, of ideas, of any desire to go on living at all.

'She probably wanted to go home because she had to make the flight to Krakow,' I whispered.

'Could be, though she didn't mention it,' said Carl. 'She didn't mention your name at all, so I thought . . . well, didn't really think much about anything. I'm really sorry, Roy. Especially now I see how upset you are.'

I lowered my head and stared at the floor. The leg had swollen up and was now pressing against the leg of my trousers.

'Because you are, aren't you?'

'Are what?'

'Upset?'

'Guess I am.'

'It must feel terrible.'

I didn't answer, just looked up at him. The light on his face, the sound of his voice, but still, it was like seeing and hearing a stranger. He seemed to be looking for something in my face too, the difference being he had found it. At least he was nodding his head, as though he had.

'Tell me if there's any way I can make it right again,' he said.

'It's OK,' I said. 'I've lost her anyway.' I swallowed and didn't say the words that crowded in on me. *And now I've lost you too.*

I went back up to reception and asked for the key card to the Bridal Suite. Said I needed to check it out for some friends who were thinking of having their wedding here. The boy looked at his screen.

'The room isn't ready yet,' he said.

'I'll look at it just as it is,' I said and held out my hand. And added, when I noticed his hesitation, 'I own thirty-six per cent of the shares here.'

The door to the suite swung closed behind me with a soft click.

Light streamed into the room, reflected off the white bedlinen on the big four-poster bed intended for the happy couple. So much light I had to squint. And squinting was enough as I pulled the duvet to one side and saw the tiny red spots of blood on the sheet.

I opened the minibar. It had obviously been replenished, and I could see it contained enough for an already half-drunk person to drink themselves all the way to oblivion.

I went back down, handed the key card in at reception, then drove up to Opgard.

It was four in the afternoon when Kurt Olsen's SUV swung into the yard at Opgard, and he and Johnny climbed out. After returning from the hotel I had changed the bandage and gone through the pills in the medicine drawer in search of painkillers. I had already found a box of anxiety suppressants, some olive-green pills I remembered Carl getting just after Shannon died, when I located a pack of tramadol, painkillers Carl had been prescribed after having his appendix removed. I'd taken three of them, and they had made me so tired I had to drag myself up out of the chair to open the door for Kurt and Johnny.

'Why don't you answer your phone?' Kurt asked, a cigarette twitching between his lips.

'Is that one of my responsibilities as a citizen?' I asked, supporting myself against the doorjamb.

'No, but if you had done and reported to the sheriff's office you would have saved yourself and us a lot of trouble.'

'So you're going to arrest me again?'

'Last time was just a detention.'

'And this time?'

'This time it's an apprehension.'

'And that is?'

Kurt moved his weight to the other foot. 'If you want you can call it an arrest.'

'For what?'

275

I didn't know what answer to expect, and the truth is that right then and there I didn't care a damn either, it felt like it would be a relief to get everything over with. To draw the line. Wind everything up.

Kurt flicked ash from his cigarette. 'We've learned that you bought plane tickets to Krakow.'

'And if I did? So what?'

'So what? If you didn't have so much trouble reading then you'd know that in that document you signed for us there was an express commitment not to make any attempt to leave the country. So what you've done is a criminal offence in itself, Roy. And it will make it a helluva lot easier to get the people at the custody meeting to agree to us holding you on remand.'

They didn't point a gun at me this time. Didn't handcuff me either. But once we were inside the sheriff's office I realised that, this time, it was serious.

28

THE FIRST THING THAT STRUCK me was that the place looked like Kurt and Johnny had prepared it for the occasion. The table that had been inside the cell had now been moved to the middle of the little office, and three people were already seated at it. Gilliani was there, with his nerdy spectacles, and a stout, pale woman I'd never seen before but who, like Gilliani, had a KRIPOS ID card around her neck. Oh, but this was serious all right. Those people don't drive all the way in from the capital to Os on a Saturday for the fun of it. There was a third guy sitting with them, wearing a suit that looked like he might have borrowed it from Vendelbo. Kurt pulled out a chair for me.

'I confess,' I said as I slumped down into it.

'You confess to what?' asked the stout lady and pressed a button on the small recorder on the table.

'That's up to you to decide,' I said, and yawned.

Yawning can indicate that you're tired, but – as any semi-educated psychologist will tell you – it can also be a nervous reaction, you see it a lot in dogs. In my case the cause was too much tramadol.

'That is not a course of action I would advise,' said the man in the Vendelbo suit.

'Who are you?' I asked.

'I'm that guy who's second and also last on the list of people the police call when they need to get hold of a defence lawyer in Notodden and surrounding areas.'

It was hard to tell from his bulldog face whether he was trying to be funny or not. I felt pretty sure they'd dragged him out of bed after the party last night. OK, so that made two of us who only wanted to sleep right now. The guy pulled out a notebook.

'First question is, do you accept me as your defence lawyer?'

'Should I?'

He grinned at me. 'I can leave now, if you want. I charge by the hour, including travel time, and there are a number of other things I would prefer to be doing today.'

Kurt Olsen cleared his throat. 'Say yes, Roy. Only professional criminals demand different lawyers from the ones the police give them.'

I looked at Gilliani, who nodded almost imperceptibly.

'Then let's say I do,' I said. 'Have I been arrested because I booked a flight to Krakow or because something new has turned up?'

'Let me rather . . .' the lawyer guy began, but I held up a hand and he did, in fact, stop.

'What we have is more than enough,' said Kurt. 'KRIPOS here

can confirm that the blood behind the licence plate came from my father. Correct?'

He turned to the stout lady, who nodded, her blonde ponytail bouncing gaily up and down. 'That's correct, we found blood that matches that of the former station head, yes.'

'Former *what*?'

'Station head.'

I turned to Kurt, who looked embarrassed. 'They don't call it sheriff any more, they—'

'So you lost the title your father had,' I said, not taking my eyes off Kurt. I could see it on him. He'd been lying. They had found something new. But what was it? 'You haven't mentioned that to anyone, Kurt. Still says Os Sheriff's Office on the sign outside.'

'It'll be changed,' Kurt hissed between his teeth. 'You ready to answer our questions or not, Roy?'

'Here I must object. If my client—'

'Shut up!' Kurt and I growled in chorus without even looking at the lawyer guy.

'Ask away,' I said.

'How would you describe your relationship with your father?' asked the stout lady.

'*My* father?' I said. 'What's this got to do with him?'

'We're asking because we have questions about that particular incident too.'

'You do? Such as?'

Gilliani coughed. 'The crime technologists found a couple of unusual faults on the car that can't be explained as a result of the accident or the crash. And since you tinkered about with cars back then—'

'Hold on,' I interrupted, for no other reason than that I needed

279

a moment to think. Because this was what Kurt didn't want to tell me. They had clearly done more than just check the Cadillac for blood. 'I was a mechanic.'

Gilliani straightened his spectacles irritably. 'Not sure what the difference is, but as I was saying—'

'The difference,' I said, 'is that being a mechanic is a trade. When people ask you what you do, do you say you play cops and robbers?'

Gilliani gave the lawyer an exasperated look, as though to encourage him to tell me to behave myself.

'Anyway,' said Gilliani, 'we found holes in the brake hoses and a piece of the steering wheel which had come loose from what I gather is called the rack and pinion. According to the ... er, mechanic we talked to, that could be the reason the car carrying your father and mother failed to make the corner up by your place. Any comment on that?'

I nodded. Long and slow.

The hung-over lawyer was probably doing his best to read the situation and chose the moment to lean forward and interject a few words.

'My client is not required to respond to hypothetical questions.'

'No he isn't, he doesn't have to answer any questions at all if he doesn't want to,' said the stout little woman without taking her eyes off me.

I yawned. I did. It wasn't intended as provocation, because my brain really did actually need more oxygen. And when it had got it, I leaned back in my chair. 'Listen, people, this has already been a long day for me. So let me make this as brief as I can. The way I understand it, Sheri—I'm sorry, Station Captain-or-whatever

Olsen first of all arrested me and then released me, hoping I might be scared enough to do something stupid that would reveal that I killed his father. Since, to his great disappointment, I didn't, he's now using this Krakow ticket as an excuse to get me held on remand, to see if I will fold after I've been cooped up for a while. To put a little extra pressure on me you've come up with this wild hypothesis that I have something to do with the death of my own parents too. Or am I wrong? No, don't answer, Kurt, the question was rhetorical, as they say. Here's my suggestion: I can provide you with a witness here and now who can give a plausible and quite unsensational explanation for how that blood got onto the car. In addition I can offer you an unconditional admission that I killed both my parents. What d'you say to that?'

Five faces gazed at me for several long moments. Then the stout lady's ponytail began bouncing again.

Erik Nerell sat beside me staring at the recorder on the table.

Normally, Kurt and KRIPOS would have questioned him without others being present, but Erik had insisted I be present, to help him remember, as he put it. When Kurt said that was out of the question Erik had told the two from KRIPOS that if they wanted to hear what he had to say then it would be with me in the room, or they could just forget about it.

So now we sat there, Erik, me and the lawyer on one side of the table, Kurt and the two from KRIPOS on the other.

'You tell them what happened,' said Erik. 'Then I can interrupt if it's not the same way I remember it.'

I could see Kurt was about to protest so I hurriedly spoke up.

'It was the winter before my parents met their deaths in the car,' I said. 'Dad and I were out driving and just passing the Nerell place. There's a gentle bend there, and we weren't going fast, but the steering was loose and the brakes none too good. Dad knew about that from the day he bought the used and overpriced Cadillac from that villain Willumsen. Anyway, we came off the road and ended up arse first in a snowdrift, see. No one got hurt and the car wasn't damaged, but we couldn't get it back on the road again. Erik and his father had seen us, and they came along and helped me push the car. We were almost there, but the wheels just kept spinning in the snow, and in the end Erik's father went off to fetch his tractor to tow us out.'

I stopped there to give Erik the chance to nod and say yes, that's right.

'Perhaps we might hear Nerell's own account of what happened from this point on,' the stout lady said.

Erik gave me an uncertain look. I nodded, and he wiped the palms of his hands down the sides of his trousers before starting to speak. 'Well, that's exactly what happened. Then the sheriff, the old sheriff that is, drove by and he stopped. When he heard my father was on his way with the tractor he said all it needed was just a little shove to get it back up on the road. Wasn't that what happened, Roy?'

Erik looked at me and I took over again before the lady could stop me.

'Right. And we said we'd tried, and then the sheriff said all you needed was to push in the right place and put your back into it. I guess he wanted to show he was stronger than Erik's dad. So he went back behind the car and took a good hold under the rear bumper bar and told us youngsters where we should push, and Dad should give it just a bit of throttle. Dad did what he said, and the sheriff pushed with all his might, pushed so hard he actually even yelled out. And the car moved all right. But then the sheriff slipped. It was probably those snakeskin boots, bloody slippery soles they have, right? Anyway, he fell and his head hit the end of the licence plate. Bleeding and everything. Remember, Erik?'

'Sure do.'

I looked straight at Kurt. 'Maybe he mentioned it when he got back home?'

'No,' said Kurt. 'Don't recall any cut on his forehead either.'

I shrugged. 'It probably wasn't an intervention for a sheriff to come home and boast about. And the cut was just above the hairline, wasn't it, Erik?'

Erik shook his head. 'It's so long ago, it's hard to remember, but it sounds about right.'

'He had a lot of hair did your dad,' I said and looked at Kurt. 'So it could be you didn't see any cut.'

I withdrew from the staring competition with Kurt and looked at the others. 'And Erik's father got the car back on the road with his tractor. So it all ended well. Or . . . *that* day did at least.'

Those on the other side of the table and the right side of the law exchanged looks. Stout whispered something into Gilliani's ear then looked back at me again. 'The confession you promised us, Opgard?'

'That's implied in what I just told you.'

'How so?'

I shrugged. 'I was a car mechanic. My dad's car was in such bad condition it was dangerous to drive. And I didn't give it the attention it deserved and needed. So obviously, the accident was my fault.'

Silence in the room.

Stout cleared her throat. 'That's the full extent of your confession?'

'It's quite a lot, if you ask me.'

She exchanged more looks with her colleagues. 'Do you have any explanation for why you neglected to repair the car for him?'

Again I shrugged. 'My only excuse would be that he never asked me to.'

Stout nodded to herself a couple of times then began straightening the papers in front of her, as though unconsciously getting ready to pack up and leave. With unfinished business. Or maybe they didn't look at it that way, maybe they were professionals through and through, and to their way of thinking had done their job and lifted the burden of suspicion from an innocent man. Maybe.

But Kurt Olsen sure didn't see it like that. He sat slumped in his chair and stared vacantly into the air as we walked out of his office. Night had fallen. Erik offered to drive me up to Opgard.

'Good job back there,' I said once we were inside the car which was parked at the other side of the square.

'Did the best I could,' he said. 'When d'you think I'll get the papers for my part ownership of Fritt Fall?'

'Next week,' I said, and looked up at the Meierigård. There was a light on in her bedroom.

29

I SAT IN THE WINTER garden with two tramadol inside me and six beers in front of me and waited. Just what for I don't know. For Natalie to ring? Carl to come home? News that someone had found Anton Moe dead? Or KRIPOS and Kurt to pull into the yard, blue lights flashing, and arrest me for one or more of the eight murders I was now guilty of or accessory to?

I opened the first bottle and started to summarise my situation. Natalie had finished with me, and it clearly had something to do with the fact that she had fucked my brother. Naturally I couldn't feel completely sure about cause and effect, if she'd already decided to end it with me and therefore thought it would be OK. Or if it just happened the way Carl said, and after that she felt she couldn't go on seeing me. Maybe she thought Carl wouldn't say anything, but that it could be kept from me if she and I stopped meeting. That a drunken Carl had taken a woman – could've been anyone – to one of his hotel rooms and fucked her wasn't exactly shocking news. But that he had deliberately crossed into my territory was more difficult to swallow. Booty call? He knew I was head over heels about the girl. So why fuck her, of all women? Was he in love with Natalie himself? No, I would have noticed, he was my brother, we knew each other inside out.

Or did we? I'd been with Shannon without his knowing about it, and as an actor I'm not exactly any kind of Oscar nominee.

I opened the second bottle.

It was perhaps strange that it hurt more to think about Natalie and Carl than the fact that I had just killed an innocent man. Although, of course, he wasn't innocent, so I knew it was something I would be able to live with, I really did know that. And that is maybe the only advantage to already having seven murders under your belt, that it makes you a little less sensitive about that kind of thing. But obviously I could be done for Moe's murder. There's always something you leave out of your calculations when the time comes to cover your tracks. Like how old Olsen bled onto the car when he fell down into Huken, or that I had made holes in the brake hose and loosened the steering column. But that had been dealt with now. Everything had been dealt with and Erik was about to become part owner of Fritt Fall. Halden and Fuhr had got their twelve million. Asle Vendelbo and Johnny Depp had my word I wouldn't be saying anything about what I knew. I almost had to smile, because it reminded me of the title of the only book I could ever remember my dad reading, back in the eighties. *The Art of the Deal* it was called. That some nutcase of an author should end up president was just ridiculous. King of America, yeah, right.

Thinking about Erik's share reminded me I hadn't informed Julie that she was going to get a one-third share as well. I pulled out my phone and looked up her number.

She managed a 'Hi' in the middle of a yawn.

'Sorry, in bed already?'

'No, no,' she said. 'Worked late yesterday, so just a little tired.'

'Thought you had yesterday off?'

'I did, but Carl asked if I could do the bar at the hotel. They had the staff party, and he wanted as many employees as possible free to attend.'

'I see. Listen, I've got an offer for you.'

'Oh yeah? In a good way, or—'

"I said *offer*, didn't I?'

'Yeah, but they call it an *offer* when they say they want you to retire early, they can't use you any more.'

I laughed. Now and then it occurred to me that, apart from Carl, Julie was the only person I could be in the same room with for hours on end without suffering my usual social exhaustion.

'You're working tomorrow?' I asked.

'Yep. We open at eleven. Same as the priest.'

'Then I'll pop in.'

We hung up. I downed the second beer and considered a third. I'd done a quick Google search for tramadol and read that it wasn't a good idea to combine it with alcohol. OK, then maybe I should treat myself to another tramadol and go to bed.

I'm not sure, but I think that's what I did. Because my dreams that night must have been opioid dreams. I saw Shannon sitting in a chair and trying to get up but unable to because of the two huge nails driven through her thighs. She was screaming and stretching her arms towards a baby in the chair next to her who was sucking on Natalie's teat. Natalie was sitting on Carl's lap, Carl's towel had slipped down so he was naked, and he was moving his hips up and down and humming *Ride a cock horse*. All at once the baby starts to sing in a deep bass voice: *Do you know Kari Midtgard from Tinn, she doesn't let the boys in*. And then I see the child has the face of an old man. It takes me a while to recognise it. And when I do I have to laugh, even though I feel more like crying. Because the old man is me.

30

THE CHURCH BELLS PEELED OUT across the valley.

Coffee and forgiveness, it said, in Erik's writing on the pavement sign outside Fritt Fall.

'You're limping,' was the first thing Julie said as I entered the club.

'I've got a shotgun shell in my leg,' I said as I looked out over the empty club. 'Isn't eleven a bit early to be opening?'

She leaned back on the counter. 'Maybe, but I get so restless hanging about waiting at home. Knock into something?'

'Guess you could say I did,' I said. 'The offer is that I transfer one third ownership to you and one third to Erik. In return you take a fifteen per cent wage cut and promise to remain as manager for at least two years, not including pregnancy leave and that kind of stuff.'

I saw the surprise in her eyes, saw the calculator working full speed. 'That works out well for me,' she said in due course. 'If we don't run this little ship aground, of course. And if we exploit the potential in this place, as I plan to do, then it's going to be worth a *lot* more to me.'

'Well then, say yes,' I said.

Julie laughed, came round the counter and gave me a big bear hug.

'Thanks,' she said, wiping away a tear.

'Thanks? I'm doing it so you and Erik will work your arses off so that I earn more money too.'

'I know that, but all the same, thanks.'

'I'll do the paperwork next week,' I said as Julie poured me a coffee. 'What was it like to be tending bar at the hotel again?'

'Same as before,' she said. 'It's funny actually, isn't it? Our generation lives completely different lives from our grandparents. We dress different, eat, drink, read and see things different. But we drink exactly the same way. Go to bars and get sloshed. Just like they did a hundred, no, a thousand years ago! At least.'

'It's a steady business when you look at it like that. A lot of drunks on Friday?'

'Yeah, I'll say.'

I took a sip of the coffee. Kept the cup in front of my mouth and thought about taking another sip, to stop myself asking what I was about to ask. It didn't work.

'Did you see Natalie Moe there?'

'Natalie? Oh yeah. She's really something these days – have you seen her?'

I looked into Julie's large, innocent blue eyes. The rumours about me and Natalie obviously hadn't reached her yet.

'Yes,' I said. 'She's been helping me on a project. Was she as drunk as everyone else?'

Julie put her own cup down, peered up into the air and looked like she was biting the inside of her cheek.

'No, not *as*.'

'*More?*'

'Yes. And no.'

'No?'

'I don't know what she had to drink with the meal, but at the bar afterwards all she ordered was water. And she seemed completely sober. And then, half an hour later, she was out of her head. As if she'd taken a pill or something. Head lolling, swaying in her chair. If she hadn't been Natalie I would have had to ask her to leave the bar, know what I mean? But I've seen it before and thought to myself, there's someone with a drug problem. Luckily Carl intervened before I had to do anything.'

I swore and cursed inside. Please, not that.

'What did he do?'

'Helped her outside, poor girl. I asked about her later in the evening and someone said they'd seen Carl helping her into a taxi. He's a good man is your brother.'

I nodded slowly. Thanked Julie for the coffee, gave her a hug and limped out.

Stood beside the car, which I'd parked right outside the door, and looked up at Natalie's flat. No lights on, but did that curtain just move?

Unlike Carl's, my car still had manual gears and my face twisted in pain every time I had to depress the clutch with my injured leg. I wasn't sure whether to drive back to Opgard or call in at the petrol station to see how things were doing. Sometimes you can leave it to your body to make decisions like that, and that's what I did this time. It chose the third option, the hotel. I could, of course, pretend not to know why. But, of course, I did.

I parked directly and illegally right outside the hotel entrance, limped into reception and asked where the housekeeping store was. They probably recognised me, and just pointed down a corridor and let me limp off without asking any questions. At the end of the corridor I opened a door with STORE written on it, and found myself in a large, garage-like room containing about a dozen trolleys. They were big and I had to really stretch to get my hand up inside one. I pulled out a white duvet cover.

'Can I help you, sir?'

I turned and looked at the woman who had spoken. The accent was East European, the demeanour a lot darker than the question.

'I'm looking for an earr . . .' I tried to think what the word for it was in English.

'I speak a little Norwegian,' said the woman. She was broad, looked strong, exuded the natural authority of someone secure in their position, regardless of where they might be in the hierarchy.

'Earring,' I said. 'My girlfriend's. She thinks she lost it in bed. It has tiny spikes on it, so she says it might have got stuck on the sheet. If it's OK I'll just look through the trolleys with sheets.'

'There are sheets in all these trolleys here.'

'All of them?' I did a quick count. Eleven. Could be a helluva job to find what I was looking for.

'When was she here?' the lady asked. The stony face was gone, her new face was the opposite. Lively, expressive.

'Before the weekend.'

'I'm sorry, but the laundry is picked up every morning.'

'Nor Tekstil only come on weekdays. And my girlfriend was here Saturday night.'

The woman looked at me. 'Which room?'

'The Bridal Suite.'

'Your new wife or your girlfriend?'

I smiled, and she smiled back and sighed. Then she pointed. 'I'm not certain, but probably in one of these three trolleys. I'll be back in two minutes, have to check.'

I had reached the bottom of the second trolley and already found one sheet where a guest had clearly had a period – at least that's what I hoped it was – when I found a second sheet, this one with tiny drops of blood on it. I hadn't a knife on me, but I hadn't cut my nails for a while, so I used them to scrape the blood off.

'Did you find anything?' the woman asked when she came back, just as I was throwing the sheet back into the trolley.

'Unfortunately no,' I said.

'I spoke with my girls now, they haven't found anything, I'm sorry.'

'The earrings weren't all that expensive, I'll just have to buy her some new ones.'

The woman gave a mischievous little twist of her lips. 'And maybe be a little more gentle next time?'

Back at Opgard I used a toothpick to clean out the dried blood from under my nails and put it in an empty tin of Berry's chewing tobacco. Then I phoned Vera Martinsen.

'Hi,' she said, and laughed.

'Eh?'

'Gilliani told me how long Olsen's face was when they found out how that blood ended up behind the licence plate.'

'Kurt never gives up,' I said.

'I told you when we last spoke you should report him, so the Special Conduct Unit can decide whether it constitutes harassment.'

'I know, but I'm calling about something else. Two things, actually. The first is, is my phone being tapped?'

'No.'

'No? You can tell me that just straight away?'

'Someone came to us asking for permission, I'll give you no guesses who it was. We told him it takes a lot to get a court order for a wiretap. A lot more than we have here. What was the other thing?'

I told her what the other thing was.

After we hung up I could feel the pains getting worse again. On the net it said tramadol was powerfully addictive and carried a strong risk of overdose. But after a few minutes I couldn't stand any more and opened the medicine drawer again. I considered trying one of the olive-green pills as well, I knew they worked as sleeping pills too, but ended up taking one more tramadol instead. Then I limped up the stairs to the next floor and into the bedroom. As I pulled off my T-shirt I looked out the window. The house at Opgard is a little too set back from Huken to see the whole village, but I could see the rise and Carl's Palace down below. There were lights on, so Carl was obviously there. Maybe he was checking something, or maybe he was showing Mari around. In case she had ideas about how things should be, I'm thinking. If they were there, would it occur to Carl that less than forty-eight hours earlier, he'd been cheating on the woman he was now talking children's bedrooms with? And with one of his own employees, the woman his brother was in love with? I thought how maybe at that exact moment he was standing by the big terrace windows looking up and seeing the lights of Opgard. That I could use the curtains to send him messages in Morse code. About how I had lost enough, that I didn't want to lose him too. That I had tried to hate him, but it was true, blood was thicker than water – and more than that, thicker than right and wrong too. In a war you didn't choose, family is on one side, and you didn't choose that either, it chose you. I never wanted to be fucking born here and to be a fucking Opgard. But I was, and I am.

The phone rang. I bent down and pulled it out of my trousers on the floor.

It was Stanley.

'I've just got back from my walking weekend and only now heard your message. You've shot yourself in the leg?'

'Yes.'

'And you didn't go to the hospital in Notodden?'

'Too far. I've bandaged it.'

'Jesus, Roy. I'll be in Os in an hour, can you be at the surgery then?'

Stanley studied the wound as I lay on the bench and studied the ceiling.

'You've been remarkably lucky,' he said.

'Yes, I think so too,' I said.

'The bullet came to rest against the shin bone, and it doesn't look as if there are any bone splinters here. The wound is so shallow I can actually see the bullet. But we'll have to get you to Notodden, get it X-rayed, get the metal out.'

'Really? If you can see the bullet, can't you just do it here?'

Stanley gave a quick laugh before realising I was serious. 'Had we been on a desert island then I would, Roy. But we need to minimise the chance of infection, and the hospital is the best bet there.'

'I don't want to.'

'I understand, but—'

'As in "I refuse". Either you nip out that bullet or I'll take a pair of pincers at home, heat them up with a lighter and do it myself.'

Stanley looked thoughtfully at me. 'Are you aware of the possible consequences of infection?'

'Yes I am,' I said. 'Amputation and early retirement. How about it?'

Stanley sighed heavily.

'Good,' I said. 'And no anaesthetic either, thank you.'

Stanley raised his shaven eyebrows. 'Sure?'

I thought about it. 'Correction. All the anaesthetic you've got.'

Here things go blank again. It's possible I neglected to inform him of the amount of tramadol I had taken, and that the combination with what he gave me knocked me out completely, but whatever it was, I don't remember much until I heard a pling and opened my eyes and said to Stanley that it sounded exactly like that scene in the Westerns, where Doc lets the bullet from his pincers drop into one of those metal bowls. Stanley laughed and showed me the metal bowl, with the blood-smeared bullet lying in it. He put a fresh bandage on my leg, wrote out a prescription for more painkillers and a sick note, and told me not to drive in my condition, said he would be happy to drive me home. I said that was kind of him, but that I'd call Dagur, driving people who were ill and sick was sort of like his calling in life.

Emerging from the surgery on the crutches Stanley had given me I saw a cigarette glowing in the dark over by the sheriff's office.

'Good evening,' I said.

'Good evening,' said Kurt. He pushed himself upright from the wall he was leaning against and dropped his cigarette. The sparks danced away over the asphalt in the wind until he put his heel down and the cigarette died. 'What you done to your leg?'

'Shooting accident at home. Tell me, are these regular office hours or are you following me?'

He gave a quick, cold laugh. 'Why would I be doing that?'

'Because you are hell-bent on proving that I killed someone, for example?'

Kurt snorted. 'You *are* a fucking murdering killer, Roy. Remember that computer game that stood in the corridor at the old Kaffistova?' He nodded over in the direction of Fritt Fall. 'The one where an asteroid exploded in front of your spaceship and the game was to dodge all the bits? It was easy to begin with. But once you moved up to the advanced levels those bits came so thick and fast that in the end you just couldn't do it any more.'

'I remember it well,' I said. 'I think I held the record, didn't I?'

Kurt shook his head. 'No one remembers your fucking record, Roy.'

Dagur's Mercedes glided up alongside me. I put my crutches on the back seat before opening the passenger door. As I got in, I said over my shoulder: 'Ask Rita, I'm sure she'll remember.'

We pulled away, and in the wing mirror I saw the flare of a lighter as Kurt lit himself another cigarette.

31

THEY FOUND ANTON MOE ON Monday morning, and by mid-morning everyone in Os knew about it. Obviously it had occurred to me that it could be Natalie who would find him, but according to Grete Smitt there was a neighbour who was puzzled that Moe had neither attended church nor hoisted his flag on Sunday but had obviously not gone travelling anywhere, since there was still a light on inside the house.

'It was gruesome,' said Grete, holding her hands to her cheeks as though it were she herself who had found the body. She was in the station shop with Egil, me and Simon Nergard for an audience. 'His whole head was smashed to pieces.'

'Not so surprising,' said Simon. 'That van of his must weigh at least two tons. What is surprising is that he was lying *under* the car when he was changing the tyres.'

'He was probably checking something in the undercarriage while he had the car up on the jack,' I said.

'OK, but then how do you manage to kick away a jack that's holding up two tons?'

I spread my arms. 'He probably didn't touch the jack, just gave the car a nudge. Checking something under the wheel arch, for example, and never noticed the jack wasn't standing straight.'

'Oh Jesus,' said Egil. 'And he gets the wheel drum right in his face.'

'Not a pretty sight,' said Grete with a heavy sigh. 'Kurt had to get Natalie to identify the body.'

'Why?' I said. It just escaped me. The other three looked at me. I moistened my mouth. 'To the best of my knowledge Kurt's seen more of Anton these last eight years than she has.'

'True,' said Grete. 'And Anton had one of his testicles removed, so they could always have identified him that way.'

Now it was her turn to be stared at.

'You mean you didn't know?' Grete said, acting surprised. 'Anton had cancer.'

All Monday I kept thinking how Natalie must be feeling. Sure, I'd promised not to get in touch, but wouldn't a death in the family nullify a promise like that? Maybe she even *hoped* I would contact her? It was, of course, more likely that I hoped that she hoped, but could I really imagine *never* talking to Natalie again? And if not, wasn't now exactly the right time to do it?

Around one o'clock Vera Martinsen called.

'I talked to the lab, and as I told you yesterday, they prefer urine samples. But they will be able to do it. They wondered if a chromatographic test would be necessary or would a simple immunological screening test be enough?'

'What's the difference?'

'The second one is quicker and simpler if you're looking for something definite.'

'I am,' I said.

'OK then,' she said. 'But before I do this favour for you I need to be absolutely sure this won't come back on me, Roy.'

'I promise,' I said. 'This has nothing to do with what's keeping Olsen so busy.'

'Then I trust you.'

'Good,' I said, hoping I sounded as convinced as I felt, and then hung up.

There was a steady stream of customers, and every time I heard the sound of an SUV pulling up to the pumps I glanced up and half expected to see Kurt. But he didn't come. Not until five, when I heard a sound that could only have come from a Land Rover. He climbed out and disappeared, clearly taking a walk around the station building. Then he appeared once more and came moseying up to the door, more bow-legged than ever. In he came and stopped in front of the counter, thumbs hooked behind his belt buckle like the cowboy sheriff I'm certain he saw himself as.

'We can't go on meeting like this, Roy.'

I wondered how long he'd spent working out that line.

'I've got a few questions I'd like to ask you, here or else at the . . .' He hesitated.

'Police station,' I finished off for him. 'Here's fine.'

He gave a slight smile. 'I'm thinking you must've heard that Anton Moe was found dead?'

I nodded. Saw that Kurt was expecting me to say something about it, so I didn't.

Kurt shifted his weight from one foot to the other. 'In that regard, where were you ten thirty on Saturday morning?'

In the silence that followed, as we stared at each other, there came the sound of flushing from the staff toilet and the door being opened.

'Egil!' I called.

He came shuffling over to us.

'Egil, where was I ten thirty last Saturday morning?'

He looked from me to Kurt and back again. Scratched his ear. 'Weren't you here?'

'The station head at Os Police Station wants a definite answer,' I said.

'Who?'

'Kurt.'

'Oh, yeah. Let's see . . . Saturday morning. Yeah, that's right, you were here. Don't you remember? You were in the back room, trying to find out where the mistake was in the bookkeeping.'

I was going to say something but wasn't fast enough.

'You locked the door and said you weren't to be disturbed,' said Egil, clearly pleased to be able to add these supplementary but superficial details. I cursed inwardly.

'And you didn't disturb him?' asked Kurt.

'Tried,' said Egil. 'The counter on one of the pumps stopped working, but he didn't answer, so I went out and fixed it myself.'

Kurt raised his eyebrows and looked at me.

'Earpods,' I said. 'JJ Cale and accounting work really well together.'

Kurt nodded. 'Would you mind showing me the back room?'

'If you want,' I said, trying to sound as if it didn't bother me.

Kurt gave me that thin smile, and again I got that feeling that he was sitting on something, that he had something up his sleeve, as they say.

'I do,' he said.

I led the way on my crutches into the narrow back room and positioned myself between him and the rear door, pointed at the overloaded desk. 'Well behind with the paperwork, as you can see.'

But Kurt wasn't interested in that, instead he was looking over my shoulder.

'Where does that door lead to?'

'This one?'

'The only one here as far as I can see,' he said. He turned the handle and opened the door.

'Well, now look at that. And look, there's your car there too.' He sounded in excellent humour now. 'How about you and me get us a little fresh air, Roy?'

Cautiously, I moved out onto the wet asphalt on the crutches. The priest rolled out of the car wash in his car, didn't see us standing there, drove off. Kurt bounced contentedly up and down in his snakeskin boots as he lit a cigarette.

'Not too hot now, that alibi of yours, is it?' he said. 'Might even sound so strange it could work the other way. What do you think the jury's going to think when the prosecutor asks Egil how many times in all these years you've locked the door to that room, or not answered when he's called and asked for help, and he says the answer is once? On the very day Anton Moe was killed.'

'Killed?' I stifled a yawn. 'I thought his van fell on him.'

'So say some,' said Kurt, dragging away on his cigarette and idly kicking the tyres of my Volvo. 'And for a while I believed that too. Until I spoke to a neighbour who told me the last sign of life from the farm was a gunshot on Saturday, at around ten thirty. The neighbour was able to be so exact about it because he was listening to his radio and the sound disturbed the opening moments of that series about the kings of Norway, you know the one.'

'Sorry. Must've missed that.'

'So that got me wondering, what does a man shoot at ten thirty on a Saturday morning?'

'Deer?'

'That's what the neighbour thought too,' said Kurt. 'It's open season after all, and you often get deer grazing on the fields out there, especially in the morning. The neighbour was telling me he shot one from his kitchen window four years ago.'

'Mystery solved,' I said.

'Not quite,' said Kurt, and took another drag on his cigarette. 'There was thick fog on Saturday. Visibility across the fields was nil. And I know what you're going to say, the deer might have been closer to the house. But for someone to have seen the animal at that point in time it must have been at the most fifty metres away, and from that distance, you don't miss. And there is no dead deer.'

I shrugged. 'Maybe it wasn't a shot. Maybe the sound came from something else.'

Kurt shook his head. 'There was a Remington rifle hanging on the wall inside the barn. I checked it. That smell will still be there a week after the gun was fired, and there is no doubt about it. Fired recently, you can bet on it.'

Kurt's knees creaked as he bounced up and down on his toes,

looking like he was having the time of his life. 'So then you start to ask yourself, well, why did he shoot? Could it have been to defend himself, for example? Against something that threatened him?'

I looked at my watch. 'Can we speed things up a bit here, Kurt?'

He laughed. 'If you like. But shall we do it somewhere we can be completely sure we won't be disturbed?'

'Why?'

'You'll see.'

I nodded in the direction of the workshop.

'Fine,' said Kurt, and stamped out his cigarette.

I let us in and walked ahead into the workshop. Leaned my crutches against the wall next to the bicycle, pulled out one chair for him and sat down on the other. Kurt remained standing in front of the bicycle.

'Broke?' he asked, indicating with the toe of his boot where the chain had been.

'Had another use for it,' I said.

'Oh yeah, they make those shifting spanners out of them, don't they?'

'Exactly,' I said, and shuddered. Maybe because the murder weapon – or at least what was left of it – was still up in that tractor grab less than a metre above his head. Or maybe because it occurred to me that what he was really looking for – his father's body – had been dissolved up in that very same grab. Or was it because it was so cold and damp in the workshop?

'The devil or the deep blue sea,' said Kurt, still standing, looking around the workshop as though he wanted an overview before he sat down. 'Difficult choice, isn't it, Roy?' He sank into the chair, folded his arms and grinned.

'No,' I said. 'The devil.'

'Oh yeah?'

'Less certain than the other one.'

'Whatever,' said Kurt. 'In that case, this is the deep blue sea.'

He reached into his pocket, then held out his hand and opened it in front of me. I saw a tiny piece of metal in his palm. 'You recognise this?'

'Should I?'

'It's the bullet that was inside your leg.'

'Cripes,' I said, and shifted in my seat. 'How did you get hold of that?'

Kurt held the bloodstained bullet between thumb and forefinger and studied it. 'When the neighbour said he'd heard a shot, I remembered you saying you'd had a shooting accident at home. And I remembered a couple of other things too. Like that time you came charging in accusing Moe of abusing his daughter.'

I remembered as well. The place I'd come 'charging' into was Grete's solarium, and all I could see as I reported my suspicion was the cigarette smoke wafting out from between the panels of the sunbed. And how Kurt had dismissed the whole thing.

'Directly afterwards Moe was walking around with his face all beat up and you with a damaged hand. Think I can't put two and two together, Roy?'

I was tempted to answer his question but let it go.

'So I phoned Stanley earlier this morning,' he said. 'Explained that we're looking at this as a murder case with the possibility of a repeat offence, and how that put him under an obligation to share information with us. I asked him to look in his rubbish for the bullet, and *voilà*.'

I ignored the French and asked what he meant by the 'possibility of a repeat offence'.

'Don't you watch TV, Roy? There's always the "possibility of a repeat offence" when the offender is a serial killer like you.' Kurt closed his hand around the bullet. 'And you and I both know that if I send this bullet and Moe's rifle to KRIPOS, the ballistic analysis will show the one came from the other. Which puts you at the scene of the crime around the time of Moe's death. Which would explain one or two things.'

'Such as what?'

'Such as that I don't think all Moe's facial injuries are commensurable with that wheel drum. And that there are fresh scratch marks on the floor, as though someone has used a knife or a plane to shave away at the timber. You think you've been so smart, Roy, but actually it's not all that fucking difficult to reconstruct what happened. You've gone to confront Moe and attacked him, he's tried to defend himself with the rifle but only managed to shoot you in the foot before you beat him to death with something, obviously not with your bare fists since you're hands look OK. You've removed the blood from Moe and yourself by scraping it away, and you've arranged the crime scene to make it look like an accident. How am I doing? No need to reply, Roy, the question is . . . what did you call it? Rhetorical?'

Kurt opened his hand again.

'This bullet means twenty years in prison for you, Roy. That's the deep blue sea. And now for the devil.'

He looked at me. Until I did what he wanted and asked what that might be.

'I want you to confess that you killed my father. That you knocked him over the edge of Huken and then pushed an empty boat out onto the water, with his boots inside to make it look like my father was some poor suicide victim. OK?'

He looked at me as though making sure I understood what he was saying.

I cleared my throat. 'Sounds similar to me.'

'Yes, doesn't it? Faking accidents. That is your . . .' He looked for the word.

'Modus operandi,' I suggested.

He shook his head. 'Your *method*,' he said.

'OK,' I said. 'But what I'm saying is that your devil and your deep blue sea sound pretty much like the same thing to me.'

'No, no. In the first place, a mitigating circumstance is that you were only nineteen when you killed my father. In the second place there'll be a reduction in sentence for a murder that took place such a long time ago. You'll get five years at the most.'

'And you'll get . . . what do you get?'

The heat in Kurt's eyes faded. 'I clear my father's name.'

I nodded. 'So what you're suggesting is?'

'A deal. That you confess to the murder of my father and I throw this bullet into Budalsvannet.'

My head-nodding slowed until it was hardly moving at all. 'So,' I said, 'Natalie Moe never gets to know who killed her father, because it's more important for you to restore your family's honour and good name? Or something along those lines?'

I could almost feel the physical chill in Kurt's eyes now. 'You won't get a better offer, Roy. So what d'you say?'

I scratched my chin. After Natalie complained about how my five-day stubble scraped her skin I'd been shaving every day. Until Saturday. And now it was itching.

'I know you'd like to be an artist of the deal, Kurt. Like you were over that campsite. But you don't quite make it.'

'That so?' he said in a dead voice.

'The best way to get a deal done is to make sure the parties involved are all sitting in the same boat.'

'Well, we are,' he said. 'You get a reduced sentence, and I make things right for my father.'

'Now listen here, Kurt. Let us – completely hypothetically – say that you're right and I've committed those two murders. As soon as I've confessed to the murder of your father then you no longer have any reason to throw away that bullet and I'll get sentenced for two murders. Let's turn it around, start with you throwing away the bullet. You do that and I no longer have any need to confess, and you're left with two unresolved murder cases. What you need to do is create a balance of terror, a situation in which defeat for one party also means defeat for the other. But of course, all that does require a certain amount of brainpower . . .'

I saw it coming but did nothing about it. Kurt didn't take a swing at me, he threw himself at me. Grabbed hold of my arm and my wrist, twisted them until the pain had me on my knees and my head bowed to the ground as Kurt stood behind me and hissed in my ear:

'I don't take lessons from a fucking dyslexic peasant with a petrol pump in one hand and a murder weapon in the other, you hear me?'

'I hear you,' I groaned from the corner of my mouth that wasn't squashed up against the cold concrete floor.

'So what'll it be?'

'The devil.'

'Eh?'

'The devil! And hey, you're beating up a man who's got a sick note.'

He released me, and I got to my feet again.

'So you'd rather be tried for Moe's murder?' Kurt straightened his denim jacket as though it was a yacht club blazer.

'I'm not confessing to anything I haven't done,' I said.

'Suit yourself. You'll regret it, Roy. Because I will find proof that you killed my father too.'

'Then you'll have got everything you want,' I said as I brushed the dirt and dust from my cheek. 'And completely mal apropos, as they say, that line about the petrol pump in one hand and a murder weapon in the other, that was pretty impressive stuff. Elegant. There's no other word for it.'

He gave me a last if-looks-could-kill look, then turned. His steps echoed briefly and angrily around the workshop. He slammed the door behind him, and I slumped down into the chair.

Took out my phone and tapped in a text.

My condolences.

Deleted it. It was too cold, even for Roy the Terrible. Not that the follow-up text was any better:

Just heard about your father. Call if you want to talk.

But then what would I do? Confess I'd meant to hurt her father because I was so sure he'd raped her while she was in a helpless condition, and ended up killing him instead? Who would benefit from that? So then, just offer to be there for her if she needed me? And leave it up to her not to reply if she now hated everything and everyone connected with the name of Opgard.

I pressed Send.

32

MY BRAIN NEEDED A BREAK.

So I concentrated on practical things, such as the daily routines involved in running a petrol station. I spoke to my accountant in Notodden. I wrote, signed and sent off the papers concerning the tripartite ownership of Fritt Fall. From the framework loan I'd transferred fifty million kroner to Os Spa and with the recent shares emission I was now the company's largest single owner with my thirty-six per cent. Carl offered to call a general meeting so that I could be voted onto the board, but I said that wasn't necessary, I was only going to have the shares for six months and would anyway have to go along with the majority on the board which, without exception, followed Carl's lead in all matters great and small.

For the time being these distractions might have kept my

thoughts away from Natalie and the ticking bombs surrounding me, but they couldn't do anything about the pain in my leg. Despite large doses of painkillers I was unable to sleep. So I decided to try one of Carl's olive-green pills. And slept like a stone that night. Of course, I knew this type of self-medication was not something to be recommended and that I risked becoming addicted to the pills, but they were just too good.

After three days I decided anyway to drop them. I lay awake until four in the morning then went down to the kitchen and took one more, telling myself it was definitely the last. Next thing I remember I was lying in bed and Carl was shaking me.

'They're calling me from the station, wondering where you are,' he said in a voice so loud I understood he had been trying to wake me for some time. I picked my phone up from the bedside table. Six missed calls from Egil. And one from Vera.

'What did you tell him?' I asked as I balanced on one leg and pulled on my trousers.

'That you're off sick. But Egil said he hadn't heard anything about that.'

'Couldn't find anyone to step in at such short notice,' I said and put both feet down experimentally on the deck. 'Anyway, the leg's a lot better.'

It was raining, the even, leftover drizzle we get from clouds making their way back from Vestlandet. My head was still swimming as I got into the car, but I phoned Vera anyway.

'Well, fuck you too,' she said before I could even say hi.

'Hey! What's up?'

'You promised none of this would come back on me. And now I'm hearing that Ballistics are checking a bullet from your leg in connection with a possible murder investigation! Have you any idea how much trouble you could get me in if it comes out that I helped you?'

'Oh shit, that, yeah. When I said that to you I had no way of knowing Kurt would get so hung up on the fact that I'd had a shooting accident at home with our rifle.'

'What shooting accident?'

'I was cleaning the gun and tried the trigger, forgot I had a bullet in the chamber.'

'And you shot yourself in the *leg*?'

In the tense silence that followed I tried to hear if she was buying the story or not. Finally she gave a little cough. 'I got an answer from the lab.'

'Good! Did they find anything?'

'No alcohol, but traces of flunitrazepam. Better known as Rohypnol, the date rape drug. I don't know if you're familiar with it?'

My head was still swimming. 'Sure,' I said. 'But I thought only addicts used it?'

'Well, it's a long time since you could buy it at the chemist's. Rohypnol's become a street drug, like amphetamine and heroin. You're sure she's not an addict?'

'You're sure it's a *she*?'

'There's not much a blood test like that doesn't tell you.'

'I thought you requested a simple screening test?'

'Sometimes you get more than you ask for, Roy.'

'What d'you mean?'

'I heard from Gilliani that you'd booked a trip to Poland along with a lady friend, and the funny thing is, it actually hurt a bit. You and me never went anywhere.'

'Does it hurt any less if I say that it wasn't my idea?'

'A bit. Is it her blood? And you want to know if she's a user?'

'Last time you said you didn't want to know the reason for the test, that way your hands were clean.'

'Yes. True. I didn't. So this conversation is now over.'

'OK. Thanks, Vera. I owe you.'

'Love you?'

'*Owe* you.'

'No you don't.'

'Yes I do.'

'OK then.'

We laughed and hung up.

I called the hotel. Got hold of the same woman I'd spoken to about the laundry and asked her about their routines involving the minibars.

Five minutes later I was in the shop, thanked Egil for staying at his post, told him I'd overslept three hours and he could have all Sunday off on full pay. He grinned happily as I pulled out the phone that was vibrating against my thigh. Read the name on the screen. Felt my body going cold and warm. Pressed Accept.

'Hi,' I said as I made my way into the back room.

'Hi,' said Natalie. 'The funeral is today.'

'I know.'

'Can you come with me?'

The priest said a few words of welcome, as holy as the spirit of the times would allow. I'd managed a trip home and changed into a black suit. I hadn't had time to iron my shirt but didn't look too out of place sitting there on the second row. Even though that's exactly what I was, attending the funeral of a man I'd sent here. Natalie had met me outside the church and we had agreed that I wouldn't sit with her and the other members of her small family on the first row but directly behind her. As the priest intoned the first prayer I used the time to look around. It probably wouldn't be accurate to say that everyone was there. There had been more at Willumsen's funeral, for example. And at the old sheriff's too, though there hadn't been anything to bury there. But there were more than at Mum and Dad's, and far more than for the memorial ceremony for Shannon who had, of course, been, a recent newcomer. Sure, I was perhaps out of place, but in a way it was a tradition. Apart from the Danish hit man's I'd been at the funerals of everyone Carl and I had put under ground. The old mayor, Jo Aas, was here. So were Grete Smitt and Kurt Olsen. Julie and Rita too.

The priest was saying that the deceased's brother wanted to say a few words. A thin man on the front row got up, and stood behind the lectern. His memorial words were short and unsentimental, read from a sheet of paper he held that was shaking so much the microphone picked up the sounds. The essence of it was that Anton Moe had been an honest, hard-working man who went about things quietly and whose only aim in life had been to look after his family and contribute to the welfare of his community. And he had apparently been funnier than many people realised. He gave an example of the time he'd pinched a cheese sandwich from Anton's packed lunch. Anton hit him on the back of the head with a soft carpet beater, and said that if he'd have taken the ham sandwich then he'd have hit him with a log. The gathering laughed politely. I don't know why that clumsily delivered anecdote should have touched me. Perhaps because it was from one brother to another. Perhaps because it bore witness to a love, a tenderness for a brother that I could recall myself from another day, another time. When he was my kid brother, the one you're told to look after, but who you couldn't protect from your dad. The person I had loved so much and – so I thought – so unconditionally, right up until the day when I realised something – that there are always conditions.

The first time I realised it was when I discovered he regularly beat Shannon up.

The second was the time he stole my share of the land with a forged signature. It was after that I went from being a killer with Carl to planning Carl's death. But, as they say, man proposes, God laughs. The day we were to put our plan into action, Carl confronted Shannon, saying he couldn't possibly be the father of the child she was carrying. They quarrelled, and he killed her with an iron.

Then something happened that I still don't really understand. As always when there was a crisis, Carl turned to his big brother for help, not knowing that Shannon and I were involved. And why I didn't turn him down is something I will never, ever understand. I mean, it's unnatural, isn't it? Or maybe it isn't. Maybe it's that same old blood thicker than water thing. At least when everything else fails. Sticking together, no matter what, is perhaps the family's great blessing, but it's also its greatest curse. Anyway, I helped Carl in the way that had become my speciality – by making the murders look like accidents or suicides. Had I ever regretted coming to his rescue? That's like asking if you regret hitting back the first time you got punched on the nose. There was no choice involved, it was all pre-programmed. Because even when I sabotaged the brakes in my father's car, it was out of loyalty. Loyalty to a kid brother who begged me to stop Dad, and loyalty to Dad who was also begging me to stop him that time when he leaned the shotgun up against the barn wall for me to shoot him. Could things be different this time round? Could I put anyone else before myself, and my family?

There was a rustle of clothing and I realised the priest was back with his Bible so I stood up too. Not long after that the bells began to chime and the coffin was carried out in the rain.

'Thanks for coming,' said Natalie, who had joined me on the way out of the cemetery after the burial was over.

'It was the least I could do,' I said, switching hands so that the umbrella now sheltered her too. 'How are you?'

She folded her arms and even though she was wearing a coat she shivered. 'Not too good. I'm off sick.'

'That's no wonder, when you've just lost your—'

'Not because of him. Because of what happened at the staff party.'

'Really?' I saw Kurt and Rita getting into his Land Rover and driving off. 'You were very clear about it, that you won't say anything about what happened, and that's OK. But of course I still do wonder.'

'Me too,' she said.

'You too?'

'I remember nothing, Roy. Or *almost* nothing.'

'Yes, well, that's what Rohypnol does to you, isn't it?'

'What?'

'There was flunitrazepam in your blood.'

She stopped and stared at me. 'How do you—'

She was interrupted by a couple of people offering their condolences. I carried on towards the car park. And then she was at my side again.

'I wondered if it was that,' she said.

'You did?'

'We sometimes scored it in Notodden, so I recognised the after-effects. Like the way you can't remember a thing. But I didn't take anything to the party with me, so I must have got it from someone there.'

'Or someone slipped it into your glass of water.'

She smiled. 'This isn't Oslo, Roy. No one spikes drinks in Os.'

'Well, someone did.'

'Who was it?'

I held open the passenger door of my car and she got in. I sat behind the wheel. Water ran like tears down the windscreen as the last of the mourners got into their cars and drove off.

'Who was it?' she asked again.

'Carl,' I said.

She looked at me in disbelief.

'You had sex,' I said. 'Do you remember that?'

She shook her head slowly, not taking her eyes off me.

'Guess that's why they call them Forget Me pills,' I said.

'But I knew I'd had sex with someone at the party,' she said. 'When I woke up I had blood and sperm stains in my knickers. Sorry about the details.'

'I'm sure you did, because you bled onto the sheets in the Bridal Suite too. That's where I found the blood and had it analysed.'

'But how do you know it was Carl?'

'He told me.'

'He *told* you?'

'Minus the detail about spiking your drink. He lied and said you were both drunk before you ended up in the Bridal Suite.'

'How do you know that isn't what happened? I could have

taken dope without him noticing the difference between whether I was high or drunk.'

'Could be. But he was lying anyway when he said you emptied the minibar in the suite. Thinking that would explain why he had to help you into the taxi afterwards. But there was no trace of alcohol in your blood.'

'I could have started drinking from the minibar after we had sex.'

'No. I checked with the hotel. The minibar in the Bridal Suite wasn't refilled on Saturday or Sunday. Because it hadn't been touched.'

Natalie blew out air that condensed on the windscreen.

'OK, so he lied about my drinking,' she said. 'Doesn't mean he lied about the rest of it. Where would he have got hold of Rohypnol?'

I put my hand into my pocket and held one of those olive-green pills up in front of her.

'You've got Rohypnol?' she said.

'Not mine, it's Carl's. He got hold of it eight years ago. For his anxiety attacks, to help him sleep.'

'He didn't get that from any doctor,' said Natalie. 'They stopped prescribing it ages ago. They would have given him some-thing else.'

'True, but he didn't want to go to a doctor.'

'Why not?'

I looked at her. What should I answer? That a man who has just killed his wife wants to avoid arousing any suspicion by tell-ing his doctor he's having anxiety attacks and can't sleep? That instead he buys what he needs from some pusher in Oslo?

'Forget it,' she said. 'It was him. It was Carl. I realise that now.'

'Now? I think you knew it was him even when you were speaking to me the morning after.'

She didn't reply.

'Isn't that the truth?'

She blinked quickly, as though I'd clapped my hands in front of her face.

'I remember him being a bit tipsy and flirting with me at the bar,' she said. 'And I thought it was weird.'

'Because he's your boss?'

She rolled her eyes. 'Because he's your *brother*, idiot.'

'Was that why you decided not to see me again? You thought you'd taken dope and had sex with my brother of your own free will?'

'I don't know what sort of idea you have of me, but it wouldn't be the first time something like that happened. Minus that bit about it being someone's brother. And it would have been the first time I've been with someone else when I was already in a relationship.'

'Yes, because that's what we had?' I said, glancing over at her. 'A relationship?'

'Don't you think so?'

'I don't know the codes, but for me that's what it was, yes.'

'Good. Because it was for me too.'

We looked at each other. For a long time. I knew that if I'd tried to kiss her then, she would have stopped me. In the first place, because her father had just been buried, and we could see his grave from where we were sitting. And in the second place, it was less than a week since she'd had my brother inside her. And in

319

the third place because there was far too much information that had to be processed first.

'What do you suggest I do now?' she asked.

'What do you think?'

'That either I report your brother to the police or I find a job somewhere else, some place where I know I won't ever have to see him again.'

'OK.'

She groaned. 'What d'you mean, OK?'

'I mean, you decide.'

'Jesus, Roy, you're the one telling me all this, you're the one with all the information.'

'And now you have it too.' I took a couple of deep breaths. 'Are you going to let a rapist drive you out of your home town, and stop you having the life you want?'

She looked thoughtful. The rain was heavier now. 'If I report it, will you help me?'

I squeezed the steering wheel hard. 'I'd like to, Natalie. But if you report it to Kurt Olsen then the best help I can probably give you is to stay out of it.'

'I get it,' she said quickly. 'He's after you. OK.'

'You've got the information I've just given you. Act like you found it all out yourself and get him to double-check it. The blood, the pills, the minibar, all of it.'

She nodded. Reached for the door handle, stopped.

'Why?' she said.

'Why what?'

'Why throw your own brother under the bus? After all, he's . . .'

'The only family I've got left? Well . . .'

'Well?'

'Some family trees spread sickness. They should've been cut down a long time ago.'

She gave me a look that was more like a shudder. Then got out of the car and walked off into the rain. My words hung in the car like an echo. I shuddered too.

33

THE FIRST DRAWINGS FROM GLEN Moore and Rocky Mountain Constructions arrived. They were actually just technical specifications drawn over Shannon's originals, but they were so beautiful and exciting I could hardly tear myself away from them. Moore wrote that the lady must have been a gifted mathematician because the stuff here wasn't the physics they were taught at architectural college, but it all added up. He also sent a timetable, a payment plan and a draft contract based on a job RMC had done in Poland. At first glance it all looked OK, but I had an arrangement with the legal firm the hotel used to vet anything to do with contracts. There weren't any potential deal breakers, but I saw we would need to go over some of the conditions here, and also a couple of things we would hope to add.

The debate over the major road had moved on from the Todde tunnel and was now focused on other options. But all of them – the likely as well as the less likely – contained plans to keep or upgrade the section of road that passed through Os.

Natalie phoned and invited me to dinner.

'You sure?' I asked.

'No,' she said. 'But it's a start.'

'I was thinking about the dinner. You said yourself you aren't much of a cook.'

'I'll make something simple.'

'Or I could come and help you.'

'Is that your way of saying you'd prefer to make something complicated?'

After we hung up I asked myself the same question, because that was what it looked like. I showered, got dressed and groomed myself as though it was our first date.

'You're not using your crutches,' she said as she opened the door.

'Didn't feel they were quite me,' I said.

It was of course overly generous of her to reward this with laughter, but I loved it anyway.

'No thanks,' she said when she saw the bottle of wine I had brought.

'It's alcohol-free,' I said.

She wrinkled her nose. 'Nasty, isn't it?'

'Probably. But I've been thinking about including it in what we're offering at the station. You know . . .'

'Desperate cabin owners on their way up who didn't make the off-licence?'

'Precisely.'

She returned to the exchange as we were eating her surprisingly good lasagne and drinking the wine that really was nasty.

'You're the only person in Os who uses that word. *Precisely.*'

'Me and Carl,' I said. 'We got it off Mum. She worked as a housekeeper in the city before moving here.'

'So is that why Carl talks like a city boy?'

'That began when he was a student in Minneapolis. He said it was to make it easier for the other Norwegian students there to understand him. Most of them were from the West End, you know, Oslo, Bærum. And because that kind of standardised Norwegian was easier for Shannon when she started learning the language.'

'Bullshit.'

'Well put, native.'

She smiled. 'I don't mean I'm an exception, but why is it we're never content simply to be what we *are.*'

'Hm. Is that a question?'

'It is if you have an answer, yes.'

'Then let me try. We're not content because we always believe we're lacking something. So we're always trying to imitate people that seem complete to us, who appear to be complete in themselves. We try to dress like them, talk, eat like them, want the same things as them, look for the same things they look for.'

'Like role models,' she said. 'Mimetic lust.'

'Wow.' I raised my glass. 'You've read René Girard.'

'No, but we had a lecturer in marketing who was very interested in his ideas. Wanting the same things as those we look up to have, our role models – d'you think that's why?'

I thought I knew what she was referring to but asked anyway what she meant.

'Carl,' she said. 'Did he want me because I was yours?'

I thought about Shannon. 'I don't think it's that simple,' I said.

'Why not? You're the big brother. The role model.'

'It was more like the other way round.'

'Other way round?'

'Maybe I was older, but he was the one who had what I wanted. He was better than me at school. Charming, smart, well liked, could get anybody he wanted. *Had* anybody he wanted.'

'And you wanted what he had?'

I shrugged.

'Still do?' she asked.

I took a swig of that disgusting wine. 'Over time perhaps you become more whole, more content with who you are and what you have. So no, I don't want what he has.'

'No? You don't want his hotel? That new house of his, the Palace? You don't want to be the king of Os?'

'Do you?'

'No!' She laughed. Then, as though recalling what we were talking about, she became serious again. Looked down and dug a fork into her food. 'So if it's the case that your brother is used to getting anyone he wants, why chase after a woman he knows his brother is involved with?'

'Because he's drunk and you're the most attractive girl at the party.'

'So a guy who can get anybody he wants has to put dope in my glass of water so he can get his end away?'

I sighed and looked out of the window. Darkness had begun to fall noticeably earlier. 'I don't know, Natalie. Maybe he doesn't even know himself. Perhaps it's some form of kleptomania.'

'I think you're going to have to explain that.'

'Maybe it's a sort of compulsive disorder. The way some people get addicted to gambling, Carl goes in search of excitement by doing something he knows might mean not just prison but full social ostracism.'

Natalie definitely did not look convinced.

'Well, all right then,' I said. 'But speaking of prison, have you . . . ?'

She nodded. 'I haven't heard yet.'

'You talked to Kurt Olsen?'

'Yes. He suggested I wait before making the complaint until he's made a few inquiries. It would be for my own good, he said.'

'Oh yeah?'

She shrugged. 'He said he wanted to check that what I gave him was enough. Because a complaint that didn't lead to anything could put me in a bad light. I can understand that. People think women want to save their good names by claiming they were raped, or get their own back on a man who doesn't want anything more to do with them. Can we talk about something else?'

'Sure,' I said.

She pushed her chair a little way back from the table, so that I could see all of her. Turned on that look of hers. I pushed back a little way myself. Crossed my arms.

'How was the lasagne?' she asked and blinked lazily.

'As I said, it was . . . very good.'

'You've only praised it twice.'

'Three times now,' I said slowly.

'Doesn't count because I had to ask you.'

'OK, so how many times do I have to compliment it?'

'Four for the main course, two for the dessert.'

'So there will be a dessert?'

'Yes,' she said and stood up. Unbuttoned her dress and let it fall to the floor and then swayed her way across the floor.

'You forgot to put on your underwear,' I called out after her.

'Oops,' she said, then crept up onto the sofa on all fours, with her bum towards me. Turned her head and gave me that veiled look.

'Very . . .' I said, and had to moisten my mouth, '. . . good dessert.'

I left Natalie's sometime after midnight since I didn't have to go to work in the morning. Carl was sitting in the winter garden with a beer. I told him from the kitchen that I was going up to bed, but he called out to me.

'What is it?' I said, standing in the doorway.

'Kurt came by the hotel,' he said, not moving his gaze from the view. 'That fucking bitch is considering filing against me.'

'Bitch?'

'Natalie Moe. Claims I drugged her with that rape-date drug. As though I would have that.'

'No? Wasn't that what you scored that time in Oslo, for the anxiety attacks and sleeplessness?'

'Was *that* Rohypnol? Maybe, but there's no way that would work now.'

'Not sure that's right. I read somewhere that most pills still work years after the use-by dates on the packet.'

'So?' He looked at me. There was something alien in the look, it reminded me of the look he could give Dad over the breakfast table, injured but at the same time hard.

'Maybe stupid of me then,' he said. 'That I didn't chuck them out long ago.'

327

I just nodded and knew that if I looked in that drawer the bag of pills would be gone. I just hoped he hadn't noticed that there fewer of them now.

'What did Kurt say?' I asked. 'Are you in trouble?'

Carl shrugged. 'Kurt's after me of course, especially since he can't get anything on you. But he admitted that the fact that she sent in a blood sample containing Rohypnol proves nothing, only that she's taken the stuff at some point or other. Which isn't exactly news, she actually has a record for possession.'

'Has she?'

'So you didn't know that? Just be glad it's all over between you and that lady, Roy. No, I'm not in trouble, she won't get anywhere with her complaint.'

'Did you tell Kurt you had sex with her that night?'

'Are you crazy?' Carl gave a mirthless laugh. 'Not that fucking her would be a crime, but I'm hardly going to complicate matters by admitting that. I said she was hammered, and I helped her to lie down in the Bridal Suite, and that was that. The rest is he-said-she-said stuff. Although actually it isn't even that, because she admits she can't remember a single bloody thing about what happened.'

'Then I guess everything should be all right then,' I said.

Carl took a drink from the bottle. 'If the police ask you if I told you anything about what happened, you won't say anything, will you?'

I put my head on one side. 'What do you think, junior?'

Carl gave a quick smile. 'No, but, I mean, we've got so much on each other. That would be, like, total nuclear war, right?'

I didn't answer. He turned round until he could see me. 'You're looking very smart. Where've you been?'

'Dined out,' I said.

'Who with?'

I thought about it. The seconds ticked by.

'Someone who's thinking about buying the petrol station,' I said.

'What? You're thinking of selling?'

'No,' I said with a yawn. 'But I was interested in hearing the offer. It's always interesting to know the *real* value of things, don't you think?'

Carl looked a bit surprised, sitting there in his chair.

'Goodnight,' I said, turned and left.

34

ERIK AND I LOOKED AT the poster I was in the act of pinning up on the wall just inside the entrance to Fritt Fall.

'I just feel I've seen that picture somewhere before.'

'That's because you have,' I said.

'But Hell Spelemannslag? Can't exactly say the name rings any bells.'

'They're good. That's enough for me.'

'They said yes to five thousand plus the door,' said Erik. '*That's* enough for me.'

'We'll see, maybe more'll turn up than you think.'

'If they do it'll be a bonus. I see it as an expense for marketing Fritt Fall as the happening place in Os.'

'In competition with . . . ?'

'We-ell. The meeting hall. Grete's haircuts and solarium. Your petrol station.'

Erik went in and I knocked in the last pins. Turned and was about to go in when I saw Natalie crossing the square from the Meierigård. I waited and watched her. Her hair was up in a top-knot and she was walking with her arms folded over a thick grey pullover in the grey, flat morning light. She was wearing a pair of narrow, faded jeans and swayed her hips as she walked. That wide, almost greedy mouth with the soft lips which I had kissed and could not wait to kiss again. That little shiver of well-being that ran through her body as we lay naked and close, and later, that greater surge just after she matter-of-factly, but almost in exasperation, whispered in my ear: 'I'm coming.' And afterwards, the way she snuggled herself catlike into me, as though now it was her turn to get inside me and make us one. But now I saw there was something uneven about her walk, like that first time we walked in the mountains together, and as she got closer I saw that her eyes were red-rimmed. She stopped some distance away from me.

'What is it?' I asked.

'Kurt Olsen rang.'

'And?'

'He says I don't have enough to make a formal complaint.'

'But that's nonsense!'

'He says he's spoken to Carl and his version is that he just helped me to find somewhere to lie down until I felt better. Kurt says it's just my word against his, and not even that, since I can't remember a single bloody thing about what happened.'

'A single bloody thing? Were those his actual words?'

'Yes.'

I shook my head and stepped towards her to give her a hug, then stopped as she held up her hand.

'What is it?'

'Kurt told me something else too.'

'Yeah?'

'He said he doesn't believe my father's death was an accident.'

'No?'

'He thinks he was beaten to death. By someone who he injured first in self-defence.' She stared at me with those red-rimmed eyes, her arms crossed so tight around her it looked like she was wearing a straitjacket. 'He says he'll have the proof very soon.'

I swallowed and nodded.

'I'd rather hear the truth from you than from Kurt Olsen, Roy. Did you kill my father?'

Of course, I should have been prepared for the question, but I wasn't. I drew a breath to activate my vocal cords, to make a sound, with no idea of what that sound would be. Because I didn't know whether I could still go on lying, whether I could face it. To others, yes, but not to her. Not to the girl who had just crossed the square and got me thinking that dammit all, that girl there has done something I didn't think was possible, and that is to make me fall in love again.

The air finally came up out of my lungs, but no sound.

Tears welled up in her eyes. 'I understand,' she whispered. 'My father said he was afraid of you. I said he had no reason to be, all that was in the past now. But now I realise he was right.'

'Natalie ...' I took another step towards her, but she backed away.

'I never want to see you again. Ever.' She turned and hurried back the way she had come. I saw her shoulders begin to shake. Then she started to run. Not until the door to the Meierigård closed behind her did I shut my eyes and whisper all the curses that came to me then.

The board meeting of Os Spa AS was held in the afternoon in the large conference room at the hotel. I'd never sat on a board before, but things went pretty much as I had imagined they would. Board members should really be voted in at a general meeting, but as chairman Jo Aas told the board that since Alpin's board member had resigned before his period of service was over, and their head office in Paris wasn't insisting on representation, the board were empowered to vote me in for the remainder of the service period.

I sat at the end of the table and listened as the others went through the agenda. Carl and Aas did most of the talking, the others nodded and seemed able to follow. The mood was good and there were no critical questions. Since I had to be voted in before I'd had a chance to read the internal accounts all I saw was the cumulative figures for the operating accounts and the balance presented at the meeting, and they all looked reasonable enough, so I thought that was why nobody was making any fuss. But it was clear that some of the items deserved a more thorough account than Carl had offered. I noted that the expenses for maintenance had risen sharply over the preceding year, not that I could remember seeing a lot of workmen around the hotel. And when I asked a few simple questions about the valuation of certain fixed assets, if the right depreciation rate lay behind it and so on, Carl looked more annoyed than helpful. 'That's for the accountant and bookkeeper to decide at the annual accounting, not now,' he said. As though it wasn't him who decided what the figures looked like on paper. And maybe it wasn't either. At least no one sitting round the table seemed to suspect anything fishy.

Jo Aas took me to one side on our way out to the car park.

'I just wanted to thank you for stepping up, Roy.'

I watched that tall, rangy man walk towards his car, an Opel he seemed to have had forever and which – to the best of my knowledge – never seemed to give him any trouble at all. Hidden faults and missing parts, we've all got those, but Aas and that car of his, they stood for something, there was a dependability there, something you could rely on. So what did he mean about *stepping up*? Stepping up – wasn't that something you did when things looked to be heading the wrong way? All I had done was provide capital to fund an expansion, hadn't I?

I sat in the Volvo, waited, and started as Carl slipped into the passenger seat.

'What did Aas want?' he asked.

'Said he was glad to have me along,' I said as I reversed out using the mirror, even though everything was shown on the video screen. We drove in silence as local radio reported on the road situation.

'By the way, did I tell you, I had a chat with Goebbel about Natalie?' said Carl.

'No.'

'She says I've got nothing to fear from the law, but if Natalie makes a complaint and it leads to other employees coming forward, that could be worse for me.'

'Is there any danger of that?'

'Others?' Carl shook his head. 'When I was working in Canada there was a couple of young girls, fresh on the job, you could probably say I had some kind of authority over them. But of course, we never thought about things like that back then. Which reminds me – I heard an interesting story about a case at a hotel in Bergen a couple of years ago. Two of the bosses had fallen for the same lady, a young receptionist, and were courting her. You know, invitations, flowers, flirtatious texts, all this. One of them hit the jackpot, married her and now he's running the hotel. The other was fired for sexual harassment and shot himself not long afterwards. Turned out later the text messages that got him fired were pretty much the same as the ones from the guy she later decided she liked and married.'

We were passing the Nergard place and I changed down for the climb up the hill.

'And the moral is?'

'That it pays to be the attractive one,' said Carl. 'And to know your audience.'

'It isn't quite that simple. Harassment is about context, not just the gist of a text message, or whereabouts on her body the boss touched the employee.'

'Not that simple, no,' said Carl. 'But for the guy who lost his job and his good name and was left there with a gun in his hand, I guess it was.'

That evening I went out for a drive alone. It's always calmed my nerves to feel a steering wheel between my hands, see the road making familiar turns, listening to the sound of the engine and knowing it's in good shape, listening to and hearing that JJ Cale isn't in such good shape, but in a way that was OK. On that evening, though, the nerves just wouldn't be calmed. I forced myself to stop thinking about Natalie, and instead my thoughts moved on to the man with the gun.

And Carl. Maybe that was why I suddenly found myself outside Kongsgården, the Palace Carl was having built. I'd been up here with him when he was looking at sites and I've no good explanation for why I hadn't been back since. I'd been invited, of course, but always managed to find some excuse, something or other that came up, and there was no hurry. After all, as I told him, the house wasn't going anywhere.

I parked behind a cement mixer and climbed out. By the light of my mobile phone I picked my way between unopened piles of planks and bricks. The main door was locked, but I walked around to the side of the house facing towards Os and found a basement window that was slightly open and crawled in. It smelled of cement dust and Rockwool. I passed through the half-finished rooms, one by one. There were many of them, so many the house seemed big even for a family of four. Finally I arrived on the top floor, where a single, glowing light bulb hung from the ceiling which was at least six or seven metres over my head at its highest. The light didn't penetrate to the walls, I barely caught the outlines of the mezzanines and had to use my phone to get a full picture of the room. I presumed it would be a living room, dining room and – judging by the plug points – a kitchen that was on its way from Germany. Scattered around the room were various tools, nail guns, saws, planers and a bench with circular saw, all carrying the same AUB logo I'd seen in the new wing of the hotel. The side of the room facing Os was glass, from floor to ceiling, with a large terrace in front. I stood by the bench and looked out.

It was a fantastic house. Cold, impersonal and fantastic. Or personal maybe for a cold person. But still absolutely fantastic. As I stood there it struck me that Carl must have thought that not only did the house have a perfect view of Os, it gave Os a perfect view of his Palace. There was no practical reason for the house to be so tall, that was just so people down below could look up and see Carl Opgard towering up to the sky at the limits of their vision. Proof-positive of who the real king of Os was.

For some reason I suddenly thought of that text on the embroidery at Moe's house. *For what is a man profited, if he shall gain the whole world, and lose his own soul?* Perhaps it wasn't a question that had exercised Carl to any noticeable degree but, of the two of us, he'd always been the toughest. Yes, it was me and not him that used the knife that put an end to Dog's sufferings. But that was a necessary killing, even a mercy killing. When it came to doing what had to be done to win world domination then Carl was the man, the tough one.

Lose his own soul.

Was that what I had understood when I could neither lie nor tell the truth to Natalie? That it was an impossible choice? That the truth would mean losing her instantly, and a lie the same, only more slowly and painfully? In that sense it would be almost a liberation when the next phase of this sombre mood arrived, where absolutely everything felt meaningless and worthless, for it would mean that not even losing the one you loved mattered all that much. And that phase was on its way. I could feel it.

I looked up at the flex holding the light bulb. Seemed like it was securely fastened to the ceiling.

The phone rang.

I considered not taking it. The screen told me it was Vera.

'Yes?'

'Hi. Are you alone?'

'Yes, I think so.'

She hesitated, sounded like she was considering asking me to expand on that answer, then continued:

'The result of the ballistic analysis is in.'

'And?'

'They can't connect the bullet from your leg to the rifle that was hanging in Moe's barn.'

'Can't?'

'There's always a possibility that is where the bullet came from. But I talked to Gilliani who agrees that it looks like what we have here is a sheriff who's pursuing some kind of personal vendetta. So he's going to present it to Kurt Olsen in such a way that . . . well, that he won't have any reason to get hung up on the fact that there is a theoretical possibility we are mistaken.'

I saw a light far out on the waters of Budalsvannet.

'Thanks, Vera.'

'I'm just relieved you told me the truth. Sorry for doubting you.'

'No apology necessary.'

'You sound a bit . . . sad?'

'Do I? Guess it must be the time of year. The dark season. We look forward to the spring, to mating time, you and me. Thanks again. I love you.'

'Hey! Now you said—'

'You hear what you want to hear, Vera. There's a word for it.'

'Aw shut up.'

We hung up, and I took a last look around me and then left the Palace the same way I had come in.

35

'YES, I DO SPEAK ENGLISH.' The man on the other end of the line sounded almost offended.

'I'm sorry, Mr Gerard,' I said. 'I wasn't sure since . . .' I left it at that.

'Since I'm French?' he asked in a challenging voice.

I searched my brain half-heartedly for some diplomatic response before realising I didn't actually care that much. 'Yes.'

The man at the other end laughed. 'I'm as busy as I'm sure you are, Mr Opgard. So, how may you help me?'

I doubted it was a linguistic slip, or some kind of joke.

I told him that for the time being I owned thirty-six per cent of the shares in Os Spa, that I'd taken over the seat on the board after Alpin had vacated it and explained why I was calling. Gerard listened. When I had finished he suggested I take a trip to Paris. He asked me what my calendar was looking like.

'If I had one, it would be empty.'

Gerard laughed again and suggested a date and time.

We hung up. It was my second international call of the day. The first had been to Vilnius, where I had to wait a quarter of an hour before the receptionist at AUB put me through to Lewi Wirkus. I got straight to the point and told him I'd been checking Os Spa's bookkeeping and found an invoice from AUB for three million kroner headed 'Preparatory work'. Could Wirkus tell me exactly what this involved? It turned out the wait had been wasted time.

'We don't give out information like that, but in general we specify our invoices the way our clients want them specified,' Lewi Wirkus answered. 'If you have more questions, talk to our client.' And with that he had hung up.

And I had called Paris.

That was stage two. A third remained. The toughest. I was so tired, but there was no other way to do it. But there was, of course, a way out of it, there always is. I left the petrol station, walked over to the slope, pushed in a plug of chewing tobacco and looked out over Budalsvannet and the fresh snow that capped Ottertind. There, under a cloudless sky with an autumn sun that was doing its best, the darkness descended. The real darkness. The intolerable darkness. Where the thought always lay wrapped. It was so long since it had moved. But now it not only moved, it rose up and took to its legs, came walking and stood there in front of me, blocking the sun.

I nodded to the invisible giant, as though we had come to an agreement. I let myself into the workshop, stood in front of the wall with the rack of tools. How to put an end to it? Imagination was the only limit. I walked into my little bedsit and looked at the registration plates. Or rather, looked at one of them, from Barbados, the one Shannon had given me. Then I pulled open a drawer, opened the red plush box lying in there. Ran my index finger over the narrow gold ring I had bought in Kristiansand. The plan had been to propose to her on the way, on the journey that would take us away from Os and all the way to Barbados. Could she and I and our child have made a life there, as we had hoped? Would things have been different, or would the darkness have caught up with me there too? I don't know. All I know is that the darkness had never been so dark before Shannon and our unborn baby died. So if anything could have brought them back to life then maybe I might have come back too, as the guy I once had been, before I killed my parents, before I turned into this cold, depressed bastard. Because I not only resembled my dad, I had actually *become* him.

I closed my eyes.

When I opened them again I pulled my phone out of my pocket and lay it on the windowsill. Let myself out again hurriedly and returned to the shop. Egil was busy cleaning the ovens, God bless the lad.

'Egil, can you hold the fort for the rest of the day?'

'No problem.'

'That boat of your uncle's up on Gudimvannet, think I could borrow it?'

'Sure. Can't guarantee it won't leak, mind you.'

'Think I'll go and do a little fishing.'

'Fishing?'

'I need time to think.'

Egil's face looked like one big question mark, as they say. Probably because the only thing he'd ever heard me say about fishing was that I didn't see the point of it.

I drove up to Opgard and considered my options. The rifle on the wall in the porch, or what was left of the tramadol and Rohypnol in the medicine drawer. For a number of reasons, the choice fell on the pills. In practical terms it meant I wouldn't have to carry the rifle with me, and Egil's uncle wouldn't have to wash his boat afterwards. There was also the thought that using the rifle would probably entail another round of ballistics that would cause all sorts of problems for those left behind. I weighed the tin of tramadol and the bag of Rohypnol in my hand. I'd read that six grams of tramadol was reckoned a deadly dose, and there was at least double that amount here.

I drove back down to the main road and headed east, passing the petrol station, and parked in the stand of trees where Rita Willumsen used to leave her Saab Sonett in the days when I was her young lover and we would meet at her cabin. I swallowed two tramadol and started walking. It was surprisingly quick and easy. My leg felt a lot better, which was a cause of some slight irritation, knowing that I would no longer be using it anyway. After twenty minutes' walking I had reached the hills. There was no wind at all, little Gudimvannet lay as smooth as a mirror reflecting the blue sky above, as though they were one and the same thing. I found Egil's uncle's green fibreglass boat, lying under the same tree as Willumsen's red boat, pushed it out and jumped in. Almost lost my balance, which was maybe the tramadol's fault. I fitted the oars into the locks and rowed out into the middle of the lake. Stared at the surface of the water, the way I had done eight years earlier, standing on a bridge and thinking on the same thing as now. The difference this time was that the thinking was over. And I had a stroke of luck, because in my jacket pocket I found that ready-written suicide note, so I wouldn't have to worry about the usual spelling mistakes.

I HAVE HAD ENOUGH OF THIS LIFE. GOODBYE. OPGARD.

Funny.

I unscrewed the lid of the tramadol and peered inside. I realised I had forgotten I would need water to swallow all of those pills. I looked around, found a baler, dipped over the gunwale into the water, emptied the tin down my throat then drank from the ladle. It felt like someone was pulling a chair down my craw, but down they went, all of them. Same thing with what was left of the Rohypnol in the bag. I lay down on the sun-warmed planks in the bottom of the boat and closed my eyes. Now that the die had been cast I welcomed the darkness of the mind and felt a quick jab of panic when it seemed as though my worst enemy was about to betray me. But then there he was. Large, dark and crushing. The best thing about pain is the knowledge that at some point it will stop.

Sleep and numbness must have come slowly, for each time I opened my eyes the sun had moved only slightly across the sky above. At least that's what I thought then. Maybe it was just the boat turning.

Everything went still inside me. Then it went black. In the good way.

I walked through a flat, desolate landscape strewn with wrecked cars. They must have rained down from the sky, I couldn't see any other way they could have got there. Some were concertinaed, some on their sides, others on their ends, some upside down with their roofs squashed flat. There were new cars and old cars, some rusting, others with dazzlingly bright paintwork. The tyres were missing from a few of them, as though grave robbers had been at work. High above me hovered birds that neither sang nor screeched. Suddenly I heard a droning sound behind me. I turned and saw a car standing upright in a cloud of dust, and I understood it had just fallen there. Then all went quiet again. I was looking for someone, and then realised I had forgotten who, and why. So I gave up, lay down on the hard, baked ground and closed my eyes. Something swishing through the air. I didn't move, just waited for the car to hit me. But the swishing changed, turned into a long, sad chime that rose and fell. I opened my eyes, and now I was lying in water. No, I was on a roller coaster, I was lying on the water in a carriage on a roller-coaster track. I pulled myself up to see where the noise was coming from. There was a girl standing on the bank, not far away. She was wearing peasant costume and strumming a *langeleik*. Now she lay down the instrument and started towards me. She walked across the water. Or no, the water was up to her knees. Then to her waist. But she kept on walking, as though she refused to sink, or else she had supernatural powers. I lay back down again, the warm sun so good on my face. Then something shadowed the sun, and it went cold.

'Roy.'

That was, in some way, my name, and someone was saying it.

'Roy.'

If I just ignored it, maybe the voice would disappear.

'Roy!'

The voice was addressing me, I understood that much. But I didn't want to go back to where it was, I wanted to stay here.

I was being moved backwards and forwards, someone was rocking the carriage.

I opened one eye. It was Natalie.

'Roy! What have you done?'

I tried to put together a sentence: *Smashed your father's head to pieces.* But my jaw wouldn't obey. Then the light went out.

36

THE LIGHT HAD COME ON again, so strong I could see it through my eyelids. I heard mumbling voices and raised one eyelid. Whiteness all around me; the walls, the curtains, the bed-clothes, the uniforms of two of the three women standing at the foot of the bed with their heads together. I closed my eye again. Picked up words like 'poison' and 'ingredients'; it reminded me of the three witches I'd learned about when Rita read to me, cooking a broth for Macbeth and prophesying that one day he'd be king.

Reluctantly I opened my eyes.

'He's awake,' said one of the white-clad witches.

'Roy?' said another. I was just about able to focus on her face, but I didn't recognise the woman. 'I am Dr Helgesen,' she said.

'Do you know where you are and what has happened over the past twenty-four hours?'

I was about to shake my head, then realised it would probably be less painful to just say no.

'I don't even know what day it is,' I said.

'You've been asleep for eighteen hours,' she said as she scanned the papers on her plastic clipboard. 'You've had your stomach pumped here at the hospital, and we've given you activated carbon.'

'How . . . did I end up here?'

'You were brought here by your girlfriend.'

'Girlfriend?'

The lady in white smiled in the direction of the third witch, the one not wearing white. 'That's what she says.'

I managed to get the third figure in focus. It was Natalie. She came towards me, took hold of something lying on the duvet which I did not realise was my own hand until I registered, after a short delay, the warmth from hers. The doctor continued her account, only parts of which I heard, for all my focus was on Natalie. Her eyes were glowing, her smile trembled.

'And now the two of you can have a few moments alone,' said Dr Helgesen.

I heard the door click shut without taking my eyes off Natalie or letting go of her hand. She sat down on the side of the bed.

'Girlfriend?' I asked.

'It was the most practical solution,' she said. 'Otherwise they would have been getting in touch with your nearest close relative, and since you've only got one and I don't want to have to deal with him . . .'

'OK,' I said. 'But how . . . ?'

'How what?'

'How everything. And why?'

'Well, you see,' she said, then looked ahead for a few moments, as though she needed the time to put her story together. 'I got a phone call yesterday from Kurt Olsen. He said they'd believed my father had shot someone in the leg in self-defence but it turns out the bullet in that person's leg didn't come from my father's shotgun after all. They now believe that the shot the neighbour heard was my father shooting at a deer, or a wolf.'

'Wolf?'

'Olsen said. Anyway, he said they'd abandoned the theory that my father was beaten to death, they think it was an accident. I was so happy, Roy. Because my father wasn't murdered, but mostly because you aren't a murderer.'

She swallowed and looked at me.

'Can you forgive me for believing what I did about you?'

'Of course,' I said. 'It's no wonder you believed it.'

'I should have known better. It's just that I had a feeling . . . that that was how it would end between you two. So I judged you. But you were innocent. After the conversation with Kurt Olsen I drove straight to the petrol station to ask you to forgive me. And ask if you would . . . yes, if you would have me back, even though I'd let you down. But you weren't there, Egil said you'd just left to go fishing. I tried to call you. Got no answer. Then I tried again. Still no answer. But I'd seen a light in one of the windows in the workshop. So I went over and saw your phone inside, on the windowsill. And that made me uneasy.'

'Because?'

'Because it looked so . . . abandoned. There's, like, no reason to leave a phone on a dirty windowsill like that. Especially no reason to forget it. And something like that is what I would have done, if I was going to . . .'

'Going to?'

'Disappear.'

I grunted something, squeezed her hand. 'And then?'

'Then I asked Egil where you'd gone, and he told me about the green boat. He found the place on Google Maps for me.'

'How did you reach the boat?'

'I sort of panicked and waded out.'

'So it *was* you. I thought I was hallucinating . . . Well, there was a little bit of that too. And then . . . ?'

'I got into the boat with you. An empty tin was rolling about in the bottom. I saw it was tramadol and worked the rest out for myself. So I took out my bottle of ipecac—'

'Aw Jesus. You mean that antidote you carry about with you?'

She smiled. 'I pretty near emptied it into you.'

'And I threw up?'

'Like Robert in *Bad Taste*.'

'And then?'

'Then I rowed ashore and got you down to the road.'

'Was I able to walk?'

'No.'

'You . . . ?'

'More or less, yes.'

'Aw Jesus.'

'Seriously, you need to work a bit on your vocabulary.'

I nodded. Could feel my eyes getting heavy-lidded again.

'A psychiatrist is coming to talk to you before they let you go home,' she said. 'What are you going to say to him?'

'About what?'

'About when you plan to make your next suicide attempt.'

I shook my head. Didn't hurt as much as I expected. 'There won't be any next attempt.'

She gave a brief smile. 'We all say that.'

'I mean it. You saved my life, and I don't want that to be wasted. Well, maybe my life is wasted, but I intend to go on living it.'

'Because?'

'Don't be afraid, Natalie, it wasn't because you broke up with me that I took those pills. None of this is on you, O K?'

'I didn't think that either. But in any case, I don't want a boyfriend who's suicidal.'

I watched her hand as it stroked mine. Took a deep breath.

'The only other time I've been close to doing something like that was eight years ago. I would say twice in forty-something years isn't all that often. If it's an average then that means I'll be seventy before I try it again, and by then I'll probably have died of something else anyway.'

She put her head on one side. 'You really think that's a good try at selling yourself as someone I should put my money on?'

'It's the best I can come up with right now, and I'm still so out of it I think you could cut me a bit of slack here.'

She nodded and got to her feet. 'I'm meeting Ola for lunch. I'll come back afterwards. Maybe they'll discharge you and we can drive home.'

I let go of her hand only when I had to. 'Boyfriend?' I asked. 'Am I?'

She smiled. 'Not yet.'

'OK. What's it going to take then?'

'A trip to Krakow.'

I thought about it. 'Think I can improve on that.'

'Improve on it?'

'How about Paris?'

37

'THAT'S OUR PRICE,' SAID GERARD.

'OK,' I said.

'OK?'

'Opgards don't haggle.'

The man whom Gerard had introduced as his financial adviser leaned over to his boss and whispered something in his ear. As he moved, the Eiffel Tower came into view behind him. Not that I know Paris, or doubted that Alpin's offices had an exclusive location, but I'd started to feel you could see that bloody thing no matter where you were in the city. We could see it from our hotel room, and Natalie had insisted we get properly dressed so we could open the doors onto the so-called balcony of our room for an even better view of the fabled tower.

'What's not to like about the Eiffel Tower?' she'd asked.

'Those lights on the top. They screw up the navigation for birds flying from Africa to Os. Stupid fucking thing.'

She'd laughed, and that was enough to make me happy.

'How come you know so much, Roy, you who've never been anywhere?'

'Reading.' That was my way of travelling.

'So tell me something you like about this city,' she demanded.

'OK,' I said. 'This.'

'This?'

'French balconies. They started here in Paris because people without a garden needed somewhere to grow flowers. In England they call them "Juliet balconies". Because it was under one like this that Romeo was standing when he declared his love for Juliet. I really like that.'

She was silent for a long time, then she said: 'Is there some kind of subtext here?'

'Absolutely not,' I said.

She gave me the slow Os nod. 'OK. So shall we take all our clothes off and fuck?'

'Definitely.'

For some reason her enthusiastic 'yes' reminded me of when Gerard had looked at me at our meeting the day before and said: 'It's all yours.'

'Good,' I had said.

And then we shook hands, and Gerard's legal adviser had pushed the papers for me to sign across the table.

I looked at the first page and raised an eyebrow.

'Sorry,' Gerard said quickly. 'There's an English copy there too, but it's French policy that all commerce in France is done in French. Actually, it's French policy to spread the French language wherever possible.'

'Why?' I asked as I read through the English version.

'Why? Pride, jealousy and world domination, of course. Are there any other reasons?'

Gerard accompanied me to the lift.

'Now that we've signed,' I said, 'can you tell me why you're selling?'

'Apart from the price you mean?'

'I don't believe it was about the price, Mr Gerard.'

'You are right, Mr Opgard. It was the accounts. We didn't like them. Or more precisely, we didn't like the accounting. I knew your brother when we were in Toronto. He's a smart man. Maybe a touch too smart.'

The lift door opened, I stepped in, turned and nodded to the Frenchman. His suit must have cost five times what I had paid for mine. I could see Gerard thinking he had outsmarted this country bumpkin. But what he couldn't know was that I had actually sold the occasional used car from my workshop in Os, and that the moment I'd entered that meeting room I'd picked up how keen the French were to sell, and that the price I had paid for a fifteen per cent share in Os Spa was about a third lower than what I would have been willing to pay. In the lift on the way down I thought about what Gerard had said about motivations. Pride, jealousy and world domination. I tried to come up with other reasons. Without success.

The following day Natalie and I hired a car and drove to Plailly, about thirty kilometres north of Paris, and visited the Parc

Astérix. The season was almost over, and we were well wrapped up, but there were a lot of people there considering it was such a cold day. The park was much smaller than Disneyland Paris, but it had seven roller-coaster rides and I planned to test them all out. I was especially curious about the Tonnerre Deux Zeus which – at least until it was rebuilt – was reckoned to be the best timber track in the world. Natalie wasn't quite so curious.

'Do I have to?' she asked as we stood looking up at the heart-shaped top of the track as the train of carriages came diving towards us, accompanied by a chorus of hysterical shrieks.

'You don't *have* to do anything,' I said. 'Only what you want to do.'

'With you I want to do almost anything,' she said, leaning into me.

'Oh yeah? Like marry me?'

She pulled on my arm. 'Don't joke about marriage!'

I laughed. 'Sorry, I just wondered.'

'No, you're checking in advance if you'd get a yes. Because you're planning to video it when you propose at the top of that wooden track and then put it on YouTube.'

'I am?'

'Hope so.'

'OK, so you've unmasked me.'

'Yeah, right!'

I sighed. 'If you want to know you'll have to come with me.'

'If you want to know you'll have to come with me,' she repeated slowly.

If the roller coaster at Os was no longer just a memorial to Shannon, my personal cathedral, then why not ask for a promise of marriage up there at the top, once the ride was built? After all, King Sigurd the Crusader got wed in the cathedral he'd built himself in Oslo. But the thought was dizzying enough, and as the train came whizzing down again of course I banished the whole thing from my mind.

We drove straight from the park to Charles de Gaulle airport. While we were waiting in the slightly shabby area reserved for Scandinavian departures, I phoned Jo Aas, informed him of the shareholding I had just bought and asked how quickly he could call an extraordinary general meeting in Os Spa. He said all shareholders with more than a ten per cent share were entitled to demand such a meeting and that it be held within one month. He asked what the hurry was.

Silence at the other end when I told him.

'Have you discussed this with Carl?' Aas said finally.

'No.'

'Are you sure this is what you want to do, Roy?'

'Do you have any objections?'

'It could ruin a lot of things for a lot of people.'

'In the short run maybe. But in the long run the company and the local community will emerge the stronger for it. You agree?'

'The danger here, Roy, is of a pebble in the road upending a great load. I think you and I should meet once you get back.'

'I asked if you agreed because I was curious, Jo, not because it would change my decision.' I could almost see the former king of Os opening his eyes wide in surprise to hear me not only disagree with him but address him by his first name. But he said nothing. Like the crafty, realpolitik dealer he was, he could sense a change coming in the weather.

'Suit yourself,' he said. 'There is, of course, another option.'

'And that is?'

'That we let the board handle the whole thing. Now I don't know exactly why you want Carl fired, but if the board is responsible for the dismissal then we can keep the reasons for it a little closer to our chests, so to speak. We'll have greater freedom in deciding how changes in the company leadership are communicated to the outside world.'

'What you're saying,' I said, 'is that we can wrap it up and make it less humiliating for Carl that he's being kicked out.'

'Well, isn't that what we want, after all?'

I saw the car with Shannon inside rolling towards Geitesvingen, saw Natalie lying unconscious on the four-poster in the Bridal Suite.

'Hello? Roy, you still there?'

'I'll have to go, we're boarding. Yes, let the board handle the whole thing.'

38

IT WAS JUST PAST MIDNIGHT when I arrived home.

Carl turned in the rocking chair and looked at me as I stood in the doorway of the winter garden.

'How was Paris?'

'Big. Take a walk with me?'

'Walk? Now? Where?'

It was something he'd inherited from Dad, I think. That there was no point in moving, in expending energy, unless you were doing something. Boxing with a punchbag was OK, it was training for something you would be doing one day. But to go for a walk, or a drive just for its own sake, that was something he didn't get at all.

Carl pulled on his wellingtons and his camel-hair coat.

I walked ahead through the heather, stepping out into the

moonlight, heard Carl already short of breath behind me. After fifteen minutes I stopped on a rise. From where I stood I could see the lights of the hotel illuminating the night some distance below us. I waited for Carl to join me.

'Remember this place?' I asked.

He nodded, panting to get his breath back. 'It was here that you, me and Shannon stood when I showed you where I wanted the hotel built.'

'Before that,' I said. He shook his head.

'You were going to prove to Dad that you weren't a cissy who couldn't kill things. So you took Dad's shotgun and Dog. You disturbed a pack of grouse when you were just a few metres from them, and when they flew up into the air you put the shotgun to your shoulder – isn't that what happened?'

'I was only doing it the way Dad taught us. I waited so long I could have shaken hands with them and then pulled the trigger.'

'Only you didn't manage to pull the trigger.'

Carl shrugged. 'I suppose I just thought they were living beings. They were together, they were a family.'

'So you lowered the gun and only then did you pull the trigger.'

'So the two of you would hear it. So Dad would see the grouse flying up.'

'But you hit Dog.'

'I hit Dog.'

'And you came running back to the house and fetched me. Just me. Because you didn't want Dad to know. All you wanted was for me to come and clear the mess up for you.'

Carl nodded.

'I killed Dog with the knife, I did the shit job for you,' I said.

'And afterwards we told Dad it was you, that you'd taken responsibility and done what had to be done after the mistake you'd made.'

Carl shifted his weight, I could see he was getting impatient. 'I already thanked you for that, Roy. So what is this? You want me to thank you again?'

'No,' I said. 'You don't owe me anything.'

'I have been in your debt. But when I built that hotel on our land, I made you a rich man too. Without that—'

'I wouldn't have been able to buy the petrol station,' I said.

'Or any of the other properties.'

'True.'

'It's late and it's cold, Roy. Shall we get to the point and go home?'

I nodded. 'I'm going to have to kill something for you again. Since you won't do it yourself.'

Carl just looked at me.

'I bought shares in Paris,' I said.

Carl lifted his chin. I recognised the gesture, it meant it was beginning to dawn on him.

'My shareholding in that hotel down there right now is 51 per cent. It means that on my own I can kill off, or at least dismiss, the CEO. And just like with Dog, you'll end up thanking me for doing it.'

We were already so pale in the moonlight it was impossible to see if Carl turned even paler. His first question was as expected.

'Why?'

'Because you told Lewi Wirkus to invoice Os Spa for the work AUB are doing on your house. You've persuaded them to call it "Preliminary—"'

'Not that,' Carl interrupted. 'I'm asking why you think I'll thank you.'

I took a deep breath. 'Sooner or later someone's going to ask questions about those invoices, Carl. If not someone on the board then someone at the general meeting. Or even worse, Dan Krane. Vendelbo got wind of it. Gerard got wind of it. But Gerard is a businessman and pragmatist. Faced with the choice of firing you or selling the shares before the scandal ran the whole thing aground he very naturally chose the latter option. And you can be glad he did. Because with me as the majority shareholder, and as of now the only person on the board who knows the unpleasant truth, we can play down your departure, tell people you need a break and are handing over the helm to me, but that we don't rule out your return at some future date.'

'*You* are going to be CEO?'

'And chairman of the board. I'll make sure the accountant corrects what is an obvious error in the invoicing from AUB and that they are resubmitted correctly – that is, to you personally. If I'm not mistaken you're going to have to sell something to cover the three million plus. The easiest thing would probably be to sell your shares in Os Spa, and if you do then I'll take them at a higher price than I paid for Gerard's shares. Let's say I give you a twenty per cent discount. At the very least I'm giving you the choice.'

Carl shook with soundless laughter. 'I do not fucking *believe* you, Roy.'

'No?'

'You steal my hotel and you've got the cheek to claim you're doing me a favour.'

'You mean you think I'm not?'

'And if I go to Vendelbo and tell him that fifty million of that

361

loan he's given for the roller coaster is being used for something else entirely, what d'you think is going to happen then?'

'I think Vendelbo will be delighted the money's being invested in something less risky. An Os Spa with a modernised highway, a new wing and without you as its leader, that is the bank's wet dream. He'll thank me, Carl.'

I could see that Carl realised I was right, which is why his reaction was a little surprising. Because he began to laugh again. He was probably drunker than I'd imagined.

'I've thought about it a bit,' he said. 'Why Dad didn't do the same to you as he did to me. You were the oldest after all, you were the first to reach that age.'

'You were the one who was most like Mum,' I said. 'The way she was when he fell in love with her.'

'Idiot,' said Carl. 'It was because he was always a bit afraid of you. He realised that if he touched you, even if you were just into your teens, you would kill him. He saw an unscrupulous killer in you, Roy. And you know what, he was right.'

'I'd say he was wrong,' I said. 'I am a scrupulous killer. Think about what I've just told you. Board meeting is in two weeks.'

I started to head back towards Opgard. Halfway there I turned. Carl's silhouette was still rooted to the same spot on the mountain. It looked like he was standing there, admiring his hotel.

I spent the next ten days with Natalie in her apartment. We were together all the time when I wasn't working at the petrol station. Slept, ate, watched movies, read, made love, talked. I am what people call the silent type, and never before had I said so many words and sentences as in the course of those days. Not even Shannon could loosen my tongue the way Natalie did. But sometimes saying nothing was the right thing to do. Like the time I accompanied Natalie to the cemetery to put flowers on her father's grave, and to my surprise I saw a tear in her eye. I longed to ask if a father who was also an abuser deserved her tears? But I desisted. Maybe because I had felt something of the same schizophrenia myself. Maybe I was afraid that if I said something critical of her father then she would see it on me, hear it in my voice, that I was somehow indirectly defending an act of murder. *Rest in peace* were the words carved into his gravestone. He didn't do that in the nightmares I'd been having recently. But if he and the others in that cemetery really rested in peace then I envied them. Yeah, some days I would gladly have changed places with them.

We went walking in the mountains and talked about life, the future and the things we saw around us. And about how to run a business – the hotel rather than the amusement park. I had, after all, been watching Carl in action at Os Spa and learned that, in principle, it wasn't much different from running a petrol station. On the other hand it was obvious Natalie had a better understanding of the service industry than me, and on top of that an intuitive understanding of the bigger picture when it came to business.

'Delegate,' she said at least five times every walk.

I had told her that I knew what the word meant, but she kept on repeating it. Said that that's what a leader does, a leader has to trust the team. Because that's what a leader was, she said, a manager whose job it was to explain each player's responsibilities to them, and why they were an important tactical element in winning the game. But the leader had to stand on the sidelines. Leaders could not get involved in the game themselves.

'When you see players throwing their arms around each other

when they score, that's when you know you've done something right as a leader. They don't just want to win for you, they want to win for themselves. They want Os Spa to be a place they're proud of working at.'

'Sounds like you should be giving one of those inspirational lectures for the employees.'

'Oh but I will, the day I'm administrative director,' she said, with a crafty smile at my raised eyebrow.

'And in the meantime do what?'

'I don't know.' Almost imperceptibly, her Os dialect had started to regain lost ground. 'But right now I know exactly what I want to do.'

'And that is?'

'Get home as quick as possible, take off all our clothes and fuck.'

It was packed at Fritt Fall the night Hell Spelemannslag played. Now of course that might have been because at that hour there were always plenty of customers at Fritt Fall, regardless of which night it was, and who was playing. But things really did take off; it was as though hard folk music on the Hardanger fiddle was exactly what the town had been waiting for. By the time Ola – with his lock of hair twisted through his earring – jumped up onto the monitor with his fiddle howling and screeching, people were already on their feet, and I saw Johnny and his pals pogoing in front of the stage as though they were at a Satyricon concert.

Ola tossed his head and his lock of hair flew free and sent a shower of sweat and holy water over the newly converted, and I saw – this was after a few beers, but I definitely do believe I saw – Egil and Børge sticking out their tongues to get some of what was going down. Then Natalie came onstage, stood at the front with her *langeleik* and stared out at her fellow villagers who had never seen her like that before, like someone able to demand complete submission and get it. Where just a few seconds earlier people had been going wild it was suddenly as quiet as a church. I felt an arm around my waist when she started to sing. It was Julie, and her other arm was round Alex. She stood on tiptoes and whispered in my ear: 'You lucky bugger. I'd have taken her too.'

When the place was finally emptied, apart from Julie and Alex, Erik Nerell, me and the band, it was almost two o'clock. We all – except Julie and Natalie – shared a bottle of cognac, and Erik was almost crying with happiness. Not because of the record takings at the bar, because actually they weren't, but because we – or actually, mostly him – had been able to give the people of Os an experience they would remember for a very long time. For the rest of their lives even, Erik was prepared to bet. And thanked me again for giving him another chance. When he went so far as to embrace me, I had to remember what Natalie had said about footballers celebrating a goal and allowing people to create their own enthusiasm; there surely was something in that.

Natalie had to support me on the way home.

'D'you think I should have stayed sober in solidarity with you?' I slurred.

'No,' she said. 'It's just good to see that Roy Opgard can let his hair down now and then too.'

For ten days I was, in a word, absurdly happy. And even though I haven't much experience of that type of happiness I like to remind myself that it was made all the better by the fact that the sun didn't shine from a cloudless sky. On the contrary, there were heavy, leaden thunderclouds on all sides. But that's when you

know to enjoy the warmth, right? When you realise it's all borrowed time, that you must savour every second, and that when
you close your eyes and feel it getting even warmer, then that's
because the sun is nearing the edge of a cloud, so that for a few
moments the beams strike at a different angle and are focused as
though through a magnifying glass. But that's also the moment
before the sun disappears, the temperature drops and – if it's a
sky like mine – the mother of all storms can break.

That's where I was, beneath my sunny sky, enjoying a desperate happiness that was at its most intense and frenetic, when
Carl called and asked me to come up to the hotel. I didn't know
what he wanted, but I know every nuance of his voice – just as he
does mine – and at that moment the temperature plummeted.
And when, an hour later, I stood in his office, sure enough, the
mother of all storms broke over me.

39

CARL WAS SITTING BEHIND HIS desk when I came in.

'Please take a seat,' he said.

Since we're brothers who don't tend to use courtesies like that I took it as a preamble, a warning that he had something serious on his mind.

As I sat down he simultaneously stood up.

Definitely something serious.

'You like this office?' he asked, patting the top of the high-backed director's chair. He continued without waiting for an answer. 'I do too.' He crossed to the window. 'I like the view of our own outfields too. I like the way they come up here with lunch from the restaurant if I ask them to. Or make room for me at the spa if I need a massage. I like the combination of freedom and responsibility that a boss's job like this gives me. I like the respect that comes with it. And the power. The power to do good things. Good things for me, for my staff, and for Os. And I like it so much, Roy, that I've made up my mind I'm going to keep it.' He turned towards me. 'Last time we spoke you said at least you were giving me the choice. But that's inaccurate because, of course, you didn't give me any choice. I had to do it.'

'Do what?'

Carl smiled, but there was both guilt and resignation in his eyes. And it was a look I recognised. The same look as when he told me he'd shot Dog. When he admitted he'd pushed the old sheriff over into Huken. And when he told me he'd beaten Shannon to death.

I swallowed. 'What is it, Carl? Tell me what you've done.'

'I've made a deal with Kurt Olsen to tell him everything. About how you killed Mum and Dad, how you made it look as though Sigmund Olsen had drowned himself, and as though Willum Willumsen shot himself.'

I looked at him as I tried to understand what he had just said. Because it didn't make sense. As I say, I'm not exactly top of the class when it comes to reading, but I'm pretty good at adding up. And this didn't. It just didn't add up.

'You're prepared to admit that you killed the old sheriff so I won't be able to move into this office?' I asked.

'I'm prepared to give evidence that it was you who killed Sigmund Olsen. And Kurt has already said he believes me. Everyone who ever went to those dances at Årtun knows that of the two of us, you're the violent one.'

I closed my eyes and clenched my jaw. 'You're saying you've already spoken to Kurt about this?'

'That's right.'

I breathed so hard through my nose it squeaked and whistled. 'You get me sentenced, but so what? You'll lose your job here anyway once the fraud is uncovered.'

'But I won't, you see,' said Carl. 'And maybe you won't have to go to jail either.'

I opened my eyes again. 'No? And how is that going to be possible? Since you've already talked?'

A smile, now broad and genuine, spread across his face. 'A statement to the police and a witness's testimony are two different things, Roy. A false statement can simply be withdrawn. I can say I felt myself pressured by Kurt, or that I just wanted to tease him and pay him back for the way he's been after us all these years. I can withdraw my statement this very day, Roy, but only on the following conditions. That you don't try anything at the board meeting, and I keep my job. And that you personally, and without drawing anyone's attention to it, pay off that invoice for three million. If the mistake shows up later we can lay the blame on AUB and show that it's all taken care of now.'

I nodded. Felt dazed. What Carl had done was follow the advice Dad gave us about boxing, to hit your opponent with everything you've got, and do it when he's on the attack and moving forward.

'You look a little shaken, big brother. But try to see it as me doing you a favour. And at least I'm giving you a choice.'

All I could do was go on nodding, like one of those nodding dogs old people used to have in the back of their cars.

'I know how you feel,' said Carl. 'But this makes us even and we can make a fresh start. Team Opgard. What d'you say?'

'*Even?*'

'Yes. Sure, I knew you were in love with Natalie Moe. Knew

369

how bad it would make you feel if I fucked her. But I had to do it. So we were even there too.'

I stared at him. And it all dawned on the idiot Roy Opgard. Of course Carl hadn't drugged Natalie just to get himself laid. He'd done it to get revenge on me. And that could mean only one thing. That he knew.

'How . . .' I began, and had to stop to clear my throat.

'Kurt,' said Carl. 'He came to see me. Wanted me to testify against you in the murder of his father. In exchange for immunity against any accusation of being involved. He said he had certain information that he thought would put a damper on brotherly love, as he phrased it. Because they hadn't just analysed old Olsen's blood they discovered behind the number plate on Dad's car, they'd also looked at Shannon's blood, in the car she was in. They learned that she was pregnant, which of course I already knew. What I didn't know was that they can tell from a pregnant woman's blood who the father is. Did you know that?'

I nodded. Could feel the skin of my neck begin to prickle.

'Fantastic, isn't it? As fantastic as the fact that it turned out to be you, dontcha know. You, Roy, my own brother, had been fucking my wife on the quiet.' He put his head on one side. 'I've been wondering what plans you and Shannon made for the future. Going to keep it a secret from me? So I'd feed and raise the little cuckoo as my own?'

I swallowed. Didn't think I could really tell him that the plan had been considerably more drastic than that.

'Kurt was convinced he was driving a wedge between two brothers. Which is not exactly untrue. I said I would think about his proposal. And I did think about it, Roy. I could throw you under a bus, get my revenge and at the same time stop having to look over my shoulder all the time, wondering when Kurt Olsen was coming after me.'

I knew now what it was, that enigmatic strangeness in the way he had been looking at me. The same way he had once looked at Dad. That it was a combination of hate, and of guilt for what he knew he was about to do.

'At first I thought it would be enough just to fuck Natalie Moe,' he said. 'I wanted to see your pain, see your heart break a little, I hoped that might be enough for me. And you know what? It was. It could have stopped there, Roy. But then you started the nuclear war, and then there was only thing for it. Same as Dad used to say about the Third World War.'

'Retaliation,' I said.

'Retaliation,' Carl echoed. 'Bomb everyone – and especially the commies – all the way back to the Stone Age.'

I had to smile.

Carl sat back down in his director's chair. 'So what do you say to you and me cheating Kurt Olsen out of his victory, brother? Shall we say we've given each other a couple of hefty punches below the belt, and leave it at that? I carry on running the hotel, and you get your funfair and your princess into the bargain?'

We studied each other. I don't know what he saw, but I saw the kid brother I had played and fought with, argued and competed with, protected when I could and comforted when he needed it. When we both needed it. Those nights when Dad had come and left, and I would climb down from the top bunk and put my arms around Carl and hold him until he stopped crying. The kid brother who had got up in the night, when he thought I was sleeping, opened my satchel, taken out the homework I was to hand in the next day and corrected all the spelling mistakes I hadn't noticed. Who had danced with all the pretty girls at Årtun so I had to step up and deal with all the jealous boyfriends.

'Is that why Natalie didn't get anywhere with her complaint?' I asked. 'Kurt was protecting you, his crown witness, in the only case Kurt Olsen really cares about?'

'Aw, I don't think Kurt told Natalie anything that isn't true, which is that most cases involving accusations of rape end up being dropped for lack of evidence.'

'Of course.' I rubbed my chin.

Carl leaned forward in his chair and held out his right hand to me.

'Handshake for peace, big brother?'

My hand continued to run back and forth over the unfamiliar smooth skin; I still hadn't got used to shaving every day. A strange thought struck me. That when I took that outstretched hand, the warm, rough feeling of the skin of the only other surviving member of the Opgard clan would seem more reassuring and familiar to me than the skin of my own chin did right at that moment.

I coughed. 'Yes, I well remember what Dad said about retaliation and world wars,' I said. 'He meant that the day we bombed each other back to the Stone Age we should do the same to everyone else too. That way we could continue fighting on an equal footing – with flint axes.'

Carl gave me an uncertain look, his hand hanging in the air like an unfinished sentence. I stood up.

'Go to Kurt with your testimony, Carl. And I'll go home to my flint axe.'

I heard the creaking of his director's chair, as though he was sitting and rocking in it, as I walked across the parquet floor and closed the door behind me.

40

THAT AFTERNOON, KNOWING NOW THAT the Third World War had started and that everyone would be a loser, I made *lapskaus* for Natalie. Not the Norwegian copy of it but real German *labskaus*. It was, of course, not the simple version they serve to seamen consisting of cheap meat and saturated ship's biscuits, but what even the rich burgers of Hamburg and Bremen eat, the recipe Mum had learned as a housekeeper, with salted beef, herring, potatoes, beetroot and onion, parsley and spices. As Natalie was tucking into her third helping I asked, rather unnecessarily, if she liked it. She just laughed and pointed at my dish. 'More to the point, do *you* like it?'

'Yeah, sure, I'm just not that hungry.'

'Anything wrong?'

'There's always *something* wrong,' I said, because you lie best when you're not lying.

'Job?'

'Job,' I said, and was still telling the truth, technically speaking, since it was about the job as hotel boss.

'Happy to listen if you want to talk about it,' she said.

'Thank you, darling, but there isn't really much to tell.' I had noticed how I was borrowing that word of hers, *darling*, with increasing frequency. In the beginning I had used it the same way she did, as an affectionate joke involving an ironic distance. But the irony had become less and less noticeable.

'OK,' she said, and sighed. 'It's just that I need something to think about. Not doing anything is beginning to get on my nerves.'

I pushed my plate away. 'And I feel like my brain needs an airing too. I'll take a walk, maybe call in on Erik at the club afterwards. Shall I get anything while I'm out?'

'Petrol station's probably the only place open now, and that's a bit far in the rain.'

'A bit far, yes,' I said. I kissed her forehead and walked out into the rain-sodden evening. I pulled up the hood of my jacket, crossed the square and turned onto the footpath leading to the petrol station. A little ahead of me I saw a woman emerging from a Skoda, the hybrid model, sensible family runaround. I recognised the car but not the woman, thought only that it was a funny place to get out of a car, with no houses or anything else along that stretch of the path. She began walking quickly along the path, heading in my direction, towards the square, and when the Skoda drove off in the same direction I pretty much got the picture. The car passed me first, and behind the back-and-forth motion of the windscreen wipers I saw Dan Krane staring stiffly ahead, as though a witness on the footpath would somehow disappear as long as he didn't look at them. As the woman came closer I recognised her too. It was the woman with the Eastern European accent who had helped me with the sheets in the hotel storeroom. I nodded, but the stony face – with, admittedly, a certain colouring of the cheeks – stared straight past me.

And yet. What I had just glimpsed wasn't happiness, not even stolen happiness. The two of them couldn't have looked more alone if I'd seen them drifting in the middle of an ocean. I took Natalie's guilty pleasure – a large bar of milk chocolate from the station – and retraced my steps. Counted them and told myself I had to make a decision before reaching three hundred and thirty-three. Would Carl really stand up in a court of law and testify against me? It was hard to imagine. If it was an empty threat then what I was planning – a pre-emptive strike – could turn out to be a catastrophic mistake. Three hundred and thirty-one. I stood outside Fritt Fall. The rain had made stripes through Erik's chalked message on the pavement sign.

I went in.

Erik repeated my question. 'What kind of friends are we? We-eell. We *used* to be the type where he made the decisions and led the way and the rest of us followed behind. In our crowd we looked up to Kurt, at least while we were growing up. Partly because he was the sheriff's son – I guess we thought he had a more exciting home life than us. Partly because he was easily the best footballer of all of us, the brightest prospect from Os from as far back as you could remember, people said. But mostly because of the superior way he carried himself, his way of being.'

Erik topped up my coffee. He'd handed the bar over to Alex and we were sitting at the table furthest away, by the door and out of earshot. I took a sip, knowing it could be a while before Erik got to the point.

'He was best and didn't he fucking know it. Not the smartest, he was never top of the class or anything, but as soon as the playground bell went he was top dog in everything. And he was the first of us who could pull the birds. They liked his self-assurance. And then of course there was the blond hair, thick as a wheatsheaf. He should've been in a band, Kurt. Worst thing was, he could actually play the guitar and wasn't too bad. Just lacked the application. And then of course he had to concentrate on his football, he was playing for the first team when he was only sixteen. Got an offer from Notodden and went to Skien for a trial for Odd. Sat on the bench for them for a couple of games, came on and didn't do too bad, but. Bit too nervous, you know. Couldn't really show how good he was. Came back home again pretty quick. Didn't enjoy Skien, he said. Didn't meet anyone. He liked Os. Safe. Secure. Liked having mates around who'd be there for him if needed.'

'Liked being a big fish in a little pond,' I said.

Erik nodded. 'If Kurt had one weakness it would have to be that he couldn't stand not winning. OK, so maybe that was his strength too, he ran and ran until he wore his opponents out. Patient. Never gave up. But he could explode too. I remember one cup game against Notodden. They had one little lad, good dribbler, nutmegged Kurt twice. People laughed and applauded because he'd got the better of our captain. The third time the lad tried it Kurt chopped him knee-high and the lad had to be stretchered off the pitch. Torn ligament. Six months later I read in the papers he had to call it a day and retire.'

I saw Johnny, in his uniform, sitting at a table with two mates. Now and then they glanced over in our direction.

'What you say about him knowing you would all back him,' I said. 'I wonder if he ever made use of that.'

'What are you thinking about?' asked Erik, raising his cup to his lips. But the cup was empty.

I was on my way out, in the entrance to Fritt Fall, when my phone rang.

It was Bent Halden.

'What's up?'

'Jon Fuhr,' he said.

'Oh yeah?'

He outlined the problem to me. It was surprising, if not actually shocking. I asked Halden how quickly he could be in Os. He said he was worried about being seen with me, but I said he could drive his car to my workshop and if anyone said anything about it he could say I had to fix something on his car I hadn't had time to when I last had it in for repair.

'OK,' he said, and we hung up.

I stood there, staring down at the worn parquet flooring in the entrance. There was a lighter square, and I realised it was from the old computer gaming machine that used to stand there. The exploding asteroid fragments were hurtling towards me now, and Kurt Olsen had been right, of course, in the end it would be impossible to dodge them. But what can you do? Just keep playing until it says Game Over, the music stops and the light goes out?

41

IT WAS ALMOST MIDNIGHT. BENT Halden had driven his Audi into the workshop, sat down on a wooden chair by the wall and explained. There was a raw cold in the workshop, and we kept our jackets on. Jon Fuhr had told Halden that he now realised how much my brother and I stood to make out of that report of theirs, and he wanted to ask for more. Six million kroner more.

'Why six?' I asked.

'Don't know,' said Halden, despair in his voice. 'I think he owes someone money . . . something he's gambled on and lost.'

'Makes no difference what it is,' I said. 'It's not going to happen. We had a deal, and I expect you to keep your side of it.'

'Jon says if you won't pay then he'll change the report.'

'If you change so much as a comma we'll come after you.'

'He doesn't believe there is a "we",' said Bent. 'He says there's just you and your brother.'

'Doesn't he understand that even if you do change the report and we *don't* come after you, suspicions will be aroused. It'll all come out and we'll all end up in jail. And you'll get longer sentences than us.'

'*I* understand,' said Halden. 'And I think Jon understands that too, but . . .'

'But?'

'He wants to go ahead anyway. He's completely . . . yeah, fearless.'

'Fearless?'

'Become unhinged, sort of.'

'Steroids,' I said.

Halden gave me a puzzled look.

'You didn't know?' I said. 'That your partner takes anabolic steroids?'

Halden shook his head. 'He takes pills he keeps in his desk drawer, but that's a nutritional supplement . . . er, he says.'

'Steroids usually have that effect. They make you fearless, aggressive, angry and generally stark raving bonkers,' I said. 'Would you say that's an accurate description of Jon these days?'

'Yes I would.'

'And that's why you've got in touch with me without his knowing? You're afraid of what he might do?'

'I don't want any part of this any more,' Halden said, shivering, rubbing his hands together. 'I've got a family to think about. I want out.'

'It's too late to jump off a roller coaster once the ride has started,' I said.

'But he . . . you don't know him, he will do it. He's already started working on a revised report. He doesn't know that I know, but I've logged on to his computer and seen it.'

I pulled out the tin of chewing tobacco, offered it to Halden – OK, so I was only joking, I knew he wasn't the type – then wedged in a big plug. Took my time. Processed what he'd just told me. Started to get some idea of what this was all about.

'Halden, what's the real reason you're telling me all this?'

'Because I want you to know that I want no part of it.'

'And because you want me to do something about it?'

'What? No!' He looked at me. 'Or yes . . . that is, if you *can* do anything?'

I met his gaze. Trying perhaps to read his thoughts. I was guessing that one of them at least was about that story I'd told him in his garage that night, about the engineer who so conveniently fell out of his hotel-room window.

'Did you know that a wolf has been seen around here?'

Halden looked confused. Shook his head.

'A lot of the sheep farmers want to shoot it of course, but that's against the law. So what they do is find out where the wolf goes to hunt for food and leave out poisoned mutton. Letting the wolf kill itself, you might say.'

Halden blinked. Saw his brain working. I'm thinking they're pretty smart guys, those geologists.

'Isn't that illegal too?' he asked.

'Probably. But a bit harder to trace, and a lot harder to find the culprit.'

'Right. Do you . . . er, is that the kind of thing you do?'

'No,' I said firmly. 'But if it was then I would use fentanyl. Fifty times stronger than heroin. If you're lucky you get hold of pills that look the same as those the wolf is already taking. And you just leave them in the place where the wolf usually goes to eat, right?'

'And the autopsy would show?'

'That the wolf had taken an overdose of a well-known drug. Surprising, but not shocking when further examination reveals that the wolf in question has been using other drugs for a long time. As it happens, I read the other day that anabolic steroids are now the second most popular drug in the USA. People aren't just using it to build muscles but to increase their sex drive and general energy level. A bit like amphetamines, if you get me?'

Halden looked at me and nodded. Not as slowly as we do in Os, but not too far off either. Oh yeah, he was smart enough. Smart enough to know when a problem has to be dealt with root and branch. Smart enough to know the difference between twelve million divided by two and by one. We exchanged a few pleasantries about the weather, I closed the bonnet of his Audi, opened the door and waved him off.

When I let myself in at Natalie's she was sitting in her nightdress on the sofa. She said she'd been waiting for me. She looked so lovely, just sitting there, silently watching me. I kissed her and we made love, no way could we have waited until we were in bed. And she was like me, wild, intense, almost desperate even. Like women and men in times of war, I read somewhere, who unconsciously know that this, this one night, may very well be their last.

As usual I held back when I felt myself on the point of coming, but this time she wouldn't let me.

'Keep going!' she hissed low in my ear.

'But—' I started to say.

'Shhh.' She dug her fingernails into the cheeks of my arse, and I closed my eyes and let it happen.

42

IT WAS SUNDAY, TWO DAYS to go before the board meeting.

At breakfast I asked Natalie if she wanted to go to the football match with me later in the day.

'I'm not all that interested in football,' she said. 'Didn't think you were either.'

I shrugged and smiled. 'Might be exciting.'

'Exciting? Haven't we already got promotion?'

'I wasn't thinking about the match.'

She studied me, her forehead wrinkled in a frown. 'Then what were you thinking of?'

'We-ell, what *was* I thinking of? Anyway, it's free.'

'Oh yeah?'

'Yes. As majority shareholder in Os Spa I've got two tickets in the VIP stand.'

I could see it dawning on her. 'You want to go to . . . show who we are?'

I nodded. In the old days in Os a girl and boy were officially recognised as a couple when they arrived at the Saturday dance together, or the Sunday service.

'You decide,' I said. 'It'll do just as well some other time. Or never. Maybe you don't want to, maybe you just want me for my body.'

She stood up, walked round the table and sat down in my lap. 'You are so bloody sweet,' she said, and kissed me on the nose. Then I felt her stiffen. 'Your brother . . . won't he be there too?'

'What would you say if I told you he won't be?'

'Then I'll come,' she answered, and this time she kissed me on the mouth.

I was sitting on the throne, phone in my hand and hearing Natalie in the living room working on her Duolingo French course. Carl answered on the second ring.

'Where are you?' I asked.

'The new house. The Germans are here with my kitchen.' I could tell by his voice – or rather by the silence after he spoke – that he was waiting for me to say what he hoped I would say. That I had changed my mind and was offering to make peace.

'Natalie wants to see the game with me today,' I said. 'But only if you aren't there. I think that would be a respectful gesture, Carl. The kind of thing that might tip the balance when she decides whether to bring you down or not.'

Carl thought about it. In the background, I could hear the whining of sawblades and the thudding of hammers.

'I'll drop the match if you drop the takeover plan,' he said.

'Not going to happen,' I said. 'I'm saving the hotel *and* you. Can't you see that?'

Carl sighed. 'Oh yes, I see it, Roy. I see it only too bloody clearly. You've got your own motives, so don't give me that bullshit about *saving you* et cetera. I was hoping you'd see sense, that's why I haven't pressed the red button. But now I'm going to have to. Just remember, it was your choice, Roy. Remember that. Goodbye.'

'Carl, wait!'

He didn't hang up, and I heard it again. Something about his breathing maybe, the way I'd heard it from the bottom bunk when we were kids and picked up every little hint. Now he was clinging on to that 'wait' as a last straw. A last straw that would prove that, when it all came down to it, I remembered those words Dad had imprinted on us: *We are family. We have each other and no one else.*

I cleared my throat. 'Are you going to the match or not?'

I could almost hear the wind go out of him. 'You're lucky, big brother.' His voice as flat as a flat tyre. 'I have to stay here today and make sure everything's done right.'

'Make sure everything's done right,' I repeated.

He hung up, and I pulled the flush.

Stepped out leaving the rush of water behind me. '*On y va!*'

Considering there was little at stake the turnout for the game at Os stadium was impressive.

'Everyone turns up for parties thrown by the successful,' said Natalie when I remarked on it. I thought that was a little extreme. After all, we were talking about the lower divisions here. A couple of years back Os had had a biathlete on the national junior team and that was by some way a bigger deal than promotion. All the same, it was mostly just parents and weirdos who turned up to watch local biathlon championships for juniors. Football attracts the masses because the masses have all played themselves. They know when they're seeing a good performance on the pitch out there and when they aren't, groaning when a player misses an open goal they knew they could have hammered into the back of the net themselves nine times out of ten. Whereas for most of us it's a miracle every time a biathlete standing fifty metres away on his skis and aiming his rifle hits a target the size of a candle flame, a thing you can hardly even see.

'A candle flame?' said Natalie as we walked towards the VIP stand. 'That I have got to try!'

She seemed unaffected by all the looks we got. I acted casual, but I could read what those gawping eyes were thinking easily enough. Like 'Wow, Moe's daughter and Roy Opgard, who would've thought it?' And 'Yup, she went for the money.' And 'Cradle-snatching.' Or 'What are those two looking so happy about?' Or even 'Grete Smitt said Carl Opgard had it away with her at the staff do. Yeah yeah, so she has to make do with the brother, Carl's got enough on his plate with Mari Aas.'

'Hi,' said Rita Willumsen as we made our way up the stand. 'Nice to see you have company. Hi, Natalie.'

'Hi, Rita.'

The two women exchanged warm smiles. They had never exchanged a single word before, the only thing they'd exchanged was me, and now here they were, like two bosom pals. Girl stuff. I didn't understand it, and if someone had explained it to me I doubt whether it would have been any clearer.

Mari Aas and Dan Krane were standing together. Dan avoided my eye, not too surprising since he knew I'd caught a glimpse of what he was up to on the side. All the more peculiar, then, that he and Mari were standing there holding hands. Because that is what they were doing. No two ways about it, the worst engine problem ever is easier to figure out than anything we human beings get up to. I nodded to Asle Vendelbo and Jo Aas, who both stood aside for Natalie and me.

'Who are we playing today?' I asked them.

'Kongsberg 2,' said Natalie. 'Mid-table.'

I looked at her in surprise and saw Vendelbo nod his confirmation.

Like I said, give me a dodgy car engine any day of the week . . .

Aas cleared his throat but said nothing, but I knew what was on his mind. Wanted to know if I'd thought about what he'd said. If I'd changed my mind about Carl. I spat the plug of tobacco out over the edge of the little stand, and from his almost imperceptible nod I knew he'd understood that that was my answer.

There was beer at half-time. I don't know how they managed it but the VIP stand was classified as a private gathering and so exempt from the football association's ban on alcohol at matches. On behalf of the bank Vendelbo treated us to beer served in small, stemmed glasses, which we sipped like it was champagne, while the commoners around the stand looked up at us and shook their heads as though we were red-coated upper-class twats on a fox hunt. But no one said anything, they understood that it was us – or rather our money – that had got the club promoted and might possibly manage to do it again.

Towards the end of the second half the crowd on one side of the stand started cheering. Since not much was happening on the pitch we turned to see why. It was Kurt, moseying bow-legged along the grass between the spectators and the touchline and heading for the VIP stand. The cheers turned to a steady chant of 'Kurt, Kurt'. He grinned, waved to show that he was going along with it, both sides knowing that it wasn't just bollocks, that here was the man who was *their* king of Os. Kurt looked up towards the stand, caught my eye and I knew what he was coming for. Johnny wasn't with him this time, but there could be no doubt, he was about to arrest me for a third time and couldn't think of a better place to do it than in the VIP stand in the middle of a game, with everybody looking on. Not least Rita. Which could only mean he was certain he had a watertight case this time.

Jo Aas – who had been talking with Natalie about the new wing at the hotel – must have realised what was happening. He fell silent, looked at Kurt, who was still advancing, looked at me. He then took the three steps which were all his long legs needed to get down to the first row of the stand and cut Kurt off. He put a hand on the sheriff's shoulders, leaned close to him, whispered in his ear. Kurt stopped and listened. Because everyone in Os listens when the old mayor Jo Aas has something to say, that's just the way it is. Kurt said something back, but Aas shook his head and did the rest of the talking. Kurt nodded. Glanced at the pitch, knowing of course that all eyes were on him, hitched up his trousers by his belt – just the way his father used to do it – and made out he was watching the game. Rita joined him, and she said something to him as well, but he shook his head. A few minutes later he looked demonstratively at his watch and left. I watched him until he disappeared round the corner of the German barracks. Listened out for the sound of the Land Rover's engine but there was too much wind.

'What did Kurt want?' asked Natalie.

'Nothing that can't wait for a more suitable occasion,' Aas said, and turned to me. 'Maybe you'll go and see him after the game, Roy? He has one or two loose ends you can help him clear up, I think.'

I nodded.

Natalie had said she could drive, so I'd drunk a few glasses of that beer, and a couple of minutes before full-time I went for a piss in the clubhouse toilet, to get there before the rush. I told her I'd see her at the car.

The clubhouse was empty.

There was a short, old-fashioned trough in the Gents, one of those that regularly flushes water according to a routine I've never taken the trouble to analyse. And it must have been the sound of that flushing which prevented me from hearing the door open behind me. I didn't notice anything until I felt a jab in the back and then heard Kurt's voice.

'This is the barrel of a Glock-17, Roy. Don't move. Put your hands behind your back.'

If it had happened at almost any other time during my whole lifetime in Os I might have laughed at the parody.

'Kurt . . .'

'Do as I say now, or we'll call it resisting arrest and that means I can do anything I like and the law will back me. And I think you know what I'd like to do . . .'

'Just let me—'

'Now!'

I did as he said. Felt and heard the handcuffs click around my wrists.

'And now turn round,' he said.

I turned.

'Shit!' Kurt screeched as the jet of urine struck him on his thighs. He staggered back, but the jet followed him, and I can't pretend I was trying to stop it. It was decreasing in strength and moving down from his thighs to his knees, but not until it hit the tops of his snakeskin boots did he really lose it and start to scream incoherently. He totally freaked out. And when the jet finally died away he took two steps forward and what happened was a repeat of something I should obviously have seen coming. He hit me. With the gun. On the forehead. I felt a straining in the stitches and then the wound burst open. Closed my eyes as it streamed warm down my cheek. When I opened my eye again, Kurt's face was poking right into mine.

'I'm going to kill you,' he said. 'You know that, Roy?'

I reacted instinctively. Not wisely, not planned, but not in a rage either, not in fear nor in any other counterproductive way. It was as though my brain carried out a very simple series of calculations and told the muscles what to do based on the answers it had come up with. That it had to save me. So with my hands locked behind me I pulled away a little and moved my head. Not Os slow, but Årtun hard. Kurt must have forgotten about it, the oldest trick in the book, the headbutt. I heard something give way, something break at the base of the nose, just like with Fuhr. Kurt lost his balance, slipped on the piss and fell. There was a nasty thud as the back of his head hit the tiled floor.

I did as I had done with Moe, sat astride his chest and pressed Kurt's underarms to the floor with my knees. Yes, it was the same thing, all over again. Everything was. My life went round and round in fucking circles and I had no idea how to break out. Blood dripped down my chin onto Kurt's face, which was maybe what brought him round. He opened his eyes and stared up at me. It looked like it took him a couple of seconds to realise where he was.

'Now you are in trouble, Roy,' he whispered hoarsely.

'You too,' I said. 'When we leave here people will see that you hit a man in handcuffs.'

Kurt blinked as a drop of blood struck him on the cheekbone. He snorted, probably felt safe enough anyway since I couldn't use my hands. He shifted a bit.

'Get up now, Roy, or I'll throw you off.'

'You'll lose your job, Kurt.'

'No way. I'll say you headbutted me first, I had to hit you to subdue you, and I handcuffed you afterwards. Word of a police officer against that of a murderer. Hard to know who they'll believe, dontcha think?'

A grin spread across Kurt's face as he lay there beneath me. He was tough all right, I'll give him that. And maybe not quite as dumb as I sometimes suspected him of being either. Just then the door opened, and there was a clatter of studs on the tiled floor. I looked up and saw a man wearing Os's strip stop dead in his tracks. It was our Nigerian striker, the one we'd paid so much for. In the sudden silence he just stared at us.

'Coach?' he said.

'Yes, Umar?'

'Do you need help?'

Kurt turned his head and looked at his striker. 'No, Umar. Leave us, please.'

Umar stood there gazing at me. More precisely, at my prick, still dangling out of my flies and – as I only now realised – in the immediate vicinity of Kurt's mouth. He looked as though he was trying to put together the various elements in the picture – blood, sex, two men, handcuffs, a public place – before nodding that he understood and accepted the situation and backing out.

The door glided shut behind him, the sound of the studs receded.

'So much for your version then,' I said.

'Move.'

'If you promise to take off the handcuffs?'

'Move!'

I stood up. Kurt did the same, picked up the gun that had slid under the sink, fished out his key and removed the handcuffs. I put the snake back where he belonged and did up my flies.

'You are under arrest,' Kurt muttered, handing me a paper towel from the container by the sink.

'For what?'

He gave a sad smile. 'I hardly know where to begin.'

'Carl?' I asked as I washed off the blood. Didn't help much, it just kept coming.

He nodded. Carefully touched his nose with his finger and winced.

'Your brother told me everything this morning. So it's all over. I don't actually need a confession from you. But it might be taken into account when it comes to the sentencing. Even though that's going to be a big ask since we're talking about several murders. So what do you say? You want to go straight to the slammer or make a statement first?'

'What did Aas say that made you decide not to arrest me with everybody watching?'

Kurt shrugged. 'Something about professional discretion. He made it sound like a sensible idea.'

'He's good at that, Aas.'

'He is.'

We stood there, cleaning ourselves up as the taps ran.

'You can't prove I hit you first,' said Kurt. 'In fact, you can't prove I hit you at all.'

'Hadn't even thought of trying,' I said.

'No? Why not?'

'Because I can well understand you reacting the way you did. I pissed on you, didn't I?'

He peered at me to see if I was kidding.

'Quite literally,' I went on. And I was kidding.

Kurt grunted. 'You could at least have tried to direct it another way.'

'Yeah, I'm sure you would have got the jury to agree with you there.'

In Kurt's mirror I could see he was grinning, actually grinning.

Damned if I know where this sudden levity came from. For Kurt it was maybe because the hunt was finally over. Roy Opgard was under arrest, and his father released from the suspicion that he had taken his own life. As for me, I've never understood the shame attached to suicide. It must be because you never managed to make a life you thought was worth living. But then who can master something as complicated and arbitrary as life?

'Am I going to get that confession?' he asked.

'We'll get to that in a while,' I said. 'First I have to stop this bleeding.'

We left the toilet and went into the changing room. The players were still getting changed but they greeted Kurt and gave him a hug, I could see he really was loved by his players. But the striker hung back.

393

'Stanley,' said Kurt.

Stanley Spind – who was squatting down in front of a player carefully bending his knee back and forth – turned to us.

'Ouch,' he said. 'What happened here?'

'We slipped,' said Kurt. 'Someone's pissed on the toilet floor and we banged our heads together when we fell. Where's your stitching kit?'

Stanley looked from Kurt to me and then back again. He clearly didn't believe a word of the story but he opened his little black bag and took out his kit.

'Lot of accidents you've been in recently,' Stanley said laconically as he stitched my forehead up again. I didn't say anything as he wrapped another turban on me. Afterwards he took a look at Kurt's nose, which was already beginning to swell.

'I can give you some painkillers and send you to the ear, nose and throat department at Notodden so you can have it X-rayed.'

'It's crooked,' said Kurt. 'Can you do anything about that?'

'I can try to straighten it but it's going to hurt.'

'Do it,' said Kurt, sitting down on the bench and closing his eyes.

I shuddered, remembering how Stanley had carried out a repositioning of my index finger eight years previously, how much that had hurt. Kurt's face gave nothing away, he didn't make a sound. But the broken nose did, and so did the players, standing around wincing and looking on with dreadful fascination. Kurt thanked Stanley, stood up and walked over to me, blinking away the tears of pain.

'Time we took a little ride, Roy.'

He laid a hand on my shoulder and we left.

The car park was empty apart from Natalie, who was standing with her arms folded next to my Volvo. She tensed when she saw us.

'Can I . . . ?'

'Yes, but make it quick,' said Kurt.

I walked over to her. Saw the confusion and worry on her face.

'What is it?'

'Carl's told him what happened when my parents died.'

'What? But . . .'

'I have to go with Kurt now. I'll call you as soon as I know more, OK?' I handed her the car keys and kissed her on the cheek. 'I love you.'

She blinked. 'Will you . . . are you coming back?'

'Yes.'

'You sure?'

'No. But probably.'

'How . . . ?'

'About seventy-one per cent.'

'Silly.'

And that was the last thing she said to me before I walked away towards Kurt's SUV, where he stood holding the passenger door open for me.

'Turned into quite a woman, that Natalie,' Kurt said as he started the car.

'Where we going?'

'Notodden.'

'Prison?'

'You need proper food and lodgings now that you're going to be locked up for a while.'

As we hit the main road and started heading east the sun broke through the layer of cloud.

'I'll tell you the whole story,' I said.

'Best wait until we can get it on tape at Notodden,' said Kurt.

'No, I won't be saying anything at Notodden. So best if we make a stop. Best for both of us. A plug of chaw, a ciggy and a story.'

Kurt gave a glance over at me. 'What do you mean, best for both of us?'

'You know what?' I said, pointing ahead. 'It would be bloody brilliant to turn off up there, the place where the story sort of comes to an end.'

Kurt peered ahead. Hesitated. But he understood what I meant. Directly ahead of us was the turn-off to the boathouse with the boat that was found drifting with Sigmund Olsen's boots on board. He indicated for the turn and braked.

'Let's see if that boat has sprung any leaks,' I said and pushed open the door.

'Easy now,' said Kurt, who looked like he was about to draw the pistol from his shoulder holster but then changed his mind. He followed after me down to the red-painted old boathouse, standing on its own by the water's edge, bathed in afternoon sunlight. There was a padlock on the door. I pushed the plank door enough to be able to peer inside. Sure enough, the boat was there.

'You've changed the padlock,' I said. 'Back then there was a big shiny one.'

'Had to,' said Kurt as he offered me a cigarette from his packet. 'The keys disappeared along with Dad.'

It was that 'Dad' which did it. Something happened to me when he said it. I understood something that should have been obvious to me a long time ago. But I had never heard him refer to his father as 'Dad', and when he did so now it was like he was lowering his guard, he was showing me something. Not his vulnerability, because even though I could see that there was something else he wanted to show me. The ties of family. Intimacy. Love for his father. Because at the same time as it's vulnerable it's also a strength, something you can't beat. I hadn't loved my father, hadn't been loved. And for that reason, Kurt Olsen would be able to beat me every time. Because there was a purpose to his hunt, it had meaning. Whereas I was just running *from* something, not *towards* anything. I knew it, Kurt knew it, and now I had finally been brought down it was as though the hatred he had directed towards me was turned off. Almost as if he wanted to thank a worthy opponent for the game. The easy sportsmanship of the winner.

I sat on the rocks in front of the boathouse and pulled out my snuffbox.

'I tampered with the brakes and the steering of the car my parents drove over into Huken,' I said. 'It was supposed to be only my father. He abused Carl.'

'Yes, Carl told me.' Kurt sat down next to me, lit a cigarette.

'Your father began to suspect something, and Carl pushed him down into Huken.'

'By accident,' said Kurt, blowing out smoke. 'He was seventeen, whatever happens, he won't do time for it now. And then?'

'Then I had to help him. We had to make sure the body disappeared. I dismembered the corpse at my workshop, put it in the tractor grab and filled it with Fritz Industrial Cleaner. As you probably know, it's a corrosive. Leaves nothing behind.'

I saw Kurt swallow.

'I took your father's boots and his key fob, let myself into the boathouse here in the middle of the night, got the boat out, tossed the boots into it and pushed it out. It drifted back in again, so in the end I had to row out until the current caught the boat, then I jumped overboard and swam ashore.'

'One murder, and one accessory to covering up a murder,' said Kurt. 'You were nineteen, so you won't get too much for that. Willumsen is worse.'

'Does Carl say I killed him?'

'He told me you planned it, and you carried out your plan.'

I sighed. Carl really had told him everything. 'Willumsen exploited the fact that Carl was in a tight spot, he lent him money at loan-shark rates and when Carl couldn't make the repayments he set a Danish hit man on him. And on me.'

'So you killed them both?'

I shrugged. 'Self-defence, I would claim. Defend the family. Do you understand that, Kurt?'

Kurt nodded slowly. 'Although the last murder wasn't self-defence, now was it?'

'The last one?'

'Carl's wife.'

That was really hitting below the belt. Had Carl really said that *I* had killed Shannon? If he had, then it must have been because Carl thought I would pay him back by telling Kurt it was Carl who killed Shannon, and he was trying to forestall me. But it didn't add up. Carl was pissed off and wanted to stop me so he could keep his job, but that didn't mean he'd turned into an idiot. He knew that I knew we both had a lot to lose if it ever came out that Shannon hadn't just driven over the edge of Huken.

'And what makes you think I killed her?' I said, spitting so hard it hit the water.

'We-ell now. When your sister-in-law is pregnant with your kid, and she apparently refuses to have an abortion, then of course the problem has to be dealt with somehow. And you did, after all, have some experience of that kind of work, so . . .' He gestured, cigarette in hand, meaning that the rest was obvious.

'So it isn't Carl who's saying Shannon was murdered?'

Kurt puffed intently on his cigarette. He probably felt his brain needed more nicotine to help him make the right decision, whether or not to carry on bluffing.

'I didn't say he said that,' said Kurt.

'So this is your own hypothesis?'

'Hypothesis and hypothesis. It's more like a natural question, bearing in mind that everybody else round here that seems to have died of more or less natural circumstances was actually killed by you and your brother. But I can see you're denying it, and that's fine . . .' He dropped the cigarette butt onto the grey sloping rock and ground it out with his heel. 'I've got more than enough on you as it is.' He put his hand in his jacket pocket, pulled out a pair of genuine Ray-Ban sunglasses, not the cheap copies we sell at the petrol station, and put them on. He lifted his face to the sun.

'You know what, Roy. It's a damn shame actually, all of this. Because I understand you. Sometimes I've even thought it could've been me. Including even knocking up my brother's wife, because that Shannon, she was a bit of all right, she sure was. I understand because we're quite similar, you and me. We don't just share the same taste in women, we're stubborn bastards. We keep going where others would just give up, until we get whatever it is we want. That's the way we are.'

He smiled at me. Not the triumphant smirk of a victor, but the smile of an equal, a smile of acknowledgement, an inviting, even a friendly smile. 'I forgive you, you did what you had to do. And I think that if the dice had rolled another way then you and I would have ended up mates, Roy.'

I nodded. The sun was nearing the peak of Ottertind. Another day would soon be over, another night ready to begin. And then off we go again. Round and round, same old thing.

'Well, best be on our way,' said Kurt and got to his feet. Stood smiling down at me. I was still sitting on the rock.

'You mean mates like you and Erik Nerell?' I asked.

Kurt's smile faded a touch around the edges.

'The kind of mate you can get to do you a dodgy little favour? A good mate who can help you out of a difficult situation you've got yourself into just because you were a little bit overhasty. Why don't you sit back down, Kurt?'

'What for?' he said, in a voice like a snowplough scraping bare road.

'Because I said I was going to tell you the whole story. And *this* is the story.'

Kurt's Adam's apple bobbed up and down. He sat down.

'Right,' I said, taking out my plug of tobacco and laying it on the rock. 'You wanted to press up the price of a piece of real estate you were going to sell for your lady friend. Not because you're greedy, but to show her you hadn't fallen off the back of a lorry or whatever that phrase is. So you fabricated an offer to make the buyer raise his bid. Seems innocent enough, sales people use it all the time – "Lots of people after this, better grab it while you have the chance." Only trouble is, there are rules when it comes to selling real estate. So when the buyer – who, in my case, knows something about these rules – asks to see written confirmation of the rival bid, you realise what you've done and you panic. If you admit the bluff you lose face not just to the buyer and to your lady friend, but because you're actually already guilty of an attempted fraud. Not just scrumping apples or something like that but genuine fraud, fraud with a capital F, the way it's defined in the Norwegian law code. The kind of thing that would mean losing your job. And with the history there is between the two of us, you doubt I'm going to show any mercy if I find out about it. You know, too, that Rita is a law-abiding and principled lady and she won't go along with fraud. On the contrary, she'll want to see that other offer as well. You think about all this, and you decide that, rather than forge something on your own with a made-up name and run the risk of Rita checking it, you'll go to Erik and ask him to pretend he was the one who made the offer. You get him to write it down on a piece of paper. Which you then show to Rita, who is bound to be a little surprised to learn that Erik is good for 6.4 million and is interested in going into the campsite management business. But fair enough, she thinks, Erik has lost Fritt Fall after all, and she knows he's the type who likes to own things and to be his own boss, so why not? When you show the piece of paper to me you avoid showing me the name, because you know I'm already suspicious and I would have checked it out. But I accept the bid without seeing the name, Rita's word is good enough. Only trouble is, when I do get to see the handwriting on that offer I realise who it is. It's the guy behind the fancy calligraphy I see on the pavement sign outside Fritt Fall every day. And since I know how little money he actually has, and what good mates the two of you are, I put two and two together. So I had a little chat with Erik the other day. He admitted everything, told me you'd said nothing about me being the other bidder, all you'd said was that he'd be doing you a favour. That the campsite had already been sold, he just wanted a bid he could show the buyer so the buyer would feel better about it and not think he'd paid over the market price. Keep everybody happy, right? So I told Erik you hadn't done it to keep it everybody happy but to trick me into raising my bid. That you'd nutmegged me and chopped him down at the knee. Now it's not unlikely that his loyalties have changed a bit after I gave him third-part ownership of Fritt Fall free of charge, and on top of that, he's realised you've used him for something that could see him charged with conspiracy to defraud.'

Sitting there beside me Kurt looked pale and nauseous.

'So Erik has signed a document describing step by step exactly what happened, and that document is now in the possession of a solicitor in Oslo. For the time being only three of us, four now, including you, are aware of its contents.'

'Wh . . .' Kurt had to moisten his lips. 'Why keep it secret?'

'Why do you think, Kurt?'

We looked at each other. Like two exhausted boxers in the fifteenth round, him with a broken nose that was still swelling, me with a bloody bandage wrapped around my head.

'Because you knew you might have a use for it,' he said.

I nodded. And something seemed to dawn on him.

'You already knew all this when you bought the campsite,' he said. 'That you'd been tricked.'

I shrugged. 'So what did I pay over the odds? More than a million? I thought it was worth it, as insurance.'

'You turned me into a fraudster.'

'Oh no, that was all your own doing, Kurt. I just didn't stop you.'

'For fuck's sake.'

He said it with such an explosive exhalation I thought he was going to throw up. Maybe I'd been imagining how it would feel, this moment. That it would be sweet, delicious. But strangely enough it didn't. Because, dammit, I felt sorry for the guy.

'So there we have it,' I said, and put a hand on his shoulder. 'The two of us in the same boat and with pretty heavy shit on each other.'

He hung his head. 'What did you mean about checking if the boat had sprung any leaks?'

'Something like,' I said, giving him a comforting pat on the back, 'if we both keep quiet then the boat should stay afloat.'

'Crazy,' whispered Kurt.

'Agreed.'

He lit another cigarette. 'I'm guessing you've been thinking ahead a bit too, Roy. So what do you suggest we do now? Abandon the whole thing and each go our own way?'

'The problem,' I said, 'is Carl.'

'Why?'

'When he realises you're not going to arrest me he might go to the police in Notodden or Oslo.'

'OK. But I can't stop him doing that.'

'You should. Or else my solicitor will publish that document. With Erik's name kept out of it, by the way.'

'For chrissakes, Roy, how do you think I can stop Carl?'

'Carl is rational. He came to you because he knew you would give him a deal that let him off the hook. That's not something he's automatically going to get somewhere else. Unless you set it up for him through colleagues. So if you don't do that favour for him, then we're pretty safe, both of us.'

'You think so?'

'Yes I do. Moreover, once the board of Os Spa has chosen a new leader then it's all over for Carl anyway.'

Kurt scratched his mop of hair. 'You're his brother, so you know best.'

We got up and walked over to the car as Kurt spoke to the police in Notodden and cancelled the interrogation and the place in a holding cell. He hung up and got in behind the wheel, with me in the passenger seat. He made a U-turn, and as we waited for the cars moving in both directions along the main road to pass, the question just popped out of me:

'Do you hate me, Kurt?'

I could see he was thinking as he looked left and right to time his entry into the traffic. Then he accelerated out, and not until we were on our way to Os, and I was thinking he must either have forgotten or be deliberately ignoring my question, did he finally answer:

'For many years I thought I did, Roy. But it was probably just the usual thing.'

'That being?'

'Whenever you hate someone in that intense way, it's because you actually hate yourself.'

We drove on in silence as I stared out of the side window and thought of Dad. The sun slid down behind Ottertind. Soon the darkness – that doesn't fall but rises up from the ground in Os – would be upon us.

*

When I got back home I told Natalie everything.

She listened, wide-eyed in astonishment.

We didn't make love that night but held tight to each other, sweating through our sleep, as though both were dreaming the other was about to fall overboard.

43

'WILL YOU MARRY ME?'

It was the first time in my life I had said those four words in precisely that order. Natalie's sleep-drenched eyes flickered in the morning light and she looked round as though seeing if my question was directed to someone else. I knelt beside the bed with a cup of coffee in one hand and a plate in the other with a serviette, a slice of bread with brown goat's cheese, and a red plush box containing a small gold ring. She picked up the slice of bread, took a bite, chewed as she studied the ceiling.

'OK then,' she said, as though everything had depended on the way that slice of bread tasted. Then she erupted in hysterical laughter and didn't manage to get her hand up to her mouth in time to stop bread and cheese spraying all over the duvet. We cleaned up with the serviette.

'Shall we try that again?' I asked.

She nodded.

I left the room, came back in and knelt by the bed. Repeated those four words in the same order, this time for the second time in my life.

'Yes,' she said in a loud and clear voice, and then began to hiccup and sob.

'Shall we try that one more time?' I asked.

'Stupid,' she said, then pulled me up onto the bed and used my T-shirt to dry her tears. 'Kiss me, stupid.'

We made up for lost opportunities the night before, and afterwards she took the ring out of its box.

'It's so lovely,' she said as she tried to slide it over her ring finger. 'Did you think I had such thin fingers?' She laughed. Then stopped and looked up, and probably read it in the look on my face.

'You didn't buy this for me, I'm guessing?'

I nodded my affirmation. 'I bought it for Shannon, but never had the chance to give it to her. Now I'm giving it to you. Is that all right?'

It was as though I could see the questions flickering behind her eyes: *Is it all right to be number two, you mean? Did you prefer to save money rather than buy a new ring? Or do you want me to wear it so you can pretend I'm Shannon, the one you really love?*

I guess she had to think all these thoughts, the same way I'd had to. But then it was as if she realised something that made the hardness in her eyes soften. That up here in the mountains we don't throw away useful things, not even the kinds of things that have symbolic value. Our love is as unsentimental as nature and as life itself. You love someone you lose, then – if you're lucky – you fall in love with someone else. You can pretend things are otherwise, write some sugary ballad about romance. But that would be telling a lie, and Natalie and I had made a pact about that. We wouldn't tell lies to each other.

'It's beautiful,' she said quietly as she stroked the ring with her fingertip. 'I'll take it to the jeweller's and get it adjusted.'

We slept, and when I woke up I was alone in the bed. I got up and found Natalie sitting at the laptop in the living room.

'I've got an interview in Lillehammer,' she said. 'I'm emailing them now.'

'The director's job?'

'It's a small hotel. But you'll like Lillehammer. And I'm certain you'll get a good price for the petrol station.'

I laughed. Before I realised she wasn't joking. Or maybe just a bit. She gave a half-smile. 'It's just a first interview.'

'You'll be getting more offers,' I said. 'What would it take to keep you in Os?'

She shrugged. 'The usual.'

'The usual?'

'More money, better job, better place to live, a husband. In that order.'

'You've got a husband now, and this place is pretty nice.'

She shook her head and went on typing. 'Too small for two. And maybe three.'

I felt my heart skip a couple of beats. She looked up from the keyboard and laughed. 'Did that make you jump? Relax, I'm kidding. Newly pregnant women don't go around applying for new jobs.' She went back to her typing.

'Should be possible to find something bigger,' I said. 'Carl's moving out.'

'Our place is bigger,' she said.

'You want to live there? With all . . .'

'With all the bad memories? Isn't the same true of Opgard? Isn't that why your brother's having a new place built?'

'Partly maybe, but mostly he's doing it for the same reason as the wren.'

Natalie looked puzzled for a moment until she remembered. And understood.

'You mean he has to build a nest Mari Aas is happy with?'

I nodded.

'So they can be king and queen of Os,' said Natalie.

'Yep. That was what Mari and Dan thought they were going to be when they moved here. But it didn't happen. So now she's got herself another mate.'

Natalie thought about it. 'But you said her and Krane were holding hands at the football match?'

'I saw them.'

'Why, if she's planning to leave him?'

I shrugged. 'Maybe they've heard there are rumours about them splitting up, and they want to show they aren't true.'

'No,' said Natalie and pushed the laptop aside. 'It's Irini.'

'Irini?'

'The housekeeper at the hotel. The woman you saw getting out of Krane's car. Mari's found out about them.'

'You think so?'

'Yes.'

'And?'

'And the strangest thing happens. Mari realises that the man she's lost interest in and lost faith in is attractive to other women.

That maybe he's the one who's going to be leaving her. She rediscovers him, she wants him back.'

'Mimetic desire?' I ran my hand over the bandage on my head. 'But according to the theory, Mari should see Irini as a role model, and even if she does come from a Socialist background she's – how shall I put this? – not exactly the egalitarian type.'

'You can't go fitting the whole of reality into these theories,' Natalie sighed and went back to her laptop.

Jo Aas phoned as I was inspecting some of the cabins at the campsite. He invited me for a coffee and I drove up to his house. He greeted me at the door wearing his woollen peasant's cardigan and his slippers. His wife, Elin, served coffee and *kransekake* in the living room, which had a view out across fields so wide and waving that if you didn't know any better you might think you were in one of the flatland towns in Østlandet. It was a handsome place and I told him so.

'Yes, well, it's too big for people of our age so we're moving into one of the farm cottages in the new year,' Aas said, with a nod in the direction of the house where his daughter and Krane lived. 'They need the room now, you know.'

I didn't respond to this. I had no idea if he was just pretending or if he really didn't know of Carl and Mari's plans.

'As retiring chairman of the board I think it would be proper to give my successor a few tips and words of advice,' he said, and waited until his wife had left the room before continuing. 'My general advice is probably what you'd expect an older man to say to a younger man, and that is not to act *übereilen*. Don't rush into things. That is the cause of so much trouble, Roy.'

I chewed and chewed. 'Good *kransekake*.'

'For most people breaking family bonds is more dramatic than they imagine beforehand. Did you know Elin comes from a family of Jehovah's Witnesses?'

'No.'

'The rule there is, either you're one of us or we can't have any contact with you. Elin stopped believing in what they preached quite early on; but that wasn't why she had to break with them. That was so she could be with an outsider like me.' He smiled, not that it did much to soften the stony severity of a face that could have fronted propaganda posters from both extremes of the political divide. 'It isn't a unique story, and everyone on our side of the fence thinks of it as the only possible happy ending. But that's where they're mistaken.'

He stirred his coffee and continued.

'Elin still has times when she wonders if she made the right decision. And I know what you're thinking; does she really in all honesty think it might have been better had she lied about believing in God and remained a member of the community, rather than live a life in truth outside of it? And some days the answer is yes, and some days it's no.' He looked at me. 'Take Mari. She's got a family, and we all know how that sometimes gets in the way of things, especially when you're young and . . . well, you're ambitious, you make demands of life, I think it's fair to put it as bluntly as that. So that sometimes you forget how important family is, and what you need then is someone older and hopefully wiser to remind you of it. To get on the right track, the one that leads to a happy ending.'

I could only nod my assent. Jo Aas knew all about Mari and Carl. Maybe about Dan and the woman up at Os Spa too. It wasn't any mimetic desire or any other fancy stuff like that which had brought Mari and Dan together again. It was a thundering speech from the old mayor. The threat of cutting family ties. Probably sweetened with the promise of taking over the big house if they did as Aas said. But why hadn't Aas acted before now? I saw the answer to that too. Now that Aas knew Carl Opgard was going to be fired and faced an uncertain future, he was no longer worth the divorce that Jo Aas had seen coming for his daughter.

'When Carl and Mari were teenage sweethearts Carl was like a son to me,' he went on. 'As you know, I helped him out so he could take up that scholarship to study in the USA. And perhaps because, in that respect, I feel some responsibility for the course he took, I feel a certain responsibility too for the situation he finds himself in now. For that reason I feel duty-bound to advise you to be extremely careful about how you treat your brother in his current predicament.'

'Thanks,' I said. 'I will try. Is that all?'

'Yes,' said Aas.

I ate the rest of my piece of *kransekake* and stood up.

'One more thing,' said Aas as we stood out in the corridor. 'I've just spoken to Dan. A man named Fuhr from GeoData has announced a press conference regarding the main road this evening.'

The *kransekake* I was still chewing suddenly doubled its size in my mouth.

'Let's hope it isn't bad news for Os and Os Spa,' said Aas as he held the door open for me. 'See you at the board meeting tomorrow?'

*

A press conference.

Fuhr was really going to do it.

I put my foot down hard as I drove down from Aas's place, as though I had some kind of urgent appointment. But it was too late, the race was already run, I could see that only too well. Because once a fucking kamikaze pilot on steroids makes up his mind to blow everything to smithereens, you've got no chance. Of course. What else had I expected, to be honest?

Having got rid of Kurt Olsen from my six o'clock, had I become so overconfident I thought I could dodge every bit of that exploding asteroid? Get up there on the heavenly heights of the game, where the horizon is clear and you can just cruise off into the sunset? As they say, Man proposes, God laughs.

I had to laugh myself.

It occurred to me that weather sort of reflected the situation, just like it did in Rita's Brontë novels. So, right now it was fair weather with light clouds; but the rain would come later in the afternoon, and I sensed rather than saw those heavy clouds building up in the west.

Natalie looked surprised when I appeared in the living room and suggested we take the same walk we had taken that very first time we walked together.

'Now?'

'The weather's too fine to last.'

She sighed. 'A walk usually means you've got several more gruesome things to confess.'

'You mean you think I can top what you already know?'

'I think probably everything can be topped. For all I know maybe you've been eating babies.'

'Are you coming with me?'

'I'm your golden plover,' she said, closed the laptop and went to get changed.

In the online edition of *Os Daily* it said the GeoData press conference was scheduled for six o'clock. That gave me four hours before all hell broke loose. Before I lost everything. And there and then I realised something. That it wouldn't be the end of the world if Os Spa, the petrol station and the roller coaster all went down the tube, as long as I still had her. Because I believed her. She was my golden plover. She was the companion of the solitary. She wasn't a wren, like Mari Aas, who looked at the nest first and only then looked at the man.

'I still don't have any walking boots,' she called from the hall.

'Carl's at work, we'll get Mum's from Opgard. I can pick up some clothes for myself too.'

'OK.'

We took her car and on the drive up to Opgard I told her about the press conference. And again the thought struck me, how liberating it felt to have someone you could tell absolutely everything to. We-ell, almost everything. At one point in my life Carl had been that person, but it felt like a hell of a long time ago now.

'So Fuhr's going to publish a revised report saying that the Todde tunnel can be built after all,' said Natalie, changing down as we approached the first steep hill.

'Looks that way.'

'So why not call and tell him you accept his conditions? Because that's probably what he's waiting for now.'

'Because it doesn't end there. He'll only make more demands.'

'But do you have any choice?'

'I can let whatever has to happen, happen now.'

'And everything you've worked for, just let it go?'

'Yes, everything. The whole fucking lot.' I didn't dare look at her, just listened and waited for her reaction. Then it came.

'OK.' Light as a linnet in April.

'OK?'

'If that's what you think, then just let it go. That's how I look at it. You can be a family man in Lillehammer. They rang not long ago and when I said I wasn't sure if I'd be coming for the interview they more or less offered me the job there and then.'

'Really?'

'Yep. So there's our choice, darling.'

I ran through it. Sell everything, including Opgard, and just leave. A fresh start. That was the dream back then, after all. Until it was taken from me, along with Shannon. Could it come true after all? I tasted it. Damn right we could move, all we had to do was do it. So what was holding me back? Had I become too old, too afraid of change? No, it wasn't that. It was her. It was the thought of putting your life in the hands of another.

'Trust me,' she said.

I turned and stared at her in disbelief. 'What did you say?'

'Trust me,' she said again.

I swallowed. Could she even read my thoughts now?

'I love you,' I said. It sounded strange, but like the right thing to say.

'How much?'

'So fucking much.' It just sounded right.

Without taking her eyes off the road she leaned over and kissed me on the cheek. Oh yes, I trusted her. Sure, the new report could lead to a closer investigation of what had happened when the first one was written, maybe certain uncomfortable facts would see the light of day even though Fuhr would do his best to make sure they didn't. But with Natalie by my side there was a limit to how great the disaster could be.

Or so I thought.

Five minutes before the disaster hit.

All disasters should have a prelude. A build-up, a warning of what's to come, like this press conference. Like those seconds in the yard when Dad looks at me before him and Mum get in the car and drive off. Like Carl ringing to tell me something's wrong. Like the baying of a sheriff who's snapping at your heels. Like the rumble in the mountains before the avalanche hits.

But it isn't always like that. Sometimes the sun is shining from a cloudless sky and the birds are chirping when you realise that the disaster isn't just on the way, it is already here. I was upstairs in the bedroom and throwing T-shirts, socks and underwear into a bag ready to put in the car and take down to Natalie's after the walk. Heard Natalie stamping her feet as she tried on Mum's hiking boots down in the hallway at the bottom of the staircase. I packed more clothes and heard the scraping of a chair down in the hall. Packed a couple of jackets and two crumpled shirts. If I ironed them I could look good for her when I made her a nice meal.

It had gone quiet down there. I looked through a couple of drawers to see if there was anything else I might need, zipped up the bag and walked down the stairs. Natalie was standing on the stool with her back to me, her body twisted at a strangely awkward angle as she reached up to touch what hung above her: the

Remington rifle. Her father's. My father's identical rifle was hanging on the wall of the barn at the Moe place. Obviously the barn door had been locked after the death, and I had still not found an excuse to ask Natalie for the key so that I could quietly switch them back. I'd been assuming the chance would come. But it wouldn't, I could see that now.

Her hand ran over the back end of the walnut stock. Over the only thing that distinguished the two guns from each other, that you would have to know about in order to spot it. A tiny little heart the daughter had engraved on it, to make her father happy.

Natalie turned. A tear ran down each cheek, the one on the right was leading. I'd stopped a couple of steps from the bottom so that we now stood at the same height, both of us almost floating a little above the ground. It was so quiet there in the porch, the only sound was her quick, trembling breathing. She climbed down from the stool and pulled off the hiking boots. Pushed her feet into her own shoes, took something from her pocket and lay it on the stool. Her movements were neither rushed nor hesitant, just efficient, and her face – apart from the tears – seemed serene, calm, like that of someone who has already made a decision, already resigned themselves to the fact that this is the only possible option. It was the fact that she didn't seem at all outraged that told me this was definite. People who get very angry reach a point at which they're no longer angry, and then perhaps they start to see things a little differently. But Natalie didn't even seem surprised, only like someone who has confirmation of something she always half suspected, and who had already decided on what the consequences must be.

'Well well,' she said. As in well well, such is life, that's how

417

things are, these things happen, well well, at least we tried. Then she gave me a shrug, reached for the door handle, and she was gone.

I just stood there, broken.

Heard the engine start and the car drive off.

Only then did I drop the bag, walk to the stool and see the ring lying there.

44

I AWOKE WITH A START in pitch-darkness. A deep, rumbling roaring dying out. Thunder. I'd had a nightmare. Not about those seven old ghosts who gave me no rest, and not the new one either, Moe the roofer. The nightmare was about Natalie leaving me for the third time, and my dad standing there shouting in my ear *third strike and yer out*, the way he used to when he was teaching me and Carl how to play baseball out in the yard. So yeah, it was a relief to wake up from the dream. Until I remembered that reality wasn't a whole lot better. I turned over in what I thought was my bed and tumbled over the side of the sofa. Hit the floor and recognised the smell of that worn Persian rug Dad had brought over from America and realised I was in the living room. The hands of my watch glowed faintly. Eleven thirty. I vaguely recalled what had happened after Natalie left. It wasn't much. I had turned off the phone and started drinking the Budweiser Carl bought on special order from the off-licence in Notodden, even though we were agreed it was pretty weak stuff. The TV and the radio remained off while I built up a high that would quell a little of the pain every time I thought of Natalie. Beer was enough, I had no plans this time to take the fast track into endless silence. Just enough to sleep.

And now that I was awake it felt quiet enough as it was. A crazy thought struck me. That Natalie had called, that she'd changed her mind and wanted me to go with her to Lillehammer, or anywhere at all. There was the clinking of empty beer bottles as I fumbled for my phone which I seemed to remember placing on the table. A flash of lightning lit the room for an instant and I saw the phone lying on top of a book. As the thunder came rolling I turned it on. Six missed calls and two text messages. None from Natalie. I groaned. Three of the calls were from Carl, two from Dan Krane, one from Jo Aas. The text messages were from Dan Krane. I opened the first one.

Tried to call you. As a significant investor in Os, Os Daily would like your comments on what emerged at GeoData's press conference regarding errors in the previous report.

I almost had to laugh. I didn't exactly know what the consequences would be for me, what I would lose, but they would mean nothing compared to what I had lost in losing Natalie. Sure, the petrol station, the amusement park, and perhaps even Os Spa would all go, but at least it would be epic. A first-class disaster, you might say. Oh sure, I felt like laughing as I opened the second text message.

Can I have your comment on the tragedy and the accusations that Fuhr and GeoData have acted dishonestly?

I could always call Krane and comment that the word 'tragedy' should be reserved for use in cases of sudden death, lovesickness and serious physical injury, and not to describe developments in the Norwegian road network and their effects on the depopulation of rural Norway. And actually it wasn't even that, because what was Os's poison would be Todde's meat. Speaking of which, I still hadn't eaten breakfast. I decided I had to get something down me, go to bed and get up early in the morning. The board meeting was still ten hours away, and there was a lot of preparation to do in light of the revised situation. One topic would be the dismissal of Carl and my own appointment as leader. Another and equally important discussion would be on the wisdom or otherwise of continuing with the new wing, now the main road would no longer be running through Os.

I stood up and headed for the kitchen. Without turning on the light I cut a couple of slices of wholemeal bread, found some cooked ham in the fridge and sat at the table by the window, chewing and staring out into the dense blackness. It struck me then how quickly my thoughts had moved on from the break-up with Natalie to concentrate on practical matters. The main road, the board meeting, food. The same thing happened when Shannon died. Maybe it was the survival instinct. If that's what it was then at least it showed I wanted to go on living, in spite of everything.

Another bolt of lightning ripped the sky.

And that was when I saw it.

Again.

The wolf.

It must have tipped over the rubbish bin that stands beside the barn, and in the flash of lightning I saw it, nose down in the trash that had tumbled out.

Then it was dark again.

I blinked. Had I really seen it? It was like the time Uncle Bernard came home from the USA with a View-Master – or mini-cinema as we called it in Os – for me and Carl. Back then it was the equivalent of VR glasses. It showed illuminated still pictures with a fascinating 3-D effect. Our View-Master had pictures of the Grand Canyon and the Rockies. Pretty stylish, but probably more impressive to people down in the valleys than to us up here in the mountains. The picture I looked at most and never tired of looking at was of a big golden puma on a mountainside. Not, as I say, because of the mountain but because it looked so alone standing there. In Dad's encyclopedia it said that the puma lived and hunted alone in a large territory. The only time it sought company was when it encountered a female on heat and mated with her – if she let him. Afterwards they would stay together for two weeks. That was it. Two weeks, no more and no less. Then the male would leave to be on his own again, to hunt and rule over his vast, deserted kingdom. It seemed so sad. But in a good way, which I'm not sure I can explain. You're born a puma, it's your nature, you do what you're supposed to do, what you have to do, there's nothing to get upset about. But if you're a wolf, a pack animal rejected by the pack, and have to survive off the contents of rubbish bins, then that's different.

I stared out into the darkness, waiting for another lightning flash. To see it. To see me. The king of trash. A poor bastard sacrificing his dignity on the altar of survival, the way we all do. We just move the limits of what we call dignity, change the definition so we can live with ourselves. Even people who kill those who stand in their way, who steal their brother's wife and his position, feel they have an honour to defend. And they defend it more desperately than most because the limit can't be moved any more, because there's no more dignity left to move.

Another bolt of lightning flashed over the yard. But the wolf was gone.

I switched on the light and carried on eating. Tried not to think, just to concentrate on that thunderstorm. It was hard to tell if it was coming or going. After a while I cleared the food away, rinsed the plate and was standing by the open door of the fridge when I heard another sound. Carl's BMW. I went to the window and saw it turn into the yard. But instead of parking in front of the house he drove up the ramp and into the barn. He switched off the ignition and for a few seconds there was complete darkness until the neon tube hanging from the roof blinked several times and then came on. Carl was hidden behind the wall where the light switch was and it was several moments before he reappeared. He walked down the ramp, noticed the upended bin and all the scattered trash in the light from the barn door but did nothing about it. What was he up to? Had he been drinking? He approached the house with the light from the barn behind him, and I knew he could see me standing by the kitchen window.

'What're you doing here?' he asked as he came into the kitchen where I was now sitting down, waiting for him.

'I guess I live here,' I said.

'You do?' He stayed standing in the doorway. His voice was low, dead. 'Where's your car?'

'Natalie was here. We used hers.'

'And now she's gone?'

I nodded.

'Then maybe you've got a moment to help me with my car.'

'Oh? Something wrong?'

'The brakes,' he said. 'They're not working properly.'

'I'll have a look at it first thing tomorrow.'

'Prefer if we could do it now.'

Our eyes met. He looked sober. I shrugged.

He led the way over the yard, with me still looking around, even though I knew the wolf must be miles away by now.

Another flash of lightning followed by a rolling peal of thunder. And as though it really had torn a hole in the sky, heavy drops of rain began to fall. We ran up the ramp and into the barn. Another lightning flash, another crash of thunder and the rain was suddenly drenching, hammering on the corrugated-iron roof and the ramp out there in the dark. Carl got into the driver's seat and released the bonnet catch. I lifted it up and leaned in. Checked the brake fluid.

'Looks normal enough,' I said.

I got no reply and realised I would have to shout to be heard above the deafening drumming on the roof.

'All looks normal here! We'll have to—'

I stopped as I looked up past the bonnet towards the driver's seat and saw that Carl wasn't sitting there any longer.

'Don't worry about it,' I heard Carl say right behind me.

And in that moment I knew.

'Maybe they're OK after all,' Carl said, and even though he was standing close to me he had to raise his voice to be heard. 'It isn't easy to tell. I mean, I started worrying when I heard today that the police think there was something wrong with the brakes in the car Shannon was driving as well, and that's why she went over the edge.'

I didn't turn round. Just listened to the rain. To another rumble of thunder. It was getting close now.

'I mean, it was my car, after all,' Carl went on. 'And I know there was nothing wrong with the brakes last time I drove it. So that got me thinking. You and Shannon were going to have a kid, perhaps you were even looking forward to it, making plans. Just that I was a problem, in so many ways. So what do you do? Well, it's pretty obvious. When you have to do something where there's a risk, but it's something you've dealt with before, you just do the same thing all over again, right? You fixed the brakes on my car the same way you fixed them on Dad's. Or actually, you must have found a cleverer way of doing it, so the police technicians wouldn't suspect anything criminal this time round. If I hadn't killed Shannon before going to that investors' meeting at Os Spa that evening, it would've been me who died, not her. Am I right, Roy?'

I turned slowly.

Carl was standing two metres from me and holding the shotgun at chest height. His finger was on the trigger, the two barrels pointing straight at me. He knew me, knew it was likely I would try something. And this time I had no bike chain with me.

'Repetition,' I said.

'Meaning?'

'You choosing the same method too. Same as when you shot Dog. But maybe we repeat our mistakes too. You didn't manage to kill Dog, just wound him. And it was an accident. How are you going to manage to kill your own brother?'

Carl smiled. 'My dear Roy, that stuff about the first one being the most difficult may be true or it may be bullshit, but I've killed twice since then anyway. The old sheriff and Shannon. No, wait, make that three, with your kid.'

I swallowed. 'What do you think you're actually going to achieve by killing me? The board won't give you your job back, not now they know about all the irregularities.'

'Ah, but you're forgetting inheritance, Roy.'

'Inheritance?'

'Yes. That was what I was thinking as I sat over there in my new place looking up towards Opgard. Saw there was a light on in the kitchen and realised you'd come home. Home to your inheritance. And then my thinking went like this. That I'm the only family you have. That if you died now, I would inherit every-thing you own. Not just Opgard, but the shares in Os Spa. That at the board meeting tomorrow you wouldn't be able to fire me and that I, as the soon-to-be majority shareholder, would in prac-tice be able to dismiss the entire board, or at least those of them not well disposed to the idea of my continuing as manager of the hotel.' Carl laughed, evidently at the surprise that was showing on my face. 'Simple, isn't it, Roy?'

'OK,' I said. 'But how do you intend to get away with it?'

'Get away with what? No one's going to blame me when they find out you've shot yourself out here in the barn.'

'Suicide. I see. The day before I take over at Os Spa and fire you. You think people will believe that?'

'At first glance it might be hard to see any obvious motive for suicide. But when it emerges that you recently had pills pumped out of your stomach at the hospital in Notodden, then the police, and everybody else, are going to think it's something that's been on your mind for a long time. It isn't unusual in men of your age. Just look at Fuhr.'

'Fuhr?'

Carl moved his head back in surprise and wrinkled his brow. 'You didn't hear?'

'Hear what?'

'Really? No, you had your phone turned off.' Carl gave a brief laugh. 'Jon Fuhr took his own life. He didn't turn up for the press conference and his body was found shortly afterwards. They think it was an overdose of something or other. But OK, maybe he had a motive. From what Bent Halden said at the press conference, it looks like Fuhr felt responsible for the mistakes in the first report.'

'Mistakes? What, in the one we ordered?'

'No, no, there's the irony of it. Turns out there's an underground stream in the mountain they didn't discover and it can't be emptied or dammed. So regardless of the geology, the Todde tunnel would have been impossible to build. Halden admitted that GeoData should have discovered it much earlier on, it would have saved the country somewhere around a hundred million in planning and pre-production costs. Fuhr was boasting about how he'd come into a lot of money recently, and that's given rise to speculation that supporters of the Todde project bribed him to deliberately avoid any mention of the river in his report.'

'So the main road . . .'

'Will still run straight through Os. And this time there's no doubt about it, it's not a question of interpreting uncertain data and loose rocks. Any tunnel that ever got built would just turn into a river.'

I had misunderstood the text message from Krane about wanting my comments on GeoData and *errors in the previous report.* And in what was obviously a later message after Fuhr had been found. *Can I have your comment on the tragedy and the accusations that Fuhr and GeoData have acted dishonestly?*

'Speaking of rivers,' said Carl, lifting the shotgun to rest against his cheek. I stared into the barrels. Saw his finger move to squeeze the trigger. I didn't feel afraid, only tired. I wanted to get it over and done with.

'Wait!' I said.

'Why?' He stared at me with one eye, the other closed.

'You can't shoot me from two metres away with a shotgun and make it look like suicide. In the first place they'll see from the scattering that I can't have done it myself. And in the second place it's not certain I'll die straight away, and that'll leave traces all over the place. People who shoot themselves with shotguns put the gun barrel in their mouths.'

'OK. So then what do you suggest?'

'That you use the rifle. Hanging in the porch. It's even got a bullet in the chamber.'

'Oh yeah?' He put his head on one side. 'Are you helping me or are you trying something on?'

I shook my head. 'In the first place I don't want to suffer unnecessarily. And in the second place, you're my brother. If I've got to die anyway – and it's not as if I don't deserve it – then I don't see any point in the last Opgard going straight to jail just because he's incapable of thinking things through in a practical way. And in the third place . . .'

'Yes?'

'If I cooperate now then I want Natalie to have the petrol station and the properties in town.'

Carl thought about it. 'She can have the petrol station.'

'And the properties in town,' I said. 'Remember, you're getting the campsite and the shares. And Opgard.'

Carl laughed. 'Deal. I mean, you've been there for me enough times. But I'm afraid it's going to be the shotgun.'

'OK, but then I'll take it on the chin, as they say.'

'You will?' He looked sceptical.

'Look, I won't try anything,' I said, dropping to my knees and putting both hands in my pockets. 'Afterwards you wipe the trigger and rub my right index finger against it. Then you touch nothing, you leave everything exactly as it is. And stay as close to the truth as possible when you talk to the police, about what time you came home and so on. You came in, didn't find me, you were about to go to bed and you heard a shot. Went out to the barn, found me, checked for any signs of life and then phoned them. You got that?'

'Got it.'

'OK then. Let's get it over with.'

I opened my mouth. Carl stared at me in disbelief. Then – with great caution – he took a step towards me. I closed my eyes. Another rumble of thunder, further off this time. Then I felt the double barrels of the shotgun against my lips and had to open my mouth wider. Carl forced the metal barrels in, and the acrid taste of powder and steel filled my mouth. I've read that theory about why you see your whole life pass before your eyes when you know you're about to die. That it's the brain, desperately searching through the entire memory bank for something that might be used to try to escape. I didn't want to escape any longer, but all the same, this was what happened. It started with Carl and me sitting carsick in the back of the Cadillac, with Dad driving and smoking and Mum reading the map. Dad stopped so we could be sick, ruffled our hair and promised us ice cream at the next petrol station. A promise he kept. And before we reached Oslo we stopped at the fjord and bathed in the sea, in the salt water. Mum bathed too, and Dad stood leaning against the car, smoking and watching. Handed us a big towel when we were finished. I can remember him smiling and thinking that Dad was happy right at that exact moment. And maybe he was. For that single moment. Then me standing in front of Carl, holding in my hand the essay I got a Very Good for. Him smiling and denying that he – my kid brother – has corrected my spelling mistakes, even though I can *see* he has. The Cadillac heading away from us, Dad and Mum inside it, Carl and me watching from the yard. Four people in that old Volvo my uncle gave me for my eighteenth birthday, heading for a dance in Årtun. Carl and Mari the sweethearts in the back seat, Grete Smitt, who is in love with Carl, in the passenger seat, and me, who is in love with Mari, at the wheel. Mari offering herself to me in revenge, after Carl got drunk and fucked Grete. And me at that moment realising it isn't Mari I'm in love with, it's anything that belongs to Carl, and she doesn't any more. Moe in the petrol station shop, hunched over in shame and fear, buying a morning-after pill. Shannon. Flame-red hair against snow-white skin, that damaged, half-closed eyelid, as though she's taking aim at me. Me by the railings on the Varodd Bridge after I moved from Os to Kristiansand to get away from her. Her on my doorstep one evening, rain dripping from her hair and asking if she can come in. Natalie lying in the heather. The miracle of finding someone else to love. Zator. The view from the top, to be up there, high above everyone else, and know at the same time that in another second you'll be hurtling down into the abyss. Then the bang. But instead of going black, it was as if everything started moving backwards. The shotgun jerked and the barrel pulled out of my mouth. Was that what happened when you died, that you lived your life again only the other way round? Was I going to win and lose Natalie three times before she grew younger? Would I meet Shannon again? Would Dad, Mum, Moe, Willumsen, the old sheriff and all the other ghosts come back from the dead? Would I see a teen-aged Natalie backing out of the petrol-station door and never see her again? I felt something warm running down my cheek and over my lips and automatically stuck out my tongue. Recognised the taste at once. Not tears, but blood.

I opened my eyes.

Carl was no longer standing in front of me, I was staring out into the darkness beyond the open barn door and all I could see was the light from the kitchen window. So I was alive, wasn't I? That bang. Must have been thunder. Another lightning flash lit up our whole house. I saw something by the wall. Maybe I was dead, maybe I was seeing what I wanted to see, maybe that's what paradise is. Because it was her, Natalie, and she was holding a *langeleik* and she was obviously playing it, though it was raining so heavily I couldn't hear a thing. Then it was dark again, and she was gone. A groan. Finally I looked down.

It was Carl.

He was on the ground, his face pale. But his white work shirt was coloured.

Blood red.

He stared at me as he fumbled for the shotgun. Got a finger to it before I pulled it away. Turned and put it on the BMW behind me. Saw the grille all covered with his blood.

'Wh . . . what happened?' Carl whispered hoarsely.

I was still on my knees, still staring out into the darkness.

And then she stepped into the light. Hair dripping wet.

'Hi,' said Natalie. I'd been mistaken. It wasn't a *langeleik* she'd been holding up. It was a rifle.

'Hi,' I said, unable to think of anything more meaningful.

'I saw you when I came round the house. He was going to . . .'

'Yes,' I said, and got to my feet. 'The rifle from the porch?'

She came closer. 'I was as quick as I could. Is he . . . ?'

'Not quite.'

We looked at Carl. His face was turning white at the edge, like chocolate that's been lying around too long. Blood was dripping from his shirt front and down onto the wooden planks. Natalie had fired from the main house, a distance of seventy or eighty metres. The bullet had hit Carl in the back and come out through his chest. Turning, I saw that the underside of the car bonnet had an almost invisible dent where the bullet had ended its flight.

'Will he be . . . ?'

'No,' I said. 'He can't survive that.'

Natalie looked at me as though she had more questions, how I could know that there was no hope for Carl, for example. But there must have been something in my face that made her desist.

'Can you go and get my hunting knife?' I asked, watching Carl as he wriggled about like a worm on a fish hook. 'It's in the bottom of the chest of drawers in the porch.'

'OK.'

Natalie disappeared back into the night. I saw her lit up by another flash of lightning. Then the thunder, rolling in behind it, like an afterthought. I squatted down by the living corpse. Carl opened and closed his eyes. Wheezing like a punctured tyre: 'I'm dying, aren't I?'

The Os dialect sounded almost alien in Carl's mouth after all these years.

'Yes,' I said. 'Any last requests?'

Carl looked as though he was trying to laugh. 'Same as yours,' he wheezed. 'That you make sure the king of Os is an Opgard.'

'Don't know if I'm all that interested in the title.'

'Maybe *you* don't know it, but I do. Because you've always wanted what I have.'

'Oh yeah?'

'The throne. Shannon. Even Mari, when we were teenagers, I knew that, of course. Even the attention from Dad, excepting that part about the . . . well, you know. Crazy but true, am I right?'

I shuddered. Was it true?

Carl's eyelids were half shut now and he looked like he was falling asleep. I took his hand and squeezed it. He squeezed back.

'What will you do with my body?' he whispered.

'I haven't had time to think about that yet.'

'Oh yes you have. You think fast when it comes to practical matters. What's the plan?'

'Sure you want to know?'

'No, not sure, so just lie to me if it's too awful.'

'I'll bury you here on the farm. With a view.'

Carl laughed and coughed at the same time. 'You can lie better than that!' Specks of blood spattered his chin and upper lip.

'In the outfields,' I said. 'Deep down, so the fox doesn't get you.'

'Better.' He smiled, the white lips looking like empty larval skins. 'Good. Thanks.'

Natalie reappeared from the dark. Handed me the broad-bladed hunting knife with both hands, as though it were a surgical instrument and I a surgeon. It was Dad's knife, the one I had used to put Dog out of his misery.

'I'm going outside,' said Natalie. 'Do it.'

I sat there, looking at the knife. The design was brutal, with a channel down one side of the blade to run the blood off when cutting up prey.

'It's bloody painful now, Roy. Please can you just get it over with?'

I nodded but I couldn't move. Cleared my throat.

'What if you can actually survive all this if I call Stanley now?'

'Think about it, Roy,' he groaned, whispering so quietly I had to lean forward to hear him above the rain. 'I survive, get fired tomorrow, declared bankrupt and have to move into that bloody house alone now that Mari isn't going to leave Dan after all. Natalie will go to jail for attempting to kill me and I will for attempting to kill you. But if I'm gone then all the problems disappear, for both of us. So can I *please* not have to survive? And can you *please* get a bloody move on?'

I sat on the floor behind him, took hold of that mane of thick, dark hair in my left hand. It hit me like a déjà vu, those nights I climbed down to him in the lower bunk after Dad had been there, lying with him and comforting him as he sobbed, stroking his hair, my little brother. I pulled his head back hard, embraced him with my right arm, pressed the point of the blade against the skin of his neck on the left side.

'What d'you think?' I whispered in his ear. 'That name Os Spa, it's a bit . . . stiff. What about renaming it "Carl's"?'

'Idiot,' he wheezed.

'I mean it.'

A smile spread across the pale lips. 'I'll think about it,' he whispered.

Then I pushed the point in and pulled the knife to the right, being sure to maintain the pressure and keeping the blade level. Blood running. Until I reached the main artery and then it began to spurt. Three arcing jets splashed to the floor. Then it was over, and Carl relaxed in my grip. I laid him down carefully and got to my feet. Saw him lying there in a pool of blood. I felt nothing. Thought nothing. Apart from that it meant another job with the plane, scraping the blood off the wood flooring.

45

I HEAR THAT AS A rule the bereaved manage to keep their grief at arm's length as long as they can keep their minds occupied with arrangements for the funeral. I don't know whether that's why I felt remarkably untouched by the fact that Carl was dead. Or perhaps I'd been destroyed years before and no longer even *had* the ability to grieve. Anyway, we didn't bury Carl in the out-fields like I'd promised him. Because he'd been right. Why take the chance on something new when you can repeat a method that worked for you before?

So we put Carl's phone on the kitchen table, wrapped Carl in bin liners, put the body in the boot of the BMW and drove it and Natalie's car to the workshop. The timing and the weather were perfect. The petrol station was closed, and there wasn't a soul to be seen out in the rain that continued to hammer relentlessly down. I opened the door, drove in, and Natalie helped me lift the body up into the tractor grab and we poured what was left of the Fritz Industrial Cleaner into the grab. I could hear the flesh already bubbling and sizzling as I raised the grab to its top position, directly up under the roof. We left our mobile phones behind, got back in the cars and drove east. We pulled in at the same remote lay-by where I'd had the meeting with Jon Fuhr. Where I'd got that typewritten letter which I now pulled out of my pocket and placed on the passenger seat.

I HAVE HAD ENOUGH OF THIS LIFE.
GOODBYE. OPGARD.

With a rag from the workshop I wiped the steering wheel and any other places I might have touched, even though there would hardly be an investigation, and finding traces of the victim's older brother on the car wouldn't seem particularly suspicious anyway. Then I got out, wiped the keys and lay them on top of one of the front tyres and rubbed out my footprints in the gravel as I walked over and sat in Natalie's Mitsubishi.

We drove in silence, the only sounds those of the rain and the wipers. So far we had only spoken to each other regarding the practical problems that required our immediate attention. Now it was time to talk about the other thing. The thing that was there, that had to come out.

But we didn't. Maybe we both needed to ease down a bit first. Allow the brain and the body to rest after what we'd been through. In the end I was the one who broke the silence.

'Why did you come back?'

Another long silence followed, but I saw how she swallowed continuously, like a kid trying to hold back her tears.

'Because I know,' she said, her voice brittle. She tried to say more, stopped, breathed heavily. I waited. Then she started again.

'You did it because you thought it was my father who had raped me. I don't know if you did it because you love me, maybe you would have done it anyway, because of what your father did to Carl. But I understand, and that's what frightens me. I realised after I left you that *if* my father had touched me, then I would have wanted you – or me – to kill him. That I'm like you. That I could be a murderer. And now . . .' A tear trickled down her cheek. '. . . now I am one.'

'No,' I said. 'You're a person who saves lives. You saved mine twice.'

She wiped away the tear with the back of her hand and snuffled. 'I don't intend to make a habit of it, if that's what you're thinking.'

I smiled. 'Lucky for me that you were in such a rush to let me know.'

'Stupid, there wasn't any hurry to tell you *that*.'

'Oh? Then what?'

'Stupid.' She sniffed and wiped her nose with the sleeve of her jacket.

'Correct. And stupid people need to have things spelled out for them.'

She gave a weary sigh. 'I thought I had to hurry up to tell you I love you, all right?'

I looked at her. 'How . . . ?'

'So fucking much,' she said.

We laughed. We really did.

Natalie waited outside the workshop while I went inside to pick up our mobile phones. I no longer heard anything from the chemical reactions up in the grab, but the air smelled poisonous and I held my breath until I was outside again. As we lay in Natalie's bed with the lights off, trying to get a few hours' sleep ahead of the board meeting, I thought she was asleep until I felt her hand stroking me on the stomach. I turned, a little surprised – was this really what she wanted, so soon after she'd helped to kill a person whose remains were at that very moment being dissolved just a few hundred metres away from where we lay? Her eyes glowed in the dark and no, I hadn't misinterpreted that hand. And I suddenly realised it wasn't in spite of what she'd just been a part of, it was *because* of it. Not that she'd turned into a psychopath who got a thrill from killing, but that the presence of death arouses our appetite for life, the desire to prolong it, to pass something of ourselves on. Less than a minute after we'd finished she was sleeping like a child, as they say.

I saw Rita Willumsen climb out of her Saab Sonett as I turned into the car park at Os Spa. She stood waiting for me as I stepped out of the Volvo.

'Good morning,' she said. 'You're looking well.'

'Thanks, you too,' I said, and I meant it. That she didn't mean it was obvious. I had hardly slept, and in the mirror that morning I looked ten years older than the guy who'd gone to bed just a few hours earlier.

'And congratulations on your girlfriend,' she said as we headed in step towards the entrance. 'You've found someone there with brains and style.'

I almost repeated that 'Thanks, you too', but managed not to.

I ran through a list of reasons why Rita Willumsen would sud-denly be acting so friendly towards Roy Opgard, a boy she had once kept as a pet, but who she also knew was almost certainly responsible for the fact that she became a widow back then.

The list was short. In fact, there were just two entries. One was that Kurt had told her I had him by the short and curlies, which meant she too was involved in the illegal proceedings surround-ing the sale of the campsite. But I doubted whether Kurt had breathed a single word about that. Instead I was betting on the second entry: that Rita had pretty much understood what was going to happen at the board meeting we were on our way to, and that afterwards it would definitely be to her advantage to have Roy Opgard on her side. Because even though Rita was a sen-sitive soul – or actually no, she wasn't, so let me rephrase that – even though Rita was capable of strong antipathies she was above all a pragmatic businesswoman who played her hand as the situation demanded.

The six other members of the board were already there as Rita and I entered the large conference room at the precise time arranged for the meeting to start. I greeted everyone and then sat down, noting that the others, consciously or not, had left vacant the chair at the head of the table where the chairman, Jo Aas, usually sat.

'We better wait for Carl,' said Aas with a glance at his watch. Everyone, me included, nodded.

While we waited the conversation round the table was mostly about GeoData's discovery of the underground stream, and how that made it even more certain that the main road would still run through Os, as well as the tragic suicide of the guy who had clearly made the initial mistake in not spotting that stream.

Maybe it was the talk of suicide that caused a change in the atmosphere around the table when I said that the last I had seen or heard of my brother was when I woke up on the sofa at Opgard late the evening before, and that he had driven off.

'I've tried to call Carl several times,' said Aas, frowning deeply. 'No answer.'

'That could be,' I said. 'When I left I saw Carl's phone was still on the kitchen table.' I glanced at my own phone. 'He's very forgetful, but it's odd that he didn't come back to fetch it. And of course, it's a little worrying that he isn't here, and hasn't contacted anyone to say he can't come or that he's been delayed.'

I showed a serious face to all the other faces around the table. And read there just what they were thinking. That it wasn't unheard of for people in Os to take their own lives after losing their jobs.

'People usually turn up,' said Jo Aas. 'As a rule. But then, of course, there are exceptions. Let us hope this isn't one of them. Anyway, we must get started on this meeting.' And it started, with an affirmation of the meeting itself and the outlined order of business, after which we went directly to the first order, the choice of a new chairman. Which was what they call a pro forma business.

'I think Roy is the right choice, and it's not just because he owns more than fifty per cent of the shares and it leaves us with no choice,' Aas said to a round of laughter. 'As you all know, Roy has ownership experience from running the petrol station, Fritt Fall and the Meierigård building, to mention just a few of his properties. And they've all given good returns, as far as I know. So if you ask me, the hotel and the board will be in the best of hands when Roy takes over the gavel.'

I was chosen with another word I'd rarely had occasion to use myself – acclamation.

'I wish I could quite literally hand a gavel over to you,' said Aas with a glint in his eye. 'But I'm afraid it's just a turn of phrase. In fact, I never had a gavel even when I was town mayor here.'

More laughter from the other members of the board. I contented myself with a small smile, it's wise not to laugh too easily when your little brother has gone missing and you're worried about him. The worst thing is that I *was* worried. Everything that had taken place during the night now seemed so unreal that a part of me wondered if in fact Carl might not just walk through the door, and I could breathe a sigh of relief knowing it had all been a bad dream.

'Anyway,' Aas continued, 'from this point on, you are formally leader of this meeting, Roy.'

'Thank you,' I said. 'But I would appreciate it if you will take us through the rest of the day's business, Jo.' A twitch in a couple of Aas's wrinkles at this, but not as much as the first time I addressed him by his first name.

'It will be an honour,' he said. 'The next point concerns the appointment of a new manager.' It was nicely done of him to avoid the use of words like dismissal, replace, terminate. All the same, something passed through the room, as though the gathering were reminded of what that empty seat at the table might imply.

'The suggestion from Roy and Carl is that Roy takes over. It's a good suggestion, given that Carl himself feels that it is time he moved on. I say this based only on the conversations I've had with Carl, and it would of course be best if he were here and able to explain it himself.'

'Strictly speaking, what Carl himself thinks doesn't matter,' one of the board members volunteered. 'If Roy wants to fire him then that's Roy's decision.'

A finger wearing red nail varnish was raised in the air.

'Yes, Rita?' said Aas.

'It matters a lot what Carl thinks,' she said. 'Like most leaders he signed a contract providing compensation on condition he doesn't invoke the usual legal protections against termination. So the board is perfectly entitled to dismiss Carl with immediate effect if it wants to, because it wants to, and without having to explain why. But if he steps down on his own initiative then he voluntarily relinquishes the compensation which, if memory serves me correctly, amounts to an exit package of two years' salary. Carl's annual wage is so high I think the board has to know whether this is a dismissal or whether Carl simply wants to step down for reasons of his own, and we need to know this before making any new appointment. If the board now dismisses Carl before his possible resignation that would be a pre-emptive strike—'

'A what?' said Aas. Rita had said it in English and it was obviously a phrase Aas was not familiar with.

'You strike before your potential opponent has launched a first attack,' I said.

Aas looked around the room with raised eyebrows, as though to reassure himself he wasn't the only one who had not heard the term before.

'On the one hand there are the short-term economic consequences,' Rita continued. 'And on the other the long-term, by which I mean how a sudden dismissal will affect Os Spa's reputation. If it turns out that Carl – despite what the former chairman believes to be the case – does not wish to resign voluntarily, then I have a suggestion for the offer the board makes to Carl. And that is that Carl is allowed to resign formally in return for a lower compensation, let's say a year and a half's salary, which we will call a bonus for a job well done and not a golden handshake. The arrangement would save the company six months' salary and damage to its reputation, and it would spare Carl quite extensive damage to his reputation. If the board agrees with my suggestion then I also suggest that while waiting for Carl's reply we postpone the appointment of a new manager and as soon as we get it arrange another meeting of the board.'

Aas looked around the table again. Nods the whole way, mine included, and I privately resolved that Rita Willumsen would be the first person I would invite to join my new board.

It was dusk when I saw Kurt Olsen's Land Rover swing into the petrol station. He parked away from the pumps, and I guessed the purpose of his visit. And as he walked in through the sliding doors I saw that, sure enough, he'd put on his priestly face, the one he wore for funerals and delivering bad news. I nodded to Egil, meaning he should deal with the customers alone while I went over to meet Kurt.

We stood behind the station. Kurt lit a cigarette and I wedged a plug of Berry's under my lip. As we stood facing the water Kurt explained that he'd had a call from Grete Smitt; a customer reported seeing Carl's car at a lay-by due east of the county line. And since she'd also heard that Carl had failed to turn up at the board meeting that morning, she thought it was her duty to report the information.

I nodded. 'Good thing we have an informal information exchange like Grete.'

'Town gossip has its function, yeah. Anyway, I drove out there to check. It was his car right enough. There was a note on the passenger seat. Never a good sign when you see something that looks like a note. Even worse when you also find the car key on top of the left-hand front wheel.'

'No it isn't,' I said. 'No need to beat about the bush, Kurt, give it to me straight.'

'Sorry.' He inhaled so hard I could see the glow creep up the cigarette. Puffed out the smoke. 'Looks like a self-slaughter note, Roy.'

'Self-slaughter?'

'Police termology. Suicide.'

Terminology, I thought. I said nothing.

'These Oslo words are driving me crazy,' he said. '*Station head?*' He snorted in contempt. Probably welcomed the digression.

'What did it say?' I asked, because it would have seemed strange if I hadn't.

'Let's see,' said Kurt as he fished out his phone, obviously having photographed the note.

I HAVE HAD ENOUGH OF THIS LIFE. GOODBYE. OPGARD.

He read it out, and I nodded very, very slowly, as though I needed to taste each word, chew on it and digest it.

'The local sheriff's out there now with dogs,' said Kurt. 'But I doubt whether they'll find anything. There's a steep slope down from the lay-by into the lake.'

'Yeah, I think I know where that lay-by is.'

'Now of course it might not be what we fear . . .'

You mean what we *hope*, I said. Because you would sleep better too, knowing that Carl couldn't now go to the police in Notodden or in Oslo and report that the sheriff in Os had failed to follow up credible information about several murders. Only I didn't say it, just thought it. Fair enough, we were all in the same boat. So I didn't feel nervous at all when I saw Kurt looking over towards the workshop and probably wondering whether history was repeating itself, and that even as we spoke, something up in the tractor grab was being corroded away to nothingness.

Kurt took a last drag and reached the tip. 'But if they do find something, then of course I'll get in touch with you at once.'

'Thanks,' I said.

Kurt dropped the smoking cigarette butt into a little puddle on the asphalt and sauntered back to his car. I stayed where I was, looking down at that fag end. Then I picked it up and took it over to the rubbish bin. I like to keep the place tidy.

46

JUST BEFORE EASTER I RECEIVED a call from Liv Goebbel.
Fresh snow covered the ice on Budalsvannet, and the bright sun
hurt my eyes as I stood in the campsite. I walked away a little
from Glen Moore and the two Norwegian engineers who were
still talking about what should go where, alternately pointing at
the drawings and up into the terrain. Goebbel informed me that
she had managed to persuade the court that death could be established beyond any reasonable doubt and she had obtained a
so-called Presumption of Death Certificate – a title that, I must
admit, had stopped me in my tracks the first time I heard it. It
meant that Carl Opgard had finally been officially declared dead,
and the inheritance settlement could commence. Although there
really wasn't much to it, since Carl had left no will and I was his
only close relative. The liquid assets didn't amount to much, Carl

had more debts than he had cash, if I can put it like that. But of course, he did have possessions, and not all of them had to be sold to pay off the outstanding debts. As his appointed executor I had already sold the BMW before Christmas, and also the shares in Os Spa, which Rita Willumsen bought, in exchange for a promise to look after the hotel as well as I had once looked after her Saab Sonett. From her grin when she said it I gathered she intended her words to convey some kind of double meaning.

'Everything should be in order within a week or two,' said Goebbel. 'Is there going to be a funeral for Carl?'

'A memorial service,' I said. 'And a stone next to Mum and Dad.'

'Oh, that's nice.'

'Thank you, Liv. See you at the board meeting next Wednesday.'

We hung up and I looked at my watch. Told Glen I had a lunch appointment at the hotel with Natalie and had to go.

'It's going to be fabulous,' he said enthusiastically. 'Imagine the ride when it's been snowing. Fuckin' fantastic.'

Natalie was sitting waiting at our regular table by the window when I arrived ten minutes late.

'Sorry, we got a bit carried away,' I said, kissing the hand she so graciously held up to me. I felt the ring against my lips.

'Good.' She smiled. 'You look happy.'

'I am,' I said, and ordered from the waiter who had arrived immediately. Tea and an Os salad for Natalie, local trout and water for me.

'It *is* good that you're so busy with this park,' she said. 'At the same time I feel almost obliged to tell you that it's starting to be noticeable that you've got less time for other things that are equally important.'

I nodded and lay my hand on top of hers on the white table-cloth. 'You're right. You and I should take a long weekend somewhere. You work too hard as well, you know. I was thinking that once the Easter rush is over we could go to San Jordi, in Barcelona.'

'San Jordi?'

'St George's Day. The Catalan festival celebrating their patron saint. The woman gives a book to the man she loves, and the man gives the woman a rose. The custom is from the olden days, before women could read, but since in our case things are the other way round, I'll be happy to get the rose.'

She laughed and flapped her serviette at me. 'Cute. But I wasn't meaning you neglecting us two, I mean the job here at the hotel.'

'OK,' I said, placing my own serviette in my lap as the waiter brought some freshly baked bread and olive pâté. 'Exactly what?'

'I've made a list.'

I smiled, but I saw from her face that she meant it literally.

'Some are decisions that *have* to be taken,' she continued. 'Some decisions that *could* be taken.'

'*Could* be taken?'

'Good, proactive suggestions.'

'From you?'

'And others. There are a lot of smart people at all levels here. And no leader can be smart at everything, so that means they have to be good listeners.'

'Darling, now listen—'

'I know, Roy, you *are* a good listener. The problem is that at the moment you don't have *time* to listen. And you need to find a solution to that, that's all I'm saying.'

I nodded. Watched Natalie's hands as she spread the pâté on her bread. She'd put the ring back on the day after the new Fritz Night, the night she'd taken the rifle down from the wall in the porch at Opgard and shot Carl. She'd come, understood what was happening, analysed the alternatives, taken her decision and done what had to be done. And I had asked myself: isn't that exactly the kind of imaginary situation they present to applicants for leadership jobs in America, to see how results-oriented they are?

'Before you show me that list, there's something I need to show you,' I said.

'Oh yeah?'

'After lunch.'

As we ate Natalie talked about another job offer she'd had, this time from one of the big hotel chains that wanted her to work in their head office. Natalie said that while it was, naturally, flattering, she wanted to work where things were happening, meaning at the front line, at the hotel. Our conversation was constantly interrupted by people coming over to say hello. The new mayor Gilbert Voss, Asle Vendelbo the bank manager, and the road boss Dag Cappelen, in charge of the improvements being made to the main road running through Os. They commented on the new wing, the weather, the prospects for Os FK in the coming season, as we nodded a subtext that was perhaps there and perhaps wasn't. Even Dan Krane came over and shook my hand, just wanted to say hello. He'd become tame now, him too realising that best for him was a continuation of the status quo, now that he and Mari had moved into the big house and were expecting number four.

'Jesus,' said Natalie after Krane had left. 'Looks like everyone just wants to pay homage and kiss your ring now.'

It took a couple of seconds before I understood she wasn't referring to a part of my anatomy as I first thought, but instead to the closing scene in *The Godfather*.

After we had paid – and I don't mix my private economy with the company's, the way Carl did – Natalie and I went for a drive in my Volvo, which both Erik and Kurt had hinted I should change now that I was director of the hotel and all that.

'What's on your mind now?' said Natalie as I turned along a forest track before we had got down to the village.

'Wait and you'll see,' I said.

A couple of minutes later I parked and we climbed out. The house – the one they call the Palace – stood there with snow glistening on its roof and covering the grounds.

'What d'you think?' I asked.

'It's fantastic. So it's almost finished now?'

'Yep. Just need to find someone to live here.'

'Maybe you'll find a buyer this Easter,' said Natalie. 'When all the rich people from Oslo come up. We can put up a sales notice at the hotel. Is it as nice inside?'

'Let's take a look,' I said.

The snow hadn't been cleared, and as it was so deep and Natalie's work shoes not really made for those conditions I went ahead and picked her up and carried her up the steps and over the threshold before putting her down.

'Oh my God!' she exclaimed.

Even here just inside the entrance you could see the view on the other side of the huge and so far unfurnished room. I had turned on the heating the evening before, and she kicked off her shoes and walked over the newly washed parquet flooring in her stockinged feet and over to the window. I stood behind her, and we looked down at the village bathed in sunshine. She leaned back into me as I put my arms around her.

'Still think we should put up the "For Sale" notice?' I whispered in her ear. At first she tensed. I didn't say more. Just waited. Then – a few moments later – her body began to shake with laughter.

'You sneaky bastard,' she said.

'You were the one who asked for it.'

'Me? I have never, ever—'

' "More money, better job, better place to live, a husband" – those were your conditions for staying on in Os. Don't you remember?'

'Oh yes, I remember. I also remember saying "in that order".'

'I know. So the next question is, what do you say to taking over as the hotel director of Os Spa? And what salary would you have in mind? Although, of course, that would be a matter for the board to decide.'

She turned, a look of disbelief on her face.

'You see,' I said, 'the job will be vacant because the current director is going to be busy building an amusement park.'

I could see some hard thinking going on behind those discoloured eyes.

'If you want to see, you'll have to come with me,' I said.

She smiled and shook her head in mock exasperation. So, OK, she wasn't quite convinced, not yet. She turned again, to face Os, and I rested my cheek against hers.

'Look,' she said, and pointed at a white cloud moving down the mountainside. It was a soundless avalanche. Soon it would hit Budalsvannet, but it was only fresh, light snow, hardly heavy enough to go through the ice. The snow would furl upwards before feathering out across the lake in the direction of the village, lying safely on the far shore. A village with scarcely more than a thousand inhabitants and only three thousand in the whole county, but a population that could quickly increase. The village lies six hundred metres above sea level. It has short but warm and dry summers, and harsh, intense winters. People here work hard. They don't speak more than is necessary, unless you count a bit of local gossip as unnecessary. Envy is human, and a degree of competition healthy, but togetherness is a precondition for survival. And even though everyone here in Os is equal, now and then what they need is a bellwether, to show them the way whenever there's fog, deep ravines and wolves.

I let my gaze wander across the landscape. There was the church. There was Årtun. Nergard with Opgard towering above it. The square, the campsite. Further off lay the meeting hall, Smitt's place and the petrol station. In this village I had lost and won everything. I hated the place and I loved it. And in the final analysis, what more can you ask of a home town?

The avalanche reached the ice on Budalsvannet, and for a few moments snow swirled up into the sunshine. Then it fell, and settled, and everything was just as it had been before.

Credits

Vintage would like to thank everyone who worked
on the publication of *BLOOD TIES*

Translator
Robert Ferguson

Agent
Niclas Salomonsson

Editor
Katie Ellis-Brown

Editorial
Liz Foley
Sania Riaz
Anouska Levy

Copy-editor
Katherine Fry

Proofreaders
Fiona Brown
Sally Sargeant

Managing Editorial
Graeme Hall

Contracts
Emma D'Cruz
Gemma Avery
Ceri Cooper

Rebecca Smith
Anne Porter
Rita Omoro
Humayra Ahmed
Kiran Halaith
Hayley Morgan
Harry Sargent

Design
Dan Mogford

Digital
Anna Baggaley
Claire Dolan
Brydie Scott
Charlotte Ridsdale
Zaheerah Khalik

Inventory
Nadine Hart
Rebecca Evans

Publicity
Bethan Jones
Mia Quibell-Smith
Amrit Bhullar

Finance
Ed Grande
Aya Daghem
Samuel Uwague

Marketing
Sophie Painter
Lucy Upton
Carmella Lowkis
Mairéad Zielinski

Production
Konrad Kirkham
Polly Dorner
Eoin Dunne

Sales
Nathaniel Breakwell
Malissa Mistry
Caitlin Knight
Rohan Hope
Elspeth Dougal
Tracy Orchard
Jade Perez
Lewis Cain
Erica Conway

Nick Cordingly
Kate Gunn
Sophie Dwyer
Neil Green
Maiya Grant
Danielle Appleton
Phoebe Edwards
Amber Blundell
Rachel Cram
David Atkinson
David Devaney

Helen Evans
Amanda Dean
Andy Taylor
Dan Higgins
Justin Ward-Turner
Charlotte Owens

Rights

Catherine Wood
Lucie Deacon
Lucy Beresford-Knox

Beth Wood
Maddie Stephenson
Agnes Watters
Sophie Brownlow
Amy Moss
Olivia Diomedes
Jake Dickson

Audio

Nile Faure-Bryan
Hannah Cawse

JO NESBO'S
EXPLOSIVE NEW THRILLER

THE *SUNDAY TIMES* NUMBER ONE BESTSELLER

JO NESBO
WOLF HOUR

THIS KILLER HAS A STORY
– TO TELL IT, HE NEEDS TO GET CAUGHT

OVER 60 MILLION BOOKS SOLD WORLDWIDE

penguin.co.uk/vintage